STONEHENGE

Also by Bernard Cornwell

The SHARPE series
(in chronological order)

SHARPE'S TIGER
SHARPE'S TRIUMPH
SHARPE'S FORTRESS
SHARPE'S TRAFALGAR
SHARPE'S PREY
SHARPE'S RIFLES
SHARPE'S EAGLE
SHARPE'S HAVOC
SHARPE'S GOLD
SHARPE'S ESCAPE
SHARPE'S BATTLE
SHARPE'S COMPANY
SHARPE'S SWORD
SHARPE'S ENEMY
SHARPE'S HONOUR
SHARPE'S REGIMENT
SHARPE'S SIEGE
SHARPE'S REVENGE
SHARPE'S WATERLOO
SHARPE'S DEVIL
SHARPE'S FURY

THE LAST KINGDOM
THE PALE HORSEMAN

The GRAIL QUEST Chronicles
HARLEQUIN · VAGABOND · HERETIC

STONEHENGE: A NOVEL OF 2000 BC

The STARBUCK Chronicles
REBEL · COPPERHEAD · BATTLE FLAG

The WARLORD Chronicles
THE WINTER KING · THE ENEMY OF GOD
EXCALIBUR

GALLOWS THIEF

By Bernard Cornwell and Susannah Kells
A CROWNING MERCY · FALLEN ANGELS

STONEHENGE

A NOVEL OF 2000 BC

BERNARD CORNWELL

HARPER

HarperCollins*Publishers*
77–85 Fulham Palace Road,
Hammersmith, London W6 8JB

www.harpercollins.co.uk

First published in Great Britain
by HarperCollins*Publishers* 1999

1

Copyright © Bernard Cornwell 1999

The Author asserts the moral right to
be identified as the author of this work

ISBN 978–0–00–786625–0

Illustrations by Rex Nicholls

Set in Postscript Linotype Meridien by
Rowland Phototypesetting Ltd,
Bury St Edmunds, Suffolk

Printed and bound by
Clays Ltd, St Ives plc

In memory of
BILL MOIR
1943–1998

'The Druid's groves are gone – so much the better:
Stonehenge is not – but what the Devil is it?'

Lord Byron, *Don Juan*
Canto XI, verse XXV.

PART ONE

The Sky Temple

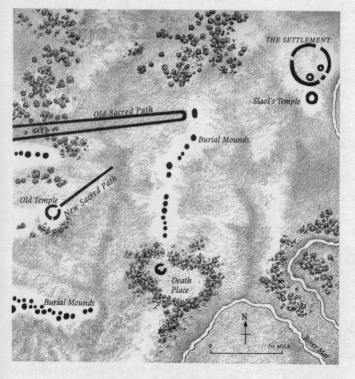

Map of the settlement and temples of Ratharryn, *c.* 2000 BC

The gods talk by signs. It may be a leaf falling in summer, the cry of a dying beast or the ripple of wind on calm water. It might be smoke lying close to the ground, a rift in the clouds or the flight of a bird.

But on that day the gods sent a storm. It was a great storm, a storm that would be remembered, though folk did not name the year by that storm. Instead they called it the Year the Stranger Came.

For a stranger came to Ratharryn on the day of the storm. It was a summer's day, the same day that Saban was almost murdered by his half-brother.

The gods were not talking that day. They were screaming.

Saban, like all children, went naked in summer. He was six years younger than his half-brother, Lengar, and, because he had not yet passed the trials of manhood, he bore no tribal scars or killing marks. But his time of trial was only a year away, and their father had instructed Lengar to take Saban into the forest and teach him where the stags could be found, where the wild boars lurked and where the wolves had their dens. Lengar had resented the duty and so, instead of teaching his brother, he dragged Saban through thickets of thorn so that the boy's sun-darkened skin was bleeding. 'You'll never become a man,' Lengar jeered.

Saban, sensibly, said nothing.

Lengar had been a man for five years and had the blue scars of the tribe on his chest and the marks of a hunter and a warrior on his arms. He carried a longbow made of yew, tipped with horn, strung with sinew and polished with pork fat. His tunic was of wolfskin and his long black hair was braided and tied with a strip of fox's fur. He was tall, had a narrow face and was reckoned one of the tribe's great hunters. His name meant Wolf Eyes, for his gaze had a yellowish tinge. He had been given another name at birth, but like many in the tribe he had taken a new name at manhood.

Saban was also tall and had long black hair. His name meant Favoured One, and many in the tribe thought it apt for, even at a mere twelve summers, Saban promised to be handsome. He was strong and lithe, he worked hard and he smiled often. Lengar rarely smiled. 'He has a cloud in his face,' the women said of him, but not within his hearing, for Lengar was likely to be the tribe's next chief. Lengar and Saban were sons of Hengall, and Hengall was chief of the people of Ratharryn.

All that long day Lengar led Saban through the forest. They met no deer, no boars, no wolves, no aurochs and no bears. They just walked and in the afternoon they came to the edge of the high ground and saw that all the land to the west was shadowed by a mass of black cloud. Lightning flickered the dark cloud pale, twisted to the far forest and left the sky burned. Lengar squatted, one hand on his polished bow, and watched the approaching storm. He should have started for home, but he wanted to worry Saban and so he pretended he did not care about the storm god's threat.

It was while they watched the storm that the stranger came.

He rode a small dun horse that was white with sweat. His saddle was a folded woollen blanket and his reins were lines of woven nettle fibre, though he hardly needed them for he was wounded and seemed tired, letting the small horse pick its own way up the track which climbed the steep escarpment. The stranger's head was bowed and his heels hung almost to the ground. He wore a woollen cloak dyed blue and in his right hand was a bow while on his left shoulder there hung a leather quiver filled with arrows fledged with the feathers of seagulls and crows. His short beard was black, while the tribal marks scarred into his cheeks were grey.

Lengar hissed at Saban to stay silent, then tracked the stranger eastwards. Lengar had an arrow on his bowstring, but the stranger never once turned to see if he was being followed and Lengar was content to let the arrow rest on its string. Saban wondered if the horseman even lived, for he seemed like a dead man slumped inert on his horse's back.

The stranger was an Outlander. Even Saban knew that, for only the Outfolk rode the small shaggy horses and had grey scars on their faces. The Outfolk were enemy, yet still Lengar did not release his arrow. He just followed the horseman and Saban followed Lengar until at last the Outlander came to the edge of the trees where bracken grew. There the stranger stopped his horse and raised his head to stare across the gently rising land while Lengar and Saban crouched unseen behind him.

The stranger saw bracken and, beyond it, where the soil was thin above the underlying chalk, grassland. There were grave mounds dotted on the grassland's low crest. Pigs rooted in the bracken while white cattle grazed the pastureland. The sun still shone here. The stranger stayed a long while at the wood's edge, looking for enemies, but seeing none. Off to his north, a long way off, there were wheatfields fenced with thorn over which the first clouds, outriders of the storm, were chasing their shadows, but all ahead of him was sunlit. There was life ahead, darkness behind, and the small horse, unbidden, suddenly jolted into the bracken. The rider let it carry him.

The horse climbed the gentle slope to the grave mounds. Lengar and Saban waited until the stranger had disappeared over the skyline, then followed and, once at the crest, they crouched in a grave's ditch and saw that the rider had stopped beside the Old Temple.

A grumble of thunder sounded and another gust of wind flattened the grass where the cattle grazed. The stranger slid from his horse's back, crossed the overgrown ditch of the Old Temple and disappeared into the hazel shrub that grew so thick within the sacred circle. Saban guessed the man was seeking sanctuary.

But Lengar was behind the Outlander, and Lengar was not given to mercy.

The abandoned horse, frightened by the thunder and by the big cattle, trotted west towards the forest. Lengar waited until the horse had gone back into the trees, then rose from the ditch and ran towards the hazels where the stranger had gone.

Saban followed, going to where he had never been in all his twelve years.

To the Old Temple.

Once, many years before, so long before that no one alive could remember those times, the Old Temple had been the greatest shrine of the heartland. In those days, when men had come from far off to dance the temple's rings, the high bank of chalk that encircled the shrine had been so white that it seemed to shine in the moonlight. From one side of the shining ring to the other was a hundred paces, and in the old days that sacred space had been beaten bare by the feet of the dancers as they girdled the death house that had been made from three rings of trimmed oak trunks. The smooth bare trunks had been oiled with animal fat and hung with boughs of holly and ivy.

Now the bank was thick with grass and choked by weeds. Small hazels grew in the ditch and more hazels had invaded the wide space inside the circular bank so that, from a distance, the temple looked like a grove of small shrubs. Birds nested where men had once danced. One oak pole of the death house still showed above the tangled hazels, but the pole was leaning now and its once smooth wood was pitted, black and thick with fungi.

The temple had been abandoned, yet the gods do not forget their shrines. Sometimes, on still days when a mist laid on the pasture, or when the swollen moon hung motionless above the chalk ring, the hazel leaves shivered as though a wind passed through them. The dancers were gone, but the power remained.

And now the Outlander had gone to the temple.

The gods were screaming.

Cloud shadow swallowed the pasture as Lengar and Saban ran towards the Old Temple. Saban was cold and he was scared. Lengar was also frightened, but the Outfolk were famous for their wealth, and Lengar's greed overcame his fear of entering the temple.

The stranger had clambered through the ditch and up the bank, but Lengar went to the old southern entrance where a narrow causeway led into the overgrown interior. Once across the causeway Lengar dropped onto all fours and crawled through the hazels. Saban followed reluctantly, not wanting to be left alone in the pasture when the storm god's anger broke.

To Lengar's surprise the Old Temple was not entirely overgrown for there was a cleared space where the death house had stood. Someone in the tribe must still visit the Old Temple, for the weeds had been cleared, the grass cut with a knife and a single ox-skull lay in the death house where the stranger now sat with his back against the one remaining temple post. The man's face was pale and his eyes were closed, but his chest rose and fell with his laboured breathing. He wore a strip of dark stone inside his left wrist, fastened there by leather laces. There was blood on his woollen trews. The man had dropped his short bow and his quiver of arrows beside the ox-skull, and now clutched a leather bag to his wounded belly. He had been ambushed in the forest three days before. He had not seen his attackers, just felt the sudden hot pain of the thrown spear, then kicked his horse and let it carry him out of danger.

'I'll fetch father,' Saban whispered.

'You won't,' Lengar hissed, and the wounded man must have heard them for he opened his eyes and grimaced as he leaned forward to pick up his bow. But the stranger was slowed by pain, and Lengar was much faster. He dropped his longbow, scrambled from his hiding place and ran across the death house, scooping up the stranger's bow with one hand and his quiver with the other. In his hurry he spilled the arrows so that there was only one left in the leather quiver.

A murmur of thunder sounded from the west. Saban shivered, fearing that the sound would swell to fill the air with the god's rage, but the thunder faded, leaving the sky deathly still.

'Sannas,' the stranger said, then added some words in a tongue that neither Lengar nor Saban spoke.

'Sannas?' Lengar asked.

'Sannas,' the man repeated eagerly. Sannas was the great sorceress of Cathallo, famous throughout the land, and Saban presumed the stranger wanted to be healed by her.

Lengar smiled. 'Sannas is not of our people,' he said. 'Sannas lives north of here.'

The stranger did not understand what Lengar said. 'Erek,' he said, and Saban, still watching from the undergrowth, wondered if that was the stranger's name, or perhaps the name of his god. 'Erek,' the wounded man said more firmly, but the word meant nothing to Lengar who had taken the one arrow from the stranger's quiver and fitted it onto the short bow. The bow was made of strips of wood and antler, glued together and bound with sinew, and Lengar's people had never used such a weapon. They favoured the longer bow carved from the yew tree, but Lengar was curious about the odd weapon. He stretched the string, testing its strength.

'Erek!' the stranger cried loudly.

'You're Outfolk,' Lengar said. 'You have no business here.' He stretched the bow again, surprised by the tension in the short weapon.

'Bring me a healer. Bring me Sannas,' the stranger said in his own tongue.

'If Sannas were here,' Lengar said, recognizing only that name, 'I would kill her first.' He spat. 'That is what I think of Sannas. She is a shrivelled old bitch-cow, a husk of evil, toad-dung made flesh.' He spat again.

The stranger leaned forward and laboriously scooped up the arrows that had spilled from his quiver and formed them into a small sheaf that he held like a knife as though to defend himself. 'Bring me a healer,' he pleaded in his own language. Thunder growled to the west, and the hazel leaves shuddered as a breath of cold wind gusted ahead of the approaching storm. The stranger looked again into Lengar's eyes and saw no pity there. There was only the delight that Lengar took from death. 'No,' he said, 'no, please, no.'

Lengar loosed the arrow. He was only five paces from the stranger and the small arrow struck its target with a sickening force, lurching the man onto his side. The arrow sank deep, leaving only a hand's-breadth of its black-and-white feathered shaft showing at the left side of the stranger's chest. Saban thought the Outlander must be

12

dead because he did not move for a long time, but then the carefully made sheaf of arrows spilled from his hand as, slowly, very slowly, he pushed himself back upright. 'Please,' he said quietly.

'Lengar!' Saban scrambled from the hazels. 'Let me fetch father!'

'Quiet!' Lengar had taken one of his own black-feathered arrows from its quiver and placed it on the short bowstring. He walked towards Saban, aiming the bow at him and grinning when he saw the terror on his half-brother's face.

The stranger also stared at Saban, seeing a tall good-looking boy with tangled black hair and bright anxious eyes. 'Sannas,' the stranger begged Saban, 'take me to Sannas.'

'Sannas doesn't live here,' Saban said, understanding only the sorceress's name.

'We live here,' Lengar announced, now pointing his arrow at the stranger, 'and you're an Outlander and you steal our cattle, enslave our women and cheat our traders.' He let the second arrow loose and, like the first, it thumped into the stranger's chest, though this time into the ribs on his right side. Again the man was jerked aside, but once again he forced himself upright as though his spirit refused to leave his wounded body.

'I can give you power,' he said, as a trickle of bubbly pink blood spilled from his mouth and into his short beard. 'Power,' he whispered.

But Lengar did not understand the man's tongue. He had shot two arrows and still the man refused to die, so Lengar picked up his own longbow, laid an arrow on its string, and faced the stranger. He drew the huge bow back.

13

The stranger shook his head, but he knew his fate now and he stared Lengar in the eyes to show he was not afraid to die. He cursed his killer, though he doubted the gods would listen to him for he was a thief and a fugitive.

Lengar loosed the string and the black-feathered arrow struck deep into the stranger's heart. He must have died in an instant, yet he still thrust his body up as though to fend off the flint arrow-head and then he fell back, shuddered for a few heartbeats, and was still.

Lengar spat on his right hand and rubbed the spittle against the inside of his left wrist where the stranger's bowstring had lashed and stung the skin; Saban, watching his half-brother, understood then why the stranger wore the strip of stone against his forearm. Lengar danced a few steps, celebrating his kill, but he was nervous. Indeed, he was not certain that the man really was dead for he approached the body very cautiously and prodded it with one horn-tipped end of his bow before leaping back in case the corpse came to life and sprang at him, but the stranger did not move.

Lengar edged forward again, snatched the bag from the stranger's dead hand and scuttled away from the body. For a moment or two he stared into the corpse's ashen face, then, confident the man's spirit was truly gone, he tore the lace that secured the bag's neck. He peered inside, was motionless for a heartbeat, then screamed for joy. He had been given power.

Saban, terrified by his brother's scream, shrank back, then edged forward again as Lengar emptied the bag's contents onto the grass beside the whitened ox-skull. To Saban it looked as though a stream of sunlight tumbled from the leather bag.

There were dozens of small lozenge-shaped gold ornaments, each about the size of a man's thumbnail, and four great lozenge plaques that were as big as a man's hand. The lozenges, both big and small, had tiny holes drilled through their narrower points so they could be strung on a sinew or sewn to a garment, and all were made of very thin gold sheets incised with straight lines, though their pattern meant nothing to Lengar who snatched back one of the small lozenges that Saban had dared pick up from the grass. Lengar gathered the lozenges, great and small, into a pile. 'You know what this is?' he asked his younger brother, gesturing at the heap.

'Gold,' Saban said.

'Power,' Lengar said. He glanced at the dead man. 'Do you know what you can do with gold?'

'Wear it?' Saban suggested.

'Fool! You buy men with it.' Lengar rocked back on his heels. The cloud shadows were dark now, and the hazels were tossing in the freshening wind. 'You buy spearmen,' he said, 'you buy archers and warriors! You buy power!'

Saban grabbed one of the small lozenges, then dodged out of the way when Lengar tried to take it back. The boy retreated across the small cleared space and, when it appeared that Lengar would not chase him, he squatted and peered at the scrap of gold. It seemed an odd thing with which to buy power. Saban could imagine men working for food or for pots, for flints or for slaves, or for bronze that could be hammered into knives, axes, swords and spearheads, but for this bright metal? It could not cut, it just was, yet even on that clouded day Saban could see how the metal shone. It shone as though a piece of the sun

15

was trapped within the metal and he suddenly shivered, not because he was naked, but because he had never touched gold before; he had never held a scrap of the almighty sun in his hand. 'We must take it to father,' he said reverently.

'So the old fool can add it to his hoard?' Lengar asked scornfully. He went back to the body and folded the cloak back over the stumps of the arrows to reveal that the dead man's trews were held up by a belt buckled with a great lump of heavy gold while more of the small lozenges hung on a sinew about his neck.

Lengar glanced at his younger brother, licked his lips, then picked up one of the arrows that had fallen from the stranger's hand. He was still carrying his longbow and now he placed the black-and-white fledged arrow onto the string. He was gazing into the hazel undergrowth, deliberately avoiding his half-brother's gaze, but Saban suddenly understood what was in Lengar's mind. If Saban lived to tell their father of this Outfolk treasure then Lengar would lose it, or would at least have to fight for it, but if Saban were discovered dead, with an Outfolk's black-and-white feathered arrow in his ribs, then no one would ever suspect that Lengar had done the killing, nor that Lengar had taken a great treasure for his own use. Thunder swelled in the west and the cold wind flattened the tops of the hazel trees. Lengar was drawing back the bow, though still he did not look at Saban. 'Look at this!' Saban suddenly cried, holding up the small lozenge. 'Look!'

Lengar relaxed the bowstring's pressure as he peered, and at that instant the boy took off like a hare sprung from grass. He burst through the hazels and sprinted across the wide causeway of the Old Temple's entrance of the sun.

There were more rotted posts there, just like the ones around the death house. He had to swerve to negotiate their stumps and, just as he twisted through them, Lengar's arrow whirred past his ear.

Thunder tore the sky to shreds as the first rain fell. The drops were huge. A stab of lightning flashed down to the opposite hillside. Saban ran, twisting and turning, not daring to look back and see if Lengar pursued him. The rain fell harder and harder, filling the air with its malevolent roar, but making a screen to hide the boy as he ran north and east towards the settlement. He screamed as he ran, hoping that some herdsman might still be on the pastureland, but he saw no one until he had passed the grave mounds at the brow of the hill and was running down the muddy path between the small fields of wheat that were being battered by the drenching rain.

Galeth, Saban's uncle, and five other men had been returning to the settlement when they heard the boy's shouts. They turned back up the hill, and Saban ran through the rain to clutch at his uncle's deerskin jerkin. 'What is it, boy?' Galeth asked.

Saban clung to his uncle. 'He tried to kill me!' he gasped. 'He tried to kill me!'

'Who?' Galeth asked. He was the youngest brother of Saban's father, tall, thick-bearded and famous for his feats of strength. Galeth, it was said, had once raised a whole temple pole, and not one of the small ones either, but a big trimmed trunk that jutted high above the other poles. Like his companions, Galeth was carrying a heavy bronze-bladed axe for he had been felling trees when the storm came. 'Who tried to kill you?' Galeth asked.

'He did!' Saban shrieked, pointing up the hill to where

17

Lengar had appeared with the longbow in his hands and a new arrow slotted on its string.

Lengar stopped. He said nothing, but just looked at the group of men who now sheltered his half-brother. He took the arrow off the string.

Galeth gazed at his older nephew. 'You tried to kill your own brother?'

Lengar laughed. 'It was an Outlander, not me.' He walked slowly downhill. His long black hair was wet with rain and lay sleek and close to his head, giving him a frightening appearance.

'An Outlander?' Galeth asked, spitting to avert ill fortune. There were many in Ratharryn who said Galeth should be the next chief instead of Lengar, but the rivalry between uncle and nephew paled against the threat of an Outfolk raid. 'There are Outfolk up on the pasture?' Galeth asked.

'Only the one,' Lengar said carelessly. He pushed the Outfolk arrow into his quiver. 'Only the one,' he said again, 'and he's dead now.'

'So you're safe, boy,' Galeth told Saban, 'you're safe.'

'He tried to kill me,' Saban insisted, 'because of the gold!' He held up the lozenge as proof.

'Gold, eh?' Galeth asked, taking the tiny scrap from Saban's hand. 'Is that what you've got? Gold? We'd better take it to your father.'

Lengar gave Saban a look of utter hatred, but it was too late now. Saban had seen the treasure and Saban had lived and so their father would learn of the gold. Lengar spat, then turned and strode back up the hill. He vanished in the rain, risking the storm's anger so that he could rescue the rest of the gold.

That was the day the stranger came to the Old Temple in the storm, and the day Lengar tried to kill Saban, and the day everything in Ratharryn's world changed.

The storm god raged across the earth that night. Rain flattened the crops and made the hill paths into streamlets. It flooded the marshes north of Ratharryn and the River Mai overflowed her banks to scour fallen trees from the steep valley that twisted through the high ground until it reached the great loop where Ratharryn was built. Ratharryn's ditch was flooded, and the wind tore at the thatch of the huts and moaned among the timber posts of its temples' rings.

No one knew when the first people had come to the land beside the river, nor how they had discovered that Arryn was the god of the valley. Yet Arryn must have revealed himself to those people for they named their new home for him and they edged the hills around his valley with temples. They were simple temples, nothing but clearings in the forest where a ring of tree trunks would be left standing, and for years, no one knew for how many, the folk would follow the wooded paths to those timber rings where they begged the gods to keep them safe. In time Arryn's people cleared away most of the woods, cutting down oak and elm and ash and hazel, and planting barley or wheat in the small fields. They trapped fish in the river that was sacred to Arryn's wife, Mai, they herded cattle on the grasslands and pigs in the patches of woodland that stood between the fields, and the young men of the tribe hunted boar and deer and aurochs and bear and wolf in the wild woods that had now been pressed back beyond the temples.

The first temples decayed and new ones were made, and in time the new ones became old, yet still they were rings of timber, though now the rings were trimmed posts that were raised within a bank and ditch that made a wider circle around the timber rings. Always a circle, for life was a circle, and the sky was a circle, and the edge of the world was circle, and the sun was a circle, and the moon grew to a circle, and that was why the temples at Cathallo and Drewenna, at Maden and Ratharryn, indeed in nearly all the settlements that were scattered across the land, were made as circles.

Cathallo and Ratharryn were the twin tribes of the heartland. They were linked by blood and as jealous as two wives. An advantage to one was an affront to the other, and that night Hengall, chief of the people at Ratharryn, brooded on the gold of the Outfolk. He had waited for Lengar to bring him the treasure, but though Lengar did return to Ratharryn with a leather bag, he did not come to his father's hut and when Hengall sent a slave demanding that his son bring him the treasures, Lengar had answered that he was too tired to obey. So now Hengall was consulting the tribe's high priest.

'He will challenge you,' Hirac said.

'Sons should challenge their fathers,' Hengall answered. The chief was a tall, heavy man with a scarred face and a great ragged beard that was matted with grease. His skin, like the skin of most folk, was dark with ingrained soot and dirt and soil and sweat and smoke. Beneath the dirt his thick arms bore innumerable blue marks to show how many enemies he had slain in battle. His name simply meant the Warrior, though Hengall the Warrior loved peace far more than war.

Hirac was older than Hengall. He was thin, his joints ached and his white beard was scanty. Hengall might lead the tribe, but Hirac spoke with the gods and so his advice was crucial. 'Lengar will fight you,' Hirac warned Hensall.

'He will not.'

'He might. He is young and strong,' Hirac said. The priest was naked though his skin was covered with a dried slurry of chalk and water in which one of his wives had traced swirling patterns with her spread fingers. A squirrel's skull hung from a thong about his neck, while at his waist was a circlet of nutshells and bear's teeth. His hair and beard were caked with red mud that was drying and cracking in the fierce heat of Hengall's fire.

'And I am old and strong,' Hengall said, 'and if he fights, I shall kill him.'

'If you kill him,' Hirac hissed, 'then you will have only two sons left.'

'One son left,' Hengall snarled, and he glowered at the high priest for he disliked being reminded of how few sons he had fathered. Kital, chief of the folk at Cathallo, had eight sons, Ossaya, who had been chief of Madan before Kital conquered it, had fathered six, while Melak, chief of the people at Drewenna, had eleven, so Hengall felt shamed that he had only fathered three sons, and even more shame that one of those sons was a cripple. He had daughters too, of course, and some of them lived, but daughters were not sons. And his second son, the crippled boy, the stuttering fool called Camaban, he would not count as his own. Lengar he acknowledged, and Saban likewise, but not the middle son.

21

'And Lengar won't challenge me,' Hengal declared, 'he won't dare.'

'He's no coward,' warned the priest.

Hengall smiled. 'No, he's no coward, but he only fights when he knows he can win. That is why he will be a good chief if he lives.'

The priest was squatting by the hut's central pole. Between his knees was a pile of slender bones: the ribs of a baby that had died the previous winter. He poked them with a long chalky finger, pushing them into random patterns that he studied with a cocked head. 'Sannas will want the gold,' he said after a while, then paused to let that ominous statement do its work. Hengall, like every other living being, held the sorceress of Cathallo in awe, but he appeared to shrug the thought away. 'And Kital has many spearmen,' Hirac added a further warning.

Hengall prodded the priest, rocking him off balance. 'You let me worry about spears, Hirac. You tell me what the gold means. Why did it come here? Who sent it? What do I do with it?'

The priest glanced about the big hut. A leather screen hung to one side, sheltering the slave girls who attended Hengall's new wife. Hirac knew that a vast treasure was already concealed within the hut, buried under its floor or hidden under heaped pelts. Hengall had ever been a hoarder, never a spender. 'If you keep the gold,' Hirac said, 'then men will try to take it from you. This is no ordinary gold.'

'We don't even know that it is the gold of Sarmennyn,' Hengall said, though without much conviction.

'It is,' Hirac said, gesturing at the single small lozenge, brought by Saban, that glittered on the earth floor between them. Sarmennyn was an Outfolk country many miles to the west, and for the last two moons there had been rumours how the people of Sarmennyn had lost a great treasure. 'Saban saw the treasure,' Hirac said, 'and it is the Outfolk gold, and the Outfolk worship Slaol, though they give him another name . . .' He paused, trying to remember the name, but it would not come. Slaol was the god of the sun, a mighty god, but his power was rivalled by Lahanna, the goddess of the moon, and the two, who had once been lovers, were now estranged. That was the rivalry that dominated Ratharryn and made every decision agonizing, for a gesture to the one god was resented by the other, and Hirac's task was to keep all the rival gods, not just the sun and the moon, but the wind and the soil and the stream and the trees and the beasts and the grass and the bracken and the rain, all of the innumerable gods and spirits and unseen powers, content. Hirac picked up the single small lozenge. 'Slaol sent us the gold,' he said, 'and gold is Slaol's metal, but the lozenge is Lahanna's symbol.'

Hengall hissed, 'Are you saying the gold is Lahanna's?'

Hirac said nothing for a while. The chief waited. It was the high priest's job to determine the meaning of strange events, though Hengall would do his best to influence those meanings to the tribe's advantage. 'Slaol could have kept the gold in Sarmennyn,' Hirac said eventually, 'but he did not. So it is those folk who will suffer its loss. Its coming here is not a bad omen.'

'Good,' Hengall grunted.

'But the shape of the gold,' Hirac went on carefully, 'tells us it once belonged to Lahanna, and I think she tried to retrieve it. Did not Saban say the stranger was asking for Sannas?'

23

'He did.'

'And Sannas reveres Lahanna above all the gods,' the priest said, 'so Slaol must have sent it to us to keep it from reaching her. But Lahanna will be jealous, and she will want something from us.'

'A sacrifice?' Hengall asked suspiciously.

The priest nodded, and Hengall scowled, wondering how many cattle the priest would want to slaughter in Lahanna's temple, but Hirac did not propose any such depredation on the tribe's wealth. The gold was important, its coming was extraordinary and the response must be proportionately generous. 'The goddess will want a spirit,' the high priest said.

Hengall brightened when he realized his cattle were safe. 'You can take that fool Camaban,' the chief said, talking of his disowned second son. 'Make him useful, crush his skull.'

Hirac rocked back on his haunches, his eyes half closed. 'He is marked by Lahanna,' he said quietly. Camaban had come from his mother with a crescent birthmark on his belly and the crescent, like the lozenge, was a shape sacred to the moon. 'Lahanna might be angry if we kill him.'

'Maybe she would like his company?' Hengall suggested slyly. 'Maybe that is why she marked him? So he would be sent to her?'

'True,' Hirac allowed, and the notion emboldened him to a decision. 'We shall keep the gold,' he said, 'and placate Lahanna with the spirit of Camaban.'

'Good,' Hengall said. He turned to the leather screen and shouted a name. A slave girl crept nervously into the firelight. 'If I'm to fight Lengar in the morning,' the chief said to the high priest, 'then I'd better make another son

24

now.' He gestured the girl to the pile of furs that was his bed.

The high priest gathered the baby's bones, then hurried to his own hut through the growing rain that washed the chalk from his skin.

The wind blew on. Lightning slithered to earth, turning the world soot-black and chalk-white. The gods were screaming and men could only cower.

Saban feared going to sleep, not because the storm god was hammering the earth, but because he thought Lengar might come in the night to punish him for taking the lozenge. But his elder brother left him undisturbed and in the dawn Saban crept from his mother's hut into a damp and chill wind. The remnants of the storm gusted patches of mist within the vast earthen bank which surrounded the settlement while the sun hid its face behind cloud, appearing only as an occasional dull disc in the vaporous grey. A thatched roof, sodden with rainwater, had collapsed in the night, and folk marvelled that the family had not been crushed. A succession of women and slaves went through the embankment's southern causeway to fetch water from the swollen river, while children carried the night's pots of urine to the tanners' pits which had been flooded, but they all hurried back, eager not to miss the confrontation between Lengar and his father. Even folk who lived beyond the great wall, in the huts up on the higher land, had heard the news and suddenly found reason to come to Ratharryn that morning. Lengar had found the Outfolk gold, Hengall wanted it, and one of the two had to prevail.

Hengall appeared first. He emerged from his hut wearing a great cape of bear fur and strolled with apparent unconcern about the settlement. He greeted Saban by ruffling his hair, then talked with the priests about the problems of replacing one of the great posts of the Temple of Lahanna, and afterwards he sat on a stool outside his hut and listened to anxious accounts of the damage done by the night's rain to the wheatfields. 'We can always buy grain,' Hengall announced in a loud voice so that as many people as possible could hear him. 'There are those who say that the wealth hidden in my hut should be used to hire weapons, but it might serve us better if we buy grain. And we have pigs to eat, and rain doesn't kill the fish in the river. We won't starve.' He opened his cloak and slapped his big bare belly. 'It won't shrink this year!' Folk laughed.

Galeth arrived with a half-dozen men and squatted near his brother's hut. All of them carried spears and Hengall understood that they had come to support him, but he made no mention of the expected confrontation. Instead he asked Galeth whether he had found an oak large enough to replace the decayed temple pole in Lahanna's shrine.

'We found it,' Galeth said, 'but we didn't cut it.'

'You didn't cut it?'

'The day was late, the axes blunt.'

Hengall grinned. 'Yet I hear your woman's pregnant?'

Galeth looked coyly pleased. His first wife had died a year before, leaving him with a son a year younger than Saban, and he had just taken a new woman. 'She is,' he admitted.

'Then at least one of your blades is sharp,' Hengall said, provoking more laughter.

The laughter died abruptly, for Lengar chose that moment to appear from his own hut, and in that grey morning he shone like the sun itself. Ralla, his mother and Hengall's oldest wife, must have sat through the stormy darkness threading the small lozenges on sinews so that her son could wear them all as necklaces, and she had sewn the four large gold pieces directly onto his deerskin jerkin over which he wore the stranger's gold-buckled belt. A dozen young warriors, all of them Lengar's close hunting companions, followed him while behind that spear-carrying band was a muddy group of excited children who waved sticks in imitation of the hunting spear in Lengar's hand.

Lengar ignored his father at first. Instead he paraded through the huts, past the two temples built within the great embankment, then up to the potters' huts and tanners' pits at the north of the enclosure. His followers clashed their spears together, and more and more folk gathered behind him so that eventually he led his excited procession in an intricate path that twisted between the rain-soaked thatch of the low round huts. Only after he had threaded the settlement twice did he turn towards his father.

Hengall stood as his son approached. He had let Lengar have his time of glory, and now he stood and shrugged the bear cloak from his shoulders and threw it, fur down, into the mud at his feet. He wiped the mist's moisture from his face with the ends of his big beard, then waited bare-chested so that all the folk in Ratharryn could see how thick the blue marks of dead enemies and slaughtered beasts clustered on his skin. He stood silent, the wind stirring his ragged black hair.

Lengar stopped opposite his father. He was as tall as Hengall, but not so heavily muscled. In a fight he would probably prove the quicker man while Hengall would be the stronger, yet Hengall showed no fear of such a fight. Instead he yawned, then nodded at his eldest son. 'You have brought me the stranger's gold. That is good.' He gestured at the bear cloak that lay on the ground between them. 'Put everything there, son,' he growled.

Lengar stiffened. Most of the watching tribe thought he would fight, for his eyes bespoke a love of violence that verged on madness, but his father's gaze was steady and Lengar chose to argue instead of striking with his spear. 'If a man finds an antler in the woods,' he demanded, 'must he give it to his father?' He spoke loudly enough for all the crowd to hear. The people of Ratharryn had clustered between the nearer huts, leaving a space for the confrontation, and some of them now called out their agreement with Lengar. 'Or if I find the honey of the wild bees,' Lengar asked, emboldened by their support, 'must I endure the stings, then yield the honey to my father?'

'Yes,' Hengall said, then yawned again. 'In the cloak, boy.'

'A warrior comes to our land,' Lengar cried, 'a stranger of the Outfolk, and he brings gold. I kill the stranger and take his gold. Is it not mine?' A few in the crowd shouted that the gold was indeed his, but not quite so many as had shouted before. Hengall's bulk and air of unconcern was unsettling.

The chief fished in a pouch that hung from his belt and took out the small lozenge that Saban had brought from the Old Temple. He dropped the scrap of gold onto the cloak. 'Now put the rest there,' he said to Lengar.

'The gold is mine!' Lengar insisted, and this time only Ralla, his mother, and Jegar, one of his closest friends, shouted their support. Jegar was a small and wiry man, the same age as Lengar, but already one of the tribe's greatest warriors. He killed in battle with an abandon that was equal to Lengar's own and he was avid for a fight now, but none of Lengar's other hunting companions had the belly to confront Hengall. They were relying on Lengar to win the confrontation and it seemed he would do that by violence for he suddenly raised his spear, but instead of stabbing with the blade he held it high in the air to draw attention to his words. 'I found the gold! I killed for the gold! The gold came to me! And is it now to be hidden in my father's hut? Is it to gather dust there?' Those words provoked sympathetic murmurs for many in Ratharryn resented the way Hengall hoarded treasures. In Drewenna or Cathallo the chief displayed his wealth, he rewarded his warriors with bronze, he hung his women with shining metal and he made great temples, but Hengall stored Ratharryn's wealth in his hut.

'What would you do with the gold?' Galeth intervened. He was standing now, and he had untied his tail of hair which hung black and ragged about his face so that he looked like a warrior on the edge of battle. His spear blade was levelled. 'Tell us, nephew,' he challenged Lengar, 'what will you do with the gold?'

Jegar hefted his spear to meet Galeth's challenge, but Lengar pushed his friend's blade down. 'With this gold,' he shouted, patting the lozenges on his chest, 'we should raise warriors, spearmen, archers, and end Cathallo for ever!' Now the voices that had first supported him shouted again, for there were many in Ratharryn who feared

Cathallo's growth. Only the previous summer the warriors of Cathallo had taken the settlement of Maden that lay between Ratharryn and Cathallo, and hardly a week passed without Cathallo's warriors scouring Hengall's land for cattle or pigs, and many in the tribe resented that Hengall appeared to be doing nothing to stop the taunting raids. 'There was a time when Cathallo paid us tribute!' Lengar shouted, encouraged by the crowd's support. 'When their women came to dance at our temples! Now we cower whenever a warrior of Cathallo comes near! We grovel to that foul bitch, Sannas! And the gold and the bronze and the amber that could free us, where is it? And where will this gold go if I give it up? There!' With that last word he turned and pointed the spear at his father. 'And what will Hengall do with the gold?' Lengar asked. 'He will bury it! Gold for the moles! Metal for the worms! Treasure for the grubs! We scratch for flint and all the while we have gold!'

Hengall shook his head sadly. The crowd that had cheered Lengar's last words fell silent and waited for the fight to start. Lengar's men must have thought the moment was close for they summoned their courage and closed up behind their leader with levelled weapons. Jegar was dancing to and fro, his teeth bared and spear blade pointing at Hengall's belly. Galeth edged closer to Hengall, ready to defend his brother, but Hengall waved Galeth away, then turned, stooped and fetched his war mace from where it had been hidden under the low thatch of his hut's eave. The mace was a shaft of oak as thick as a warrior's wrist topped with a misshapen lump of grey stone that could crush a grown man's skull as if it were a wren's egg. Hengall hefted the mace, then nodded at the cloak of bear fur.

'All the treasure, boy,' he said, deliberately insulting his son, 'all of it, in the cloak.'

Lengar stared at him. The spear had a longer reach than the mace, but if his first lunge missed then he knew the stone head would break his skull. So Lengar hesitated, and Jegar pushed past him. Hengall pointed the mace at Jegar. 'I killed your father, boy,' he snarled, 'when he challenged me for the chiefdom, and I crushed his bones and fed his flesh to the pigs, but I kept his jawbone. Hirac!'

The high priest, his skin mottled with dirt and chalk, bobbed at the edge of the crowd.

'You know where the jawbone is hidden?' Hengall demanded.

'I do,' Hirac said.

'Then if this worm does not step back,' Hengall said, staring at Jegar, 'make a curse on his blood. Curdle his loins. Fill his belly with black worms.'

Jegar paused for a heartbeat. Although he did not fear Hengall's mace, he did fear Hirac's curse, so he stepped back. Hengall looked back at his son. 'In the cloak, son,' he said softly, 'and hurry! I want my breakfast!'

Lengar's defiance crumpled. For a second it seemed he would leap at his father, preferring death to dishonour, but then he just sagged and, with a despairing gesture, dropped the spear, unlooped the gold from his neck and cut the stitches holding the great lozenges to his jerkin. He placed all the lozenges in the bear cloak, then unclasped the belt and tossed it with its great gold buckle onto the lozenges. 'I found the gold,' he protested lamely when he had finished.

'You and Saban found it,' Hengall agreed, 'but you found it in the Old Temple, not in the woods, and that means the gold was sent to all of us! And why?' The chief had raised his voice so that all the folk could hear him. 'The gods have not revealed their purpose, so we must wait to know the answer. But it is Slaol's gold, and he sent it to us, and he must have had a reason.' He hooked the bear cloak with his foot, dragging it and the treasures towards his hut's doorway from where a pair of woman's hands reached out to haul the glittering pile inwards. A faint groan went through the crowd, for they knew it would be a long time before they ever saw that gold again. Hengall ignored the groan. 'There are those here,' he shouted, 'who would have me lead our warriors against the folk of Cathallo, and there are folk in Cathallo who would like their young men to attack us! Yet not all in Cathallo wish war on us. They know that many of their young men will die, and that even if they win the war they will be weakened by the fight. So there will be no war,' he finished abruptly. That had been a very long speech for Hengall, and a rare one in that he had revealed his thinking. Tell someone your thoughts, he had once said, and you give away your soul, but he was hardly giving away secrets when he declared his abhorrence of war. Hengall the Warrior hated war. The business of life, he liked to say, is to plant grain, not blades. He did not mind leading war bands against Outlanders, for they were strangers and thieves, but he detested fighting against the neighbouring tribes, for they were cousins and they shared Ratharryn's language and Ratharryn's gods. He looked at Lengar. 'Where's the dead Outlander?' he asked.

'In the Old Temple,' Lengar muttered. His tone was surly.

'Take a priest,' Hengall instructed Galeth, 'and get rid of

the body.' He ducked back into his hut, leaving Lengar defeated and humiliated.

The last of the mists vanished as the sun broke through the thin cloud. The moss-covered thatch steamed gently. The excitement in Ratharryn was over for the moment, though there were still the after-effects of the storm to marvel at. The river flowed above its banks, the great ditch which lay inside the encircling embankment was flooded and the fields of wheat and barley were beaten flat.

And Hengall was still the chief.

The vast earthen embankment defined Ratharryn. Folk still marvelled that their ancestors had made such a wall for it stood five times the height of a man and ringed the huts where close to a hundred families lived. The bank had been scraped from soil and chalk with antlers and ox-blades, and was topped by the skulls of oxen, wolves and enemy spearmen to keep away the spirits of the dark forest. Every settlement, even the mean houses up on the higher land, had skulls to frighten the spirits, but Ratharryn mounted its skulls on the great earth bank that also served to deter and awe the tribe's enemies.

The families all lived in the southern part of the enclosure, while in the north were the huts of the potters and carpenters, the forge of the tribe's one smith and the pits of the leather workers. There was still space inside the bank where herds of cattle and pigs could be sheltered if an enemy threatened, and at those times the people would throng to the two temples built inside the earthen ring. Both shrines were rings of timber poles. The largest had five rings and was a temple to Lahanna, the goddess of the moon, while the smaller, with just three rings, was for Arryn, the god of the valley, and for Mai, his wife, who was goddess of the river. The highest poles of those temples stretched three times the height of Galeth, who was the tribe's tallest man, but they were dwarfed by the third temple which lay just to the south of the encircling embankment. That third temple had six rings of timber, and two of the rings had wooden lintels spanning their posts' tops, and that temple belonged to Slaol, the sun god. The Sun Temple had been deliberately built outside the settlement for Slaol and Lahanna were rivals and their temples had to be separated so that a sacrifice at one could not be seen from the other.

Slaol, Lahanna, Arryn and Mai were the chief deities of Ratharryn, but the people knew there were a thousand other gods in the valley, and as many again in the hills, and countless more beyond the hills, and a myriad in the winds. No tribe could build temples for each of the gods, nor even know who they all were, and besides that multitude of unknown gods there were the spirits of the dead, spirits of animals, spirits of streams, spirits of trees, spirits of fire, spirits of the air, spirits of everything that crept and breathed and killed or grew. And if a man was silent, standing on a hill in the evening quiet, he could sometimes hear the murmuring of the spirits, and that murmur could make a man mad unless he constantly prayed at the shrines.

Then there was a fourth shrine, the Old Temple, that lay on the southern hill where it was overgrown with hazel and choked with weeds. That temple had been dedicated to Slaol, but years before, no one could remember when,

the tribe had built Slaol the new temple close to the settlement and the old shrine had been abandoned. It had just
decayed, yet it must still possess power, for it was there
that the gold of the Outfolk had come. Now, on the morning after the great storm, Galeth took three men to the
ancient temple to find and bury the Outlander's body.
The four men were accompanied by Neel, the youngest of
Ratharryn's priests, who went to protect them from the
dead stranger's spirit.

The group stopped at the brow of the hill and made a
bow to the grave mounds that stood between the Old
Temple and the settlement. Neel howled like a dog to
attract the attention of the ancestors' spirits, then told those
spirits what errand brought the men to the high ground.
Galeth, while Neel chanted his news to the dead, stared
at the sacred way that ran straight as an arrow's flight off
to the west. The ancestors had built that path but, like the
Old Temple, it was now overgrown and abandoned, and
not even the priests could say why its long straight ditches
and banks had been scratched from the earth. Hirac
thought it had been made to placate Rannos, the god of
thunder, but he did not really know nor did he care. Now,
as Galeth leaned on his spear and waited for Neel to detect
an omen, it seemed to him that the world was wrong. It
was decaying, just as the ancient sacred path and the Old
Temple were decaying. Just as Ratharryn was decaying
under the siege of sad harvests and persistent sickness.
There was a tiredness in the air, as though the gods had
become weary of their endless circling of the green world,
and that tiredness frightened Galeth.

'We can go,' Neel declared, though none of the men
accompanying him had seen what sign the young priest

had detected in the landscape. Perhaps it was the brush of a mist tendril against a tree bough, or the banking flight of a hawk, or the twitch of a hare in the long grass, but Neel was confident that the ancestral spirits had given their approval. So the small party walked on into a small valley and up the further slope to the Old Temple.

Neel led the way through the rotted posts on the causeway and into the hazels. The young priest, his deerskin tunic soaked from the wet leaves, stopped with surprise when he reached the old death house. He frowned and hissed, then touched his groin to avert evil. It was not the stranger's body that caused that precaution, but rather because the space in the shrine's centre had been deliberately cleared of weeds and hazel. It looked as though someone worshipped here in secret, though the presence of the ox-skull suggested that whoever came to this forgotten place prayed to Slaol for the ox was Slaol's beast, just as the badger and the bat and the owl belonged to Lahanna.

Galeth also touched his groin, but he was warding off the spirit of the dead stranger who lay on his back with the three arrows still protruding from his chest. Neel dropped onto all fours and barked like a dog to drive the dead man's spirit far from the cold flesh. He barked and howled for a long time, then suddenly stood, brushed his hands and said the corpse was now safe. 'Strip him,' Galeth told his men, 'and dig a grave for him in the ditch.' The stranger would be given no ceremony in his death, since he was not of Ratharryn. He was a mere Outlander. No one would dance for him and no one would sing for him, for his ancestors were not Ratharryn's ancestors.

Galeth, despite his huge strength, found it hard to free

the arrows for the stranger's cold flesh had tightened on the wooden shafts, but the shafts did at last come loose, though their flint heads stayed inside the corpse as they were supposed to do. All the tribes tied their arrow-heads loosely so that an animal or an enemy could not pull out the barbed flint which, instead, would stay in the wound to fester. Galeth tossed the three shafts away, then stripped the body naked, leaving only the flat piece of stone that was tied to the dead man's wrist. Neel feared that the stone, which was beautifully polished, was a magical amulet that could infect Ratharryn with a dark spirit from the Outfolk's nightmares, and though Galeth insisted that it had merely protected the man's wrist from his bowstring's lash, the young priest would not be persuaded. He touched his groin to avert evil, then spat on the stone. 'Bury it!'

Galeth's men used antler picks and ox shoulder-blade shovels to deepen the ditch beside the temple's entrance to the sun, then Galeth dragged the naked body through the hazels and dumped it in the shallow hole. The stranger's remaining arrows were broken and tossed in beside him, and then the spoil was kicked over the body and trampled flat. Neel urinated on the grave, mumbled a curse on the dead man's spirit, then turned back into the temple.

'Aren't we finished?' Galeth asked.

The young priest raised a hand to demand silence. He was creeping through the hazels, knees bent, stopping every other pace to listen, just as though he were stalking some large beast. Galeth let him go, presuming that Neel was making certain the stranger's spirit was not clinging to the temple, but then there was a rush of feet, a yelp and a piteous howl from deep within the hazels and Galeth

38

ran into the shrine's centre to find Neel holding a struggling creature by the ear. The priest's captive was a dirty youth with wild black hair that hung matted over a filthy face, so filthy that he seemed as much beast as human. The youth, who was skeletally thin, was beating at Neel's legs and squealing like a pig while Neel flailed wildly in an attempt to silence him.

'Let him go,' Galeth ordered.

'Hirac wants him,' Neel said, at last succeeding in landing a stinging blow on the youth's face. 'And I want to know why he's been hiding here! I smelt him. Filthy beast,' he spat at the boy, then clouted him again. 'I knew someone had been interfering here,' Neel went on triumphantly, gesturing with his free hand at the carefully cleared space where the ox-skull sat, 'and it's this dirty little wretch!' The last word turned into an agonized scream as the priest suddenly let go of the boy's ear and doubled over in pain, and Galeth saw that the boy had reached under Neel's bone-fringed tunic to squeeze his groin, and then, like a fox cub unexpectedly released from a hound's jaws, dropped to all fours and scrambled into the hazels.

'Fetch him!' Neel shouted. His hands were clutched to his groin and he was rocking back and forward to contain the agony.

'Let him be,' Galeth said.

'Hirac wants him!' Neel insisted.

'Then let Hirac fetch him,' Galeth retorted angrily. 'And go. Go!' He drove the injured priest from the temple's cleared centre, then crouched beside the hazels where the strange creature had vanished. 'Camaban?' Galeth called into the leaves. 'Camaban?' There was no answer. 'I'm not going to hurt you.'

'Everyone hurts m-m-me,' Camaban said from deep in the bushes.

'I don't,' Galeth said, 'you know I don't.' There was a pause and then Camaban appeared nervously from deep inside the hazel thicket. His face was long and thin, with a prominent jaw and large green eyes that were wary. 'Come and talk to me,' said Galeth, retreating to the centre of the clearing. 'I won't hurt you. I've never hurt you.'

Camaban crept forward on hands and feet. He could stand, he could even walk, but his gait was grotesquely dipping since he had been born with a clubbed left foot, for which reason he had been named Camaban. The name meant Crooked Child, though most of the tribe's children called him Pig, or worse. He was Hengall's second son, but Hengall had disowned him and banished him from Ratharryn's walls, dooming the child to scavenge a living among the folk who lived beyond the great embankment. Camaban had been ten when he was cast out, and that had been four summers before, and many marvelled that Camaban had lived since his banishment. Most cripples died very young, or else were chosen to die for the gods, but Camaban had survived. By now, if he had not been a cripple and an outcast, he would have taken the ordeals of manhood, but the tribe would not take him as a man so he was still a child, the crooked child.

Hengall would have preferred to kill Camaban at birth because a crippled son was a disastrous omen, worse than a daughter, but the boy had been born with the red mark on his belly and the mark was shaped like a crescent moon and Hirac had declared that the baby was marked by Lahanna. The child might yet walk, the high priest had said, so give him time. Camaban's mother had also begged for his life. She had then been Hengall's oldest wife and had been barren for so long that it was thought she would never give birth. She had prayed to Lahanna, as all childless women do, and she had made a pilgrimage to Cathallo where Sannas, the sorceress, had given her herbs to eat and made her lie one full night wrapped in the bloody pelt of a newly killed wolf. Camaban came nine moons later, but was born crooked. His mother pleaded for him, but it was the moon mark on Camaban's belly that persuaded Hengall to spare the boy. Camaban's mother never had another child, but she had loved her wolf-son and when she died Camaban had wailed like an orphaned cub. Hengall had struck his son to silence and then, in disgust, had ordered that the cripple be cast outside Ratharryn's wall.

'Are you hungry?' Galeth now asked the boy. 'I know you can talk,' he said after waiting for an answer, 'you talked just now! Are you hungry?'

'I'm always hungry,' Camaban answered, peering suspiciously from under his tangle of matted hair.

'I'll have Lidda bring you food,' Galeth said. 'But where should she leave it?'

'B-b-by the river,' Camaban said, 'where Hirac's son died.' Everyone knew that benighted place downstream from the settlement. The high priest's child had drowned there, and now a sloe bush, which Hirac claimed was his son's spirit, grew among the alders and willow.

'Not here?' Galeth asked.

'This is secret!' Camaban said fiercely, then pointed up to the sky. 'Look!' he said excitedly. Galeth looked and saw nothing. 'The p-p-post!' Camaban stuttered. 'The p-post.'

Galeth looked again. 'The post?' he asked, then remembered that there had been one post of the death house left in the Old Temple. It had been a familiar enough landmark, jutting and leaning from the clump of hazels, but now it was broken. The lower half was still planted in the earth, but the upper part lay charred and shattered among the undergrowth. 'It was struck by lightning,' Galeth said.

'Slaol,' Camaban said.

'Not Slaol,' Galeth said, 'Rannos.' Rannos was the god of lightning.

'Slaol!' Camaban insisted angrily. 'Slaol!'

'All right! Slaol,' Galeth said good-naturedly. He looked down at the wild-haired boy, whose face was contorted with rage. 'And what do you know of Slaol?'

'He t-t-talks to me,' Camaban said.

Galeth touched his groin to deflect the god's displeasure. 'Talks to you?'

'All night sometimes,' Camaban said. 'And he was angry because L-L-Lengar came back and t-t-took the treasure away. It's Slaol's treasure, see?' He said this last very earnestly.

'How do you know Lengar took the treasure?' Galeth asked.

'B-b-because I watched him! I was here! He t-t-tried to kill Saban and didn't see me. I was in here.' Camaban twisted round to burrow back into the hazel bushes. Galeth followed, crawling down a passage that had been trampled through the weeds to where Camaban had woven supple branches together into a living hut. 'Here's where I live,' Camaban said, staring defiantly at his uncle. 'I'm the g-g-guardian of the temple.'

Galeth could have cried for pity at the boy's pathetic boast. Camaban's bed was a pile of soaking bracken, beside which lay his few belongings: a fox's skull, a broken pot and a raven's wing. His only clothing was a rotting sheep's pelt that stank like a tanner's pit. 'So no one knows that you live here?' Galeth asked.

'Only you,' the boy said trustingly. 'I haven't even t-t-told Saban. He brings me food sometimes, b-b-but I make him take it to the river.'

'Saban brings you food?' Galeth asked, surprised and pleased. 'And you say Slaol talks to you here?'

'Every d-d-day,' Camaban stuttered.

Galeth smiled at that nonsense, but Camaban did not see for he had turned and reached further into the leaves where, from a hiding place, he brought out a short bow. It was an Outfolk bow, the stranger's bow with its wrappings of sinew lashed about the strips of wood and antler. 'L-L-Lengar used it last night,' Camaban said. 'The m-m-man was d-d-dying anyway.' He paused, looking worried. 'Why does H-H-Hirac want me?' he asked.

Galeth hesitated. He did not want to say that Camaban was to be sacrificed, though there could be no other reason for Hirac's demand.

'He wants to k-k-kill me,' Camaban said calmly, 'doesn't he?'

Galeth nodded reluctantly. He wanted to tell his outcast nephew to run away, to go west or south into the woods, but what good would such advice do? The child would die anyway, caught by beasts or captured by slavers, and it would be better if he were given to Lahanna. 'You will go to the goddess, Camaban,' Galeth said, 'and you'll become a star and will look down on us.'

'When?' Camaban asked, seemingly unmoved by his uncle's promise.

'Tomorrow, I think.'

The boy gave Galeth a mischievous grin. 'You c-c-can tell Hirac that I'll b-b-be at Ratharryn in the morning.' He turned to push the precious bow back into its hiding place. Other things were concealed there: the stranger's empty quiver, a snake's skin, the bones of a murdered child, more bones that had small marks scratched on their flanks and, most precious of all, two of the small golden lozenges that Camaban had retrieved while Lengar had pursued Saban. Now he took those lozenges and held them tight in his fist, but did not show them to Galeth. 'You think I'm a fool,' he asked, 'don't you?'

'No,' Galeth said.

'B-b-but I am,' Camaban said. He was Slaol's fool, and he dreamed dreams.

But no one took any notice, for he was crippled. So they would kill him.

Next morning Neel had two men dig a shallow grave in Lahanna's temple, just beside the outer ring of poles. It was, the men agreed, an auspicious day for the sacrifice for the clouds that had trailed the storm were thinning fast and Lahanna was showing her pale face in Slaol's sky.

A few darker clouds appeared as the crowd gathered about the temple's five rings and some feared that Hirac would delay the sacrifice, but he must not have been concerned about the clouds for at last the dancers appeared from the high priest's hut. The dancers were women who carried leafy ash branches with which they swept the ground as they capered ahead of the seven priests whose naked bodies had been whitened with the slurry of chalk in which finger patterns swirled. Hirac wore a pair of antlers tied to his head with leather laces and the horns tossed dangerously as he danced behind the women. A ring of bones circled his waist, more bones hung from his mud-crusted hair, and a shining talisman of amber dangled at his neck. Neel, the youngest priest, played a flute made from the leg bone of a swan and its notes skittered wildly as he danced. Gilan, who was next oldest after Hirac, led Camaban by the hand. The boy had been allowed back into Ratharryn for this one day, and while he was inside the embankment the women had woven flowers into his black hair that had been untangled with bone combs so that it now fell straight to his thin waist. He too was naked, and his washed skin looked unnaturally clean. The red mark of Lahanna showed on his flat belly. Like Hengall's other two sons he was tall, though each time he stepped on his left foot his whole body made a grotesque twisting dip. Hengall and the tribe's elders followed the priests.

Four men began to beat wooden drums as the procession approached, and the tribe, ringing the temple, began to dance. At first they just swayed from side to side, but as the drummers increased the speed of their beating they stepped sunwise about the circle. They paused only to make way for the priests and the elders and, once the procession had passed through them, the dancing ring closed up.

Only the priests and the victim were allowed through the gap in the shallow bank that ringed the temple. Hirac was first, and he went to the newly dug grave where he howled up at the faded moon to draw the goddess's attention while Gilan led Camaban to the circle's far side as the other priests capered about the temple rings. One held the tribe's skull pole high so that the ancestors could see what important thing was being done in Ratharryn this day, while another carried the massive thigh bone of an aurochs. One end of the bone was a gnarled and knobbly mass that had been painted with red ochre. It was the tribe's Kill-Child, and the watching children, who danced with their parents to the beat of the drums, eyed it warily.

Hengall stood in the temple entrance. He alone did not dance. At his feet lay gifts for the goddess: a stone mace, an ingot of bronze and an Outfolk jar with its pattern of cords pressed into the clay. The priests, who did no work in the fields and raised no flocks or herds, would keep those gifts and trade them for food.

The tribe danced until their legs were tired, until they were almost in a trance induced by the drums and by their own chanting. They called Lahanna's name while the sweepers, who had driven away any spirits that might try to intrude on the ceremony, dropped their ash branches and began to sing a repetitive song that called on the moon goddess. Watch us, they sang, see what we bring to you, watch us, and there was happiness in their voices for they knew that the gift would bring pleasure to the goddess.

Hirac danced with closed eyes. The sweat was making runnels through the chalked pattern on his skin and it seemed, in his ecstasy, as though he might fall into the newly dug grave, but he suddenly became still, opened his eyes, and howled again at the moon that still glimmered between the white clouds.

A quiet dropped on the temple. The dancers slowed and stopped, the song faded, the drummers rested their fingers and Neel let the swan-bone flute fall silent.

46

Hirac howled again, then reached out with his right hand and took the Kill-Child. The priest with the skull pole moved close behind the high priest so that the ancestors could see all that happened.

Gilan urged Camaban forward. No one expected the boy to go willingly, but to their surprise the naked youth limped unhesitatingly towards the grave and a sigh of approval sounded from the tribe. It was better when the sacrifice was willing, even if the willingness did come from stupidity.

Camaban stopped beside his grave, exactly where he was supposed to stop, and Hirac forced a smile to soothe any fears the boy might have. Camaban blinked up at the priest, but said nothing. He had not spoken all day, not even when the women had hurt him by tugging at the knots in his hair with their long-toothed combs. He was smiling.

'Who speaks for the boy?' Hirac demanded.

'I do,' Hengall growled from the temple's entrance.

'What is his name?'

'Camaban,' Hengall said.

Hirac paused, angry that the ritual was not being observed. 'What is his name?' he called again, louder this time.

'Camaban,' Hengall said, and then, after a pause, 'son of Hengall, son of Lock.'

A cloud covered the sun, casting a shadow over the temple. Some in the tribe touched their groins to avert ill luck, but others noted that Lahanna still showed in the sky.

'Who has the life of Camaban, son of Hengall, son of Lock?' Hirac demanded.

'I do,' Hengall said, and opened a leather pouch that hung from his belt and took from it a small chalk ball. He gave it to Neel who carried it to Hirac.

The ball, no larger than an eye, was the token carved at the birth of a child which was destroyed when the child became an adult; until then it was the possessor of the child's spirit. If the child died the ball could be ground into dust, and the dust mixed with water or milk and then drunk so that the spirit would pass to another body. If the child vanished, snatched by the spirits or by an Outfolk hunting party seeking slaves, then the ball might be buried by a temple post so that the Gods would offer the missing child protection.

Hirac took the ball, rubbed it in his groin, and then held it high in the air towards the moon. 'Lahanna!' he cried. 'We bring you a gift! We give you Camaban, son of Hengall, son of Lock!' He threw the ball onto the grass beyond the grave. Camaban smiled again, and for a moment it looked as though he might lurch forward and pick it up, but Gilan whispered at him to be still and the boy obeyed.

Hirac stepped over the grave. 'Camaban,' he shouted, 'son of Hengall, son of Lock, I give you to Lahanna! Your flesh will be her flesh, your blood her blood and your spirit her spirit. Camaban, son of Hengall, son of Lock, I cast you from the tribe into the company of the goddess. I destroy you!' And with those words he raised the Kill-Child high over his head.

'No!' a frightened voice called, and the whole astonished tribe looked to see that it was Saban who had spoken. The boy seemed aghast himself, for he placed a hand over his mouth, but his distress was plain. Camaban was his half-brother. 'No,' he whispered behind his hand, 'please, no!'

Hengall scowled, but Galeth put a comforting arm on Saban's shoulder. 'It has to happen,' Galeth whispered to the boy.

'He's my brother,' Saban protested.

'It has to happen,' Galeth insisted.

'Quiet!' Hengall growled, and Lengar, who had been sullen ever since his loss of face the previous morning, smiled to see that his younger brother was also out of favour with their father.

'Camaban,' Hirac shouted, 'son of Hengall, son of Lock, I give you to Lahanna!' Annoyed by Saban's interruption, he brought the great bone club down so that its ochred end smashed the chalk ball into fragments. He pounded the fragments into dust, and the watching crowd moaned as Camaban's spirit was thus obliterated. Lengar grinned, while Hengall's face showed nothing. Galeth flinched and Saban was weeping, but there was nothing they could do. This was business for the gods and for the priests.

'What is the boy's name?' Hirac demanded.

'He has no name,' Gilan responded.

'Who is his father?' Hirac asked.

'He has no father,' Gilan said.

'What is his tribe?'

'He has no tribe,' Gilan intoned. 'He does not exist.'

Hirac stared into Camaban's green eyes. He did not see a boy, for the boy was already dead, his life-spirit shattered and crushed into white dust. 'Kneel,' he ordered.

The youth obediently knelt. To some of the tribe it seemed odd that such a tall youth was to be killed by the aurochs' bone, but, other than Saban, few in Ratharryn regretted Camaban's death. Cripples brought ill luck, so

49

cripples were better dead, to which end Hirac raised the
Kill-Child high above his head, looked once at Lahanna
then down to Camaban. The high priest tensed to give the
killing blow, but never gave it. He was motionless, and
there was a sudden horror on Hirac's face, and the horror
was compounded because at that moment a rift opened in
the clouds covering Slaol and a beam of sunlight lanced
into the temple. A raven settled on one of the tallest poles
and called loudly.

The Kill-Child quivered in Hirac's hands, but he could
not bring it down.

'Kill it,' Gilan whispered, 'kill it!' But Gilan was standing
behind Camaban and he could not see what Hirac could
see. Hirac was staring down at Camaban who had stuck
out his tongue and on the tongue were two slivers of gold.
Outfolk gold. Slaol's gold.

The raven called again and Hirac looked up at the bird,
wondering what its presence portended.

Camaban tucked the gold pieces back into his cheek,
wet a finger and dabbed it into the powdered chalk of his
soul. 'Slaol will be angry if you kill me,' he said to Hirac
without stuttering, then he licked the chalk off his finger.
He collected more, assembling his shattered spirit and eating it.

'Kill it!' Neel screamed.

'Kill it!' Hengall echoed.

'Kill it!' Lengar called.

'Kill it!' the crowd shouted.

But Hirac could not move. Camaban ate more chalk,
then looked up at the priest. 'Slaol commands you to spare
me,' he said very calmly, still without any stutter.

Hirac stepped back, almost into the grave, and let the

Kill-Child fall. 'The goddess,' he announced hoarsely, 'has rejected the sacrifice.'

The crowd wailed. Saban, his eyes full of tears, was laughing.

And the crooked child went free.

There was fear in Ratharryn after the failed sacrifice for
there were few omens worse than a god rejecting a gift.
Hirac would not say why he had refused to kill the child,
only that he had been given a sign, then he took himself
to his hut where his wives claimed he was suffering from
a fever, and two nights later those same wives wailed in the
darkness because the high priest was dead. They blamed
Camaban, saying the cripple had cursed Hirac, but Gilan,
who was now Ratharryn's oldest priest, claimed that it
had been a nonsense trying to kill a child marked with
Lahanna's sign. Hirac had only himself to blame, Gilan
said, for Hirac had woefully mistranslated the message of
the gods. The gold had gone to the Old Temple and that
was surely a sign that Slaol wanted the temple remade.
Hengall listened to Gilan, who was a cheerful, efficient
man, but distrusted because of his admiration for Cathallo.
'In Cathallo,' Gilan urged Hengall, 'they have one great
temple for all the gods and it has served them well. We
should do the same.'

'Temples cost treasure,' Hengall said gloomily.

'Ignore the gods,' Gilan retorted, 'and what will all the
gold, bronze and amber in the world do for you?'

Gilan wanted to be high priest, but age alone would not give him that honour. A sign was needed from the gods and all the priests were seeking signs before, together, they would choose one of their number to succeed Hirac. Yet all the signs seemed bad for in the days following the failed sacrifice the warriors of Cathallo became ever bolder in their forays into Ratharryn's territory. Day after day Hengall heard of stolen cattle and pigs, and Lengar argued that the war drum should be sounded and a band of spearmen sent north to intercept the raiders, but Hengall still shied away from war. Instead of sending spears he sent Gilan to talk with Cathallo's rulers, though everyone knew that really meant talking to Sannas, the terrifying sorceress. Cathallo might have a chief, it might have great war-leaders, but Sannas ruled there, and many in Hengall's tribe feared that she had put some curse on Ratharryn. Why else had the sacrifice failed?

The omens became worse. A child drowned in the river, an otter tore apart a dozen fish-traps, a viper was seen in Arryn and Mai's temple, and Hengall's new wife miscarried. Grey bands of rain swept from the west. Gilan returned from Cathallo, spoke with Hengall, then walked north again; the tribe wondered what news the priest had brought and what answer Hengall had returned to Cathallo, but the chief said nothing and the folk of Ratharryn went on with their work. There were pots to be made, flints to be dug, hides to tan, pigs to herd, cattle to milk, water to fetch, buildings to repair, willow fish-traps to be woven and boats to be hacked out of the vast forest trees. A trading party arrived from the southern coast, their oxen laden with shellfish, salt and fine stone axes, and Hengall took his levy from the men before letting them travel north towards Cathallo. Hengall buried one of the axes in Slaol's temple and another in Lahanna's, but the gifts made no difference for the next day wolves came to the high pasture and took a heifer, three sheep and a dozen pigs.

Lengar alone seemed unaffected by the terrible omens. He had suffered the humiliation of yielding the gold to his father, but he retrieved his reputation by his prowess as a hunter. Day after day he and his companions brought back carcasses, tusks and hides. Lengar hung the tusks either side of his doorway as proofs that the gods smiled on him. Hengall, summoning the last shreds of his authority, had sternly ordered Lengar to stay out of the northern woods and thus avoid any confrontation with the spearmen of Cathallo, but one day Lengar came across some Outfolk in the south country and he brought back six enemy heads that he mounted on poles on the embankment's crest. Crows feasted on the grey-tattooed heads and, seeing the trophies on their skyline, more and more of the tribe was convinced that Lengar was favoured by the gods and that Hengall was doomed.

But then the Outfolk messengers came.

They arrived just as Hengall was dispensing justice, a thing that was done with each new moon when the chief, the high priest and the tribe's elders gathered in Arryn and Mai's temple and listened to wrangles about theft, threats, murder, infidelity and broken promises. They could condemn a man to death, though that was rare for they preferred to make a guilty man work for the wronged party. On that morning Hengall was frowning as he listened to a complaint that a field's boundary marker had been moved. The argument was passionate, but was broken off when Jegar, Lengar's friend, announced that Outfolk horsemen were coming from the west.

The Outlanders were blowing a ram's horn to proclaim that they travelled in peace and Hengall ordered Lengar to take a group of warriors to greet the strangers, but to allow them no nearer to Ratharryn than Slaol's temple. Hengall wanted time to consult with the priests and elders, and the priests wanted to don their finery. Food needed to be prepared, for though the Outfolk were regarded as enemies, these visitors came in peace and so would have to be fed.

The younger priests prepared a meeting place on the river bank just outside the settlement. They planted the skull pole in the turf, then splashed water to mark out a circle within which the visitors could sit, and outside that circle they placed ox-skulls, chalk axes and sprigs of holly to constrain whatever malevolence the Outfolk might have brought. The people of Ratharryn gathered excitedly outside the circle, for no one could remember any such thing ever happening before. Outfolk traders were common enough visitors, and there were plenty of Outfolk slaves in the settlement, but never before had Outfolk emissaries arrived and their coming promised to make a story to tell and retell in the long nights.

Hengall was at last ready. The tribe's best warriors were dispatched to escort the strangers to the meeting place while Gilan, who had just returned from his last mission to Cathallo, wove charms to prevent the strangers' magic doing harm. The Outfolk had their own sorcerer, a lame man whose hair was stiffened with red clay; he howled at Gilan and Gilan howled back, and then the lame man put a deer's rib between his naked legs, clamped it there for a heartbeat, then tossed it away to show that he was discarding his powers.

The lame sorcerer lay flat on the ground in the meeting place and thereafter did nothing except stare into the sky, while the other eight strangers squatted in a line to face Hengall and his tribal elders. The Outfolk had brought their own interpreter, a trader whom many of Ratharryn's folk knew and feared. He was called Haragg and he was a giant; a huge, brutal-faced man who travelled with his deaf-mute son who was even taller and more frightening. The son had not come with this embassy, and Haragg, who usually arrived at Ratharryn with fine stone axes and heavy bronze blades, had brought nothing but words, though his companions all carried heavy leather bags that Hengall's people looked at expectantly.

The sun was at its height when the talking began. The strangers first announced that they came from Sarmennyn, a place as far west as a man could walk before he met the wild sea and a country, they said, of hard rock, high hills and thin soil. Sarmennyn, they went on, was far away, very far, which meant they had come a long distance to talk with the great Hengall, chief of Ratharryn, though that flattery went past Hengall with as much effect as dawn mist drifting by a temple post. Despite the day's warmth the chief had draped his black bear pelt across his shoulders and was carrying his great stone mace.

The leader of the strangers, a tall, gaunt man with a scarred face and one blind eye, explained that one of their own people, a young and foolish man, had stolen some paltry treasures belonging to the tribe. The thief had fled. Now the strangers had heard that he had come to Hengall's land and there died, which was no more than he deserved.

Small as the treasures were, the strangers still sought their return and were willing to pay well for them.

Hengall listened to Haragg's long translation, then objected that he had been sleeping and did not understand why the Outlanders had woken him if all they wanted was to exchange a few trifles. Still, he conceded, since the strangers had disturbed his sleep, and since they were being respectful, he was willing to waste a little time in seeing what offerings they had brought. Hengall did not trust Haragg to interpret for him, so instead his speech was translated by Valan, a slave who had been captured from the Outfolk many years before. Valan had served Hengall a long time and was now the chief's friend rather than his slave and was even allowed to keep his own hut, cattle and wife.

The one-eyed man apologized for waking the great Hengall and said he would have happily conducted the transaction with one of Hengall's servants, but since the chief had been gracious enough to listen to their plea, would he also be kind enough to confirm that the missing treasures were indeed in his keeping?

'We normally throw trifles away,' Hengall said, 'but perhaps we kept them.' He gestured to the embankment where a group of small children, bored with the talk, were tumbling among the woad plants growing just beneath the Outlanders' heads that Lengar had brought back from the forest. Those heads had not come from the Outfolk of Sarmennyn, but from other Outfolk tribes who lived closer to Ratharryn, but their presence was still unsettling to the visitors. 'Children like bright things,' Hengall said, nodding towards the impaled heads, 'so maybe we kept your treasures to amuse the young ones? But you say you have brought other things to exchange for them?'

The strangers laid their gifts on the turf. There were some fine otter hides and seal skins, a basket of sea-shells, three bronze bars, a rod of copper, some curious sharp teeth that they claimed came from ocean monsters, a portion of shiny turtle shell and, best of all, some lumps of amber that were scarce as gold. Hengall must have noted that the bags were still half full for he stretched his arms, yawned again, tugged at the tangles in his beard and finally said that so long as he was awake he might go and talk to the goddess Mai about the prospect of catching some fish from her river. 'We saw some large pike there yesterday, did we not?' he called to Galeth.

'Very large pike.'

'I like eating pike,' Hengall said.

The strangers hastily added more bronze ingots and the people of Ratharryn murmured astonishment at the value of the gifts. And still the offerings came; some finely carved bone needles, a dozen bone combs, a tangle of fish-hooks, three bronze knives of great delicacy, and finally a stone axe with a beautifully polished head that had a blueish tinge and glittered with tiny shining flecks. Hengall lusted after that axe, but he forced himself to sound unimpressed as he wondered why the Outfolk had bothered to carry such miserable offerings so far from their own country.

The leader of the strangers added one final treasure: a bar of gold. The bar was the size of a spearhead and heavy enough to need two hands to carry it, and the watching crowd gasped. By itself that shining lump contained more gold than was in all the lozenges. The Outfolk were well known to be grudging with their gold, yet now they were offering a great piece of it, and that was a mistake for it contradicted their assertion that the missing treasures were mere trifles. Hengall, still pretending to be indifferent, pressed the strangers until, reluctantly, they confessed that the missing treasures were not trivial at all, but sacred objects that arrayed the sun's bride each year. The treasures, the grim-faced Haragg admitted, had been gifts from their sea god to Erek himself and the people of Sarmennyn feared that their loss would bring ill fortune. The strangers were pleading now. They wanted their treasures back, and they would pay for them dearly because they were terrified of Erek's displeasure.

'Erek is their name for Slaol,' Valan told Hengall.

Hengall, pleased to have forced the admission from the strangers, stood. 'We shall think on this matter,' he announced.

Food was fetched from the settlement. There was cold pork, flat bread, smoked fish, and bowls of chickweed and sorrel. The strangers ate warily, fearful of being poisoned, but afraid to give offence by rejecting the food. Only their priest did not eat, but just lay staring into the sky. Gilan and Ratharryn's priests huddled together, whispering fiercely, while Lengar and his friends formed another small group at the circle's far side. Folk came to inspect the offered gifts, though none crossed the charm-ringed circle to touch them for the gifts had still not been cleansed of Outfolk sorcery by Ratharryn's priests. Hengall talked with the elders and sometimes asked questions of the priests, though it was mainly with Gilan that he talked. The priest had now made two visits to Cathallo and he spoke urgently with Hengall who listened, nodded and finally seemed convinced by whatever Gilan urged on him.

The sun was sliding down to its western home when Hengall resumed his place, but custom demanded that any man in the tribe could have his opinion heard before Hengall pronounced a decision. A few men did stand and most advised accepting the Outfolk's payment. 'The gold is not ours,' Galeth said, 'but was stolen from a god. How can it bring us good luck? Let the strangers have their treasures.' Voices murmured in support, then Lengar beat the ground with his spear staff and the murmurs died as Hengall's son stood to address the crowd.

'Galeth is right!' Lengar said, causing surprise among those who thought that the two men could never agree. 'The Outfolk should have their treasures back. But we should demand a higher price than these scourings from their huts.' He gestured at the goods piled in front of the strangers. 'If the Outfolk want their treasures returned, then let them come from their far country with all their spears and all their bows and offer themselves to our service for a year.'

Haragg, the Outfolk interpreter, whispered to his companions, who looked worried, but Hengall shook his head. 'And how are we to feed this horde of armed Outfolk?' he asked his son.

'They will feed from the crops and cattle that they capture with their weapons.'

'And what crops and cattle are they?' Hengall asked.

'Those that grow and graze to the north of us,' Lengar answered defiantly, and many in the tribe voiced their agreement. The tribe of Sarmennyn was famous for its warriors. They were lean, hungry men from a bare land and they took with their spears what their country could not provide. Such feared warriors would surely make brief work of Cathallo and more of Hengall's folk raised their voices in Lengar's support.

Hengall raised his vast club for silence. 'The army of Sarmennyn,' he said, 'has never reached this far into the heartland. Yet now you would invite them? And if they do come with their spears and their bows and their axes, how do we rid ourselves of them? What is to stop them turning on us?'

'We shall outnumber them!' Lengar declared confidently.

Hengall looked scornful. 'You know how many spears they muster?' he demanded, pointing to the strangers.

'I know that with their help we can destroy our enemies,' Lengar retorted.

Hengall stood, a sign that Lengar's time of talking was over. Lengar stayed on his feet for a few heartbeats, then reluctantly squatted. Hengall spoke in a loud voice that reached the outermost part of the crowd. 'Cathallo is not our enemy! Cathallo is powerful, yes, but so are we! The two of us are like dogs. We can fight and maim each other, but the wounds we would inflict would be so deep that neither of us might live. But if we hunt together we shall feed well.' The tribe stared at him in silent surprise. They had expected a decision about the gold lozenges and instead the chief was talking of the problem of Cathallo.

'Together!' Hengall shouted. 'Together, Cathallo and Ratharryn will be as strong as any land in this earth. So we shall bind ourselves in a marriage of tribes.' That news caused a loud gasp from the crowd. 'On midsummer's eve we shall go to Cathallo and dance with their people.' The crowd thought about that, then a slow-growing murmur of agreement spread among them. Only a moment before they had been eagerly supporting Lengar's idea of conquering Cathallo, now they were seduced by Hengall's vision of peace. 'Gilan has talked with their chief and he has agreed that we shall not be one tribe,' Hengall declared, 'but two tribes united like a man and a woman in marriage.'

'And which tribe is the man?' Lengar dared to shout.

Hengall ignored him. 'There will be no war,' he said flatly, then he looked down at the strangers. 'And there will be no exchange,' he went on. 'Your god was given the treasures, but you lost them, and they were brought to us. They came to our Old Temple, which tells me they are meant to stay here. If we give back the gold, we insult the gods who sent the treasures to our keeping. Their coming is a sign that the temple must be restored, and so it shall be! It will be rebuilt!' Gilan, who had been urging that course, looked pleased.

The one-eyed man protested, threatening to bring war to Ratharryn.

'War?' Hengall brandished his great club. 'War!' he shouted. 'I will give you war if you come to Ratharryn. I will piss on your souls, enslave your children, make playthings of your women and grind your bones to powder. That is war as we know it!' He spat towards the strangers. 'Take your belongings and go,' he ordered.

The stranger's priest howled at the sky and their leader tried a last appeal, but Hengall would not listen. He had rejected the exchange and the Outfolk had no choice but to pick up their gifts and return to their horses.

But that evening, when the sun was tangled among the western trees like a fish caught in a woven-willow trap, Lengar and a dozen of his closest supporters left Ratharryn. They carried bows and spears and had their hounds leashed on long leather ropes, and they claimed they were going

62

back to their hunting grounds. But it was noted that Lengar also took an Outfolk slave, a woman, and that shocked the tribe for women were not taken on hunting expeditions. And that night a half-dozen more young women slipped out of Ratharryn, so next morning the horrified tribe realized that Lengar had not gone hunting at all, but had fled, and that the women had followed their warrior lovers. Hengall's anger overflowed like the river flooding with storm water. He raged at the malign fate that had sent him such an elder son, then he sent warriors on Lengar's trail, though none expected to catch up with the fugitives who had too long a start. Then Hengall heard that Jegar, who was reckoned Lengar's closest friend, was still in Ratharryn and the chief summoned Jegar to his hut door and there ordered him to abase himself.

Jegar lay flat on the ground while Hengall raised his war club over the young man's head. 'Where has my son gone?' he demanded coldly.

'To Sarmennyn,' Jegar answered, 'to the Outfolk.'

'You knew they planned this,' Hengall asked, his rage mounting again, 'and did not tell me?'

'Your son put a curse on my life if I betrayed him,' Jegar said.

Hengall kept the club poised. 'And why did you not go with him? Are you not his soul's friend?'

'I did not go,' Jegar answered humbly, 'because you are my chief and this is my home and I would not live in a far country beside the sea.'

Hengall hesitated. He plainly wanted to slam the club down and spatter the earth with blood, but he was a fair man and he controlled his anger and so lowered the weapon. Jegar had answered his questions well and though Hengall had no liking for the young man, he still raised him to his feet, embraced him, and gave him a small bronze knife as a reward for his loyalty.

But Lengar had gone to the Outfolk. So Hengall burned his son's hut and pounded his pots to dust. He killed Lengar's mother, who had been his own first wife, and he ordered Gilan to use the Kill-Child on a boy who was popularly supposed to be Lengar's son. The child's mother screamed, begging for mercy, but the aurochs' bone swung and the boy died. 'He never lived,' Hengall decreed of Lengar. 'He is no more.'

Next day was the eve of midsummer and the tribe would walk to Cathallo. To make peace. And to face Sannas.

At the dawn of the day on which the tribe was to walk north, Saban's father brought him a deerskin tunic, a necklace of boar's teeth and a wooden-handled, flint-bladed knife to wear in the belt. 'You are my son,' Hengall told him, 'my only son. So you must look like a chief's son. Tie your hair back. Stand straight!' He nodded curtly to Saban's mother, his third wife, whom he had long since ceased to summon to his hut, then went to examine the white sacrificial heifer that would be goaded to Cathallo.

Even Camaban went to Cathallo. Hengall had not wanted him to go, but Gilan insisted Sannas wanted to see Camaban for herself. So Galeth had fetched the crippled boy from his lair in the Old Temple, and now Camaban limped a few paces behind Saban, Galeth and Galeth's pregnant woman, Lidda. They walked north along the hills above the river valley and it took a whole morning to reach the edge of that high land which meant they were now halfway to Cathallo. For most of the people who stood on the crest and gazed at the woods and marshes ahead, that was the greatest distance they had ever walked from home.

Their path now dropped steeply into thick woods dotted with small fields. This was Maden's land, a place of rich soil, tall trees and wide bogs.

The men of Hengall's tribe moved close to their women as they entered the trees and small boys were given bundles of straw bound tight to sticks, and the straw was set alight from smouldering coals carried in perforated clay pots. The boys then raced up and down the path, waving their smoky clubs and shrieking to drive away the malevolent spirits who might otherwise come and impregnate the women. The priests chanted, the women clutched talismans, and the men beat their spear staves against the tree trunks. Even more chants were needed to propitiate the spirits as the tribe crossed a tangle of small streams close to Maden.

Hengall walked at the head of his tribe, but he waited on the bank of one of the bigger streams for Saban to catch up. 'We must talk,' he told his son, then glanced at Camaban who limped just a few steps behind. The boy had found another rotting sheep's pelt to replace his old tunic, and carried a crude leather bag in which his few belongings, his bones and snakeskin and charms, were stored. He stank, and his hair was once again tangled and dirty. He looked up at his father, gave a shudder, then spat onto the path.

Hengall turned disgustedly away and paced ahead with Saban. After a while he asked Saban if he had noticed how plump Maden's wheat looked? It seemed the storm had spared those fields, Hengall said enviously, then commented that there had been some fine fat pigs in the woods by the river. Pigs and wheat, he said, were all folk needed for life, and for that he thanked the gods. 'Maybe only pigs,' he mused, 'maybe that's all we need to eat. Pigs and fish. The wheat's just a nuisance. It won't seed itself, that's the trouble.' Hengall was carrying a leather bag that clinked as he walked and Saban guessed it contained some of the tribe's treasures. The people far ahead had started singing and the song grew louder as folk caught up the tune. It passed to the walkers behind, but neither Hengall nor Saban joined in. 'In a few years,' Hengall said abruptly, 'you'll be old enough to become chief.'

'If the priests and the people agree,' Saban said cautiously.

'The priests just need bribes,' Hengall said, 'and the people do as they're told.' A pigeon clattered through the leaves and Hengall looked up to see in what direction the bird flew, hoping that it would be a good omen. It was, for the bird made towards the sun.

'Sannas will want to see you,' Hengall said ominously. 'Kneel to her and bow your head. I know she's a woman, but treat her like a chief.' He frowned. 'She's a hard woman, hard and cruel, but she has powers. The gods love her, or else they fear her.' He shook his shaggy head in amazement. 'She was already old when I was a boy!'

Saban felt fear at the prospect of meeting Sannas. 'Why will she want to see me?'

'Because you're to marry a Cathallo girl,' Hengall said flatly, 'and Sannas will choose her. There's no decision made in Cathallo without Sannas. They call Kital chief, but he sucks on the old woman's tits. They all do.'

Saban said nothing. He knew he could not marry anyone until he had passed the ordeals of manhood, but he liked the idea.

'So you're to take a bride from Cathallo,' Hengall said, 'as a sign that our tribes are at peace. You understand that?'

'Yes, father.'

'But Cathallo doesn't know you're my only son now,' Hengall said, 'and they won't be happy that you're still a boy. That's why you must impress Sannas.'

'Yes, father,' Saban said again. He understood now that Kital and Sannas were expecting Lengar to come to Cathallo and claim a bride, but Lengar was gone and so he must take his place.

'And you will be chief,' Hengall said heavily, 'and that means you have to be a leader of our people. But being chief doesn't mean you can do what you want. Folk don't realize that. They want heroes, but heroes get their people killed. The best chiefs know that. They know they can't turn night into day. I can only do what's possible, nothing more. I can break down beaver's dams to stop the fish-traps drying out, but I can't order the river to do it for me.'

'I understand,' Saban said.

'And we can't have war,' Hengall said forcibly. 'I'm not worried that we'd lose, but that we'd be weakened whether we won or lost. You understand that?'

'Yes,' Saban.

'Not that I mean to die yet!' Hengall went on. 'I must be close to thirty-five summers. Think of that, thirty-five! But I've plenty of good years left! My father lived more than fifty years.'

'So will you, I hope,' Saban said clumsily.

'But you must prepare yourself,' Hengall said. 'Pass your ordeals, go hunting, take some Outfolk heads. Show the tribe the gods favour you.' He nodded abruptly and, without another word, turned and signalled for his friend Valan to join him.

Saban waited for Galeth to catch up. 'What did he want?' Galeth asked.

'To tell me I'm to marry a girl from Cathallo,' Saban said.

Galeth smiled. 'And so you should.' Galeth knew the decision meant that Saban was favoured to become the next chief, but Galeth bore no grudge for that. The big man was happiest when he was working with wood, and had no great desire to succeed his elder brother. He cuffed Saban lightly across the head. 'I just hope the girl's pretty.'

'Of course she will be,' Saban said, though he was suddenly afraid that she might not be.

The tribe crossed the last of the marshes, then climbed into hills that were thick with trees, though the woods gradually thinned to reveal the splendours of Cathallo. They passed an ancient shrine, its timber posts rotting and its circle as overgrown with hazels as Ratharryn's Old Temple, then saw grave mounds on the hill slopes ahead. Those hills were as low as the slopes about Ratharryn, but were steeper, and among them was the famous sacred mound. There was nothing like it in Ratharryn, and though some of the tribe's travellers had brought back stories of other sacred mounds, all agreed that none was the size of Cathallo's. It was vast, a hill fit to stand among other hills, but this hill had been made by man; it reached from a valley to touch the sky and it was all gleaming white for it had been made by heaping chalk on top of more chalk. It was taller, far taller than Ratharryn's embankment; as tall, indeed, as the surrounding hills.

'Why did they make it?' Lidda asked Galeth.

'It's Lahanna's image,' Galeth said, his voice touched with awe and explained that the moon goddess, staring down from the stars, could see herself remade upon the earth and would know that Cathallo revered her. Lidda, hearing the explanation, touched her forehead in obeisance to the goddess for she, like most women, revered Lahanna above all the gods and spirits, but Camaban, who was still limping close behind, suddenly laughed. 'What's funny?' Galeth asked.

'They have giant moles in C-C-Cathallo,' Camaban said.

Lidda touched her groin. She was uncomfortable being so close to the cripple, fearing for the child in her belly, and she wished Camaban would fall behind, but he had stubbornly stayed close all day and still dogged her steps as they splashed through a small river and climbed a hill to the east of the mound. The hill was crowned by a temple that came as a relief to many of Hengall's people for it was much smaller than any of the temples at Ratharryn, though it did have stone markers in place of timber poles. The low stones were rough-hewn, mere stumps of rock, and some folk reckoned they were ugly compared to a properly trimmed pole. A group of Cathallo's priests waited at the temple, and it was to them that the first of Ratharryn's gifts was given: the white heifer that had been goaded bloody on the long journey and was now driven through the gap in the temple ditch. Cathallo's priests examined the beast warily. It was not, perhaps, the whitest heifer in Ratharryn, but she was still a good animal with a nearly

69

unblemished hide and there were murmurs of resentment among Hengall's people as the priests appeared to doubt the beast's quality. At last, after prodding and smelling the animal, they grudgingly deemed her acceptable and dragged her to the centre of their small temple where a young priest, naked but for a pair of antlers tied onto his head, waited with a pole-axe. The heifer, seeming to understand what was about to happen, strained to escape the men holding her, so the priests cut the tendons of her legs and the immobilized beast bellowed mournfully as the great axe swung.

Hengall's folk sang Lahanna's lament as they filed through the heifer's wet blood and followed the priests along a path of paired stones. The temple might have failed to impress them, but the avenue of stones did not, for these stones were larger than the temple markers and they led far across the open country. The boulder-edged avenue dipped from the temple to the valley, but swerved before it reached the great chalk mound to stride north towards the crest of a wide down. There were so many stones flanking the sacred track that they could not be counted, and all were as tall or even taller than a man. Some were pillars, symbolizing Slaol, and each pillar was paired with a vast lozenge-shaped slab that honoured Lahanna. Cathallo's wonders really were true, and Hengall's people fell silent as they followed the priests north. They danced as they climbed, clumsily for they were tired, but dutifully shuffling from one side of the avenue to the other, zig-zagging their way up to the crest where some folk from Cathallo had assembled to see the visitors. One group of warriors, their bodies greased and hair plaited, leaned on their spears to watch the women pass, though the sight of Camaban prompted the young men to cover their eyes and spit in case his clubbed foot brought them evil.

Saban, who had never visited Cathallo before, had assumed that the massive paired stones lined a path that led from Cathallo's settlement to the small stone temple where the heifer had been sacrificed, but as he crossed the crest of the down he suddenly realized that the small temple, far from being the end of the sacred path, was merely its beginning, and that the true wonders of Cathallo still lay ahead.

The settlement, unwalled, lay to the west, and that was not where the path went. Rather it led towards a great chalk embankment that reared up from the low ground. Word passed down the column of travellers that the white embankment surrounded Cathallo's shrine and Hengall's folk fell silent as they marvelled at the vast wall which looked to be as high and as extensive as the embankment which surrounded Ratharryn. The wall's long summit was crowned with animal and human skulls, while from within the great enclosure came the heavy beat of wooden drums.

The path did not lead direct to the vast temple, but instead, just outside the shrine's entrance, made a double turn so that the wonders within the high chalk circle would not be revealed until the very last moment of the approach. Saban shuffled his dance steps about the double bend and there, suddenly visible beyond the shoulders of the great encircling bank, was Cathallo's shrine. Saban's first impression was of stones. Stones and more stones, for the great space within the soaring chalk wall seemed filled with heavy, high, grey boulders, and some had been newly wetted so that glints of light shone from their rough surfaces. The giant stones lay ringed by a ditch that had been dug inside the chalk wall, and the ditch was as deep as the rampart was high, and the area enclosed by the ditch and wall was almost as large as Ratharryn itself and Ratharryn was a tribe's settlement with winter room for cattle, while this was just one temple.

Some of Ratharryn's women hesitated before entering the temple for women were not allowed inside their tribe's own shrines except when they married, but Cathallo's women urged them onwards. In Cathallo, it seemed, both men and women could enter the circle and so all Hengall's folk danced across the ditch and into the shrine of stones.

There was one wide ring of boulders skimming the ditch's edge, and each of those boulders was the size of the stacks made from the summer's hay in Ratharryn. There were dozens of those massive stones, too many to count, and within their wide circle stood two more rings of stone, each the size of Slaol's temple at Ratharryn, and still more stones stood between those inner rings. One of those stones was a ringstone, a boulder with a great hole in it, and that pierced rock had been lifted up on another, while nearby was a death house made from three massive stone slabs. Saban stared in stupefied awe. He did not understand how any man could raise such stones and he knew he must have come to a place where the gods worked marvels. Only Camaban, wincing every time he stepped on his clubbed foot, seemed unimpressed.

The people of Cathallo were massed on the embankment's inner slope and they let out a great cry of welcome as the visitors danced into the sacred ring. The shout echoed all around the vast enclosure and then they began to sing.

Kital, chief of Cathallo, waited to greet Hengall's folk.

Kital wished to impress, and he did, for he was dressed in an ankle-length deerskin cloak that had been whitened with chalk and urine, then thickly sewn with rings of bronze that reflected the sun so that it seemed to glint when he moved forward to greet Hengall. The chief of Cathallo was tall, with a long thin clean-shaven face, and fair hair that was circled with a fillet of bronze into which he had pushed a dozen long swan feathers. Kital was of an age with Hengall, but there was an animation in his face that stole the years and he walked with a lithe, eager step. He spread his arms wide in a gesture of welcome and in so doing lifted the edges of his cloak to reveal a long bronze sword hanging from a leather belt. 'Hengall of Ratharryn,' he announced, 'welcome to Cathallo!'

Hengall looked shabby beside Kital. He was taller and broader than Cathallo's chieftain, but his bearded face was blunt compared to Kital's sharp features and his clothes were dirty and ragged, for Hengall had never been a man to worry about cloaks or jerkins. He kept his spear sharp, combed the lice from his beard, and reckoned that was the extent of a man's duty towards his appearance. The two chiefs embraced and the watching tribes murmured their appreciation for any public embrace between great men betokened peace. The chiefs held each other close for a heartbeat, then Kital pulled away and, leading Hengall by the hand, took him to where Sannas waited beside one of the great stones that formed the death house.

The sorceress wore a swathing cloak made from badger skins, and a woollen shawl hooded her long white hair. Saban stared at her, and for a heart-stopping moment she looked directly back and he flinched because the eyes that peered from her hood's shadows were malevolent, clever and terrifying. She was old, Saban knew, older, it was said, than any man or woman had ever been before.

Kital and Hengall knelt to talk with Sannas. The drummers, who were beating great hollow trunks, kept up their rhythm and a group of girls, all naked to the waist and with dog-roses, meadowsweets and poppies woven into their hair, danced to the sound, shuffling their feet back and forth, stepping sideways, advancing and retreating, offering a welcome to the strangers who had come to their great shrine. Most of the visitors gaped at the girls, but Galeth gazed at the stones and felt an immense sadness. No wonder Cathallo was so strong! No other tribe could match a shrine like this, so no other tribe could hope to win the favour of the gods like these people. Ratharryn, Galeth thought unhappily, was nothing to this, its temples were risible and its ambitions petty.

Saban was watching the sorceress, and it was evident that Sannas was unhappy with the news Hengall brought, for she turned away from him with a dismissive gesture. Hengall looked at Kital, who shrugged, but then Sannas turned back and snarled something before walking to a hut that stood close to the nearest stone circle. Hengall stood and came back to Saban. 'You're to go to Sannas's hut,' he said. 'Remember what I told you.'

Saban, conscious that he was being watched by two tribes, crossed to the hut that stood between the two smaller stone circles and was the only building inside the temple. It was a round hut, a little bigger than most living huts, with a tall pointed roof but a wall so low that Saban had to drop onto all fours to crawl through the entrance. It was dark inside, for scarce any sunlight came through the door or through the smoke-hole in the roof's peak that was supported by a thick pole. That pole was a bark-stripped trunk which had been left studded with the stubs of its many branches from which hung nets that were filled with human skulls. A burst of giggling alarmed Saban and he looked around to see a dozen faces peering from the hut's low edges. 'Never mind them,' Sannas ordered in a hoarse, low voice, 'come here.'

The sorceress had seated herself on a pile of furs beside the pole and Saban dutifully knelt to her. A small fire smouldered close to the pole, sifting the dark hut with a pungent smoke that made Saban's eyes water as he bowed his head in respect.

'Look at me!' Sannas snapped.

He looked at her. He knew she was old, so old that no one knew how old she was, older than she even knew herself, so old that she had been old when the next oldest person in Cathallo had been born. There were those who said she could never die, that the gods had given Sannas life without death, and to the awed Saban that seemed true, for he had never seen a face so wizened, so wrinkled and so savage. She had taken off her hood and her unbound hair was ashen and lank, hanging over a face that was like a skull, only a skull with warts. The eyes in the skull were black as jet, she had only one tooth left, a yellow fang in the centre of her upper jaw. Her hands protruded from the edge of her badger fur cape like hooked claws. Amber showed at her scrawny throat; to Saban it looked like a gem pinned to a dried-out corpse.

As she stared at him, Saban, his eyes becoming accustomed to the hut's smoky gloom, glanced nervously about to see that a dozen girls were watching him from the hut's margins. There were bat wings pinned to the hut post, between round-bottomed pots that hung with the skulls in their string nets. There was a pair of antlers high on the central pole, while clusters of feathers and bunches of herbs hung from the roof, all swathed in cobwebs. The jumbled bones of small birds lay in a wicker basket beside the fire. This was not, Saban thought, a hut where people lived, but rather a storage place for Cathallo's ritual treasures, the sort of place where the tribe's Kill-Child would be kept.

'So tell me,' Sannas said in a voice that was as harsh as bone, 'tell me, Saban, son of Hengall, son of Lock, who was whelped of an Outfolk bitch taken in a raid, tell me why the gods frown on Ratharryn?'

Saban did not answer. He was too frightened.

'I hate dumb boys,' Sannas growled. 'Speak, fool, or I shall turn your tongue into a worm and you will suck on its slime all the days of your miserable life.'

Saban forced himself to answer. 'The gods . . .' he began, then realized he was whispering, so spoke up, determined to defend his tribe, 'the gods sent us gold, lady, so how could they frown on us?'

'They sent you the gold of Slaol,' Sannas said bitterly, 'and what has happened since? Lahanna refused a sacrifice, and your elder brother has slunk off to the Outfolk. If the gods sent Ratharryn a pot of gold, all you'd do is piss in it.' The girls giggled. Saban said nothing and Sannas glowered at him. 'Are you a man?' she demanded.

'No, lady.'

'Yet you wear a man's tunic. Is it winter?'

'No, lady.'

'Then take it off.' She demanded. 'Take it off!'

Saban hastily undid his belt and pulled the tunic over

his head, prompting another chorus of giggles from the hut's edges. Sannas looked him up and down, then sneered. 'That's the best Ratharryn can send us? Look at him, girls! It looks like something that oozed from a snail's shell.'

Saban blushed, glad that it was so dark in the hut. Sannas watched him sourly, then reached into a pouch and took out a leaf-wrapped package. She peeled the leaves away to reveal a honeycomb from which she broke a portion that she pushed into her mouth. 'That fool Hirac,' she said to Saban, 'tried to sacrifice your brother Camaban?'

'Yes, lady.'

'But your brother lives. Why?'

Saban frowned. 'He was marked by Lahanna, lady.'

'So why did Hirac try to kill him?'

'I don't know, lady.'

'You don't know much, do you? Miserable little boy that you are. And now Lengar has fled, and you are to take his place.' She glowered at him, then spat a scrap of wax onto the fire. 'But Lengar never liked us, did he?' she went on. 'Lengar wanted to make war on us! Why did Lengar not like us?'

'He disliked everyone,' Saban said.

She rewarded that comment with a crooked smile. 'He feared we'd take away his chiefdom, didn't he? He feared we'd swallow little Ratharryn.' She pointed a finger into the shadows of the hut's edge. 'Lengar was to marry her. Derrewyn, daughter of Morthor who is the high priest of Cathallo.'

Saban looked where Sannas pointed and his breath checked in his throat, for he was staring at a slender girl with long black hair and an anxious, pretty face. She looked no older than Saban himself and had large eyes and seemed tremulously nervous, as though she was as uncomfortable in this smoke-reeking hut as Saban was himself. Sannas watched Saban and laughed. 'You like her, eh? But why should you marry her in your brother's place?'

'So we can have peace, lady,' Saban said.

'Peace!' the skull face spat at him. 'Peace! Why should we buy your miserable peace with my great-granddaughter's body?'

'You are not buying peace, lady,' Saban dared to say, 'for my tribe is not for sale.'

'Your tribe!' Sannas leaned back, cackling, then suddenly jerked forward and darted out a crooked hand that gripped Saban's groin. She squeezed, making him gasp. 'Your tribe, boy,' she spat at him, 'is worth nothing. Nothing!' She squeezed harder, watching his eyes for tears. 'Do you want to be chief after your father?'

'If the gods wish it, lady.'

'They've wished for stranger things,' Sannas said, at last letting him go. She rocked back and forth, spittle dribbling from her toothless mouth. She watched Saban, judging him, and decided he was probably a decent boy. He had courage, and she liked that, and he was undeniably good-looking, which meant he was favoured by the gods, but he was still a boy and it was an insult to her people to present a boy for marriage. Yet there would be advantages in a marriage between Cathallo and Ratharryn, so Sannas decided she would swallow the insult. 'So you'll marry Derrewyn to keep the peace?' she asked him.

'Yes, lady.'

'Then you are a fool,' Sannas said, 'for peace and war are

not in your gift, boy, and they certainly don't lie between Derrewyn's legs. They lie with the gods, and what the gods want will happen, and if they choose to let Cathallo rule in Ratharryn then you could take every girl in this settlement to your stinking bed and it would make no difference.' She closed her eyes and rocked back and forth again, and a dribble of honey and saliva ran down her chin where white hairs grew from dark moles. It was time, she decided, to scare this boy of Ratharryn, to make him so scared of her that he would never dare think of crossing her wishes. 'I am Lahanna,' she said in a deep voice scarce above a whisper, 'and if you thwart my desire I shall swallow your petty tribe, I shall swill it in my belly's bile and piss it into a ditch filled with scum.' She laughed then, and the laughter turned to a fit of coughing that made her gasp for breath. She groaned as the coughing bout passed, then opened her black eyes. 'Go,' she said dismissively. 'Send your brother Camaban to me, but you go. Go, while I decide your future.'

Saban crawled back into the sunlight where he hurriedly pulled on his tunic. The dancers shuffled back and forth, the drummers beat on, and Saban shuddered. Behind him, from inside the hut, he heard laughter and he was ashamed. His tribe was so little, his people so weak, and Cathallo was so strong. The gods, it seemed to Saban, had turned against Ratharryn. Why else had Lengar fled? Why had Lahanna refused the sacrifice? Why was he forced to crawl to a hag in Cathallo? Saban believed her threats, he believed his tribe was in danger of being swallowed and he did not know how he could save it. His father had warned him against heroes, but Saban thought Ratharryn needed a hero. Hengall had been a hero in his youth, but he was cautious now, Galeth had no ambition and Saban was not yet a man – he did not even know if he would pass the ordeals. Yet he would be a hero if he could, for without a hero he foresaw nothing but grief for his people. They would just be swallowed.

That night the people of Cathallo lit the midsummer fires that sparked and billowed smoke across the landscape. The fires burned to drive malignant spirits from the fields, and more fires burned inside Cathallo's great temple where twelve men dressed in cattle hides romped among the stones. The skins formed grotesque costumes, for the beasts' heads and hooves were still attached. The monstrous horned shapes capered between the flames while the men beneath the skins bellowed their challenges to the evil spirits that could bring disease to the tribe and to its herds. The beast-men guarded Cathallo's prosperity, and there was much competition between the young warriors to be given the honour of dancing in the bulls' hides for, when the night's dark was full and the furious flames were rushing towards the stars, a dozen girls were pushed naked into the fire circle where they were pursued by the roaring men. The crowd, which had been dancing about the ring of flames, stopped to watch as the girls dodged and twisted in feigned panic away from their horned pursuers who were half blinded and made clumsy by their cumbersome skins. Yet one by one the girls were caught, thrust to the ground and there covered by the horned monsters as the onlookers cheered.

Both tribes leapt the fires when the bull dance was over. The warriors competed to see who could jump through the highest, widest fires, and more than one fell into the flames and had to be dragged screaming from the blaze. The old folk and the children skipped across the smallest fires, and then the tribe's new-born livestock were goaded through the glowing beds of embers. Some folk showed their bravery by walking barefoot across the embers, but only after the priests had pronounced a charm to stop their feet from burning. Sannas, watching from her hut doorway, jeered at the ritual. 'It has nothing to do with any charm,' she said sourly. 'So long as their feet are dry it doesn't hurt, but have damp feet and you'd see them dancing like lambkins.' She hunched by her thatch and Camaban squatted beside her. 'You can jump the flames, child,' Sannas said.

'I c-c-cannot jump,' Camaban answered, wrenching his face in an effort not to stutter. He stretched out his left leg so that the firelight flickered on the twisted lump of his foot. 'And if I tried,' he went on, looking at the foot, 'they would l-l-laugh at me.'

Sannas was holding a human thigh bone. It had belonged to her second husband, a man who had thought to tame her. She reached out with the bone and lightly tapped the grotesque foot. 'I can mend that,' she said, then waited for Camaban's reaction, and was disappointed when he said nothing. 'But only if I want to,' she added savagely, 'and I may not want to.' She drew her cloak about her. 'I once had a crippled daughter,' she said. 'Such a strange little thing, she was. A hunchback dwarf. She was all twisted.' She sighed, remembering. 'My husband expected me to mend her.'

'And did you?'

'I sacrificed her to Lahanna. She's buried in the ditch there.' She pointed the bone towards the shrine's southern entrance.

'Why would Lahanna want a c-c-cripple?' Camaban asked.

'To laugh at, of course,' Sannas snapped.

Camaban smiled at that answer. He had gone to Sannas's hut in the daylight and the girls had gasped at the horror of his left foot, shuddered at the stink of his filthy pelt, then mocked his stammer and his wildly tangled hair, but Sannas had not joined their mockery. She had examined the moon mark on his belly, then had abruptly ordered all the girls out of her hut. And after they were gone she had stared at Camaban for a long while. 'Why did they not kill you?' she asked at last.

'B-B-Because the g-g-gods look after me.'

She had struck his head with the thigh bone. 'If you stutter to me, child,' she threatened, 'I shall turn you into a toad.'

Camaban had looked into the black eyes of her skull-face, and then, very calmly, he had leaned forward and taken the sorceress's leaf-wrapped honeycomb.

'Give it back!' Sannas had demanded.

'If I am to be a t-t-toad,' Camaban had said, 'I shall be a honeyed toad.' And Sannas had laughed at that, opening her mouth wide to show her single rotting tooth. She had ordered him to throw his filthy sheepskin tunic out of the hut, then found him an otterskin jerkin, and afterwards she had insisted he comb the tangles and dirt from his hair. 'You're a good-looking boy,' she said grudgingly, and it was true, for his face was lean and handsome, his nose long and straight and his dark green eyes were full of power. She had questioned him. How did he live? How did he find food? Where did he learn about the gods? And Camaban had answered her calmly, showing no fear of her, and Sannas had decided that she liked this child. He was wild, stubborn, unafraid and, above all, clever. Sannas lived in a world of fools, and here, though only a youth, was a mind, and so the old woman and the crippled boy had talked as the sun sank and the fires were lit and the bull-dancers drove the wild-haired girls down to the shadowed turf between the boulders.

Now they sat watching the dancers whirl past the fires. Somewhere in the dark a girl whimpered. 'Tell me about Saban,' Sannas commanded.

Camaban shrugged. 'Honest, hard-working,' he said, making neither attribute sound like a virtue, 'not unlike his father.'

'Will he become chief?'

'Given time, maybe,' Camaban said carelessly.

'And will he keep the peace?'

'How would I know?' Camaban answered.

'Then what do you think?'

'What does it matter what I think?' Camaban asked. 'Everyone knows I am a fool.'

'And are you, fool?'

'It is what I w-w-want them to think,' Camaban said. 'That way they leave me alone.'

Sannas nodded her approval at that. The two sat in silence for a while, watching the sheen of the flames colour the slab-sided stones. Sparks whirled in the sky, rushing between the hard white stars. A cry sounded from the shadows where two young men, one from Ratharryn and the other from Cathallo, had started fighting. Their friends dragged them apart, but even as that fight ended, others began. The folk of Cathallo had been generous with their honey-liquor that had been specially brewed for the midsummer feast. 'When my grandmother was a girl,' Sannas said, 'there was no liquor. The Outfolk showed us how to make it and they still make the best.' She brooded on that for a while, then shrugged. 'But they cannot make my potions. I can give you a drink to make you fly, and food to give you bright dreams.' Her eyes glittered under the hood of her shawl.

'I want to learn from you,' Camaban said.

'I teach girls, not boys,' the old woman said harshly.

'But I have no soul,' Camaban said. 'It was broken by the K-K-Kill-Child. I am neither boy nor man, I am nothing.'

'If you are nothing, what can you learn?'

'All you c-c-can teach me.' Camaban turned to look at the sorceress. 'I will p-p-pay you,' he said.

Sannas laughed, the breath wheezing in her throat as she rocked back and forth. 'And what,' she asked when she had recovered, 'can a crippled outcast from little Ratharryn pay me?'

'This.' Camaban uncurled his right hand to reveal a single gold lozenge. 'Part of the Outfolk gold,' he said, 'the b-b-bride of Slaol's treasure.' Sannas reached for the lozenge, but Camaban closed his fist.

'Give it to me, child!' the old woman hissed.

'If you say you'll teach me,' Camaban said, 'I shall give it to you.'

Sannas closed her eyes. 'If you do not give it to me, you

crippled lump of horror,' she intoned in a voice that had terrified three generations of her tribe, 'I shall give your body to the worms and send your soul to the endless forest. I shall curdle your blood and beat your bones to a paste. I shall have the birds peck out your eyes, the vipers suck at your bowels and the dogs eat your guts. You will plead for my mercy and I shall just laugh at you and use your skull as my pissing pot.' She stopped suddenly, for Camaban had climbed to his feet and was limping away. 'Where are you going?' she hissed.

'I have heard,' Camaban said, 'that there is a sorcerer at Drewenna. He c-c-can teach me.'

She glared at him, her eyes bright in her corpse's face, but he stayed quite calm, and Sannas shuddered with anger. 'Take one more step, cripple,' she said, 'and I will have your twisted bones put beside that dwarf in the ditch.'

Camaban held up the gold lozenge. 'This p-p-pays you to t-t-teach me,' he said, and then he produced a second lozenge. 'And this p-p-piece of gold,' he went on, 'will p-p-pay you to mend my foot.'

'Come here!' Sannas ordered. Camaban did not move, but just held the scraps of gold that glittered in the firelight. Sannas stared at them, knowing what mischief she could make with such powerful talismans. She hoped to gain more of this gold in the morning, but every scrap was precious to her and so she governed her anger. 'I will teach you,' she said calmly.

'Thank you,' Camaban said calmly, then knelt in front of her and reverently placed the two lozenges in her out-stretched hand.

Sannas spat on the gold, then shuffled back into the deep darkness of the hut where her fire was little more than a heap of charred embers. 'You can sleep inside the door,' she said from the darkness, 'or outside. I do not care.'

Camaban did not answer, but just stared at the great temple stones. The shadows of the lovers were motionless now, but the dying firelight flickered and it seemed to him that the ring of stones was shimmering in the smoky night. It was as though the stones were alive and the people were dead, and that made him think of the Old Temple, so far away, that was his home, and he leaned forward and put his forehead on the ground and swore to whatever gods were listening that he would make the Old Temple live. He would make it dance, he would make it sing, he would make it live.

Hengall was pleased with the results of his negotiations with Kital. Peace was assured, and that peace would be sealed by the marriage of Saban and Derrewyn. 'Not that she's the girl I'd have chosen for you,' Hengall grumbled to his son as they walked south towards Ratharryn. 'She's much too thin.'

'Too thin?' Saban asked. He had thought Derrewyn beautiful.

'Women are no different from cattle,' Hengall said. 'The best have wide rumps. It's no use marrying a thin thing, they just die in childbirth. But Sannas decided you're to marry Derrewyn and the marriage will seal our peace, so that's the end of it.'

Hengall had not only agreed to the marriage, he had also bought eight great boulders with which Gilan could remake the Old Temple. The price for the stones had been one of the large gold lozenges and nine of the small, which Hengall reckoned cheap. It was right, he thought, to exchange a small part of Sarmennyn's gold for the stones for he was sure now that the arrival of the treasures had been a message from Slaol to remake the Old Temple and Gilan had convinced him that Ratharryn must possess a temple made of stone.

There was no stone at Ratharryn. There were pebbles in the river, and a few larger rocks that could be shaped into hammers or axes, but the settlement had no big stones to rival the pillars and slabs that ringed Cathallo's temple. Ratharryn was a place of chalk, grass and trees, while Cathallo's land was rich in the great boulders which lay so thickly scattered on their hills that from a distance they looked like a flock of giant grey sheep. Sannas contended that the stones had been flung there by Slaol in a vain attempt to stop the people of Cathallo from raising the sacred mound to Lahanna, though others said that the rocks had been cast onto the hills by Gewat, the god of the clouds, who had wanted to see his own likeness on the earth's green face, but however the stones had reached Cathallo, they were the closest boulders to Ratharryn.

Saban liked the idea of building something new and impressive at Ratharryn. A few of Hengall's folk muttered that timber temples had always served Ratharryn well enough, but the traders, those men who carried hides and flint and pots to exchange for axes and shellfish and salt, pointed out that Drewenna possessed a large stone temple and that nearly all the shrines in the distant west were also made of boulders, and the prospect of a stone temple of their own served to revive the spirits of most of Hengall's people. A new temple, made of stone, might restore the tribe's luck, and that belief was enough to persuade the priests that Gilan should be the new high priest. They reported as much to Hengall, and the chief, who had bribed four of the priests with bronze bars, Outfolk slave girls and lumps of amber to make just such a choice, gravely accepted the verdict as having come from the gods.

So Gilan became the new high priest and his first demand was that the tribe should clear the Old Temple of its weeds and hazels so that the shrine would be ready for the arrival of Cathallo's stones in the new year.

The men did the work, while the women stayed outside the bank and danced in a ring. They sang as they danced and their song was the wedding chant of Slaol. Only women ever sang that beautiful song, and only on occasions of the deepest solemnity. It went in snatches, with long pauses between the music, and during the pauses the dancers would stand quite motionless, before, seemingly without anyone telling them when, the steps and the singing would begin again. Their voices overlaid each other in a twisting harmony and, though they never practised the song together, it always sounded hauntingly lovely and the steps always stopped and started in perfect unison. Mothers taught the parts of the song to their daughters, and some learned one part and others learned another, and then they came together and everything fitted. Many of the women cried as they danced, for the song was a lament. On the day before the marriage of Slaol and Lahanna the sun god had fought with his bride and deserted her, but the women lived in hope that Slaol would relent and come back to his bride.

Gilan supervised the work, sometimes stopping to listen

to the women's song and at other times helping the men grub out the weeds and shrubs. A few of the hazels were good-sized trees and their roots needed loosening with antler picks before they could be dragged clear of the soil. The trees could not simply be cut down, for hazel will grow again from its stump, so the bigger trees were hauled out and their root holes filled with a chalky rubble dug from the ditch. The ox-skull that Camaban had placed in the temple's centre was buried in the ditch, his lair was pulled down, the weeds were grubbed out, the grass cut with flint knives and the waste burned. The smoke from the fire disturbed the dancers so that they moved farther away from the temple as the men cleared the grass and weeds from the ditch and inner bank so that the shrine was again ringed with its bright chalk-white circle.

The old rotting posts that had stood so thick in the entrance of the sun and about the death house were tossed onto the fire. Some of the posts had been huge and their remains were buried deep: those were snapped off at ground level and their stubborn stumps left to decay. And once all the weeds, trees and posts had been cleared, the men danced across the wide circle to the haunting rhythm of the women's song. The temple was bare again, clean. It was a low grassy bank, a ditch and a high bank ringing a circle that held nothing.

The tribe returned to Ratharryn in the evening light. Galeth was one of the last to leave and he paused at the brow of the hill above the settlement to turn and look at the temple. The clump of hazels which had broken the southern skyline was gone so that only the grave mounds of the ancestors could be seen on that horizon, but in front of the mounds, white against the darkening hillside, the temple's ring seemed to shine in the dying light. The shadows of the bank stretched long and Galeth noticed, for the very first time, how the ring of chalk had been placed on a slope so that it was very slightly tilted towards the place where the sun rose in midsummer.

'It looks beautiful,' Lidda, Galeth's woman, said.

'It does look beautiful,' Galeth agreed. It was Galeth, practical, strong and efficient, who would have to raise the stones, and he tried to imagine how the eight great boulders would look in that clean setting of grass and chalk. 'Slaol will be pleased,' he decided.

There was thunder that night, but no rain. Just thunder, far off, and in the darkness two of the tribe's children died. Both had been sick, though no one had thought they would die. But in the morning the sun rose to make the newly cleared chalk-ring shine, and the gods, folk reckoned, were once again smiling on Ratharryn.

Derrewyn was not yet a woman, but it was a custom in both Ratharryn and Cathallo that betrothed girls would live with their prospective husband's family, so Derrewyn came to Ratharryn to live in the hut of Hengall's oldest surviving wife.

Her arrival disturbed the tribe. She might be a year from womanhood, but her beauty had blossomed early and the young warriors of Ratharryn stared at her with undisguised yearning, for Derrewyn of Cathallo was a girl to stir men's dreams. Her black hair hung below her waist and her long legs were tanned dark by the sun. About her ankles and her neck she wore delicate chains of pure white sea-shells, all the shells alike and of a size. Her eyes were dark, her face was slender and high-boned, and her spirit as quick as a kingfisher's flight. The young warriors of Hengall's tribe noted her, watched her, and reckoned she was too good for Saban who was still only a child. Hengall, seeing their desire, ordered Gilan to work a protective charm on the girl, so the high priest placed a human skull on the roof of Derrewyn's hut and beside it he put a phallus of unfired clay and every man who saw the charm understood its threat. Touch Derrewyn without permission, the skull and phallus said, and you will die, and from that time the men looked, but did nothing more.

Saban also looked and yearned, and some in the tribe noted how Derrewyn gazed back at Saban, for he was promising to be a handsome man. He was still growing, but already he was as tall as his father and he had all Lengar's quickness of eye and hand. He was accurate with a yew bow, was one of the fastest runners in the tribe and yet was modest, calm-tempered and well liked in Ratharryn. He promised to be a good man, but if he failed his ordeals he would never be reckoned an adult, so, in the months after his first meeting with Derrewyn, he was kept busy learning the secrets of the woods and the ways of the beasts. He watched the stags fighting and rutting, found where the otters had their dens and learned how to steal honey from irate bees. He was not allowed to sleep in the woods for he was still a child, but he killed his first wolf in early winter, felling it with a well-aimed arrow and ending the wounded beast's life with a blow of a stone axe. Galeth's woman, Lidda, pierced the wolf's claws and threaded them on a sinew, then gave the necklace to Saban.

Saban might have been the son of the chief, but he was expected to work like everyone else. 'A man who does nothing,' Hengall liked to say, 'eats nothing.' Galeth was the tribe's best woodworker, and for seven years Saban had been learning his uncle's trade. He had learned all the names of the tree gods and how to placate them before an axe was laid to a trunk, and he had learned how to shape oak and ash into beams, posts and rafters. Galeth taught him how to make an adze blade from flint, and how to tie it to the haft with wet oxhide strips that shrank tight so that the head did not loosen during work. Saban was allowed to use flint tools, but neither he nor Galeth's son, who had been born to Galeth's first wife, were ever permitted to touch the two precious bronze axes that had been carried long distances across the land and had cost Galeth dearly in pigs and cattle.

Saban learned to carve beechwood into bowls and willow into paddles. He learned how to whittle a branch of stone-hard yew wood into a deer-killing bow. He learned to joint wood, and how to auger it with spikes of flint, bone or holly. He learned how to take an elm trunk and shape it into a hollow boat that could float all the way down the river to the sea and bring back bags of salt, shells and dried fish. He learned how to peg green oak so that it shrank into place, and he learned well, for in the winter before Saban's ordeals Galeth trusted him to raise a new roof on the hut where Derrewyn slept.

Saban stripped the rotting thatch, but first handed the skull down to Derrewyn who, knowing that it protected her, kissed its forehead and then looked up at Saban. 'And the rest,' she said, smiling.

'The rest?'

'The clay,' she said. The unfired clay phallus had crumbled in the weather, but Saban collected what he could from among the rotting thatch and gave it to her. She grimaced at the dirty scraps of clay, but found one fragment that was cleaner than the rest and reached up to give it back to Saban. 'Swallow it,' she ordered him.

'Swallow it?'

'Do it!' she insisted, then laughed at his expression as he forced the lump down his throat.

'Why did I do that?' Saban asked her, but she just laughed and then the laugh faded as Jegar came round the hut's corner.

Jegar was now the tribe's best hunter. He went into the forest for days, leading a band of young men who brought back carcasses and tusks. There were some in the tribe who believed Jegar should succeed Hengall, for it was plain the gods favoured him, though if Jegar shared that opinion he showed no sign of it. Instead he was respectful to Hengall and took care to offer the chief the best cuts of meat from his kill and Hengall, in turn, dealt cautiously with the man who had once been Lengar's closest companion.

Jegar now stared at Derrewyn. Like the other men of the tribe he had been deterred by the skull on her roof, but he could not hide his longing for her, nor his jealousy of Saban. In the new year, when Saban undertook the ordeals of manhood, he would be hunted in the deep forest and all the tribe knew that Jegar and his hounds would be on Saban's trail. And if Saban failed, then Saban could not marry.

Jegar smiled at Derrewyn who clutched the skull to her breasts and spat. Jegar laughed, then licked his spear blade

94

and pointed it at Saban. 'Next year, little one,' he said, 'we shall meet in the trees. You, me, my hunting companions and my hounds.'

'You need friends and hounds to beat me?' Saban asked. Derrewyn was watching him and her gaze made him reckless. 'Tell me about next year, Jegar,' he said. He knew it was dangerously foolish to taunt Jegar, but he feared Derrewyn would despise him if he meekly allowed Jegar to bully him. 'What will you do if you catch me in the forest?' he demanded, jumping down to the ground.

'Thrash you, little one,' Jegar said.

'You don't have the strength,' Saban said, and he picked up a long ash pole that was used to measure the lengths of the replacement rafters. He was taller than Jegar, and he also knew that Jegar would not dare kill him here in the settlement where so many were watching, but he was still risking a painful beating. 'You couldn't thrash a kitten,' he added scornfully.

'Go back to work, boy,' Jegar said, but Saban just slashed the pole at him, making the smaller man step back. Saban slashed again, and the clumsy weapon whipped past Jegar's face. This time the hunter snarled and levelled his spear. 'Careful,' he said.

'Why should I be careful of you?' Saban asked. Fear and exhilaration were competing in him. He knew this was stupidity, but Derrewyn's presence had driven him to it and his own pride would not let him back down. 'You're a bully, Jegar,' he said, drawing back the pole, 'and I'll thrash you bloody.'

'You child!' Jegar said, and ran at Saban, but Saban had guessed what Jegar would do and he let the pole's tip fall so that it tangled Jegar's legs, and then he twisted the pole, tripping Jegar, and as Jegar fell Saban jumped on him and beat his enemy's head with his fists. He landed two hard blows before Jegar managed to twist round and lash back. Jegar could not use his spear for Saban was on top of him, so first he tried to punch the boy away, then he clawed at Saban's eyes. Saban bit one of the probing fingers and tasted blood, then hands seized and dragged him off Jegar. Other hands pulled Jegar away.

It was Galeth who had hauled Saban away. 'You fool!' Galeth said. 'You want to die?'

'I was beating him!'

'He's a man. You're a boy! And you're going to have a black eye.' Galeth pushed Saban away, then turned on Jegar. 'Leave him alone,' he ordered. 'Your chance comes next year.'

'He attacked me!' Jegar said. His hand was bleeding where Saban had bitten it. He sucked at the blood, then picked up his spear. There was rage in his eyes, for he knew he had been humiliated. 'A boy who attacks a man has to be punished,' he insisted.

'No one attacked anyone,' Galeth said. He was huge, and his anger was frightening. 'Nothing happened here. You hear me? Nothing happened!' He drove Jegar back. 'Nothing happened!' He turned on Derrewyn who had watched the fight with wide eyes. 'Be about your work, girl,' he ordered, then pushed Saban back to the roof. 'And you've got work to do, so do it.'

Hengall chuckled when he heard about the fight. 'Was he really winning?' he asked Galeth.

'He wouldn't have lasted,' Galeth said, 'but yes, he was winning.'

'He's a good boy,' Hengall said approvingly, 'a good boy!'

'But Jegar will try to stop him passing the ordeals,' Galeth warned.

Hengall dismissed his younger brother's fears. 'If Saban is to be chief,' he said, 'then he must be able to deal with men like Jegar.' He chuckled again, delighted that Saban had shown such courage. 'You'll keep an eye on the boy through the winter?' he asked. 'He deserves better than to be speared in the back.'

'I shall watch him,' Galeth promised grimly.

It proved a cruelly hard winter, and the only good news of that cold season was that the warriors of Cathallo abandoned their raids on Hengall's land. The peace, which would be sealed by Saban's marriage, was holding, though some folk reckoned Cathallo was just waiting for Hengall's death before snapping up Ratharryn as they had conquered Maden. Others reckoned that it was the weather that kept Kital's men at bay, for the snow lay thick for days and the river froze so that the women had to break the ice to fetch their daily water. There were days when the snow on the hills blew from the low crests like smoke, when the fires seemed to give no warmth and the ice-bound huts crouched in a grey-white land that offered no hope of warmth or life. The weak of the tribe, the old, the young, the sick and the cursed, died. There was hunger, but the warriors of the tribe hunted in the forests. None rivalled Jegar and his band who, day after day, brought back carcasses that were butchered outside the settlement where the guts steamed in the cold air as the tribe's dogs circled in hope of spoil. The hunters gave the stags' skulls to women who fed their cooking fires with wood till they burned fierce, then held the roots of the antlers in the flames so that they would snap clean from the bone. There would be work to be done on the Old Temple in the spring, and the tribe would need scores of antler picks to make holes for the new stones that were to be fetched from Cathallo.

That winter never seemed to end. Wolves were seen by the river, but Gilan assured the tribe that all would be well when the new temple was made. This winter is the last of our woes, the high priest said, the last ill fortune before the new temple changed Ratharryn's fate. There would be life again, and love, and warmth and happiness, and all things, Gilan assured the tribe, would be good.

Camaban had gone to Cathallo to learn. He had been alone for years, scavenging a thin living beyond Ratharryn's embankment, and in those years he had listened to the voices in his head and he had thought about what they told him. Now he wanted to test that knowledge against the world's other wisdom, and no one was wiser than Sannas, sorceress of Cathallo, and so Camaban listened.

In the beginning, Sannas said, Slaol and Lahanna had been lovers. They had circled the world in an endless dance, the one ever close to the other, but then Slaol had glimpsed Garlanna, the goddess of the earth who was Lahanna's daughter, and he had fallen in love with Garlanna and rejected Lahanna.

So Lahanna had lost her brightness, and thus night came to the world.

But Garlanna, Sannas insisted, stayed loyal to her mother by refusing to join Slaol's dance and so the sun god sulked and winter came to the earth. And Slaol still sulked, and would not listen to the folk on earth, for they reminded him of Garlanna. Which is why, Sannas insisted, Lahanna should be worshipped above all other gods because she alone had the power to protect the world from Slaol's petulance.

Camaban listened, just as he listened to Morthor, Derrewyn's father, who was high priest at Cathallo, and Morthor told a similar tale, though in his telling it was Lahanna who sulked and who hid her face in shame because she had tried and failed to dim her lover's brightness. She still tried to diminish Slaol, and those were fearful times when Lahanna slid herself in front of Slaol to bring night in the daytime. Morthor claimed that Lahanna was the petulant goddess, and though he was Sannas's grandson and though the two disagreed, they did not fight. 'The gods must be balanced,' Morthor claimed. 'Lahanna might try to punish us because we live on Garlanna's earth, but she is still powerful and must be placated.'

'Men won't condemn Slaol,' Sannas told Camaban, 'for they see nothing wrong with him loving a mother and her daughter.' She spat. 'Men are like pigs rolling in their own dung.'

'If you visit a strange tribe,' Morthor said, 'to whom do you go? Its chief! So we must worship Slaol above all the gods.'

'Men can worship whatever they want,' Sannas said, 'but it is a woman's prayer that is heard, and women pray to Lahanna.'

On one thing, though, both Sannas and Morthor agreed: that the grief of this world had come when Slaol and Lahanna parted, and that ever since the tribes of men had striven to balance their worship of the two jealous gods.

It was the same belief that Hirac had held, a belief that gripped the heartland tribes and forced them to be cautious of all the gods.

Camaban heard all this, and he asked questions, but kept his own opinions silent. He had come to learn, not to argue, and Sannas had much to teach him. She was the most famous healer in the land and folk came to her from a dozen tribes. She used herbs, fungi, fire, bone, blood, pelts and charms. Barren women would walk for days to beg her help and each morning would find a desperate collection of the sick, the crippled, the lame and the sad waiting at the shrine's northern entrance. Camaban collected Sannas's herbs, picked mushrooms and cut fungi from decaying trees. He dried the medicines in nets over the fire, he sliced them, infused them and learned the names that Sannas gave them. He listened as the folk described their ills and he watched what Sannas gave them, then marked their progress to health or to death. Many came complaining of pain, just pain, and as often as not they would rub their bellies and Sannas would give them slices of fungi to chew, or else made them drink a thick mixture of herbs, fungus and fresh blood. Almost as many complained of pain in their joints, a fierce pain that doubled them over and made it hard for a man to till a field or for a woman to grind a quern stone, and if the pain was truly crippling Sannas would lay the sufferer between two fires, then take a newly chipped flint knife and drag it across the painful joint. Back and forth she would cut, slicing deep so that the blood welled up, then Camaban would rub dried herbs into the wounds and place more of the dried herbs over the fresh cuts until the blood no longer seeped and Sannas would set fire to the herbs and the flames would hiss and smoke and the hut would fill with the smell of burning flesh.

One man went mad in that hard wintertime, beating his wife until she died, then hurling his youngest child onto his hut fire and Sannas decreed that the man had been possessed of an evil spirit. He was brought to her, then pinioned between two warriors as Sannas cut open his scalp, peeled back the flesh, and chipped a hole in his skull with a small stone maul and a thin flint blade. She levered out a whole circle of bone, then spat onto his brain and demanded that the evil thing come out. The man lived, though in such misery it would have been better had he died.

Camaban learned to set bones, to fill wounds with moss and spider web, and to make the potions that give men dreams. He carried those potions to Cathallo's priests who treated him with awe because he had been chosen by Sannas. He learned to make the glutinous poison that warriors smeared on their arrow-heads when they hunted Outfolk in the wide forests north of Cathallo. The poison was made from a mixture of urine, faeces and the juice of a flowering herb that Sannas prized as a killer. He made Sannas's food, grinding it to a paste because, only having the one tooth, she could not chew. He learned her spells, learned her chants, learned the names of a thousand gods, and when he was not learning from Sannas he listened to the traders when they returned with strange tales from their long journeys. He listened to everything, forgot nothing and kept his opinions locked inside his head. Those opinions had not changed. The voices that had spoken in his head still echoed there, still woke him at night, still filled him with wonder. He had learned how to heal and how to frighten and how to twist the world to the gods' wishes, but he had not changed. The world's wisdom had left his own untouched.

In the winter's heart, when Slaol was at his weakest and Lahanna was shining brightly on Cathallo's shrine to touch the boulders with a sheen of glistening cold light, Sannas brought two warriors to the temple. 'It is time,' she told Camaban.

The warriors laid Camaban on his back beside one of the temple's taller stones. One man held Camaban's shoulders, while the other held the crippled foot towards the full moon. 'I will either kill you,' Sannas said, 'or cure you.' She held a maul of stone and a blade that had been made from the scapula of a dead man and she laid the bone blade on the grotesquely curled ball of Camaban's foot. 'It will hurt,' she said, then laughed as if Camaban's pain would give her pleasure.

The warrior holding the foot flinched as the maul hammered on the bone. Sannas hammered again, showing a remarkable strength for such an old woman. Blood, black in the moonlight, was pouring from the foot, soaking the warrior's hands and running down Camaban's leg. Sannas beat the maul on the blade again, then wrenched the scapula free and gritted her teeth as she forced the curl of Camaban's clenched foot outwards. 'You have toes!' she marvelled, and the two warriors shuddered and turned away as they heard the cracking of cartilage, the splintering of bone and the grating of the broken being straightened. 'Lahanna!' Sannas cried, and hammered the blade into Camaban's foot again, forcing its sharpened edge into another tight part of the bulbous flesh and fused bone.

Sannas bent the foot flat, then splinted it in deer bones

that she bound tight with strips of wolfskin. 'I have used bone to mend bone,' she told Camaban, 'and you will either die or you will walk.'

Camaban stared at her, but said nothing. The pain had been more than he had ever expected, it had been a pain fit to fill the whole wide moonlit world, but he had not whimpered once. There were tears in his eyes, but he had made no sound and he knew he would not die. He would live because Slaol wanted it. Because he had been chosen. Because he was the crooked child who had been sent to make the world straight. He was Camaban.

Winter passed. The salmon returned to the river and the rooks to the high elms that grew west of Ratharryn. The cuckoo called and dragonflies darted where winter ice had locked the river. Lambs bleated among the ancestors' grave mounds, and herons feasted on ducklings in Mai's river. The blackbird's song rippled across the woods where, when spring was full, the deer lost their grey winter coats and shed their antlers. Hengall's father had once claimed to have seen deer eating their old antlers, but in truth it was Syrax, the stag god who roamed the woods, who took them back to himself. The shed antlers were prized as tools, and so men sought to find them before Syrax.

The fields were ploughed. The wealthier folk tugged the fire-hardened plough stake behind an ox, while others used their families to drag the gouging point across the soil. They broke the ground from east to west, then north to south before the priests came to scatter the first handfuls of seed. The previous harvest had been bad, but Hengall had hoarded seed in his hut and now he released it for the fields. Some fields were abandoned to grass, for their soil was tired, but the previous spring the men had ringed trees on the forest's edge, then burned the dead trees in the autumn, and the newly cleared land was ploughed and sown while the women made a sacrifice of a lamb. Kestrels floated above the Old Temple where orchids flowered and blue-winged butterflies flew.

In summer, just when the thrushes fell silent, the boys of Hengall's tribe faced their ordeals of manhood. Not every boy passed the ordeals and some did not even survive them. Indeed it was better, the tribe said, for a boy to die than to fail because in failure they risked ridicule for the rest of their lives. For a whole moon after the ordeal a boy who failed would be forced to wear a woman's clothes and toil at woman's work and squat like a woman to pass water. And for the rest of his life he could not take a wife, nor own slaves, cattle or pigs. A few of those who failed might display some talent for augury and dreams, and those boys might become priests and would then receive the privileges of those who had passed the ordeals, but most of those who failed were scorned for ever. It was better to die.

'You're ready?' Hengall asked Saban on the morning of the first day.

'Yes, father,' Saban said nervously. He was not sure that was true, for how could anyone prepare to be hunted by Jegar and his hounds? In truth Saban was terrified, but he dared not show his fear to his father.

Hengall, whose hair had turned grey in the previous winter, had summoned Saban to give the boy a meal. 'Bear meat,' Hengall said, 'to give you strength.'

Saban had no appetite, but he ate dutifully and Hengall watched each mouthful. 'I have been unlucky in my sons,' he said after a while. Saban, his mouth full of the pungent flesh, said nothing, and Hengall groaned as he thought of

Lengar and Camaban. 'But in you I have a proper son,' he said to Saban. 'Prove it in these next days.'

Saban nodded.

'If I died tomorrow,' Hengall growled, touching his groin to avert the ill luck implied in the words, 'I suppose Galeth would become chief, but he wouldn't be a good leader. He's a good man, but too trusting. He would believe everything Cathallo tells us, and they lie to us as often as they speak the truth. They claim to be our friend these days, but they would still like to swallow us up. They want our land. They want our river. They want our food, but they fear the price they'd pay. They know we would maul them grievously, so when you become chief you must have proved yourself a warrior whom they would fear to fight, but you must also be wise enough to know when not to fight.'

'Yes, father,' Saban said. He had hardly heard a word for he was thinking about Jegar and his long-haired dogs with their tongues lolling between sharp teeth.

'Cathallo must fear you,' Hengall said, 'as they fear me.'

'Yes, father,' Saban said. His chin was dripping with bear's blood. He felt sick.

'The ancestors are watching you,' Hengall went on, 'so make them proud of us. And once you're a man we shall marry you to Derrewyn. We'll make it the first ceremony of the new temple, eh? That should bring you Slaol's favour.'

'I like Derrewyn,' Saban said, blushing.

'Doesn't matter whether you like her or hate her, you just have to give her sons, a lot of sons. Wear the girl out! Breed her, then breed other women, but make yourself sons! Blood is all.'

With these injunctions fresh in his ears, and with his

gullet sour from the rank taste of the bear, Saban went to Slaol's temple just beyond the settlement's entrance. He was naked, as were the twenty-one other boys who gathered beneath the high temple poles. All the boys would now have to go into the wild woods for five nights and there survive even though they were being hunted, and the hunters, who were the men of the tribe, surrounded the temple and jeered at the candidates. The hunters all carried bows or spears and they called the boys woman-hearted, said they would fail, and warned them that the ghouls and spirits and beasts of the woods would rend them. The men invited the boys to abandon the quest before they began, saying that there was small point in their attempting to become men for they were so obviously puny and feeble.

Gilan, the high priest, ignored the jeers and taunts as he prayed to the god. The small chalk balls that were the symbols of the boys' lives were laid in the temple's centre, above the grave of a child who had been sacrificed to the god at the temple's consecration. The balls would stay there until the end, when those who became men would be allowed to break them and those who failed would have to return the chalk symbols to their shamed families.

Gilan spat on the boys as a blessing. Each was allowed one weapon. Most clutched spears or bows, but Saban had chosen to take a flint knife that he had made himself from a rare piece of local flint big enough to make a blade as long as his hand. He had flaked the dark stone into a white and wicked edge. He did not expect to hunt with the knife, for even if he succeeded in killing a beast he would not dare light a fire to cook its flesh in case the smoke should bring the hunters. 'You might as well take no weapon,'

Galeth had advised him, but Saban wanted the small knife for the touch of it gave him comfort.

Jegar taunted Saban from the temple's edge. The hunter had hung a bunch of eagle feathers from his spearhead and more eagle feathers were tucked into his long hair. 'I'm loosing my hounds on you, Saban!' Jegar called. The dogs, huge and hairy, salivated behind their master. 'Give up now!' Jegar shouted. 'What chance does a pissing child like you have? You won't survive a day.'

'We'll drag you back in disgrace,' one of Jegar's friends called to Saban, 'and you can wear my sister's tunic and fetch my mother's water.'

Hengall listened to the threats, but did nothing to alleviate them. This was the way of the tribe and if Saban survived the enmity of Jegar and his friends then Saban's reputation would grow. Nor could Hengall try to protect Saban in the woods for then the tribe would declare that the boy had not passed the ordeal fairly. Saban must survive by his own wits, and if he failed then the gods would be saying he was not fit to be chief.

The boys were given a half-day's start. Then, for five summer nights, they had to survive in the forest where their enemies would not just be the hunters, but also the bears, the great wild aurochs, the wolves and the Outfolk bands who knew that the boys were loose among the trees and so came searching for slaves. The Outfolk would shave the boys' heads, chop off a finger and drag them away to a life of whipped servitude.

Gilan at last finished his invocations and clapped his hands, scattering the frightened boys out of the temple. 'Run far!' Jegar shouted. 'I'm coming for you, Saban!' His leashed dogs howled and Saban feared those animals for the gods had given hounds the ability to follow men deep through the trees. Dogs could sense a man's spirit so that even in the dark a dog could find a man. They can track any creature with a spirit and the great shaggy hounds would be Saban's worst enemies in the coming days.

Saban ran south across the pastureland and his path took him close to the Old Temple which stood waiting for Cathallo's stones. He thought, as he ran past the ditch, that he heard Camaban's voice calling his name and he stopped in puzzlement and looked into the cleared shrine, but there was nothing there except two white cows cropping the grass. His fears told him to keep running towards the trees, but a stronger instinct made him cross the shallow outer bank, clamber through the chalk ditch and climb the larger bank inside.

The sun was warm on his bare skin. He stood motionless, wondering why he had stopped, and then another impulse drove him to his knees on the grass inside the shrine where he used the flint knife to cut off a hank of his long black hair. He laid the hair on the grass, then bowed his forehead to the ground. 'Slaol,' he said, 'Slaol.' It was here that Lengar had tried to kill him, and Saban had escaped that enmity, so now he prayed that the sun god would help him evade another hatred. Saban had been praying for days now, praying to as many gods as he could remember, but now, in the warm ring of chalk on the wind-touched hill, Slaol sent him an answer. It came as if from nowhere, and Saban suddenly knew he would survive the ordeal and that he would even win. He understood that in his anxiety he had been praying for the wrong thing. He had begged the gods to hide him from Jegar, but Jegar was the tribe's best hunter and Slaol had given Saban the thought that he should let Jegar find him. That was the god's gift. Let Jegar find his prey, then let him fail. Saban raised his head to the brightness in the sky and shouted his thanks.

He ran into the woods where he felt his fears rise again. This was the wild place, the dark place where wolves, bears and aurochs stalked. There were Outfolk hunting bands looking for slaves and, even worse, there were outcasts. When a man was banished from Ratharryn the tribe did not say that he was gone from the settlement, but that he had gone to the woods, and Saban knew that many such outcasts roamed the trees, men said to be as savage as any beast. It was rumoured they lived off human flesh and they knew when the tribes' boys were hiding among the trees and so they searched for them. All those dangers frightened Saban, but there were still more horrible things among the leaves: those dead souls who did not pass into Lahanna's care haunted the woods. Sometimes hunters vanished without a trace and the priests reckoned they had been snatched by the jealous dead who so hate the living.

The forest was all dark danger, which is why the woods were for ever being felled and why women were not allowed into it. They could forage for herbs among the copses close to the settlement, or they could travel through the woods if they were accompanied by men, but they could not go alone into the trees that lay beyond the outermost fields for fear of being assaulted by ghouls and spirits, or of being captured by the outcasts. Some women, very few, actually ran to join those fugitives and once there, hidden in the deep trees, they formed small savage clans who preyed on crops, children, herds and flocks.

Yet Saban saw no dangers as he headed westwards

through the woods. The sun made the green leaves shine and the warm wind whispered in the branches. He followed the same path on which he and Lengar had tracked the stranger who had brought the treasure to Ratharryn, and though he knew there was a risk in walking such a path so openly when the woods were filled with enemies, he took the chance for he wanted Jegar's dogs to have no trouble in following his spirit through the tangling trees.

In the afternoon, when he had reached the high crest from where he could stare far across the western forests, Saban heard the faint sound of ox horns blowing. That ominous booming told him that Ratharryn's hunters had been released. They would be carrying glowing embers in pots so that if they chose to stay in the woods at night they could build vast fires that would deter the spirits and the beasts. Saban could use no such defence. He had only Slaol's help and one short-bladed knife of brittle flint.

He spent a long time searching for a tree that would suit Slaol's purpose. He knew Jegar's dogs would be lunging along the path, but he had a long start and time enough, and after a while he settled on an oak tree that grew low and broad, though halfway up its trunk there was a space from which no branches sprang. A man could easily climb the first length of the tree, then he would need to leap to catch hold of a convenient branch that was the thickness of a man's arm. That branch made the perfect handhold, and if Jegar thought Saban was hidden in the upper leaves of the tree he would leap for it. Saban leapt for it now, and held on tight as his feet scrabbled for purchase on the trunk. Then he hauled himself up and straddled the tree's narrow limb.

He sat facing the oak's trunk, said a brief prayer to the

tree so that it would forgive the wound he was about to inflict, then used his knife's tip to gouge a narrow slit along the branch's topmost surface. Then, when the cut was wide and deep enough, he jammed the flint blade into the wood so that its wicked, white-flaked edge stood proud of the bark. He did his work well, for the blade sat firm in the tree's grip when he was finished. He spat on the flint to give it luck, then dropped down from the branch. He looked up to make sure that his small trap was invisible, then collected and hid the small scraps of freshly chipped wood that had fallen by the oak's bole.

He ran downhill to find the stream that flowed at the ridge's foot and once there he waded through the shallow water because everyone knew that spirits could not cross water. While he was in the stream his own spirit would shrink into his body, thus leaving no trace for Jegar's dogs. He waded a long way, occasionally muttering a prayer to placate the stream's spirit, then climbed back up the hill to discover a place where he could rest.

He found a place where two branches sprang from an elm tree's trunk, and he placed smaller branches across the two to make a platform where he could lie safely. He was hidden, but high enough to see between the leaves to where the white clouds rode the bright sky, and, by craning his neck, he could just see a patch of mossy ground at the tree's foot. For a long while nothing happened. The wind rustled the leaves, a squirrel chattered its teeth and two bees drifted close. Somewhere a woodpecker rattled at bark, stopped, began again. A rustle of dead leaves made Saban peer down, fearing discovery, but all he saw was a fox carrying a dabchick in its jaws.

Then the living noises of the woods, all the small sounds

of claw and beak and paw, just stopped, and there was only the sigh of the wind among the leaves and the creak of the trees. Everything that breathed was crouching motionless because something new and strange had come. There was danger; the forest held its breath, and Saban listened until at last he heard the noise that had silenced the world. A hound bayed.

It was a warm day, but Saban's naked skin was suddenly chill. He could feel the hairs prickling at his neck. Another dog howled, then Saban heard men's voices far away. The men were high above him on the slope. Hunters.

He could imagine them. There would be a half-dozen young men, Jegar their leader, all tall and strong and sun-browned, with their long hair twisted into hunter's braids and hung with feathers. They would be peering up the oak tree, leaning on their spears and calling insults to where they thought Saban was hiding. Perhaps they loosed a few arrows into the leaves, hoping to drive him down so they could walk him back to Ratharryn and parade his shame in front of his father's hut, but in a small while they would become bored and one of them – let it be Jegar, Saban prayed – would clamber up the oak's trunk to find him.

Saban lay, his eyes closed, listening. Then he heard a shout. Not just a shout, but a yelp of protest and pain and anger, and he knew his small trap had bitten blood. He smiled.

Jegar fell from the tree, cursing because his right hand was cut deep across the palm. He shrieked and forced his bleeding hand between his thighs as he bent over to allevi-ate the agony. One of his friends placed moss on the wound, and bound the hand with leaves, and afterwards, furious, they rampaged along the ridge, but neither they nor their howling dogs came close to Saban. They followed his spirit down to the stream, but there the hounds lost him and after a while they abandoned the hunt. The sound of dogs faded and the myriad small sounds of the woods were heard again.

Saban grinned. He relived the moment when he had heard the scream and he thanked Slaol. He laughed. He had won.

He had won, yet still he did not move. He was hungry now, yet he dared not forage in case Jegar was still stalking the slope, so he stayed on his small platform and watched the birds fly home to their nests and the sky turn red with Slaol's anger because the world was being given over to Lahanna's care. The chill seeped up from the stream. A deer and her fawn stepped slow and delicate beneath the ash as they went to the water and their appearance suggested there were no hunters concealed on the ridge above, yet still Saban did not move. His hunger and thirst could wait. In the gaps between the high leaves he could see the sky turning smoky and misty, then the first star of Lahanna's flock appeared. The tribe called that star Merra and it reminded Saban that all his ancestors were gazing down, but it also brought fears of those folk who had died in shame and who were now rousing from their day sleep to let their famished spirits wander the dark trees. Strange claws were being unsheathed and rabid teeth bared as the night terrors of the forest were unleashed.

Saban hardly slept, but instead lay and listened to the noises of the night. Once he heard the crackling of twigs, the sound of a great body moving through the brush, then silence again in which he imagined a monstrous head, fangs bared, questing up into the elm. A scream sounded higher on the ridge, and Saban curled into a ball and whimpered. An owl screeched. The boy's only comforts were the stars of his ancestors, the cold light of Lahanna silvering the leaves and his thoughts of Derrewyn. He thought of her a lot. He tried to conjure up a picture of her face. Once, thinking about her, he looked up and saw a streak of light slither across the stars and he knew that a god was descending to the earth which he took to be a sign that he and Derrewyn were destined for each other.

For five days and nights he hid, foraging only in the half-light of dawn and dusk. He found a clearing at the bottom of the ridge where the stream had made a wide bend in its course and there he found chervil and garlic. He plucked sorrel and comfrey leaves, and found some broom buds, though they were bitter for their season was almost done. Best of all were the morels that he found higher on the ridge where a great elm had fallen. He carried them back to his platform in the ash and picked the wood-lice from their crannies before eating them. One day he even tickled a small trout up from the weeds of the stream and gnawed greedily at its raw flesh. At night he chewed the gum that oozes from birch bark, spitting it out when all the flavour was gone.

Jegar had given up the hunt, though Saban did not know that, and one twilight, seeking for more morels by the rotting elm, he heard a footfall in the leaves and froze. He was concealed by the fallen tree, but the hiding place was precarious and his heart began to thump.

A moment later a file of Outfolk spearmen went past. They were all men, all with bronze-tipped spears and all had grey tattooed streaks on their faces. They had no dogs with them, and they seemed more intent on leaving the ridge than searching for prey. Saban heard them splash through the stream, heard the flutter as the waterbirds fled their presence, then there was silence again.

The last night was Saban's worst. It rained, and the wind was high so that the noises of the trees were louder than ever as they tossed their heads in the wet sky. Branches creaked and, far off, Rannos the god of thunder tumbled the blackness. And it was dark, utterly dark, without a scrap of Lahanna's light piercing or thinning the clouds. The darkness was worse than a cold hut, for this was a limitless night filled with horrors and in its black heart Saban heard something huge and cumbersome crash through the woods and he huddled on his platform thinking of the dead souls and their yearning for human flesh until, wet, cold and hungry, he saw a grey dawn dilute the damp darkness above the ridge. The rain eased as the sky brightened, and then the ox horns sounded to say that the first ordeal was done.

Twenty-two boys had left Ratharryn, but only seventeen returned. One had vanished and was never seen again, two had been found by hunters and had been driven back to Ratharryn, while two more had been so terrified of the darkness of the trees that they had willingly gone back to their humiliation. But the seventeen who gathered at Slaol's temple were permitted to tie their hair in a loose knot at the nape of their necks and then they followed the priests down the track that led to Ratharryn's entrance and their path was lined with women who held out platters of flat bread and cold pork and dried fish. 'Eat,' they urged the boys, 'you must be hungry, eat!' But hungry as they were, none touched the food for that too was an ordeal, though an easy one to survive.

The men of the tribe waited beside a raging fire inside the great wall and they thumped their spear butts on the ground to welcome the seventeen. The boys still had two tests to face, and some could yet fail, but they were no longer jeered. Saban saw Jegar, and saw the leaves bound with twine on his hand, and he could not resist dancing a few steps of victory. Jegar spat towards him, but it was mere petulance. He had missed his chance and Saban had survived the woods.

The boys had to wrestle against men for their next test. It did not matter if they won or lost, indeed no one expected a half-starved boy to beat a full-grown man, but it was important that they fought well and showed bravery. Saban found himself pitted against Dioga, a freed Outfolk slave noted for his bear-like strength. The crowd laughed at the mismatch between boy and man, but Saban was faster than any of them expected. He slipped Dioga's rush, kicked him, slipped past him again, slapped him, jeered at him and landed one blow that stung Dioga's face and then the bigger man at last caught the boy, threw him down and began to throttle him with his big hands. Saban clawed at Dioga's tattooed face, attempting to hook his fingers into the man's eye sockets, but Dioga just grunted and bore down with his thumbs on Saban's windpipe until Gilan hit him with a staff and made him let go. 'Well done, boy,' the high priest said. Saban choked as he tried to answer, then sat with the other boys and heaved breath into his starving lungs.

The seventeen boys endured the fire last. They stood with their backs to the flames as a priest heated the sharpened tip of an ash branch until it was red hot, then placed the glowing tip on their shoulder blades and left it

117

there until the skin bubbled. Gilan stared into their faces to make certain they did not cry. Saban sang the rage song of Rannos as the fire scorched his back, and the heat was such that he thought he would have to cry aloud, but the pain passed and Gilan grinned his approval. 'Well done,' the high priest said again, 'well done,' and Saban's heart was so full of joy he could have flown like a bird.

He was a man. He could take a bride, own a slave, keep his own livestock, give himself a new name and speak in the tribal meetings. Neel, the young priest, presented Saban with the chalk ball that was his childhood's spirit shelter and Saban danced up and down on it, breaking and powdering the chalk as he whooped with delight. His father, unable to conceal his pleasure, gave him a wolfskin tunic, a fine spear and a bronze knife with a wooden handle. His mother gave him an amulet of amber, which had been a gift to her from Lengar, and Saban tried to make her keep it for she was sick, but she would not take it back. Galeth gave him a yew longbow, then sat him down and tattooed the marks of manhood on his chest. He used a bone comb that he dipped in woad, then hammered into Saban's skin; the pain meant nothing to Saban for now he was a man. 'You can take a new name now,' Galeth said.

'Hand-Splitter,' Saban said jokingly.

Galeth laughed. 'I thought that was your work. Well done. But you've made a lifelong enemy.'

'An enemy,' Saban said, 'who will find it hard to hold a bow or wield a spear.'

'But a dangerous man,' Galeth warned him.

'A crippled man now,' Saban said, for he had heard that

the flint knife had bitten right through the sinews of Jegar's hand.

'A worse enemy for that,' Galeth said. 'So will you change your name?'

'I shall keep it,' Saban said. His birth name meant Favoured One and he reckoned it was apt. He watched the blood and woad trickle down his skin. He was a man! Then, with the sixteen others who had passed the ordeals, Saban sat down to a feast of meat, bread and honey, and while they ate, the women of the tribe sang the battle song of Arryn. By the meal's end the sun was going down and the girls who had been sequestered all day in the Temple of Lahanna were taken to the Temple of Slaol. The tribe lined the path from the settlement to the temple and they danced and clapped as the seventeen men followed the girls who would now become women.

Derrewyn was not among the girls. She was too valuable as a bride to be given to that night's revelry, but next morning, as Saban walked back into the settlement to find a place where he could build his own hut, Derrewyn greeted him. She gave him one of her precious necklaces of white sea-shells. Saban blushed at the gift and Derrewyn laughed at his confusion.

And that same day Gilan began to plan how the eight stones would be placed.

The new men were not expected to work on the day after their ordeals, so Saban wandered up onto the hill to watch Gilan begin his work in the Old Temple. Butterflies were everywhere, a host of blue and white scraps being blown across the flower-studded grass where a score of people were digging the chalk with antler picks to make ditches and banks that would flank a new sacred path leading to the temple's gate of the sun.

Saban walked to the western side of the temple and sat on the grass. His new spear was beside him and he wondered when he would first use it in battle. He was a man now, but the tribe would expect him to kill an enemy before he was reckoned a proper adult. He drew out the bronze knife his father had given him and admired it in the sunlight. The blade was short, scarce as long as Saban's hand, but the metal had been incised with a thousand tiny indentations that made a complex pattern. A man's knife, Saban thought, and he tilted the blade from side to side so that the sun flashed from the metal.

Derrewyn's voice spoke behind him, 'My uncle has a sword just like that. He says it was made in the land across the western sea.'

Saban twisted round and stared up at her. 'Your uncle?' He asked.

'Kital, chief of Cathallo.' She paused. 'Of course.' She crouched beside him and placed a delicate finger to the blue-red scabs of his new tattoos. 'Did that hurt?' she asked.

'No,' Saban boasted.

'It must have done.'

'A little,' he conceded.

'Better those scars than being killed by Jegar,' Derrewyn said.

'He wouldn't have killed me,' Saban said. 'He just wanted to drag me back to Ratharryn and make me carry the chalk to my father.'

'I think he would have killed you,' Derrewyn said, then gave him a sidelong glance. 'Did you cut his hand?'

'In a way,' Saban admitted, smiling.

She laughed. 'Geil says he might never use the hand again properly.' Geil was Hengall's oldest wife and the woman with whom Derrewyn lived, and she had famous skills as a healer. 'She told Jegar he should go to Sannas because she's much more powerful.' Derrewyn plucked some daisies. 'Did you know Sannas has straightened your brother's foot?'

'She did?' Saban asked in surprise.

'She cut his foot right open,' Derrewyn said. 'There was blood everywhere! She did it on the night of the full moon and he didn't make a sound and afterwards they strapped his foot to some deer bones and he had a fever.' She began making the daisies into a chain. 'He got better,' she added.

'How do you know?' Saban asked.

'A trader brought the news while you were in the woods,' she said. She paused to slit a daisy's stem with a sharp fingernail. 'And he said Sannas is angry with your brother.'

'Why?'

'Because Camaban just walked away,' Derrewyn said with a frown. 'Even before the foot was healed he just walked away, and no one knows where he's gone. Sannas thought he might have come here.'

'I haven't seen him,' Saban said, and felt somehow disgruntled that he had not heard this news of his brother before, or perhaps he was disappointed that Camaban had not come to Ratharryn, though he could think of no reason why he should want to visit his father's tribe. But Saban liked his awkward, stuttering half-brother and felt distressed that Camaban had gone away without any leave-taking. 'I wish he had come here,' Saban said.

Derrewyn shuddered. 'I only met him once,' she said, 'and I thought he was frightening.'

'He's just clumsy,' Saban said and half smiled. 'I used to take him food and he liked to try and frighten me. He'd gibber and jump about, pretending to be mad.'

'Pretending?'

'He likes to pretend.'

She shrugged, then shook her head as if Camaban's fate were of no importance. South of the temple a group of men were tearing the wool from the backs of sheep, making the beasts bleat pitifully. Derrewyn laughed at the naked-looking animals, and Saban watched her, marvelling at the delicacy of her face and the smoothness of her sun-browned legs. She was no older than he was, yet it seemed to Saban that Derrewyn had a confidence he lacked. Derrewyn herself pretended not to notice that she was being admired, but just turned to look at the Old Temple where Gilan was being helped by Galeth and his son, Mereth, who was just a year younger than Saban. Just a year, though because Saban was now a man the gap between him and Mereth seemed much wider.

Gilan and his two helpers were trying to find the centre of the shrine, and to do it they had stretched a string of woven bark fibre across the grassy circle within the inner bank. Once they were sure that they had discovered the widest space across the circle they doubled the string and tied a piece of grass about its looped end. That way they knew they had a line that was as long as the circle was wide, and that the grass knot marked the exact centre of the line, and now they were stretching the line again and again across the circle's width in an attempt to find the temple's centre. Galeth held one end of the string, Mereth the other, and Gilan stood in the middle for ever wanting to know if his two helpers were standing right beside the bank, or on it, or just beyond it, and whenever he was satisfied that they were in their right places he would mark where the scrap of grass was tied about the string by planting a stick in the ground. There were now a dozen sticks, all within a few hands' lengths of each other, though no two were marking exactly the same place and Gilan kept taking new measurements in the hope of finding two points that agreed.

'Why do they need to find the middle of the temple?' Saban asked.

'Because on midsummer's morning,' Derrewyn said, 'they'll find exactly where Slaol rises and then they'll draw a line from there to the temple's centre.' She was a priest's daughter and knew such things. Gilan had now decided on one of the many sticks, so he plucked the others out of the soil before clumsily banging a stake into the ground to mark the shrine's centre. It seemed that was the extent of this day's work, for Gilan now rolled the string into a ball and, after muttering a prayer, walked back towards Ratharryn.

'You want to go hunting?' Galeth called to Saban.

'No,' Saban called back.

'Getting lazy now you're a man?' Galeth asked good-naturedly, then waved and followed the high priest.

'You don't want to hunt?' Derrewyn asked Saban.

'I'm a man now,' Saban said. 'I can have my own hut, keep cattle and slaves, and I can take a woman into the forest.'

'A woman?' Derrewyn asked.

'You,' he said. He stood, picked up his spear, then held out his hand.

Derrewyn looked at him for a heartbeat. 'What happened last night in Slaol's temple?'

'There were seventeen men,' Saban said, 'and fourteen girls. I slept.'

'Why?'

'I was waiting for you,' he said and his heart was full and tremulous for it seemed that what he did now was far more dangerous than sleeping in the dark trees among the Outfolk and outcast enemies. He touched the necklace of sea-shells she had given him. 'I was waiting for you,' he said again.

She stood. For an instant Saban thought she would turn away, but then she smiled and took his hand. 'I've never been into the forest,' she said.

'Then it is time you went,' Saban said, and led her eastwards. He was a man.

Saban and Derrewyn went eastwards across Mai's river, then north past the settlement until they reached a place where the valley was steep and narrow and thick trees arched high above the running water. Sunlight splashed through the leaves. The call of the corncrakes in the wheatfields had long faded and all they could hear now was the river's rippling and the whisper of the wind and the scrabble of squirrels' claws and the staccato flap of a pigeon bursting through the high leaves. Orchids grew purple among the water mint at the river's edge while the haze of the fading bluebells clouded the shadows beneath the trees. Kingfishers whipped bright above the river where red-dabbed moorhen chicks paddled between the rushes.

Saban took Derrewyn to an island in the river, a place where willow and ash grew thick above a bank of long grass and thick moss. They waded to the island, then lay on the moss and Derrewyn watched air bubbles breaking the leaf-shadowed water where otters twisted after fish. A doe came to the farther bank, but sprang away before she drank because Derrewyn sighed too loudly in admiration. Then Derrewyn wanted to catch fish, so she took Saban's new spear and stood in the shallows and every now and then she would plunge the blade down at a trout or a grayling, but always missed. 'Aim below them,' Saban told her.

'Below them?'

'See how the spear bends in the water?'

'It just looks that way,' she said, then lunged, missed again and laughed. The spear was heavy and it tired her, so she tossed it onto the bank, then just stood letting the river run about her brown knees. 'Do you want to be chief here?' she asked Saban after a while.

He nodded. 'I think so, yes.'

She turned to look at him. 'Why?'

Saban did not have an answer. He had become accustomed to the idea, that was all. His father was chief, and though that did not mean that one of Hengall's sons should necessarily be the next chief, the tribe would look to those sons first and Saban was now the only one who might succeed. 'I think I want to be like my father,' he said carefully. 'He's a good chief.'

'What makes a good chief?'

'You keep people alive in winter,' Saban said, 'you cut back the forests, you judge disputes fairly and protect the tribe from enemies.'

'From Cathallo?' Derrewyn asked.

'Only if Cathallo threatens us.'

'They won't. I shall make sure of that.'

'You will?'

'Kital likes me, and one of his sons will be the next chief and they're all my cousins, and they all like me.' She looked at him shyly, as though he would find that surprising. 'I shall insist that we all be friends,' she said

126

fiercely. 'It's stupid being enemies. If men want to fight they should go and find the Outfolk.' She suddenly splashed him with water. 'Can you swim?'

'Yes.'

'Teach me.'

'Just throw yourself in,' Saban said.

'And I'll drown,' she said. 'Two men in Cathallo drowned once and we didn't find them for days and they were all swollen.' She pretended to half lose her balance. 'And I'll be like them, all swollen and nibbled by fish and it'll be your fault because you wouldn't teach me to swim.'

Saban laughed, but stood and stripped off his new wolf-skin tunic. Until a few days before he had always gone naked in summer, but now he felt embarrassed without the tunic. He ran fast into the water that was wonderfully cold after the heat under the trees and swam away from Derrewyn, going into a deep pool where the river swirled in dark ripples. Splashing to keep his head above water, once he had reached the pool's centre, he turned to call Derrewyn into the river, only to find that she was already there, very close behind him. She laughed at his shocked expression. 'I learned to swim a long time ago,' she said, then took a deep breath, ducked her head and kicked her bare legs into the air so that she could dive down beneath Saban. She too was naked.

Saban splashed back to the island where he lay on his belly in the grass. He watched Derrewyn dive and swim, and still watched her as she came to the river's edge and slowly walked from the water with her long black hair sleek and dripping. To Saban she appeared like the river goddess Mai herself, coming from the water in awesome beauty, and then she knelt beside him, making the skin of his back shiver where her hair touched the burn scars on his shoulder blades. He lay very still, conscious of her, but scarce daring to move in case he frightened her away. This, he told himself, was why he had asked her to come into the forest, though now that the moment was on him he was consumed by nervousness. Derrewyn must have known what he was thinking for she touched his shoulder, making him turn over, then she lowered herself into his arms. 'You ate the clay, Saban,' she whispered, her wet hair cold on his shoulders, 'so the skull's curse cannot touch you.'

'You know that?'

'I promise that,' she whispered, and he shivered because it seemed to him as if Mai really had come in her splendour from the water. He held her close, very close, and like a fool he thought his joy could last for ever.

That afternoon, as Derrewyn and Saban waited for the sun to sink and the twilight to bring the shadows through which they could creep secretly home, they heard singing from the hill above the river's western bank. They dressed, waded across the branch of the river, and climbed towards the sound that became louder with their every step. The two went slowly and cautiously, but they need not have worried about being seen for the singers were too intent on their task to notice two lovers among the leaves.

The singers were women from Cathallo and they were lined up either side of seventy sweating men who were hauling on long ropes of twisted leather which were attached to a great oak sledge on which the first of Ratharryn's eight stones sat. It was one of the smaller stones, yet its weight was such that the men were heaving and grunting to keep the cumbersome sledge moving along the rough woodland path. Other men went ahead to smooth the way, cutting out roots and kicking down tussocks of grass, but after a while the men on the ropes were simply too exhausted to continue. They had hauled all day, they had even pulled the great sledge up the hill south of Maden, and now they were spent so they left the sledge in the middle of the wood and walked south towards Ratharryn where they expected to be fed. Derrewyn gripped Saban's arm. 'I'll go with them,' she whispered.

'Why?'

'Then I can say I came to meet them. That way no one will wonder where I've been.' She reached up, kissed his cheek, then ran after the retreating people.

Saban waited until they had gone, then went and stroked the stone on its oak sledge. It was warm to the touch and, where the sun pierced the leaves to shine on the boulder, tiny flecks of light glinted in the rock. Touching the stone coincided with a great surge of happiness. He was a man, and he had a woman as beautiful as any in the land. He had held Derrewyn on the river's bank and it seemed to Saban that life was as rich and hopeful as it could ever be. The gods loved him.

Hengall hardly felt that the gods loved him for that evening a great crowd of Cathallo folk arrived at Ratharryn and they all needed to be fed and given places to sleep and he had not realized, when he paid the gold pieces for the eight stones, that they would cost him so much in food. He also had to provide more folk to help haul the stones, and those were found among the poorer families in the settlement and they had to be paid in meat and grain. Hengall saw his herds diminish and he began to doubt the wisdom of his bargain, but he did not try to repudiate it. He sent men to haul the stones and, day by day as the summer neared its height, the great boulders crept towards Ratharryn.

The four larger stones proved difficult. There was a path across the stream-cut marshlands near Maden, but it was too narrow for the bigger stones and so Kital's men hauled those boulders far to the west before turning south towards Ratharryn. But there was a hill in their path, not so steep as the hill up which the four smaller stones had already been hauled, but still a formidable obstacle that proved too much for the men dragging the first of the big boulders. More ropes were fetched and more men were harnessed to the sledge, but still the stone would not shift up the slope. They tried pulling the sledge with oxen, but when the beasts took the strain they bunched together and impeded each other and it was not until Galeth devised the idea of harnessing the oxen to a great bar of oak, and then attaching ropes from the oak bar to the sledge, that they managed to shift the great stone and so drag it to the hilltop where, with its runners now crushing the level grass, it was hauled onwards. The other three heavy stones were fetched in the same way. The priests hung flowers from the oxen's horns, the beasts were surrounded by singers and there was joy in Ratharryn for the summer was kind, the stones had come safely and it seemed that the ill omens of the past had all faded.

Midsummer arrived. The fires were lit and Ratharryn's men wore the bullskins and chased the women about

Slaol's temple. Saban did not run with the bull-men, though he could have, but instead he sat with Derrewyn and, as the fires died, they jumped the flames hand in hand. Gilan dispensed the liquor brewed for the night's celebrations; some folk screamed as they saw visions, while others became belligerent or ill, but eventually they slept, except Saban, who stayed awake, for Jegar had been drunkenly searching for him with a spear in his left hand and revenge on his liquor-fuddled mind. Saban stayed close to the temple that night, sitting guard over the sleeping Derrewyn, though he dozed towards morning when he was woken by footfalls and quickly lifted his spear. A man was coming up the path from the settlement and Saban crouched, ready to lunge, then saw the reflection of dying firelight glint from the man's bald head and realized it was Gilan, not Jegar.

'Who's that?' the high priest asked.

'Saban.'

'You can help me,' Gilan said cheerfully. 'I need a helper. I was going to ask Neel, but he's sleeping like a dog.'

Saban woke Derrewyn and the two of them walked with Gilan to the Old Temple. It was the year's shortest night and Gilan kept glancing at the north-eastern horizon for fear that the sun would rise before he reached the Old Temple. 'I need to mark the rising sun,' he explained as they passed through the grave mounds. He bowed to the ancestors, then hurried on to where the eight stones waited on their sledges just outside the Old Temple's ditch. The north-eastern sky was perceptibly lightening, but the sun had yet to blaze across the far wooded hills. 'We need some markers,' Gilan said, and Saban went down into the ditch and found a half-dozen large lumps of chalk, then he stood in the entrance causeway while Gilan went to the stake that marked the temple's centre. Derrewyn, forbidden to enter the temple because she was a woman, waited between the ditches and banks of the newly cut sacred path.

Saban turned to face the north-east. The horizon was shadowy and the hills in front of it were grey and sifted with the smoke from the dying midsummer fires that rose from Ratharryn's valley. The cattle on the nearer slopes were white ghostly shapes.

'Soon,' Gilan said, 'soon,' and he prayed that the scatter of clouds on the horizon would not hide the sun's rising.

The clouds turned pink and the pink deepened and spread, becoming red, and Saban, watching where the blazing sky touched the jet black earth, saw a gap of sky above the trees and suddenly there was a fierce brightness in those distant woods as the sun's upper edge slashed through the leaves.

'To your left!' Gilan called. 'Your left. One pace. No, back! There! There!'

Saban placed a chalk marker at his feet, then stood to watch the sun chase away the stars. At first Slaol appeared like a flattened ball that leaked an ooze of fire along the wooded ridge, and then the red turned to white, too fierce for the eyes, and the first light of the new year shone straight along the new sacred path that led to the Old Temple's entrance. Saban shaded his eyes and watched the night shadows shrink in the valleys. 'To your right!' Gilan called. 'To your right!' He made Saban place another marker at the spot where the sun was at last wholly visible above the horizon, and then he waited until the sun just showed above Saban's head and made him place a third marker. The sound of the tribe singing its welcome to the sun came gently across the grass.

Gilan examined the markers Saban had laid and grunted happily when he saw that some of the old posts which had decayed in their sockets had evidently marked the same alignments. 'We did a good job,' he said approvingly.

'What do we do next?' Saban asked.

Gilan gestured either side of the temple's entrance. 'We'll plant two of the larger stones here as a gate,' he said, then pointed to where Derrewyn stood in the sacred path, 'and put the other two there to frame the sun's midsummer rising.'

'And the four smaller stones?' Saban asked.

'They'll mark Lahanna's wanderings,' the priest answered, and pointed across the river valley. 'We'll show where she appears farthest to the south,' he said, then turned and gestured in the opposite direction, 'and where she vanishes in the north.' Gilan's face seemed to glow with happiness in the early light. 'It will be a simple temple,' he said softly, 'but beautiful. Very beautiful. One line for Slaol and two for Lahanna, marking a place where they can meet beneath the sky.'

'But they're estranged,' Saban said.

Gilan laughed. He was a kindly man, portly and bald, who had never shared Hirac's fear of offending the gods. 'We have to balance Slaol and Lahanna,' he explained. 'They already have a temple apiece in Ratharryn, so how will Lahanna feel if we give Slaol a second shrine all of his own?' He left that question unanswered. 'And we were wrong, I think, to keep Slaol and Lahanna apart. At Cathallo they use one shrine for all the gods, so why shouldn't we worship Slaol and Lahanna in one place?'

'But it's still a temple to Slaol?' Saban asked anxiously, remembering how the sun god had helped him at the beginning of his ordeal.

'It's still a temple to Slaol,' Gilan agreed, 'but now it will acknowledge Lahanna too, just like the shrine at Cathallo.' He smiled. 'And at its dedication we shall marry you to Derrewyn as a foretaste of Slaol and Lahanna's reunion.'

The sun was high enough to give its warmth as the three walked back to the settlement. Gilan talked of his hopes, Saban held his lover's hand, the smoke of the midsummer fires faded and all was well in Ratharryn.

Galeth was the temple's builder, and Saban became his helper. They placed the four smaller boulders first. Gilan had calculated the positions for the stones, and they had to be placed by calculation rather than by observation for the four stones formed two pairs and each pair pointed towards Lahanna. In her wanderings about the sky, she stayed within the same broad belt year after year, but once in a man's lifetime she went far to the north and once in a lifetime far to the south. The poles in her existing temple inside the settlement marked the limits of those northern and southern wanderings and if a man drew a line between the points on the horizon where the moon rose and set at her extremes it would cross the line of the sun's mid-summer rising at a right angle. That made Gilan's task simple. 'It isn't so everywhere,' he explained to Saban. 'It's only here in Ratharryn that the lines cross square. Not at Drewenna, not at Cathallo, nowhere else! Only here!' Gilan was in awe of that fact. 'It means we are special to the gods,' he said softly. 'It means, I think, that this is the very centre of all the world!'

'Truly?' Saban asked, impressed.

'Truly,' Gilan said. 'Cathallo, of course, say the same about their Sacred Mound, but I fear they're mistaken. This is the world's centre,' he said, gesturing at the Old Temple, 'the very place where man was first made.' He shuddered at that thought, moved by the joy of it.

The high priest then laid a nettle string along the line of midsummer's rising, taking it from the chalk marker which showed where the sun rose, through the very centre of the temple and on to the south-eastern bank. Galeth had jointed two pieces of thin timber to make a square angle and, by laying the timber against the string, and then running another string along the crosswise timber, they could mark a line that crossed the sun's line at a right angle. That new line pointed to the extremes of the moon's wandering, but Gilan wanted two parallel lines, one to point to the northernmost limit and the other to the southernmost, so he drew his second line and told Galeth that the four small stones must be placed inside the bank at the outer ends of both scratched lines. One of each pair was to be a pillar and the other a slab, and by standing beside the pillar and looking across the opposite slab a priest could watch where Lahanna rose or set and judge how close she approached her most distant wanderings.

Galeth had thirty men working and at first they simply dug the holes for the stones. They scraped away the turf, then prised at the hard chalk with the picks and broke it into clumps that could be scooped out with shovels. They dug the holes deep, and Galeth made them slope one side of the hole to make a ramp so that the stones could be slid down into their sockets. It was, he told Saban, no different from raising one of the big temple poles. When all four holes were dug, more men were fetched up from the settlement and the first stone, the smallest pillar, was dragged on its sledge through the entrance of the sun. Saban had thought there might be some ceremony as the stone was brought to its new sacred home, but there was no ritual other than a silent prayer that Gilan offered with his hands reaching to the sky. The sledge runners left scars of crushed grass. Galeth lined the stone up with the hole and kept the men hauling until the tip of the sledge just overhung the ramp that Saban had lined with three smoothed timbers that had been greased with pig fat to serve as a slide.

It took twelve men using long oak levers to shift the stone off the sledge. Saban thought the levers must break, but instead the stone moved bit by bit, heave by heave, and each heave lifted and carried the boulder another finger's breadth forward. The men sang as they worked, and the sweat poured off them, but at last the weight of the stone tipped it forwards off the sledge and down onto the ramp. Men scattered, fearing the stone would fall back on them, but instead, just as Galeth had planned, it slid ponderously down the greased timbers to lodge at the ramp's bottom. Galeth wiped his face and let out a great breath of relief.

When he erected the great temple poles Galeth would haul them upright by pulling their tops into the sky by means of a great tripod over which the ropes were led, but he reckoned this stone pillar was small enough to be pushed upright without any such help. He chose the twelve strongest men and they took their places beside the uppermost part of the stone that now tilted up from the ramp's edge. The men got their shoulders under the stone and heaved. 'Push!' Galeth shouted. 'Push!' and they did push, but the stone still stuck halfway. 'Heave on it!' Galeth urged them and added his own huge strength to theirs, but still the stone would not move. Saban peered down the hole and saw that the stone was catching on the upright face of rubbly chalk. Galeth saw it too, swore, and seized a stone axe with which he hacked at the chalk face to make room for the stone.

The dozen men had no trouble holding the stone's weight and, once the obstruction was cleared, they pushed it upright. The stone now stood a little less than the height of a man, with almost as much again buried in the socket, and all that was needed was to fill the ramp and press earth and chalk into the hole about the boulder. Galeth had collected some great river stones and they were packed about the pillar's base, then the chalk rubble was scooped in, and with it the antlers that had broken while the hole was being dug, and all was stamped down and stamped down again until at last the hole and the ramp were filled and the first of the temple's stones was standing. The tired men cheered.

It took until harvest to raise the other three moon stones, but at last they were done and the four grey boulders stood in a rectangle. Galeth had rigged a short tripod of oak beams to raise the slabs, for they were heavier than the pillars, but what made raising the stones even easier was Saban's notion of lining the upright face of the hole with greased timbers so that the stone's corner, grinding down into the earth, did not lodge against the chalk. The fourth stone they raised, even though it was one of the heavier slabs, took only half as long to raise as the first pillar.

'The gods made you clever,' Galeth complimented him.

'You too.'

'No.' Galeth shook his head. 'The gods made me strong.'

The moon stones were finished. Now, if a man could draw a line through the pairs, and extend that line on either side to the very ends of the earth where the fogs lingered across grey seas in perpetuity, he could see where the moon rose and fell at the limits of her wanderings and Lahanna, endlessly travelling among the stars, could look down and see that the people of Ratharryn had marked her journeying. She would know that they watched her, know that they loved her, and she would hear their prayers.

The four larger stones stayed outside the temple while Ratharryn's folk cut the year's wheat and barley. It was a fair harvest and the women sang as they stood about the threshing floor that had been flattened and hardened by a day-long harvest dance. Saban and Derrewyn led the dance, and the women swayed and smiled because Derrewyn was young and happy, and Saban, they knew, was a good young man, decent and strong, and their imminent marriage was taken as a good augury. Only Jegar, who could still not hold a bow in his right hand and could only use a spear with his clumsy left hand, resented them, but there was little he could do. And Jegar's jealousy grew worse when a band of Outfolk tried to raid the harvest from Cheol, which was an outlying settlement of Ratharryn, and Hengall led a war band against them, defeated them, and brought back six heads. One of those heads was taken by Saban, though in truth Galeth had held the shrieking Outfolk warrior still so that Saban could kill him, but still Saban was allowed to wear a blue kill mark on his chest.

After that skirmish, and after the harvest was stored, the men went back to finish the remaining work, and Saban, going with them to begin the new work, stopped to stare at the Old Temple with its four new stones. It looked different suddenly. It was a chill day, with autumn's first bite in the air, but the sun shone between a gap in the clouds to light the new white banks of the sacred path and the clean chalk circle of the temple's ditch and bank. And in that circle, their shadows stark in the morning light, the four stones stood.

Galeth paused beside Saban. 'It looks good,' he said, sounding surprised, and it did. It looked splendid. It looked clean, purposeful, even calm. The temple was not massive and grand like Cathallo's shrine, but instead was lifted up on the hill's green breast so that the four stones seemed to float in the sky. Cathallo's temple, with its great squat boulders dwarfed by the massive embankment, was more like a thing of the earth while this shrine was airy and delicate.

'It's a sky temple,' Saban said.

Galeth liked that. 'A sky temple,' he said, 'why not? It's a good name.' He clapped Saban on a shoulder. 'It's the right name, the Sky Temple!' He hefted a timber and walked on, peering intently at the southern horizon. He was looking for smoke that might betray where a hunting band had its camp, but he saw nothing. There was a rumour that a large band of Outfolk was in the forest, though Hengall, taking another war band west and south, had found no sign of them. 'Let's hope they've moved on,' Galeth said, touching his groin. 'They can find someone else's land, not ours.'

The Outfolk had lived in the land for generations now,

indeed no one living could remember when they had first come from the land across the eastern sea, but all knew they spoke a different language and had different customs. Some of them, like the men of Sarmennyn who had lost their gold lozenges, had found great tracts of empty land to make their home, but others still wandered the forest in search of places to live and it was those homeless bands that caused trouble to Ratharryn, for the bigger Outfolk settlements were all far away.

'They won't come near us,' Saban said, 'not while their tribesmen's heads are on our embankment.'

'I pray not,' Galeth said, touching his groin again, but he still stared southwards. Hengall might not have found the hungry Outlanders, but a hunting party had discovered a campsite with its ashes still warm and a trader had glimpsed a large band of grey-tattooed men prowling in the deep trees. 'We had a good harvest,' Galeth said, 'and if the Outlanders had a bad one then they'll be eyeing us.'

They walked on to the temple and there the difficulty of raising the last stones drove away any fears of an Outfolk raid. Two of the boulders were to be raised on either side of the entrance of the sun, and those two were twice as long, twice as thick and, it seemed, many times the weight of the moon stone pillars. It took four days to raise the first, and that did not count the days digging the hole, and another three days to put up the second. The last two stones, the sun stones, that were to serve as a doorway in the avenue for the rising midsummer sun, were bigger still. They saved the largest stone till last and the hole they dug was so deep that a man could stand at its foot and not see over the lip. They made the ramp and lined it with timber and another pig died so that its fat could grease the wood.

Then, when all was ready, they set about planting the stone.

It took sixty men to move the big sun stone off its sledge. Galeth tied ropes about the boulder, harnessed them to forty men and had them haul it forward while the others used levers to ease the great stone along its oak bed. It took a whole day to shift the stone off the sledge and the best part of the next day to seat it properly in the ramp, for it had gone in crooked, so they had to straighten it with levers, but at last, after two days' work, it rested on the ramp.

Galeth had built a new tripod of oak to raise the taller stones. The tripod stood four times the height of a man and, because he feared that the hide ropes going over the peak would stick, he set a smooth piece of elm in the joint and greased it with fat. He strapped the four ropes around the upper end of the stone, led them over the elm block and tied those ropes to a beam of oak to which he harnessed sixteen oxen. Then the men whipped and goaded the beasts and slowly the stone moved, but agonizingly slowly, and so more ropes were tied to the oak beam and men were harnessed alongside the beasts and again the whips slashed down and the goads jabbed and the men fought for footing on the grass and slowly, so very slowly, the tall stone edged upwards. The higher it went the easier it became because the ropes were now pulling the stone's top straight towards the tripod's peak, while at the beginning of the raising the ropes made a narrow angle between themselves and the stone. The stone's foot crunched and splintered the greased wood lining the hole, then suddenly Galeth was shouting at the men driving the oxen to hold their whips. 'Gentle now!' he shouted. 'Gentle!' The stone was almost upright. 'Pull again!' Galeth shouted and the ropes creaked and the tripod quivered and Saban feared that the stone had lodged against an unseen obstruction at the base of the hole, but then it crashed forward against the timber-clad face and Galeth screamed at the men to stop hauling in case they pulled the stone clean over the hole's brink. The ropes slackened, but the big sun stone did not fall. It stood there, huge and grey, more than two times the height of a man.

They rammed the stone's base with stones, filled the hole, untied the ropes and thus the work was finished. The Old Temple was no more and Ratharryn had its sanctuary of stone. They had the Sky Temple.

The day chosen for the dedication of the Sky Temple proved to be propitious for it was warm and cloudless, a day that late autumn had stolen from high summer. All Hengall's people came to the ceremony. They arrived from the outlying settlements and from the upland farmsteads, and the women assembled at Lahanna's shrine while the men danced around the poles of the temple where they had stacked their spears and piled their bows for no man would carry a weapon this day. This day was given to the gods.

In the late afternoon Gilan led the tribe up from the settlement. They stopped at the grave mounds where the skull pole was paraded and the ancestors were told what was happening, and then they danced to where the new sacred path scarred the grassland. The tribe's priests were naked, their bodies chalked white with patterns swirled by spread fingers, while their heads were crowned with antlers and their hair and beards hung with animal bones and teeth. The folk who followed the priests had all dressed in their best pelts. Saban and Derrewyn were to be married after the sun set. Derrewyn wore a dress of sewn deerskins that were very pale in colour so that her skin looked even darker, while her long hair had been threaded with creamy meadowsweets. Her parents had come to see the ceremony and her father, Morthor, high priest at Cathallo, danced with Ratharryn's priests; those priests led with them a small child, a fair-haired girl just three years old, who had been born deaf. The child, like Derrewyn, wore meadow-sweets in her hair.

The sun blazed into the faces of the folk as they crossed the rim of the down from where the sacred path stretched clean and white to the eight new stones of the Sky Temple. Gilan carried the tribe's skull pole, which had been decorated with ivy, while Neel, the youngest priest, had an axe with a beautifully carved greenstone head that Galeth had sharpened that same afternoon.

The people stamped their dance between the newly made chalk banks of the sacred path, scattering the grazing sheep as they advanced. Four of the men carried goatskin drums and they set the rhythm of the dance and, as the priests neared the four taller stones, the drumming became more frantic and the tribe swooped from side to side. The women led the singing, praising Slaol, while the men echoed the last line of each verse.

The tribe swerved aside at the temple to dance about its edge. The priests went inside and, once they had driven out the sheep and cattle that were grazing on the temple's grass, they formed a circle where they stamped the intricate steps of their own dance. The priests danced inside and the people sang and danced outside. The men circled closest to the ditch, with the women outside them, and all danced sunwise as Slaol sank towards the horizon. The singing and dancing seemed to induce a trance that gripped the folk as the sun sank. Some women called out in ecstasy as on and on they danced, not noticing the tiredness in their legs but swept up by the music, and they only stopped when the men who had carried pots of fire from the settlement put the embers in the great heaps of wood that were piled on either side of the temple. The flames caught fast, the small twigs crackled and the smoke whirled the sparks upward. Galeth had broken up the great sledges and put their huge timbers in the piles. He rued such a waste of good wood, but the sledges had served a sacred purpose and so must be returned to the gods. The fires became fierce as the tribe gathered about the twin stone pillars of the sun's gate which stood in the centre of the sacred path. The drummers were silent now, but the dance was still inside the people and some could not be still, but swayed from side to side and some of the women moaned as they stared towards the great swollen ball of the sun where it flattened on the far horizon. 'Slaol,' they called. 'Slaol!'

'Slaol!' Gilan shouted at the sun, raising his arms, and Hengall now took the deaf child's hand and led her to the very centre of the temple where Galeth had dug a hole. It was not a deep hole, nor was it long, but it was enough and the child with flowers in her hair was taken to the hole's edge and there her tunic was lifted over her hair so she was naked and Gilan knelt and gave her a pot. 'Drink,' he said gently and, because she was deaf, motioned what

144

she should do. The girl took the pot in both hands and laughed at the high priest's kindly face.

The pot contained a potion to bring dreams: a potion made from mushrooms and herbs, a potion to carry the deaf child to the gods, and all the folk watched, utterly silent, as she drank. She made a face as if the liquid were bitter, but then she laughed again and dropped the pot. Gilan stood and stepped back from her, watching to see what omens the potion brought.

The girl began to gasp as if her breath were being stolen, then she screamed for her mother in a half-formed voice, and then she tried to run back towards the watching crowd, but Neel caught her and forced her back to the hole where she screamed again. Her watching mother wailed for the child. The omens were bad. She should have been smiling, laughing, dancing, but she was struggling and frantic, and her screams were scratching at the tribe's souls. To stop her noise Gilan shook her hard, so hard that she went still with terror and in that moment Gilan thrust her out at arm's length and took the greenstone axe from Neel.

Gilan raised the blade to the dying sun, paused, then struck down hard so that bloody flowers fell to the grass as the child, her skull nearly split in two, died without a sound.

She had gone to the sky. She had gone to Slaol. There would be no death place for the child and no gifts on her behalf for she was herself a gift. That was why she was not killed with the Kill-Child, for she was not really dead, but instead, even as her tribe watched in awed silence, her soul was rising to the sky to tell Slaol about this place that had been made for him. The golden-haired child was

Ratharryn's messenger and she would watch the Sky Temple until time itself was ended.

Gilan laid the little body in the grave. He broke the pot that had held the potion and dropped it beside her, placed the chalk ball of her life on her bloodied breast, and then the priests kicked the heap of earth onto her body. The child's mother still shrieked with grief and the other women clustered about to comfort her, telling her that her daughter was not dead at all, but happy in the skyworld where she was a playmate of the gods.

The sun sank beneath the horizon just as Lahanna, huge and pale, rose above the western trees. The fires were roaring now, the great timbers at their heart burning bright so that the smoke made a red-tinged pall above the temple. In a moment or two the temple's first ceremony would begin as Derrewyn and Saban danced their marriage steps in the shrine's centre, but first Hengall stood by the sun child's grave and raised his hand.

It was Hengall's task to tell the tribe what they had done. To tell the tale of the Sky Temple so that his folk would remember it and tell their children and their children's children, and so he stood with his arm raised, summoning the words, and the murmuring crowd fell silent. It was twilight, and the blinding glare of the sun had vanished to leave behind a red-rimmed sky smudged by smoke and in that livid haze Saban saw a flicker. At first he thought it was the dead child's spirit and he was glad, for it showed that the sacrifice had worked.

The flicker was red, reflecting the dying sunlight, and then Saban saw it was not the child's soul, but an arrow streaking up from the black crest of the southern upland where more of the ancestors' bones lay in their mounds.

The arrow's flight seemed to take a long time, though of course it took no time at all. Indeed Saban had scarcely time to open his mouth, let alone call out, yet he ever remembered it as being a long, long time. He saw the arrow reach up to the sky and then begin to fall. Its head glittered, the black flint flashing back the firelight, and then it slammed into Hengall's back.

Hengall stumbled forward. Most in the crowd still did not know what was happening, but they recognized an ill omen and they moaned. Then Hengall fell and they saw the arrow in his back, its black feathers dark, and still they did not understand, and it was not until the priests rushed to the chief's side that the wailing began.

Saban ran forward, then checked, for more arrows were flickering in the sky. They thumped into the turf, struck the priests, and one glanced off a moon stone with a click. Then Saban saw the naked creatures who came from the southern skyline that was all aflame with red.

The creatures themselves were red. They screamed as they capered forward and the sight of them made Ratharryn's people howl, but when they turned to flee towards the settlement there were more of the creatures behind and some of the attackers were mounted on small shaggy horses that galloped across the low chalk banks of the sacred path.

They were Outfolk warriors and they had smeared their bodies with red ochre, the same substance that was sometimes used to colour the skins of the important dead, and now these living dead-men screamed as they closed on the tribe that had no weapons. There were dozens of the enemy and Hengall's orphaned folk could do nothing but crouch in terror. Morthor, Derrewyn's father, was

147

wounded, Gilan lay dead, while Neel, the young priest, crawled on the temple's turf with an arrow in his thigh.

The leader of the red warriors appeared last of all and he alone was clothed and he alone had not used ochre to make his face look dreadful. He strode towards the temple and in his right hand was the long yew bow which he had used to kill Saban's father.

And to kill his own father too, for the man who came to the Sky Temple with a smile on his face was Lengar.

Who had come home.

PART TWO

The Temple of Shadows

The Outfolk quickly stopped their killing for Lengar had not returned to become the chief of a slaughtered tribe. When the screaming ended, he stood above his father's body and held up the bloodstained axe that had sent the child to the skies. He had shrugged off his cloak to reveal a jerkin sewn with bronze strips that glittered in the fire-light and, at his waist, a long bronze sword. 'I am Lengar!' he shouted. 'Lengar! And if any of you dispute my right to be chief in Ratharryn, then come and dispute it now!'

None of the tribe looked at Saban for he was reckoned too young to confront Lengar, but a few did stare at Galeth. 'Do you challenge me, uncle?' Lengar asked.

'You have murdered your father,' Galeth said, gazing in horror at his brother's body, which had fallen across the grave of the sacrificed child.

'What better way to become chief?' Lengar asked, then walked a few paces towards his rival. His companions, those men who had fled Ratharryn with him on the day that the emissaries from Sarmennyn had been rebuffed, climbed up from the ditch at the temple's far side, but Lengar stayed their progress with a gesture. 'Do you challenge me?' he asked Galeth again, then waited in silence.

When it was plain that neither Galeth nor any other man in the tribe would confront him he tossed the axe on to the grass behind him and walked to the temple's entrance of the sun where he stood, tall and terrible with the bloody axe in his hand, between the two high stones. 'Galeth and Saban!' he called. 'Come here!'

Galeth and Saban walked nervously forward, both half expecting arrows to come from Lengar's companions who waited at the temple's far side, but no bowstring sounded. Lengar drew his sword as they approached. 'There are men here who might expect one of you to challenge me,' Lengar said. 'Even you, little brother.' He bared his teeth at Saban, pretending to smile.

Saban said nothing. He saw that Lengar had tattooed a pair of horns on his face, one outside of each eye, and the horns made him look even more sinister. Lengar held the sword out so that its tip touched Saban's breast. 'It is good to see you, brother,' he said.

'Is it?' Saban asked as coldly as he could.

'You think I have not missed Ratharryn?' Lengar asked. 'Sarmennyn is a bare place. Raw and cold.'

'You came home to be warm?' Saban asked sarcastically.

'No, little one, I came home to make Ratharryn great again. There was a time when Cathallo paid us tribute, when they were proud that their women married a man from Ratharryn, when they came to dance in our temples and begged our priests to keep them from harm, but now they sell us rocks.' He slapped the closest stone. 'Rocks!' He spat the word again. 'Why did you not buy oak leaves from them? Or water? Or air? Or dung?'

Galeth glanced at his brother's body. 'What do you want of us?' he asked Lengar dully.

'You must kneel to me, uncle,' Lengar said, 'in front of all the tribe, to show that you accept me as chief. Otherwise I shall send you to our ancestors. Greet them for me, if I do.'

Galeth frowned. 'And if I kneel, what then?'

'Then you shall be my honoured adviser, my kinsman and my friend,' Lengar said effusively. 'You shall be what you have always been, the builder of our tribe and the counsellor of its chief. I did not come back to let the Outfolk rule here. I came to make Ratharryn great again.' He gestured at the red warriors. 'When their work is done, uncle, they will go home. But till then they are our servants.'

Galeth looked again at his brother's body. 'There will be no more killing in the tribe?' he asked.

'I will kill no one who accepts my authority,' Lengar promised, glancing at Saban.

Galeth nodded. He paused for a heartbeat then sank to his knees. There was a sigh from the watching tribe as he leaned forward and touched his hands to Lengar's feet.

'Thank you, uncle,' Lengar said. He touched Galeth's back with the sword, then turned to Saban. 'Now you, brother.'

Saban did not move.

'Kneel,' Galeth muttered.

Lengar's yellow-tinged eyes, oddly bright in the gathering dark, stared into Saban's face. 'I do not mind, little brother,' Lengar said softly, 'whether you live or die. There are those who say I should kill you, but does a wolf fear a cat?' He reached out with the sword and stroked the cold blade down Saban's cheek. 'But if you do not kneel to me, I shall take your head and use your skull as a drinking pot.'

Saban did not want to submit, but he knew Lengar's madness, and he knew he would be killed like a frothing dog if he did not yield. He bit back his pride and made himself kneel, and another sigh sounded from the tribe as he too leaned forward to touch Lengar's feet. Lengar, in turn, touched the nape of Saban's neck with the bronze blade. 'Do you love me, little brother?' Lengar asked.

'No,' Saban said.

Lengar laughed and took the sword away. 'Stand,' he said, then stepped back to look at the silent, watching crowd. 'Go home!' he called to them. 'Go home! You too,' he added to Saban and Galeth.

Most of the crowd obeyed, but Derrewyn and her mother ran to the temple's ditch where Morthor lay wounded. Saban joined them to see that an arrow had struck high on the priest's shoulder and its force had driven the head clean through his body. Saban pulled the flint free, but left the shaft in place. 'The arrow will come out cleanly,' he reassured Derrewyn. The chalk slurry on Morthor's chest was stained pink and he was breathing in short panicked gasps. 'The wound will mend,' Saban told the frightened priest, then twisted back because Derrewyn had suddenly screamed.

Lengar had taken hold of Derrewyn's arm and was hauling her round so that he could see her face in the light of the great fires. Saban stood, but immediately found himself staring at the point of Lengar's sword. 'You want something of me, little brother?' Lengar asked.

Saban looked at Derrewyn. She was in tears, flinching from Lengar's tight grip on her arm. 'We are to marry,' Saban said, 'she and I.'

'And who decided that?' Lengar asked.

'Father,' Saban said, 'and her great-grandmother, Sannas.'

Lengar grimaced. 'Father is dead, Saban, and I rule here now. And what that moonstruck hag of Cathallo wants does not matter in Ratharryn. What matters, little brother, is what I want.' He snapped an order in the harsh Outfolk language and a half-dozen of the red warriors ran to his side. One took the sword from Lengar, while two others faced Saban with their spears.

Lengar put both hands on the neck of Derrewyn's deer-skin tunic. He looked into her eyes, smiled when he saw the fear there, then tore the tunic with sudden force. Derrewyn cried out; Saban instinctively leapt forward, but one of the Outfolk spears tangled his ankles, and the other clouted him across the skull then came to rest on his belly as he fell to the ground.

Lengar ripped off the remnants of the tunic, leaving Derrewyn naked. She tried to hide her body, but Lengar pulled her out of the crouch and spread her arms. 'A thing of Cathallo,' he said, looking her up and down, 'but a pretty thing. What does one do with such pretty things?' He asked the question of Saban, but expected no answer. 'Tonight,' he went on, 'we must show Cathallo what the power of Ratharryn means,' and with that he took Derrewyn's wrist and dragged her towards the settlement.

'No!' Saban shouted, still pinned to the ground by the Outfolk spear.

'Quiet, little brother,' Lengar called. Derrewyn tried to pull away from him and he struck her hard across the face, scattering meadowsweets from her hair, and, when he was sure she would be obedient, he tugged her onwards. She pulled away from him again, but he gave her a second blow, much harder than the first; she whimpered and this time followed him in a daze. Her mother, still kneeling beside her husband, shouted a strident protest, but a red-painted warrior kicked her in the mouth and silenced her.

And Saban, bereft at the Sky Temple, could do nothing except weep. Two Outfolk warriors guarded him. Neel and Morthor, the wounded priests, were carried away to leave the bodies of Hengall and Gilan in the moonlight where Saban sobbed like a child. Then the Outlanders prodded him to his feet and drove him like a beast towards the settlement.

The Sky Temple had been consecrated but disaster had come to Ratharryn. Saban's world had turned dark. The gods were screaming again.

Most of the Outfolk warriors stationed themselves on the embankment's crest from where, with their short bows and sharp arrows, they could threaten the folk inside Ratharryn's settlement, but a handful of Outfolk spearmen stood guard outside Hengall's hut where Lengar took Derrewyn. Most of the tribe had gathered beside Arryn and Mai's temple; they heard a blow, heard Derrewyn scream, then heard no more.

'Should we fight them?' Galeth's son, Mereth, asked.

'There are too many of them,' Galeth said softly, 'too many.' He looked broken, sitting in the temple's centre with his head low. 'Besides,' he went on, 'if we fight them, how many of us will die? How many will be left? Enough to resist Cathallo?' He sighed. 'I knelt to Lengar, and so he is my chief . . .' He paused. 'For now.' The last two words were said so low that not even Mereth could hear them. The women outside the temple cried for Hengall, because he had been a good chief, while the men inside watched the enemy on the high earth bank. Lahanna stared down, unmoved by the tragedy. After a while the frightened folk slept, though their sleep was broken by people crying aloud in their nightmares.

Lengar appeared just before the dawn. The tribe woke slowly, becoming aware that their new chief was stepping over sleeping bodies to reach the centre of Arryn and Mai's temple. He still wore the bronze-plated jerkin and had the long sword at his waist, but he carried no spear or bow.

'I did not mean that Gilan should die,' he said without any greeting. Folk were sitting up and shuffling off the cloaks in which they had slept, while the women outside the temple's rings leant forward to catch Lengar's quiet words. 'My companions showed more zeal than I wanted,' he continued ruefully. 'One arrow would have been enough, but they were frightened and thought more were necessary.'

All the people were awake now. Men, women and children – the whole tribe – gathered in a protective cluster in and around the small temple and all listened to Lengar.

'My father,' Lengar went on, raising his voice just a little, 'was a good man. He kept us alive in hard winters and he cut down many trees to give us land. Hunger was rare and his justice was fair. For all that he should be honoured, so we will make him a mound.' People responded for the first time, muttering their agreement, and Lengar let the murmuring continue for a while before raising a hand. 'But my father was wrong about Cathallo!' He spoke louder now, his voice touched with hardness. 'He feared it, so he let Kital and Sannas rule you. It was to be a marriage of two tribes, but in marriage it is the man who should be master and in time Cathallo would have mastered you! Your harvest would have been carried to their storehouses, your daughters would have danced the bull dance in their temple and your spears would have fought their battles. But this is *our land*!' Lengar cried, and some folk shouted that he was right.

'Our land,' Mereth shouted angrily, 'and filled with Outfolk!'

Lengar paused, smiling. 'My cousin is right,' he said after a while. 'I have brought Outfolk here. But there are not many. They have fewer spears than you do! What is to stop you killing them now? Or killing me?' He waited for an answer, but none of the men moved. 'Do you remember,' Lengar asked, 'when the Outfolk came and begged for the return of their treasures? They offered us a high price. And what did we do? We turned them down and used some of the gold to buy stone from Cathallo. Stone! We used Slaol's gold to buy rocks!' He laughed, and many of his listeners looked ashamed for what the tribe had done.

'We shall buy nothing more from Cathallo,' Lengar said. 'They claim to want peace, but war is hidden in their hearts. They cannot bear to think that Ratharryn will be great again, and so they will try to crush us. In our ancestors' time this tribe was stronger than Cathallo! They paid us tribute and begged our approval. But now they despise us. They want us helpless, and we shall have to fight them. How do we defeat them?' He pointed at the embankment where the Outfolk warriors squatted. 'We will defeat Cathallo by buying the help of the Outfolk, for they will pay almost any price to have their gold returned. But to receive their gold they must do our bidding. We are masters here, not them! And we shall use the Outfolk warriors to become the mightiest tribe in all the land.' He watched his listeners, judging the effect of his words. 'And that is why I came back,' he finished softly, 'and why my father had to join his ancestors, so that Ratharryn will be known through all the land, feared through all the land, and honoured through land and sky.'

The tribe began to thump their hands on the earth, and then the men were standing and cheering. Lengar had persuaded them.

Lengar had won.

Saban spent the night in his hut, guarded there by two of Lengar's red-painted spearmen. He wept for Derrewyn, and the knowledge of what she endured in the dark gave him such pain that he was tempted to take the knife that had been a gift from his father and slit his own throat, but the lure of revenge stayed his hand. He had knelt to Lengar in the Sky Temple's gate, but he knew the gesture had been hollow. He would kill his brother. He swore as much in the awful dark, then cursed himself for not showing more fight at the temple. But what could he have done? He had possessed no weapon, so how could he have fought warriors armed with swords, spears and bows? Fate had crushed him, and he was close to despair. Only as dawn neared did he fall into a dream-racked, shallow sleep.

Gundur, one of the men who had fled Ratharryn with Lengar, woke him. 'Your brother wants you,' Gundur said.

'What for?' Saban asked resentfully.

'Just get up,' Gundur said scornfully. Saban put the bronze knife into his belt and picked up one of his hunting spears before following Gundur from the hut. He would kill his brother now, he had decided. He would spear Lengar without warning, and if he died under the blades of Lengar's companions then at least he would have avenged his father. The ancestors would approve of that and welcome him to the afterlife. He gripped the spear shaft tight and stiffened his resolve to strike as soon as he entered the chief's big hut.

But an Outfolk warrior waiting just inside the hut seized Saban's spear before he had even stooped beneath the lintel. Saban tried to keep hold of the ash shaft, but the man was too strong and the brief struggle left Saban sprawling ignominiously on the floor. Galeth, he saw, waited for him, and three more Outfolk warriors sat behind Lengar who had watched the scuffle with amusement. 'Did you think to avenge our father?' Lengar asked Saban.

Saban rubbed his wrist that was sore from the Outlander's grip. 'The ancestors will avenge him,' he said.

'How will the ancestors even know who he is?' Lengar asked. 'I chopped off his jawbone this morning.' He grinned, and pointed to Hengall's bloody and bearded chin that had been spiked to one of the hut poles. If a dead man's jawbone was taken then he could not tell tales to the ancestors. 'I took Gilan's too,' Lengar said, 'so the pair of them can mumble away in the afterlife. Sit beside Galeth, and stop scowling.'

Lengar was draped in his father's bearskin cloak and was surrounded by treasures, all of them unearthed from the floor or dug out of the piles of hides where Hengall had concealed his fortune. 'We are rich, little brother!' Lengar said happily. 'Rich! You look tired. Did you not sleep well?' Gundur, who had sat beside Lengar, grinned, while the three Outfolk warriors, who did not understand what was being said, just stared fixedly at Saban.

Saban glanced towards the leather curtain that hid the women's portion of the hut, but he saw no sign of Derrewyn. He squatted in front of the tribe's heaped treasures. There were bars of bronze, beautifully polished knives of stone and flint, bags of amber, pieces of jet, great axes, loops of copper, carved bone, sea-shells and, most curious of all, a wooden box filled with strangely carved pebbles. The stones were small and smoothly rounded, none of them bigger than the ball of a man's thumb, but all had been deeply cut with patterns of whorls or lines. 'Do you know what they are?' Lengar asked Galeth.

'No,' Galeth said curtly.

'Magic, I suspect,' Lengar said, tossing one of the stones from hand to hand. 'Camaban would know. He seems to know everything these days. It's a pity he's not here.'

'Have you seen him?' Galeth asked.

'He came to Sarmennyn in the spring,' Lengar said carelessly, 'and so far as I know he's still there. He was walking properly, or almost properly. I wanted him to come with me, but he refused. I'd always thought him a fool, but he isn't at all. He's become very strange, but he isn't foolish. He's very clever. Perhaps it runs in our family. What is the matter, Saban? You're not going to cry, are you? Father's death, is it?'

Saban thought of seizing one of the precious bronze axes and hurling himself across the hut, but the Outfolk spearmen were watching him and their weapons were ready. He would stand no chance.

'You will notice, uncle,' Lengar said, 'that the gold pieces of Sarmennyn are not here?'

'I noticed,' Galeth said.

'I have them safe,' Lengar said, 'but I won't display them because I don't want to tempt our Outfolk friends. They've only come here to get the gold.' Lengar jerked his head at the Outfolk warriors who sat silent behind him, their tattooed faces like masks in the shadowed gloom. 'They don't speak our tongue, uncle,' Lengar went on, 'so insult them as much as you like, but smile while you do it. I need them to think we truly are their friends.'

'Aren't we?' Galeth asked.

'For the moment,' Lengar said. He smiled, pleased with himself. 'I had originally decided to give them back their gold if they defeated Cathallo for me, but Camaban had a much better idea. He really is clever. He went into a trance and cured one of their chief's wives of some loathsome disease. Have you ever seen him in a trance? His eyes go white, his tongue sticks out and he shakes like a wet dog, and when the whole thing is over he comes out with messages from Slaol!' Lengar waited for Galeth to share his amusement, but Galeth said nothing. Lengar sighed. 'Well, clever Camaban cured the chief's wife and now the chief thinks that Camaban can do no wrong. Imagine that! Crippled Camaban, a hero! So our hero told the Outfolk that not only would they have to defeat Cathallo to get their gold back, but also give us one of their temples. Which means they have to move a temple across the country, which they can't do, of course, because their temples are all made of stone.' He laughed. 'So we'll defeat Cathallo and keep the gold.'

'Maybe they will bring you a temple,' Galeth said drily.

'And maybe Saban will smile,' Lengar said. 'Saban! Smile when you look at me. Have you lost your tongue?'

Saban was gouging his fingernails into his ankles, hoping that the pain would keep him from crying or betraying his hatred. 'You wanted to see me, brother,' he said harshly.

'To say goodbye,' Lengar said ominously, hoping to see fear on his brother's face, but Saban's expression showed nothing. Death, Saban thought, would be better than this humiliation and the thought made him touch his groin, a gesture that made Lengar laugh. 'I'm not going to kill you, little brother,' Lengar said. 'I should, but I am merciful. Instead I shall take your place. Derrewyn will marry me as a symbol that Ratharryn is now superior to Cathallo and she will breed me many sons. And you, my brother, will be a slave.' He clapped his hands. 'Haragg!' he shouted.

The Outfolk trader, the grim giant who had come to interpret when the folk of Sarmennyn had pleaded with Hengall for the return of the treasures, stooped to enter the hut. He had to bend double to get through the low doorway and when he stood he seemed to fill the hut for he was so tall and broad-shouldered. He was balding, had a thick black beard, and a face that was an implacable mask. 'Your new slave, Haragg,' Lengar said courteously, indicating Saban.

'Lengar!' Galeth appealed.

'You would prefer me to kill the runt?' Lengar enquired silkily.

'You can't put your own brother into slavery!' Galeth protested.

'Half-brother,' Lengar said, 'and of course I can. Do you think Saban was honest when he knelt to me last night? I trust you, uncle, but him? He'd kill me in an eyeblink!

He's been thinking of nothing else ever since he came into this hut, haven't you, Saban?' He smiled, but Saban just stared into his brother's horned eyes. Lengar spat. 'Take him, Haragg.'

Haragg leaned over and put a vast hand round Saban's arm and hauled him upright. Saban, humiliated and miserable, plucked the small knife from his belt and swung it wildly towards the giant, but Haragg, without any fuss, merely caught his wrist and pinched hard so that Saban's hand was suddenly nerveless and feeble. The knife dropped. Haragg picked up the blade then dragged Saban from the hut.

Haragg's son, the deaf-mute who was even larger than his gigantic father, waited outside. He took hold of Saban and threw him to the ground while his father went back into Lengar's hut, and Saban listened as Lengar sought assurances from the huge trader that the new slave would not be allowed to escape. Saban thought of trying to run now, but the deaf-mute loomed over him and then a wailing made him turn to see Morthor's wife leading her husband from Gilan's old hut. Outfolk warriors were prodding the couple towards Ratharryn's northern entrance.

'Morthor!' Saban called out, then gasped, for when the high priest of Cathallo turned Saban saw that Morthor's eyes had been gouged out. 'Lengar did that?' Saban asked.

'Lengar did this,' Morthor said bitterly. His arm hung limp and blood was thickly crusted on his wounded shoulder from which the arrow shaft had been pulled, but his face was nothing but a dreadful mask. He pointed to his ravaged eyes. 'This is Lengar's message to Cathallo,' he said, then the spearmen pushed him on.

Saban closed his eyes as though he could blot out the

horror of Morthor's face, and then he was assailed by the image of Derrewyn stripped naked in the night and his shoulders heaved as he tried to suppress the tears.

'Cry, little one.' A mocking voice spoke above him and Saban opened his eyes to see Jegar standing over him. Two of Lengar's friends were with Jegar and they levelled spears at him and, for a moment, Saban thought they meant to kill him, but the spears were merely there to keep him still. 'Cry,' Jegar said again.

Saban stared at the ground, then shuddered because Jegar had begun to piss on him. The two spearmen laughed and, when Saban tried to jerk aside, they used their spear points to hold him steady so that the urine splashed on his hair. 'Lengar will marry Derrewyn,' Jegar said as he pissed, 'but when he is tired of her, and he will tire of her, he has promised her to me. Do you know why, Saban?'

Saban did not answer. The liquid dripped from his hair, ran down his face and puddled between his knees while the deaf-mute watched with a look of faint puzzlement on his broad face.

'Because,' Jegar went on, 'ever since Lengar went to Sarmennyn, I have been his eyes and his ears in Ratharryn. How did Lengar know to come last night? Because I told him. Did I not tell you?' He asked this last question of Lengar, who had just come from his hut to watch his brother's humiliation.

'You are the most loyal of friends, Jegar,' Lengar said.

'And a friend who has a maimed right hand.' Jegar stooped suddenly and seized Saban's hand. 'Give me a knife!' he demanded of Lengar.

'Let him go,' Haragg said.

'I have business with him,' Jegar spat.

'He is my slave,' Haragg said, 'and you will leave him alone.'

The big man had not spoken loudly, but there was such force in his deep voice that Jegar obeyed. Haragg stooped in front of Saban, holding Saban's own bronze knife in his right hand, and Saban thought the huge Outlander planned to do what Jegar had meant to do, but instead Haragg seized a hank of Saban's hair. He sawed at it, cutting it through and tossing it aside. He worked roughly, slashing off great handfuls of hair and scraping Saban's scalp to make it bleed. All slaves were shaved like this, and though the hair would grow again, it was meant to show that the newly shorn captives were now mere nothings. Saban was now a nothing, and he flinched as the hard blade grazed down his scalp and the blood trickled down his cheeks where it was diluted by Jegar's urine. Saban's mother came from her hut as Haragg cut his hair and she screamed at the big man to stop, then threw clods of earth at him until two of Lengar's spearmen, laughing at her anger, dragged her away.

Haragg finished cutting off the hair, then took Saban's left hand and placed it flat on the ground.

'I will do this,' Jegar offered eagerly.

'He is my slave,' Haragg answered, and again the power in his voice made Jegar step back. 'Look at me,' Haragg ordered Saban, then nodded to his son who clamped a huge hand across Saban's wrist.

Saban, his eyes blurred with tears, looked into Haragg's harsh face. His left hand was being held hard against the ground and he could not see the knife, but then there was a terrible pain in his hand, a pain that streaked up to his shoulder and made him cry aloud, and Haragg pulled the bleeding hand up and clapped a piece of fleece over the severed stump of Saban's small finger. 'Hold the fleece,' Haragg ordered him.

Saban clamped his right hand over the fleece. The pain was throbbing, making him feel faint, but he clamped his teeth together and rocked back and forth as Haragg scooped up the chopped hair and the severed bloody finger and carried them to a fire. Jegar interceded again, demanding that the trader give him the hair so he could use it to have a spell made against Saban, but the grim Haragg doggedly ignored the demand, instead throwing both hair and finger onto the fire and watching them burn.

The deaf-mute now dragged Saban north through the huts to where Morcar, Ratharryn's smith, had his forge. Morcar was a friend of Galeth's and his usual work was making spearheads from bronze bars, but today he was heating bronze that Haragg had given him. The smith avoided Saban's eyes as he worked. Haragg pushed Saban onto the ground where Saban closed his eyes and tried to will away the pain in his hand, but then he felt an even greater pain in his right ankle and he whimpered, opened his eyes and saw that a bronze manacle was being placed around his leg. The manacle had already been bent so that it was nearly a closed circle and Morcar now hammered the heated bronze quickly so that the two ends of the curved bar met. The manacle was joined by a bronze chain to its twin that was forced over Saban's left ankle and hammered shut. The metal was scorching hot, making Saban gasp.

Morcar poured water onto the metal. 'I'm sorry, Saban,' he whispered.

'Stand,' Haragg said.

Saban stood. A small crowd of Ratharryn's folk watched from a distance. His feet were chained so he could walk, but not run, his head was shaved, and now Haragg stood behind him and slit his tunic all the way down the back with his knife. He pulled it away so that Saban was naked. Last of all he cut the necklace of sea-shells around Saban's neck and crushed them into the ground with a massive foot and pocketed the amber amulet that had been a gift from Saban's mother. Jegar laughed and Lengar applauded.

'You are now my slave,' Haragg said tonelessly, 'to live or die at my whim. Follow me.'

Saban, his humiliation complete, obeyed.

Lengar feared the gods. He did not understand them, but he understood himself and he knew that the treachery of the gods could far outdo anything man could contrive, so he feared them and took good care to placate them as best he knew how. He gave gifts to the priests; he buried symbolic chalk axes in all Ratharryn's temples; and he permitted Hengall's surviving wives to live and even promised to make certain they did not starve.

His father's spirit was about to go to the afterworld where it would live with the ancestors and gods, but it would go without a jawbone and without a right foot so that Hengall could neither tell of his own murder nor, if his spirit remained earthbound, pursue Lengar. The jaw and foot were fed to pigs, but the rest of the corpse was treated with respect. Hengall was burned on a great pyre in the manner of the Outfolk. The fire was lit three days after

Hengall's death and it was allowed to burn for another three days, and only then was a mound of chalk and soil thrown up over the smouldering embers.

On the night that the mound was raised Lengar knelt on its summit and bent his head to the chalky rubble. He was alone for he wanted no one else to witness this conversation with his father. 'You had to die,' he told Hengall, 'because you were too cautious. You were a good chief, but Ratharryn now needs a great chief.' Lengar paused. 'I have not killed your wives,' he went on, 'and even Saban still lives. He was always your favourite, wasn't he? Well, he lives, father, he still lives.'

Lengar was not sure that letting Saban live had been a good idea, but Camaban had persuaded him that to kill his half-brother would be fatal. Camaban had gone to Lengar in Sarmennyn, no longer the stuttering fool Lengar had always despised. Instead he had become a sorcerer, and Lengar found himself strangely nervous in Camaban's presence. 'The gods might forgive you Hengall's death,' Camaban had told him, 'but not Saban's,' and when Lengar demanded to know why, Camaban claimed to have spoken with Slaol in a dream. Lengar had yielded to the dream's message. He still half regretted it, but he feared Camaban's sorcery. At least Camaban had suggested that Saban should become Haragg's slave and Lengar was certain that the big trader's slaves did not live long.

Lengar rested his forehead on the mound's summit. The soil and chalk had been roughly piled on the fire's remains and the fumes still seeped through the mound to sting Lengar's eyes, but he dutifully kept his head down. 'You will be proud of me, father,' he told Hengall, 'because I will raise Ratharryn and humble Cathallo. I will be a great chief –' He went very still for he heard footsteps.

The footsteps were close to him, very close, then they were on the mound itself and despite having cut off his father's foot Lengar was suddenly terrified that this was Hengall's spirit come to avenge itself. 'No,' he whispered, 'no.'

'Yes,' said a deep voice, and Lengar let out a great sigh of relief and straightened his back to look up at Camaban. 'I decided to follow you from Sarmennyn after all,' Camaban explained.

Lengar found he had nothing to say. He was sweating with fear.

Camaban was a man now. His face was thinner than before and much harder, with high cheekbones, deep eyes and a wide, sardonic mouth. His hair, that used to be a tangled mat of filth, was now neatly tied at the back of his scalp with a leather thong from which a rattling tassel of small bones hung. He wore a necklace of children's rib bones and carried a staff tipped with a human jawbone. He now rammed the butt of the staff into the grave mound. 'Did you feel that, father?'

'Don't,' Lengar croaked.

'Are you frightened of Hengall?' Camaban asked derisively. He rammed the staff into the mound again, then spat. 'Did you feel that? I spit on you!' He gouged the staff in the chalk rubble. 'Can you feel it, Hengall? Feel it burning? This is Camaban!'

Lengar scrambled off the grave. 'Why did you come here?' he asked.

'To make sure you did the right thing, of course,' Camaban said, then, with a farewell spit to his father, he clambered down the mound and walked towards the Sky

Temple. He still had a limp, but it was much less noticeable than before. Although Sannas had straightened his foot by forcing the bones straight, they did not flex properly, so he still had a halting step, though it was nothing like the grotesque and twisting dip with which he used to walk.

Lengar, following Camaban, spoke. 'I don't need you to tell me what is the right thing to do.'

'Got your courage back, have you?' Camaban sneered. 'You were shaking when I found you! Thought I was Hengall's spirit, did you?' He laughed.

'Take care, brother,' Lengar said in warning.

Camaban turned and spat at him. 'Kill me, would you? But I am Slaol's servant, Lengar, Slaol's friend. Kill me, you fool, and the sky will burn you and the earth will refuse your bones and even the beasts will shrink from the stench of your death. Even the worms and maggots will refuse your putrid flesh, brother, and you will dry to a yellow husk and the winds will carry you to the poisoned marshes at the world's end.' He pointed his staff at Lengar as he spoke, and Lengar backed away from the threats. Lengar might be older, he might have an enviable reputation as a warrior, but Camaban commanded powers that Lengar did not understand. 'Did you kill Saban?' Camaban asked.

'I enslaved him to Haragg.'

'Good,' Camaban said carelessly.

'And I have taken his bride.'

'And why shouldn't you?' Camaban asked. 'Someone has to. Is she pretty?' He did not wait for an answer, but walked on to the Sky Temple where he crossed the low outer bank, limped through the ditch and climbed up to the high inner bank. He stopped there, staring at the four

173

moon stones. 'They have been busy,' he said sarcastically. 'Gilan's work?'

Lengar shrugged, for he knew nothing about the new temple. 'Gilan is dead.'

'Good,' Camaban said, 'for this has to be his doing. Either him or some priestly scum from Cathallo. They didn't have the courage to make a temple to Slaol without bowing to Lahanna as well.'

'Lahanna?'

'Those are moon stones,' Camaban said, pointing his staff to the paired pillars and slabs inside the ring.

'You want them removed?' Lengar asked.

'What Slaol wants,' Camaban said, 'I will arrange, and you will do nothing unless I tell you.' He walked on into the temple's centre where the high moon cast a small shadow from the hummock that marked the body of the deaf child. Camaban thrust his staff deep into the soft earth and tried to lever the corpse upwards, but though he disturbed the soil he could not shift the body.

Lengar recoiled from the stench which wafted from the loosening soil. 'What are you doing?' he asked in protest.

'Ridding the place of her,' Camaban said.

'You can't do that!' Lengar said, but Camaban ignored him and dropped to his knees so he could scratch and claw the soil and chalk away from the body and, once it was almost free, he stood and used his staff again, this time heaving the decaying corpse into the moonlight.

'Now she'll have to be buried again,' Lengar said.

Camaban turned on him savagely. 'This is my temple, Lengar, not yours. It is mine!' He hissed the last word, scaring Lengar. 'I kept it clear when I was a child! I loved this place, I worshipped Slaol in this circle when the rest

174

of you were sucking on Lahanna's tits. This place is mine!' He rammed the butt of his staff into the dead child, smashing through her ribcage. 'That thing was a messenger sent before her time, for this temple is not finished.' He spat on the corpse, then tugged his staff free. 'The birds and beasts can have her,' he said dismissively, then went to the entrance of the sun. He ignored the two pillars flanking the entrance, making instead for the paired sunstones. He frowned at the two stones. 'This one we shall keep,' he said, laying a hand on the larger of the pair, 'but that one you can throw down.' He pointed to the smaller stone. 'One stone is enough for the sun.' He waved a laconic farewell to his brother and, with as little ceremony as he had arrived, began to walk northwards.

'Where are you going?' Lengar called after him.

'I still have things to learn,' Camaban said, 'and when I know them I shall return.'

'To do what?'

'To build the temple, of course,' Camaban said, turning. 'You want Ratharryn to be great, don't you? But do you think you can achieve anything without the gods? I am going to give you a temple, Lengar, which will raise this miserable tribe to the sky.' He walked on.

'Camaban!' Lengar shouted.

'What is it?' Camaban asked irritably, turning again.

'You are on my side, aren't you?' Lengar asked anxiously.

Camaban smiled. 'I love you, Lengar,' he said, 'like a brother.' And he walked on into the dark.

* * *

Saban learned that it had been Haragg who had guided Lengar and his men from Sarmennyn to Ratharryn, for only an experienced trader would know the roads, would know where the dangers lay and how to avoid them, and Haragg was one of the land's most experienced traders. For ten years he had been crossing the world with his train of three shaggy horses that were loaded with bronze, axes and anything else that he could exchange for the flint, jet, amber and herbs that Sarmennyn lacked. Sometimes, Haragg told Saban, he carried the teeth and bones of sea monsters cast onto Sarmennyn's shores that he could exchange for rich metals and precious stones.

Most of this he grunted to Saban as they walked north. Part of the time he spoke in Saban's own tongue, but most of the time he insisted on speaking the Outfolk tongue and he would lash Saban with a stick if he did not understand or if he failed to reply in the same language. 'You will learn my language,' he insisted, and Saban did because he feared the stick.

Saban's tasks were simple. At night he made the fire which cooked the food and deterred the forest beasts from attacking, while by day he led the three horses, fetched water, cut forage and blew Haragg's ox-horn as they approached a settlement to warn that strangers were coming. The deaf-mute, who was called Cagan, could do these things, but Saban realised the huge boy, who was a few years older than himself, had also been born simple. Cagan was enormously willing and watched his father constantly for a sign that would allow him to be useful, but then he would stumble over the task. If he lit a fire he burned himself, if he tried to lead the horses he used too much strength, yet Haragg, Saban noted, treated Cagan with an extraordinary gentleness as though the deaf-mute, who was half as tall again as Saban, was a much-loved hound, and Cagan responded to his father's kindness with a touching pleasure. If his father smiled he would shudder with joy, or else bob up and down and smile back and make small whimpering noises deep in his throat. Each morning Haragg dressed his son's hair, combing it, plaiting it and tying it with a thong, and then he would comb Cagan's beard and Cagan would wriggle with happiness, and Haragg, Saban noted, would sometimes have a tear in his eye.

The trader shed no tears for Saban. The bronze manacles rubbed weals into Saban's skin, and the weals erupted with blood and pus. Haragg treated them with herbs then tucked leaves under the manacles to stop them chafing, though the leaves always fell away. After a few days he grudgingly allowed Saban a mangy wolfskin to tie around his waist, but became annoyed when Saban scratched at the lice that crawled from the pelt. 'Stop itching,' he would growl, lashing out with his stick. 'I can't bear itching! You're not a dog.'

They travelled eastwards and then northwards, usually in the protective company of other traders but sometimes alone for, though the woods were full of outcasts and hunters, Haragg reckoned there was small risk of ambush. 'If one trader is attacked,' he told Saban, 'then all traders will be attacked, so the chiefs protect us. But there are still dangerous places and there I always travel in company.' Many traders, Haragg explained, went by sea, paddling their wooden boats around the coast and exchanging goods only with the tribes that lived on the shore, but those seafarers missed the far larger inland settlements where Haragg made his living.

When they reached a settlement it was Saban's task to unpack Haragg's goods from the horses and lay them on otter skins in front of the chief's hut. Cagan would lift the heavy bags from the horses, then he would sit and watch, while the folk stared at him for he truly was a giant. The women would giggle, and sometimes the men, realising that Cagan had the mind of a small child, would try to provoke him, but then Haragg would shout at them and the men would back off, terrified of his height and fierceness.

There were some goods that were never unpacked: mainly scraps of gold and a handful of elegant bronze brooches that were saved for the chieftains Haragg reckoned would pay best. The haggling would last all day, sometimes two, and when it ended Saban would place the goods for Sarmennyn into one great leather bag, and the remaining trade goods into another, and Cagan would hang them on the horses' backs. One smaller bag contained nothing but fine large sea-shells which were wrapped in a strange weed that Haragg said grew in the ocean, but as Saban had never seen the sea it meant little to him. The shells were exchanged for food.

Haragg was not unkind. It took Saban a long time to learn this, for he feared the trader's expressionless face and quick stick, but he discovered that Haragg did not smile at anyone except his own son, but nor did he frown; instead he faced each man, woman and circumstance with the same grim determination, and if he spoke little, he listened much. He would speak to Saban, if only to while away the long journeys, but he spoke tonelessly, as though the information he provided was of small interest.

They were far to the north when the first hints of winter

came with cold winds and spitting rains. The folk here spoke a strange language which even Haragg found difficult to understand. By now he was exchanging his bronze bars and black stone axes for small bags of herbs which, he said, flavoured the liquor that the folk of Sarmennyn brewed, but he grudgingly exchanged one small bronze spearhead for a fleece tunic and a pair of properly sewn ox-hide boots that he gave to Saban.

The boots would not fit over the manacles so Haragg sat him down and took a stone axe-head from one of his bags, then levered and beat the manacles far enough apart to force them off Saban's ankles. 'If you run away now,' he said tonelessly, 'you will be killed, for this is dangerous country.' He stowed the manacles among his cargo and at the next settlement sold them for twenty bags of the precious herbs. That was one of the settlements where, when the horn sounded the trader's approach, all the women were hidden away in their huts so that the strangers would not see any of their faces. 'They behave oddly up here,' Haragg said.

By now Haragg and Saban conversed only in the Outfolk tongue. Ratharryn was a memory – a sharp one, to be sure, but fading. Even Derrewyn's face had blurred in Saban's head. He could still feel a terrible pang of remorse when he thought of her, but now, instead of self-pity, he was filled with a burning desire for revenge. Night after night he consoled himself with images of Lengar's death and of Jegar's humiliation, but those consolations were being diluted by the new wonders he saw and the strange things he learned.

He saw temples. Many were great temples: some of wood, more of stone. The stones made vast circles, while the wooden temples soared to the sky and were hung with holly and ivy. He saw priests who cut themselves with flint so that their chests were smothered in blood as they prayed. He saw a place where the tribe worshipped a stream and Haragg told him how the folk drowned a child in its pool every new moon. In another place the men worshipped an ox, a different ox each year, and killed the beast at midsummer and ate its flesh before selecting a new god. One tribe had a mad high priest who twitched and dribbled and spoke nonsense, while another would only allow cripples to be priests. They worshipped vipers in that place, and nearby was a settlement ruled by a woman. That seemed strangest of all to Saban, for she was not merely an influential sorceress like Sannas, but the chief of all the tribe. 'They've always had women chiefs,' Haragg said, 'ever since I've known them. It seems their goddess ordered it.' The woman chief insisted that Haragg sleep a night in her bed. 'She won't buy anything if I say no,' the big man explained. It was in that settlement that Haragg ordered Saban to cut a branch of yew and make himself a bow. Haragg bought arrows for him, content that Saban would not now use the weapon against his master. 'But don't let Cagan have the arrows,' Haragg warned him, 'for he will only injure himself.'

The scar from Saban's missing finger had become a hard callus, but Saban found he could use a bow as well as ever. The missing finger was a mark of his servitude, but it was no handicap. His hair had grown back thickly and there were days when he even found himself laughing and smiling; one morning he woke with the strange realisation that he was enjoying this life with the dour Haragg. That thought gave him a pang of guilt about Derrewyn, but

Saban was still young and his misery was fast being diluted by novelty.

They waited in the woman-ruled settlement as more traders assembled. The next journey, Haragg said, was dangerous and sensible men did not travel the track alone. The woman chief was paid a piece of bronze to provide twenty warriors as an escort and on a cold morning the traders walked north, climbing onto wide bleak moors that were dark under the clouded sky. No trees grew here and Saban did not understand how any folk could live in such a place, but Haragg said there were deep rocky clefts in the moors, and caves hidden in the clefts, and outcasts made their homes in such dank places. 'They are desperate,' Haragg said.

Late that day a band of men did attack. They rose from the heather to loose arrows, but they were few and cautious, and they showed themselves too soon. The hired spearmen tried to frighten the outcasts away by shouting and waving their spears, but the enemy was stubborn and still blocked the path. 'You must attack them,' Haragg shouted at the warriors, but they were unwilling to die for a few traders. Cagan wanted to charge the ragged men, howling like a beast, but Haragg held him back and let Saban advance instead. Saban loosed an arrow and saw it fall short so he ran a few more paces and let another fly. It fluttered just wide of his target and he guessed that was because the arrow had been slightly out of true rather than because of the wind, and he released a third and watched it thump home into a man's belly. The enemy's arrows were being aimed at Saban now, but they had poor bows, and Saban ran another few steps and hauled the sinew back and let it go to drive another man back. He screamed at them, mocking their courage and their marksmanship, then slashed a third flint arrow-head into a wild-haired man in a dirty fleece tunic. He danced as they ran away. 'Your mothers were swine!' Saban called. 'Your sisters lie with goats!' None of the enemy would have understood the insults, even if they had been close enough to hear them.

Haragg actually grinned at Saban. He even clapped his shoulder and laughed. 'You should have been a warrior, not a slave,' he said, and Cagan, following his father's example, bobbed his head and grinned at Saban.

'I always wanted to be a warrior,' Saban confessed.

'All boys do. What good is a boy who wants to be anything else?' Haragg asked. 'But all men are warriors, except the priests.' He said the last three words with an intense bitterness, but refused to explain why.

Next day the traders spread out their goods at a settlement north of the moors. Tribes from other settlements had come, and hundreds of folk wandered in the pasture where the haggling went on from dawn until dusk. Haragg exchanged most of his goods that day, taking in return more herbs and the promise of a pile of white pelts to be delivered to him at winter's end. 'Till then,' he told Saban, 'we shall stay here.'

It seemed a bleak place to Saban for it was nothing but a deep valley between soaring hills. Pine trees clothed the lower slopes and a cold stream tumbled over grey rocks between the dark trees. There was a stone temple lower down the valley and a huddle of huts higher; Haragg and Saban took a dilapidated hut for themselves and Saban repaired its rafters, then cut turfs and laid them as a roof. 'Because I like it here,' Haragg said when Saban asked why he did not return to Sarmennyn for the winter. 'And it will be a long winter,' Haragg warned him, 'long and cold, but when it is over I shall take you back to your brother.'

'To Lengar?' Saban asked bitterly. 'You'd do better to kill me here.'

'Not to Lengar,' Haragg said, 'Camaban. It was not Lengar who wanted you to be my slave, but Camaban.'

'Camaban!' Saban exclaimed in astonishment.

'Camaban,' Haragg confirmed calmly. 'Lengar wanted to kill you when he returned to Ratharryn, but Camaban was determined you should live. It seems that you protested once when your father was going to kill him?'

'I did?' Saban asked, then remembered the failed sacrifice and his involuntary cry of horror. 'So I did,' he said.

'So Camaban persuaded Lengar that it would bring him bad luck if he killed you. He suggested slavery instead, and to a man of Lengar's mind slavery is worse than death. But you had to become my slave, not any man's slave, so Camaban claimed to have been told as much in a dream. Your brother and I planned all this. We sat for whole nights discussing how it could be done.' Haragg looked at Saban's hand where the scar of the missing finger was now a wrinkle of dried skin. 'And it had to be done properly,' he explained, 'or Lengar would never have agreed and you would be dead.' He opened his pouch and took from it the precious knife that had been Hengall's gift to Saban and with which Saban's finger had been cut off. He held the knife to Saban. 'Take it,' he said, then gave him back the amber amulet.

Saban hung his mother's amber about his neck and pushed the blade into his belt. 'I am free?' he asked, bemused.

'You are free,' Haragg said solemnly, 'and you may go if you wish, but your brother wished me to keep you safe until we can join him in Sarmennyn. He knew no other way of keeping you alive, except to doom you to my slavery, but he charged me to protect you because he has need of you.'

'Camaban needs me?' Saban asked, utterly bemused by all that Haragg was so tonelessly revealing. Saban still thought of his brother as a crippled stutterer, a thing of pity, yet it had been the despised Camaban who had arranged his survival and Camaban who had recruited the daunting Haragg to his own purposes. 'Why does Camaban need me?' he asked.

'Because your brother is doing a marvellous thing,' Haragg said, and for once his voice held emotion, 'a thing that only a great man could do. Your brother is making the world anew.' Haragg lifted the leather curtain at the hut door and peered out to see that a new snow was falling thick and slow to smother the world. 'For years,' Haragg said, still staring at the snow, 'I struggled with this world and its gods. I was trying to explain it all.' He dropped the curtain and gave Saban a look that was almost defiant. 'It did not give me pleasure, that struggle. But then I met your brother. He cannot know, I thought, he is too young! But he did know. He did. He has found the pattern.'

'The pattern?' Saban asked, puzzled.

'He has found the pattern,' Haragg repeated gravely, 'and all will be new, all will be well, and all will be changed.'

In a winter night when the earth lay hard as ice and the trees were rimed with a frost that glowed under a pale misted moon, a man limped from the trees north of Cathallo and crossed the fallow fields. It was the longest night, the darkness of the sun's death, and no one saw him come. The huts of the settlement seeped a small smoke as the night fires settled to embers, but the dogs of Cathallo slept and the wintering oxen, sheep, goats and pigs were safe in the huts where they could not be disturbed by the stranger.

Wolves had seen the man and in the previous dusk a dozen of the grey beasts had followed him, their tongues lolling as they looped around behind him, but the man had turned and howled at them and the wolves had first whimpered, then fled into the black, white-frosted trees. The man walked on. Now, in the starlit moments before the dawn, he came to the northern entrance of the great shrine.

The great stones within the high earth bank glimmered with frost. For a heartbeat, pausing in the entrance, it seemed to him that the great ring of boulders was shimmering like a circle of dancers shifting their weight from foot to foot. The dancing stones. He smiled at that idea, then hurried across the grass to Sannas's hut.

He gently pulled aside the leather curtain that hung over the entrance and let in a gust of cold air that gave the dying fire a sudden glow. He ducked into the hut, let the curtain fall and went very still.

He could see almost nothing. The fire was mere embers in ash and no moonlight came through the small smoke-hole in the roof, and so he just squatted and listened until he detected the sound of three people breathing. Three sleepers.

He crept across the hut on his knees, going slowly so that he made no noise, and when he found the first of the sleepers, a young slave, he put one hand over her mouth and sliced a knife down with his free hand. Her breath bubbled harsh in her cut gullet, she twitched for a while, but at last went still. The second girl died the same way, and then the man discarded caution and went to the fire to blow on the smouldering embers and feed them with tinder of dried puffball and small twigs so that the flames flickered bright to illuminate the hanging skulls and bat wings and herb bunches and bones. The fresh blood glistened on the furs and on the killer's hands.

The last sleeper shifted on the hut's far side. 'Is it morning?' her ancient voice asked.

'Not quite, my dear,' the man said. He was putting some larger pieces of wood on the fire now. 'It's almost dawn, though,' he added comfortingly, 'but it will be a cold one, a very cold one.'

'Camaban?' Sannas sat up in the pile of furs that was her bed. Her skull-like face, framed by a tangle of white hair, showed surprise and even pleasure. 'I knew you'd come back,' she said. She did not see the new blood, and the stench of smoke masked its smell. 'Where have you been?' she demanded querulously.

'I have walked the hills and worshipped in temples older than time,' Camaban said softly, feeding more wood onto the revived fire, 'and I have talked with priests, old women and sorcerers until I have sucked the knowledge of this world dry.'

'Dry!' Sannas laughed. 'You've hardly licked the tit, you young fool, let alone sucked on it.' In truth Sannas knew Camaban had been her best pupil, a man to rival her own skills, but she would never tell him as much. She leaned to one side, revealing a leathery flap of breast as she reached for her honeycomb. She put a piece in her mouth and sucked noisily. 'Your brother is making war on us,' she said sourly.

'Lengar loves to make war,' Camaban said.

'And loves to make babies,' Sannas said. 'Derrewyn is pregnant.'

'I heard as much.'

'May her milk poison the bastard,' Sannas said, 'and its father too.' She pulled the furs round her shoulders. 'Lengar takes our men prisoner, Camaban, and sacrifices them to his gods.'

Camaban rocked back on his heels. 'Lengar thinks the gods are like hounds that can be whipped into obedience,' he said, 'but he will learn soon enough that their whips are bigger than his. But for the moment he does Slaol's work so I imagine he will prosper.'

'Slaol!' Sannas hissed.

'The great god,' Camaban said reverently, 'the god above all gods. The only god who has the power to change our sad world.'

Sannas stared at him as a dribble of honey trickled from her lips. 'The only god?' she asked in disbelief.

'I told you that I wished to learn,' Camaban said, 'so I have learned, and I have discovered that Slaol is the god above all the gods. Our mistake has been to worship the others, but they are much too busy worshipping Slaol to take any notice of us.' He smiled at Sannas's appalled expression. 'I am a follower of Slaol, Sannas,' he said, 'and I always have been, ever since I was a child. Even when I listened to you talk of Lahanna, I was a worshipper of Slaol.'

She shuddered at his impiety. 'Then why come back here, fool?' she demanded. 'You think I love Slaol?'

'I came to see you, my dear, of course,' Camaban said calmly. He put a last piece of wood on the fire, then moved to her side where he sat and cradled her shoulders. 'I paid you to teach me, remember? Now I want my final lesson.'

The old woman saw the blood on his hands then and tried to claw his face. 'I will give you nothing,' she said.

Camaban turned his body to face her. 'You will teach me the last lesson, Sannas,' he said gently. 'I paid for it with Slaol's gold.'

'No!' she hissed.

'Yes,' Camaban said gently, then he leaned forward and kissed her on the mouth. She struggled, but Camaban used his weight to push her down. He still kissed her, his mouth fixed on hers, and for a few heartbeats she tried to escape his kiss by twisting her head, but her strength was no match for his.

She glared up at his eyes, then he moved the furs from her breasts and put one arm around her body and began to squeeze. The old woman struggled again and a small whimper escaped her, but Camaban pushed his mouth hard down on hers, squeezed with his arm and pinched her nostrils with his left hand. All the time he kept his green eyes on her black eyes.

It took a long while. A surprisingly long while. The old woman kicked and twitched under the furs, but after a while the spasmodic movements ended, and still Camaban kissed her. The fire was almost dead again by the time Sannas's small, birdlike movements had ended, but her eyes were still open and Camaban stared into them until at last, though cautiously, as if expecting a trick, he slowly pulled his face from hers. He waited, his mouth just a finger's breadth from her mouth, but she did not move. And still he waited, scarce daring to breathe, but finally he smiled. 'What a honey-sweet kiss that was,' he said to the corpse, then touched his finger to her forehead. 'I took your last breath, lady. I have stolen your soul.'

He sat for a moment, savouring the triumph. With her last breath he had stolen her power and engulfed her spirit, but then he remembered the closeness of dawn and he hurriedly crossed the hut. He cleared away the stones that ringed the small hearth and then, using a piece of firewood, shifted the burning wood, embers and hot ashes aside. He found a broken antler and used it to dig into the hot soil beneath the hearth, scrabbling the earth away where he knew Sannas hid her most precious possessions.

He uncovered a leather pouch. He prised it gently from the earth's grip, then pulled aside the leather curtain at the hut entrance where the first seeping grey of the morning provided a sullen light. He untied the pouch and spilt its contents on to his palm. There were eleven of Sarmennyn's small lozenges and one large one. It was the gold Hengall had exchanged for Cathallo's stones and the two lozenges Camaban himself had paid to Sannas. He gazed at the treasure for an instant, then returned it to the pouch, tied the pouch to his belt and went out into the cold.

He went north, and a child saw him leave the shrine in the misty greyness but did not raise any alarm. He limped across the frost-whitened fields to the dark woods in which he vanished before the sun rose to blaze across Cathallo's shrine.

Where Sannas the sorceress lay dead.

Haragg hired three slave women for the winter. They came from a tribe that lived yet farther north and spoke a language that even Haragg did not understand, but they knew their duties. The youngest slept with Haragg, and Saban and Cagan shared the other two. 'A man should sleep with a woman,' Haragg told Saban. 'It is a natural thing, the proper thing.'

Haragg seemed to take small pleasure from his own woman. Instead his joy came from the spare, cold life of that long winter. Each morning he would go to the temple to pray and afterwards he would bring water or ice to the fire while Cagan fed hay or leaves to the three horses that shared the hut. The chief of the settlement regarded Haragg as an honoured guest and provided food for all of them, though Saban supplemented those gifts by hunting. He preferred hunting by himself, stalking the scarce prey through an ice-bound land, though he did once join the men of the settlement when a bear was found sleeping in a cave. They woke the beast with fire and killed it with flint and bronze and afterwards Saban carried a bleeding haunch of meat back to the hut. There was never quite enough food, at least for the giant Cagan, but none of them starved. They ate berries and nuts that were stored in jars, eked out their bags of grain and herbs, and occasionally gorged on venison, hare or fish.

And day after day the snow glittered on the hills and the air seemed filled with a sparkling frost and the sun came for a short time and the nights were endless. They burned peat, which Saban had never seen before, but sometimes, to make the light in the hut brighter, they would add logs of resinous pine that burned smoky and pungent. The long evenings were usually silent, but sometimes Haragg talked. 'I was a priest,' the big man said one night, startling Saban. 'I was a priest of Sarmennyn, and I had a wife and a son and a daughter.'

Saban said nothing. The peat glowed red. The three horses stamped their feet and Cagan, who loved the horses, felt the vibration and turned and gurgled soothingly to them. The three women watched the men, sheltering under a shared pelt. They had tangled masses of black hair that half hid the scars on their foreheads, which showed they were slaves. Saban was learning their language, but now he and Haragg spoke in the Outfolk tongue.

'My daughter was called Miyac,' Haragg said, staring into the fire's steady glow. It was almost as though he were talking to himself, for he spoke softly and did not look at Saban. 'Miyac' – his voice caressed the name – 'and she was a creature of great loveliness. Great loveliness. I thought she would grow to marry a chief or a war leader, and I was glad, for her husband's wealth would keep my wife and me in our old age and would preserve Cagan when we were dead.'

Saban said nothing. There was a slithering noise from the roof as a mass of snow slid down the roof turfs. 'But, in Sarmennyn,' Haragg went on, 'we choose a sun bride each year. She is chosen in the spring and for three moons' – he rocked his hand back and forth to show that the three moons were an approximation – 'she is a goddess herself. And then, at midsummer, at the sun's glory, we kill her.'

'Kill her?' Saban asked, shocked.

'We send her to Erek.' Erek was the Outfolk's name for Slaol. 'And one year,' Haragg went on, 'we chose Miyac.'

Saban flinched. 'You chose her?'

'The priests chose her,' Haragg said, 'and I was a priest. My wife screamed at me, she hit me, but I thought it was an honour to our family. What greater husband could Miyac have than Erek? And so my daughter went to her death and my wife died within a moon, and I fell into a black sadness, and when I came from that sadness I no longer wanted to be a priest and my ideas were unwelcome and so I began to wander the land. I traded.' The sadness showed on his face and Cagan whimpered so that Haragg leaned over and patted his son's hand to show that everything was well.

Saban shifted closer to the fire, dragged the pelt around his shoulders and wondered if the world would ever be warm again.

'My twin brother was the high priest in Sarmennyn,' Haragg said, 'and when I told him I no longer believed in sacrifice he allowed me to become a trader instead of a priest. His name is Scathel. You will meet him, if he still lives.'

Something about the way Haragg said his brother's name suggested that Saban did not want to meet Scathel. 'Is your brother still the high priest?' he asked.

Haragg shrugged. 'He lost his wits when the treasures were stolen and fled into the mountains, so now I do not know if he is alive or dead.'

'Who stole the treasures?' Saban asked.

'His name is never spoken,' Haragg answered, 'but he was a son of our chief and he wanted to be chief himself, except he had three older brothers and all were greater men than he and so he stole the tribe's treasures to bring ill luck on Sarmennyn. He had heard of Sannas, and he believed she could use the treasures to make a magic that would kill his father and brothers and give him the chieftainship. We know that, for he said as much to his woman, and she told us before we killed her, and then Scathel averted the ill luck by killing the chief and all his family. So the gold never did reach Sannas, but Scathel still went mad.' He paused. 'And perhaps the ill luck was not averted, I don't know. What I do know is that my people will do anything, give anything, to have the treasures returned.'

'They must give a temple,' Saban said, remembering what Lengar had told him on the morning of his enslavement.

'They must listen to Camaban,' Haragg said softly, and once again Saban was filled with wonderment that his awkward, crippled brother had suddenly gained such an awesome reputation.

A few days later, when a thaw had melted some of the snow on the passes through the hills and Haragg's precious white pelts had been delivered, and as the days lengthened again as Slaol recovered his strength, Haragg took Saban and Cagan westwards. Ostensibly they went to buy some axes made from black stone that were much prized in the south country, but Saban suspected there was another purpose in the journey. It took half a day until, quite unexpectedly, they reached a high hill that ended abruptly at a sea cliff. This was the first time Saban had ever seen the sea and he whimpered at the sight. He had never imagined anything so dark, grey, cold and venomous. It heaved constantly, as though muscles worked beneath its white-flecked surface, and where it met the land it broke into a myriad wind-whipped fragments, then sucked and drained and surged to shatter again. Shrieking white birds filled the air. He could have gazed at it for ever, but Haragg stirred him northwards along the shore. Monsters' bones littered the small beaches in the cliff bends and, when they came to the settlement that sold the axes, Saban found himself sleeping in a hut whose rafters were made of those vast curved bones that arched above him to support a low roof of wood and turf.

Next morning Haragg took Cagan and Saban to a narrow fragment of high land that jutted into the vast ocean and, at the land's end, atop a cliff that seemed to shake with the endless thunder of the sea, there was a temple. It was a simple enough shrine, a mere ring of eight tall stones, but one stone stood proud of the circle. 'Erek again,' Haragg said, 'for wherever you travel, you will find Erek is worshipped. Always Erek.' The outlying stone, Saban guessed, stood towards the place where the sun rose in midsummer and its shadow would pierce the circle as the sun gave life to the earth. Small sprigs of dead heather lay at the foot of the stones, evidence of prayers made, and not even the skirling sea wind could wholly snatch away the blood stink of a beast that had been sacrificed at the temple not long before. 'We have a shrine like this in Sarmennyn,' Haragg said softly, 'and we call it the Sea Temple, though it has nothing to do with Dilan.' Dilan, Saban now knew, was Sarmennyn's sea god. 'Our Sea Temple doesn't face the rising sun,' Haragg went on, 'but looks to where it sets in midsummer, and if I had my way I would pull it down. I would take its stones and cast them into the sea. I would obliterate it.' He spoke with an uncommon bitterness.

'The sun bride?' Saban guessed diffidently.

Haragg nodded. 'She dies at the Sea Temple.' He closed his eyes for a few heartbeats. 'She goes to the temple arrayed in Erek's gold and there she is stripped naked, just as a bride should go to her husband, and sent to her death.' Haragg hugged his knees, and Saban could see tears on his face, or perhaps that was just the effect of the wind that flecked the sea ragged and whirled the shrieking birds about the sky. Saban understood now why Haragg had come to this high place, because from here he could gaze into the vastness above the sea where his daughter's spirit flew with the soaring white birds. 'The gold was a gift from Dilan,' Haragg went on. 'The treasures were washed ashore in a swamped boat, close to where the Sea Temple stands, and so our ancestors decided the gold was a gift from one god to the other, and perhaps they were right.'

'Perhaps?'

'Boats do get swamped,' Haragg said, 'and traders from the land across the sea do bring us gold.'

Saban frowned at the scepticism in the big man's voice. 'Are you saying . . .' he began to ask.

Haragg turned on him fiercely. 'I am saying nothing.

195

The gods do talk to us, and maybe the gods did send us the gold. Perhaps Dilan swamped the boat and steered it to that beach under the cliff, but why?' Haragg frowned into the wind. 'We never did ask why, we just wrapped a girl in gold and killed her, and we went on doing it year after year after year!' He was angry now, spitting at the temple stone where the sacrificial blood, stuck with brown hairs, still showed. 'And it is always the priests who demand sacrifice,' Haragg went on. 'From every beast that is killed they get the liver and kidney and brain and the meat of one leg. When the sun bride is a goddess she is given treasure, but who keeps it when she is dead? The priests! Sacrifice, the priests say, or else the harvest will be bad, and when the harvest is bad anyway they simply say you did not sacrifice enough and so demand more!' He spat again.

'Are you saying there should be no more priests?' Saban asked.

Haragg shook his head. 'We need priests. We need people who can translate the gods to us, but why do we choose our priests from the weakest?' He gave Saban a wry look. 'Just like your tribe, we choose our priests from those who fail the ordeals. I failed! I cannot swim and I almost drowned, but my brother saved me, and in so doing he failed his own ordeal too, but Scathel always wanted to be a priest.' He shrugged, dismissing the story. 'So most priests are weak men, but like all men, given some small authority, they become tyrants. And because so many priests are fools they will not think, but simply repeat the things they learned. Things change, but priests do not change. And now things are changing fast.'

'Are they?' Saban asked.

Haragg gave him a pitying look. 'Our gold is stolen! Your father is killed! These are signs from the gods, Saban. The difficulty is knowing what they mean.'

'And you do?'

Haragg shook his head. 'No, but your brother Camaban does.'

For a moment Saban's soul rebelled against this fate, which had brought him to a strange temple above an unforgiving sea. Camaban and Haragg, he thought, had entangled him in madness, and he felt a huge resentment against the destiny that had snatched him from Ratharryn and from Derrewyn's arms. 'I just want to be a warrior!' he protested.

'What you want counts for nothing,' Haragg said curtly, 'but what your brother wants is everything, and he saved your life. You would be dead now, cut down by Lengar's spear, if Camaban had not arranged otherwise. He has given you life, Saban, and the rest of that life must be in his service. You have been chosen.'

To make the world anew, Saban thought, and was tempted to laugh. Except that he was trapped in Camaban's dream and, whether he wanted to or not, he was expected to fulfil that vision.

Camaban returned to Sarmennyn at the beginning of spring. He had wintered in the forest at an ancient timber temple. It was overgrown and decaying, but he had cleared the undergrowth and watched the sun retreat about the ring of poles and then start back again towards its summer fullness, and all the time he had talked with Slaol – even argued with the god, for at times Camaban resented the burden laid on him. He alone understood the gods and the world, and he knew he alone could turn the world back to its beginnings, but sometimes, as he tested his ideas, he would groan in agony and rock backwards and forwards. Once a hunting party of Outfolk, seeking slaves, had heard him, seen him and fled from him because they understood he was a holy man. He was also a hungry man by the time he reached Sarmennyn: hungry, sour and gaunt, and he came to the tribe's chief settlement on a day of festival like a mangy crow alighting amid a flock of swans. The settlement's main gate was hung with white garlands of cow parsley and pear blossom, for this was the day on which the new sun bride would be greeted by her people.

Kereval, the chief of Sarmennyn, greeted Camaban warmly. At first glance Kereval was an unlikely chief for such a warlike nation, for he was neither the tallest nor the strongest man in the tribe. However, he was reckoned to have wisdom and, in the wake of their treasures' loss, that was what the people of Sarmennyn had sought in their new leader. He was a small and wiry man with dark eyes that peered from the tangle of grey tattoos that covered his cheeks; his black hair was pinned with fish-bones; his woollen cloak was dyed blue. His people asked only one thing of him: that he retrieve the treasures, and that Kereval was seeking to do by his alliance with Lengar. A bargain had been struck by which a small war band of Sarmennyn's feared warriors would help Lengar defeat Cathallo and a temple of Sarmennyn would be given to Ratharryn, and in return the golden lozenges would be sent home.

'There are those who think your brother cannot be

198

trusted,' Kereval told Camaban. The two men squatted outside Kereval's hut where Camaban greedily ate a bowl of fish broth and a piece of hard flat bread.

'Of course they think that,' Camaban retorted, though in truth he did not care what people thought for his head was dizzy with the glory of Slaol.

'They believe we should go to war,' Kereval said, peering towards the gate to see if the sun bride had yet appeared.

'Then go to war,' Camaban said carelessly, his mouth full. 'You think it matters to me whether your miserable treasures are returned?'

Kereval said nothing. He knew he could never hope to lead an army to Ratharryn for it was too far away and his spearmen would meet too many enemies on the way, despite the fact that those spearmen were famous for their bravery, and were feared by all their neighbours for they were as hard and pitiless as the land they came from. Sarmennyn was a rocky land, a bitter place trapped between the sea and the mountains where even the trees grew bent as old folk, though few in the tribe ever did grow old. The hardships of life bent the people as the wind bent the trees, a wind that rarely ceased from wailing about the rocky tops of the mountains beneath which the folk of Sarmennyn lived in low huts made of stone and thatched with driftwood, seaweed, straw and turf. The smoke from their crouched huts mixed with mist, rain and sleet. It was a land, the people said, that no man wanted, and so the Outfolk tribe had occupied it and made a living from the sea, by carving axes from the dark stones of the mountains and by stealing from their neighbours. They had thrived in their barren country, but since their treasures had been stolen nothing had gone well in the land.

There had been more disease than usual, and the disease had afflicted the tribe's cattle and sheep. A score of boats had been lost at sea, their crew's bodies washed ashore all white and swollen and sea-nibbled. Storms had flattened the land's few crops so there was hunger. Wolves had come down from the hills and their howling was like a lament for the lost treasures.

'If your brother does not keep our bargain –' Kereval began.

'If my brother breaks his word,' Camaban interrupted the chief, 'then I will undertake to return the gold. I, Camaban, will send you the gold. You trust me, do you not?'

'Of course,' Kereval said, and he did, for Camaban had cured the chief's favourite wife who had been dying of the wasting disease when Camaban had first visited Sarmennyn. Kereval's priests and healers had achieved nothing, but Camaban had given the woman a potion he had learned from Sannas and she had recovered swiftly and wholly.

Camaban wiped the broth from the clay bowl with the last of the bread then turned towards the crowd at the garlanded gate who had suddenly sunk to their knees. 'Your newest bride is here?' he asked Kereval sarcastically. 'Another child with twisted teeth and tangled hair to throw at the god?'

'No,' Kereval said, standing to join the crowd at the gate. 'Her name is Aurenna, and the priests tell me we have never sent a girl so lovely to the sun. Never. This one is beautiful.'

'They say that every year,' Camaban said, and that was true, for the sun brides were always reckoned beautiful. The tribe gave their best to the god, but sometimes, in years past, when parents had a beautiful daughter, they would hide the girl when the priests came to search for the bride. But the parents of this year's sun bride had not hidden her, nor married her to some young man who, by taking her virginity, would have made her ineligible for the sun god's bed. Instead they had kept her for Erek, although Aurenna was a girl so lovely that men had offered her father whole herds of cattle for her hand, while a chieftain from across the sea, a man whose traders brought gold and bronze into Sarmennyn, had said he would yield Aurenna's own weight in metal if she would just take ship to his far island.

Her father had rejected all the suitors, even though he desperately needed wealth for he had no cattle, no sheep, no fields and no boat. He chipped stone every day. He and his wife and their children all chipped the dark, greenish stone that came from the mountains to make axe-heads, which his children polished with sand, and then a trader would come and take away the heads and leave a little food for Aurenna's family. Aurenna alone had not chipped or polished stone. Her parents would not permit it for she was beautiful and a local priest had prophesied that she would become the sun bride, and so her family had protected her until the priests came to take her away. Her father had wept and her mother had embraced her when that moment arrived. 'When you are a goddess,' her mother pleaded, 'look after us.'

Now the new sun bride came to Kereval's settlement and the waiting crowd touched their foreheads to the ground as the priests escorted her through the blossom-hung gate. Kereval lay flat just inside the settlement's gateway and did not move until Aurenna gave him permission to stand, though one of the priests had to prompt her for she still did not fully understand that she was about to become a goddess. Kereval stood and felt a great relief that Aurenna was all that she had been reported to be. Her name meant 'golden one' in the Outfolk tongue, and it was a good name for her hair shone like pale gold. She had the whitest, cleanest skin Kereval had ever seen, a long face, calm eyes and a strange air of authority. She was, indeed, beautiful – Kereval would have liked to have taken her into his own household, but that was impossible. Instead he escorted her to the hut where the priests' wives would wash her, comb her long golden hair and dress her in the white woollen robe.

'She is beautiful,' Camaban grudgingly said to Kereval.

'Very,' Kereval said, and dared to hope that the sun god would reward the tribe for giving him a bride of such ethereal beauty.

'Beautiful,' Camaban said softly, and he knew suddenly that Aurenna must be part of his great scheme. In a world where folk were bent and scarred, toothless and dirty even when they were not wall-eyed, crippled and wart-covered, Aurenna was a pale, serene and dazzling presence, and Camaban understood that her sacrifice made this year a special one for Slaol. 'But what if the god rejects her?' Camaban asked.

Kereval touched his groin in the same gesture that Camaban's people used to avert ill fortune. 'He won't,' Kereval said fiercely, but in truth he did fear just such a rejection. In the past the sun brides had gone calmly to their deaths to be snatched in a blaze of light, but since the loss of the treasures the brides had all died hard. The last one had been the worst for she had screamed like a clumsily killed pig. She had writhed and shrieked and her moans of pain were worse than the howling of the wolves or the sigh of the ever-cold sea as it sucked at the dark rocks which edged Sarmennyn's bleak land. Kereval believed that the manner of Aurenna's death would be a touchstone for his wisdom. If the god approved of the bargain with Lengar then Aurenna would die cleanly, but if he disapproved then Aurenna would die in agony and Kereval's enemies within the tribe would reject his leadership.

At the southern edge of the settlement, beside the river where a score of boats had been pulled above the high tide, there stood a circle of rough stone pillars: the temple of the sun bride. The tribe danced about the circle, singing as they waited for the bride to appear from the hut where she was being washed and dressed. Leckan, the lame sorcerer who had gone to Ratharryn when the folk of Sarmennyn had attempted to trade for the gold, and who was now the senior priest in Kereval's settlement, glanced up at the sky and saw that the clouds were thinning so that there was a chance that the sun might see the girl. That was a good omen. Then the singing and the dancing stopped as the tribe dropped to the ground.

Aurenna had appeared and, led by two priests, walked to her temple. Her hair had been combed, then gathered into a plait that was bound with a leather thong and laced with cowslips and sloe-blossom. The robe, so clean and white, hung straight from her shoulders. She would normally have been arrayed in gold, with a cascade of lozenges around her neck and the larger pieces sewn to the robe, but the gold was gone, yet even so she was dazzling. She was a tall girl, and slender, and straight-backed, so that it seemed to Camaban, who alone watched as she walked through the prostrate tribe, that she moved with an unworldly grace.

Aurenna was unsure of what she should do. She was hesitant to enter the circle until one of the priests whispered that this was the moment when she became a goddess and this was her temple and she could do as she wished, but that it was customary for the bride to go to the circle's centre and there instruct the tribe to stand and dance. Aurenna did as she was told, though there was a catch in her voice as she spoke. And just at that moment the sun broke through the clouds and the people sighed with delight for that good omen.

Kereval, the chief, carried a leather bag which he handed to Leckan, and Leckan opened it to discover new treasures inside. These were treasures that Kereval had ordered made in the land across the western sea, and they had cost him dearly in bronze and amber and jet, and though they could not replace the lost treasures, they could still do honour to Erek and his bride. The priest drew out one large golden lozenge and three chains of smaller lozenges that had been strung on strings of sinews and he hung them about Aurenna's neck. Then he produced a bronze-bladed knife that had pins of gold pierced into its wooden handle. He kept the knife himself as a symbol that the thread of Aurenna's life would be cut when her time was done.

Gifts were brought to the goddess. There were bags of grain, oysters, mussels and many dried fish. There were axe-heads and slivers of bronze, and those gifts the priests tucked away for their own use, but the food was piled before Aurenna, fetched into the temple by men who dared take a glance at the goddess before they prostrated themselves. She thanked each one with a diffidence that was alluring. She even laughed when one man brought some dried fish, all threaded by their gills onto a stick, and one fish fell off. As the man turned to retrieve it another fell from the opposite end of the stick, and as he turned to retrieve that so a third fell off. Aurenna's laughter was as bright as her betrothed who still shone down from the gap in the clouds.

'It is customary to give the food to the widows,' Leckan the priest told her in a low voice.

'The food must go to the widows,' Aurenna said in a clear voice.

Leckan gave her more instructions. She was a goddess now, so she must not be seen eating or drinking, though wherever she went in Sarmennyn a hut would be provided for her privacy. Two women would be her constant attendants and four young spearmen her guards. 'You are free to go wherever you wish, great one,' he murmured to Aurenna, 'but it is customary to travel throughout the land to bring blessings on it.'

'And . . .' Aurenna began a question, but the words dried in her throat. 'When . . .' she began again, but still could not finish.

'And, at the end,' Leckan said calmly, 'you will be here and we shall escort you to your husband. It does not hurt.' He pointed to the sun, which now blazed between the clouds. 'Your husband will not wish to wait one heartbeat longer than is necessary. There will be no pain.'

'No pain?' a voice suddenly shouted behind them. 'No pain? There must be pain! What bride does not feel pain? Pain and blood! Blood and pain!' The man who had shouted these words now came into the temple where he dropped to the ground and stretched his hands towards Aurenna's feet. 'Of course there is pain!' he shouted into the grass. 'Unimaginable pain! Your blood will boil, your bones crack and your skin shrivel. It is agony. You could never imagine such pain, not if you were to live in torment till the end of time!' He scrambled to his feet again. 'You should scream in pain,' he spat at Aurenna, 'for you are a bride!'

The man had come with a dozen followers, all naked like their leader and all priests, but only the man who shouted had come close to Aurenna. He was a tall, gaunt creature with a starved face and blazing eyes, long yellow teeth and tangled black hair and a scar-flecked skin. His voice was like a raven's jeer, his heavy bones were as knobbled as flint and his blackened fingers were hooked like claws. 'Pain is the price you pay!' he shouted at the terrified girl. He carried a heavy flint-headed spear which he flourished wildly as he capered among the stones. 'Your eyes will burst, your sinews will shrink and your screams will echo from the cliffs!' he shouted.

Camaban had watched this display and grinned at it, but Kereval had run into the temple. 'Scathel?' he shouted angrily. 'Scathel!'

Scathel was the high priest of Sarmennyn, and had been the high priest when the treasures were stolen, but he had blamed himself for the gold's loss and so he had gone away into the hills where he had howled at the rocks and scarred his body with flints. Others of the priests had followed him and, when Scathel's madness had passed, they had built themselves a new temple in the high rocks and there they had prayed, starved and abased themselves, making amends for the loss of the treasures. Many in the tribe believed that Scathel had vanished for ever, but now he had returned.

He ignored Kereval and prodded Leckan out of the way with his spear so that he could advance on the frightened Aurenna. If Scathel was impressed by her beauty he did not show it, but instead thrust his raw-skinned face at her. 'You are a goddess?' he demanded.

Aurenna could not speak, but did give one small nod in nervous acknowledgement of the question.

'Then I have a petition for you,' Scathel shouted so that every soul in the settlement could hear him. 'Our treasures must be returned! They must be returned!' His spittle flecked her face as he shouted and she stepped back to avoid it. 'I have built a temple!' Scathel bellowed over Aurenna's shoulder, addressing the whole crowd, who stared at him aghast. 'I have made a temple with my own hands and I have bled for the god, and he has spoken to me! We must fetch the treasures back!'

'The treasures will be returned,' Kereval intervened.

'You!' Scathel turned on the chief, and even levelled his spear so that a dozen warriors ran to Kereval's side. 'What have you done to retrieve the treasures?' Scathel demanded.

'We have lent men to Ratharryn,' Kereval replied courteously, 'and will send them a temple.'

'Ratharryn!' Scathel sneered. 'A small place, a miserable place, a bog of stunted people, goitred pigs and twisted serpents. You are a chief, not a trader! You do not bargain for our gold, you take it! Take our spears, take our arrows, and take back the treasures!' He stepped aside and raised his arms to attract the tribe's attention. 'We must go to war!' he shouted. 'To war!' He began to beat his spear against one of the stones. 'We must take our spears, our swords, our bows and we must kill and maim until the things at Ratharryn scream for our mercy!' The spear shaft broke and the crude stone head flew harmlessly away. 'We must burn their huts and raze their temples and slaughter their livestock and throw their infants into Erek's fires!' He turned back on Kereval and thrust out the splintered spear staff. 'Lengar has our men to fight his wars, and he has our gold, and when his wars are won he will turn on our men and kill them. You call yourself a chief? A chief would even now be leading the young men to war!'

Kereval drew his sword. It was a bronze blade, beautifully balanced, part of the tribute that each trader who came from the island across the western sea had to pay to the folk of Sarmennyn before he was allowed to carry his goods further eastwards. Kereval suddenly slashed at the spear staff and the ferocity of the attack drove Scathel backwards. 'War?' Kereval asked. 'What do you know of war, Scathel?' He slashed again, knocking the staff violently aside. 'To go to war, Scathel, I must lead my men across the black hills, then through the land of Salar's people. You would fight them?' The sword cut a third time, slicing a thick splinter from the rough ash staff. 'And when we have buried our dead, priest, and crossed the further hills, we shall come to the tribes of the great river. They have no love for us. But perhaps we can fight them too?' He slapped the staff aside again with his sword. 'And when we have fought our way across the river, and up into the farther hills, then Ratharryn's allies will wait for us with spears. With hundreds of spears!'

'Then how did Vakkal reach Ratharryn?' Scathel

demanded. Vakkal was the man who had led the forces to help Lengar take the chieftainship.

'They went by hidden paths, led by your brother,' Kereval said, 'but they were only fifty men. You think I can take all our spearmen secretly? And to conquer Ratharryn, Scathel, will take all our men, and who will stay here to protect our womenfolk?'

'The god will protect them!' Scathel insisted.

Kereval slashed the sword again. This time Scathel dropped the staff and spread his hands as though inviting Kereval to drive the heavy sword into his belly, but the chief just shook his head. 'I have given my word,' Kereval said, 'and we shall give Lengar of Ratharryn time to keep his word.' He raised the sword so that its tip disappeared into the filthy tangle of Scathel's wild beard. 'Be careful of what you stir in this tribe, priest, for I still rule here.'

'And I am still high priest,' Scathel spat back.

'The treasures will be returned!' Kereval shouted. He turned to look at his tribe. 'We have chosen a bride who is more lovely than any girl we have ever sent to Erek's bed,' Kereval announced. 'She will carry our prayers.'

'And what will you do' – Scathel repeated Camaban's grim question – 'if the god rejects his bride?' He suddenly turned and snatched the bronze knife from Leckan's hand. For a heartbeat men thought he was about to attack Aurenna, but instead he held his own beard with his left hand and slashed at it with the knife, slicing off great tangled hanks of matted hair. Then he threw the hair into the temple's centre. 'With my beard I put a curse on Kereval if the god refuses this bride! And if he does, then it will be war, nothing but war! War and death and blood and slaughter until the treasures are back!' He stalked towards his old hut and the tribe parted, letting him through, while behind him, at her temple, Aurenna shuddered in horror.

Camaban watched, and afterwards, when no one watched him, he retrieved the hanks of Scathel's hair and wove them into a ring through which he stared at a cloud-shrouded Slaol. 'He will fight me,' he told the god, 'even though he loves you as I do. So you must turn his thoughts as I have turned his hair,' and with that he cast the circlet of hair into the river that flowed past Kereval's settlement. He doubted the small charm would effect the change by itself, but it might help, and Camaban knew he needed help for the god had given him a gigantic task. That was why he had returned to Sarmennyn in the time of their sun bride's rule for it was then that the Outfolk tribe was most vulnerable to suggestion, to magic and to change.

And Camaban had a whole world to change.

Haragg, Saban and Cagan reached Kereval's settlement on the same day as Aurenna, but it was evening when they came and the good weather had turned into a heavy downpour that beat on the dark land and soaked Saban's hair and tunic. Haragg unloaded his horses, then led the weary beasts into a decrepit hut, evidently his home, before taking Saban and Cagan to a great hut that stood on the highest ground within the settlement's timber palisade. Water streamed from the thatched roof of the hut that was larger than any Saban had ever seen, so large that, when he ducked inside, he saw that its ridge pole needed the support of five great timbers. The hall stank of fish, smoke, fur and sweat, and was crowded with men who feasted in the light of two great fires. A drummer beat skins while a flautist played a heron-bone flute in the hut's corner.

A silence fell as Haragg entered and Saban sensed that the men were wary of the big trader, but Haragg ignored them, pointing instead at a small man sitting at one end of the hall close to a smoky fire. The man's wiry hair was crammed into a bronze circlet, while his face was thick with ash-grey scars. 'The chief,' Haragg whispered to Saban. 'Called Kereval. A decent man.'

Camaban was sitting next to Kereval, though at first Saban did not recognise his brother, seeing instead a hollow-cheeked, sunken-eyed sorcerer with a frightening face framed by bones woven into his hair. Then the sorcerer pointed a long finger at Saban, crooked it and gestured that he should come and sit between himself and the chief, and Saban realised it was his brother.

'It took you long enough to get here,' Camaban grumbled, without any other greeting, then he grudgingly named his brother to Kereval who smiled a welcome then clapped his hands for silence so he could tell the feasters who the newcomer was. Men stared at Saban when they heard he was Lengar's brother, then Kereval demanded that a slave bring Saban some food.

'I doubt he wants to eat,' Camaban said.

'I do,' Saban said. He was hungry.

'You want to eat this filth?' Camaban demanded, showing Saban a bowl of stewed fish, seaweed and stringy mutton. He lifted a strand of seaweed. 'Am I supposed to eat this?' he asked Kereval.

Kereval ignored Camaban's disgust and spoke to Saban. 'Your brother cured my best wife of a disease that no one else could mend!' The chief beamed at Saban. 'She is well again! He works miracles, your brother.'

'I simply treated her properly,' Camaban said, 'unlike the fools you call healers and priests. They couldn't cure a wart!'

Kereval took the seaweed out of Camaban's hand and ate it. 'You have been travelling with Haragg?' he asked Saban.

'A long way,' Saban said.

'Haragg likes to travel,' Kereval said. He had small beady

eyes in a face that was good-humoured and quick to smile. 'Haragg believes,' he went on, leaning close to Saban, 'if he journeys far enough, he will find a magician to give his son a tongue and ears.'

'What Cagan needs is a good blow on the head,' Camaban snarled. 'That would cure him.'

'Truly?' Kereval asked eagerly.

'Is that liquor?' Camaban asked, and helped himself to a decorated pot that stood beside Kereval. He tipped it to his mouth and drank greedily.

'You will stay now? Through the summer, perhaps?' Kereval asked Saban with a smile.

'I don't know why I'm here,' Saban confessed, glancing at Camaban. He was taken aback by the change in his brother. Camaban, the stuttering cripple, was now seated in the place of honour.

'You are here, little brother,' Camaban said, 'to help me move a temple.'

Kereval's smile vanished. 'Not everyone believes we should give you a temple.'

'Of course they don't!' Camaban said, not bothering to lower his voice. 'You have as many fools here as in any other tribe, but it doesn't matter what they think.' He waved a dismissive hand at the feasters. 'Do the gods seek the opinion of these fools before they send rain? Of course they don't, so why should you or I? It only matters that they obey.'

Kereval quickly diverted the conversation, talking instead about the change in the weather, and Saban looked about the firelit hall. Most of the men had drunk enough of the Outfolk's famously fierce liquor to be loud and boisterous. Some were arguing about hunting exploits while others bellowed for silence so they could listen to the flautist whose thin notes were being overwhelmed by the uproar. Women slaves brought in food and drink, and then Saban saw who sat beyond the hall's farther fire and his world changed.

It was a moment when his heart seemed to cease its beating, when the world and all its noises – the rain on the thatch, the harsh voices, the splintering of burning wood, the airy notes of the flute and the pulse of the drums – vanished. All was suspended in that moment as if there were nothing left but himself and the white-robed girl who sat on a wooden platform at the hall's far end.

At first, when he glimpsed her though the swirling smoke, Saban thought she could not be human for she was so clean. Her robe was white and hung with shining lozenges, while her hair fell in a cascade of shining gold to frame a face that was the palest and most beautiful he had ever seen. He felt a surge of guilt for Derrewyn, a surge that was swept away as he looked at the girl. He stared and stared, motionless, as though he had been struck by an arrow like the one that had flickered through the twilight to kill his father. He did not eat, he refused the liquor that Camaban offered, he just gazed through the smoke at the ethereal girl who seemed to hover above the brawling feast. She did not eat, she did not drink, she did not speak, she just sat enthroned like a goddess.

Camaban's harsh voice sounded in Saban's ear. 'Her name is Aurenna, and she is a goddess. She is Erek's bride, and this feast is to welcome her to the settlement. Is she not beautiful? When you speak to her, you must kneel to her. But if you touch her, brother, you will die. If you even dare to dream of touching her, you will die.'

'She's the sun bride?' Saban asked.

'And she will burn in less than three moons,' Camaban said. 'That's how the sun brides get married. They jump into a fire at the sea's edge. Hiss of fat and splinter of bone. Flame and screaming. She dies. That's her purpose. That's why she lives, to die. So don't stare at her like a dumb calf, because you can't have her. Find yourself a slave girl to rut with because if you touch Aurenna you'll die.'

But Saban could not take his eyes from the sun bride. It would be worth dying, he thought recklessly, just to touch that golden girl. He guessed she was fourteen or fifteen summers old, the same age as himself, a bride in her perfection, and Saban was suddenly assailed by a gaping sense of loss. First Derrewyn, and now this girl. Had Miyac, Haragg's daughter, presided over a feast like this? Had she been as beautiful? And had some young man gazed at her with longing before she went to the flames at the sea's edge?

And then his thoughts were broken as the leather curtain in the wide doorway was snatched aside so violently that it tore from the wooden pegs holding it to the lintel. A gust of chill damp wind flickered the two fires as a tall, gaunt and wild-haired man strode into the hut. 'Where is he?' he shouted, his wolf pelt cloak dripping rainwater.

Haragg, thinking the wild-haired man sought him, stood, but the newcomer just spat at Haragg and turned on Kereval instead. 'Where is he?' he shouted. Three other men had followed him into the hut – all priests, for they had bones woven into their beards.

'Where is who?' Kereval asked.

'Lengar's brother!'

'Both Lengar's brothers are here,' Kereval said, gesturing at Camaban and Saban, 'and both are my guests.'

'Guests!' the wild man sneered, then he threw his arms wide and turned to stare at the feasters who had fallen silent. 'There should be no guests in Sarmennyn,' he cried, 'and no feasts, no music, no dances, no joy until the treasures are returned to us! And those things' – he whipped round to point a bony finger at Saban and Camaban – 'those two bits of dirt can bring Erek's gold back.'

'Scathel!' Kereval shouted. 'They are guests!'

Scathel pushed past the seated men and stared down at Saban and Camaban, frowning when he saw the bones tied into Camaban's hair. 'Are you a priest?' he demanded.

Camaban ignored the question. He yawned instead, and Scathel suddenly bent and seized Saban's tunic and, with an astonishing strength in a man so thin and bony, pulled him upright. 'We shall use the brother magic,' he told Kereval.

'He is a guest!' Kereval protested again.

'The brother magic?' Camaban asked in a tone of genuine enquiry. 'Tell me of this magic.'

'What I do to him,' Scathel said, digging a finger into Saban's ribs, 'will be done to his brother also. I take his eye; Lengar loses an eye.' He slapped Saban. 'There,' he crowed, 'Lengar's cheek is stinging.'

'Mine isn't,' Camaban said.

'You are a priest,' Scathel said, explaining why Camaban had failed to feel Saban's pain.

'No,' Camaban said, 'I am no priest, but a sorcerer.'

'A sorcerer who does not know the brother magic?' Scathel jeered. 'What kind of sorcerer is that?' He laughed, then turned Saban around so that all the hall could see

216

him. 'Lengar of Ratharryn will never yield the treasures!' he shouted. 'Not if we give him every temple in Sarmennyn! Not if we take every stone from every field and lay them at his feet! But if I take his eyes, his hands, his feet and his manhood, then he will yield.'

The listening men beat their hands on the floor in approval and Camaban, watching silently, saw how much opposition there was in Kereval's tribe to the agreement with Lengar. They did not believe Ratharryn would ever yield the gold. They had agreed to the bargain for, at the time, there had seemed no alternative, but now Scathel had come roaring from the hills and proposed using magic, torture and sorcery. 'We shall dig a pit,' Scathel said, 'and drop this louse inside, and there he shall stay shut up until his brother yields us the treasures!' The feasters shouted their approval.

'Put my brother in a pit,' Camaban said when there was silence, 'and I shall fill your bladder with coals, so that when you piss you will writhe from the agony of liquid fire.' He leaned over and took a morsel of fish from Kereval's bowl and calmly ate it.

'You? A crippled sorcerer? Threaten me?' Scathel gestured at Camaban's left foot, which was still misshapen, though no longer grotesquely clubbed. 'You think the gods listen to things like you?'

Camaban took a fishbone from his mouth, then delicately bent it between a thumb and forefinger. 'I will make the gods dance on your entrails,' he said quietly, 'while dead souls suck your brains out of your eye-sockets. I shall feed your liver to the ravens and give your bowels to the dogs.' He snapped the bone in two. 'Let my brother go.'

Scathel leaned down to Camaban, and Saban, watching,

thought how alike the two men were. The Outfolk sorcerer, Haragg's twin brother, was the older man, but like Camaban he was lean, gaunt and powerful. 'He will go in the pit tonight, cripple,' Scathel hissed at Camaban, 'and I will piss on him.'

'You will let him go!' a woman's voice commanded, and there was a gasp in the hall as the men turned to look at Aurenna. She was standing, pointing a finger at the angry priest. 'You will release him,' she insisted, 'now!'

Scathel quivered for a heartbeat, but then he swallowed and reluctantly released his grip on Saban. 'You risk losing everything!' he said to Kereval.

'Kereval does Erek's will,' Camaban said, still quietly, answering for the chief, and then he leaned forward and dropped the two scraps of fishbone into the fire. 'I have long wanted to meet you, Scathel of Sarmennyn,' he went on, smiling, 'for I had heard much of you and thought, fool that I am, that I might learn from you. I see, instead, that I will have to teach you.'

Scathel looked into the fire where the two slivers of bone lay on a burning log. For a heartbeat he stared at them, then he reached down and carefully picked them up, one after the other; the hairs on his arm shrivelled in the flames and there was a rank smell of burning flesh that made men wince, but Scathel did not flinch. He spat on the bones, then pointed one at Camaban. 'You will never take one of our temples, cripple, never!' He flicked the bone scraps at Camaban, plucked the damp wolf pelts close about his thin body and walked away leaving the feast hall in silence.

'Welcome to Sarmennyn,' Camaban said to Saban.

'What am I doing here?' Saban demanded.

'I will tell you tomorrow. Tomorrow I give you a new life. But tonight, my brother, if you can, eat.' And he would say no more.

Next day, in the fresh swirling wind that followed the night's rain, Camaban led Haragg, Saban and Cagan to the Sea Temple. It lay a fair walk west of the settlement on a low rocky headland where the sea broke white. Cagan would not go near the temple where his sister had died, but cowered in some nearby rocks, whimpering, and Haragg soothed his huge son, patting him like a small child and crooning to him even though Cagan could hear nothing. Then Haragg left Cagan in his cleft of stone and followed the brothers to the deserted temple, which was loud with the plaintive calls of the white birds.

The temple was a simple ring of twelve stones, each about a man's height, while from the ring a short corridor flanked by a dozen smaller stones led to the cliff's edge. The cliff was neither high nor sheer and just beyond its upper edge, and not far beneath it, was a wide ledge heaped with timber. 'They've already begun stacking the fire,' Haragg said in disgust.

'Kereval tells me they're making the fire bigger this year,' Camaban said. 'They want to make sure this girl dies quick.' The wind lifted his hair and rattled the small bones tied to the fringes of his tunic. He looked at Saban. 'The girl is stripped inside the circle, then waits till the sun touches the sea when she must walk the stone avenue and leap into the flames. I watched it last year,' he went on, 'and the girl took fright. Tried to jump straight through

219

the fire.' He laughed at the memory. 'What a death she had!'

'So they don't go willingly?' Saban asked.

'Some do,' Haragg said. 'My daughter did.' The big man was weeping now. 'She walked to her husband as a bride should and she smiled every step of the way.'

Saban shuddered. He looked at the cliff's edge and tried to imagine Haragg's daughter stepping into the blazing fire. He heard her scream, saw her long hair flare brighter than the sun she would marry, and suddenly he wanted to cry for Aurenna. He could not shake her face from his thoughts.

'And Miyac's burned bones were pounded to powder and scattered on the fields,' Haragg went on. 'And for what? For what?' He shouted the last two words.

'For the good of the tribe,' Camaban replied sourly, 'and you were a priest then, and you'd burned other men's daughters without scruple.'

Haragg flinched as if he had been struck. He was much older than Camaban, but he bowed his head as if accepting the younger man's authority. 'I was wrong,' he said simply.

'Most people are wrong,' Camaban said. 'The world is stuffed with fools, which is why we must change it.' He motioned for Haragg and Saban to squat, though he stayed standing like a master addressing his pupils. 'Lengar has agreed to return Erek's gold if Sarmennyn gives him a temple. He made that agreement because he believes no temple can be moved to Ratharryn, but we are going to prove him wrong.'

'Take this temple,' Haragg said, nodding at the Sea Temple's stark pillars.

'No,' Camaban said. 'We shall find Sarmennyn's best temple and take that one.'

'Why?' Saban asked.

'Why?' Camaban snapped at him. 'Why? Slaol sent Ratharryn his gold. That is a sign, fool, that he wants something of us. What does he want? He wants a temple, of course, because temples are where the gods touch the earth. Slaol wants a temple, and he wants it in Ratharryn, and he sent us gold from Sarmennyn to show us where the temple must come from. Is that so very hard to understand?' He gave Saban a pitying look, then began pacing up and down the short turf. 'He wants a temple from Sarmennyn because here Slaol is worshipped above all the other gods. Here the people have glimpsed part of the truth, and that truth we must carry to the heartland. But there is a greater truth.' He stopped his pacing and stared at his two listeners with a fierce expression. 'I have seen to the heart of all things,' he said softly, then waited for either man to challenge him, but Haragg was just watching him with a worshipful face and Saban had nothing to say.

'The priests believe the world is fixed,' Camaban went on scornfully. 'They believe that nothing changes and that if we obey their rules and make our sacrifices, then nothing will ever change. But the world is changing. It has changed. The pattern is broken.'

'The pattern?' Saban said. Haragg had mentioned the pattern in the north country, but would not explain it. Now Camaban would tell him.

To do so Camaban stooped and plucked an arrow from Saban's quiver, for Saban went nowhere without his yew bow, which was a symbol that he was no longer a slave.

Camaban used the arrow's flint point to scratch a wide circle in the turf, gouging it so that the soil showed brown through the sallow grass. He said, 'The circle is the sun's year. We know that circle. We mark it. Here in Sarmennyn they kill a girl each midsummer to show when one circle ends and the same circle begins again. Do you understand that?' He was looking at Saban for Haragg already knew of the broken pattern.

'I understand,' Saban said. At Ratharryn they also marked the circle's end and beginning at midsummer, though they did it by killing a heifer at sunrise rather than a girl at sunset.

'Now for the mystery,' Camaban said, and he gouged a much smaller circle, placing it on the larger scratched ring like a bead on a bronze wire circlet. 'That is Lahanna,' he said, tapping the small circle. 'She is born, she grows' – he was tracing his finger about the bead – 'and dies again. Then she is born again' – he made a new circle, the same size as the first and next to it – 'she grows and dies, and then is born again.' He scratched a third circle. What Camaban had drawn now looked like three beads that almost, but not quite, filled one quadrant of the big circle of the sun. 'She is born, she dies,' he said again and again, drawing more circles until he had made twelve beads, and then he stopped. 'You see?' he said, pointing the arrow's head to the gap between the last and the first bead.

The circle now had twelve beads. 'Twelve moons in each year,' Camaban said, 'but the mystery is here.' He tapped the small space that was left between the first and the last of the moon circles.

Haragg turned to Saban, eager that he should understand. 'The moon's year is shorter than the sun's year.'

Saban understood that. The priests at Ratharryn, indeed priests everywhere, had long noted that the moon's year of twelve swellings and shrinkings was shorter than the sun's great circuit about the sky, but Saban had never thought much about the disparity. It was one of life's constant mysteries, like why stags only wore antlers for part of the year, or where the swallows went in winter. He watched now as Camaban brought a human thigh bone from his bag.

'When I was a child,' Camaban said, 'I sat in our Old Temple and watched the sky. I would go to the Death Place and steal bones, and I would mark the bones like this one.' He gave the bone to Saban. 'Look,' he instructed him, pointing to a series of small marks that had been cut into one long side of the bone. 'Those marks are the days of the sun's year.'

Saban had to hold the bone close, for the marks were tiny, but he could see hundreds of nicks, far too many to count, and each tiny scratch marked a day and a night, adding to a year. 'And these marks' – Camaban showed Saban a second set of scratches that lay parallel to the first – 'are the days of the moon's growing and dying. They show twelve births and twelve deaths.' The second set of marks was fractionally shorter than the first.

Saban again held the bone close to his eyes and used his fingernail to count the extra days on the sun's line. 'Eleven days?' he asked.

'So far as I can tell,' Camaban said. His scornful tone was gone, replaced by an earnest humility. 'But the days are hard to count. I used many bones over many years, and sometimes there was too much cloud and I had to guess the days of the moon, and some years the gap came to more than eleven, and sometimes it was less.' He took the bone back from Camaban. 'But this bone came from the best year, and it tells the same message as all the bones. It tells me that the pattern is broken.'

'The pattern?'

'The circles should meet!' Camaban said fiercely, tapping the diagram he had scratched into the turf. 'That gap' – he put his finger on the space between the beads – 'is eleven days long. But it should not be there.' He stood again and began to pace. 'To everything in the world there is a purpose,' he said, 'for without purpose there is no meaning. And the meaning is in the pattern. Night and day, man and woman, hunter and prey, the seasons, the tides! They all have a pattern! The stars have a pattern. The sun follows a pattern, the moon follows a pattern, but the two patterns are different, and the world is being split into two.' He pointed towards the sea. 'Some patterns follow the sun, others the moon. The crops come and are cut with the sun, but the tides follow the moon – why? And why did Dilan send the gold to Erek?' He used the Outfolk names for the gods of the sea and the sun, then answered his own question fiercely. 'He sent it so that the sun would take the sea tides back into his pattern!'

'Women follow the moon pattern,' Haragg said gloomily.

'They do?' Camaban sounded surprised.

'In their bleeding,' Haragg said, then shrugged, 'or so I'm told.'

'But everything,' Camaban declared, 'everything should follow the sun! All should be regular, but it isn't.' He pointed again at the pattern in the turf. 'The mystery is how to make the pattern right.'

'How?' Saban asked.

'You tell me,' Camaban said, and Saban understood that the question was not lightly asked.

He stared at the pattern. Think of it, he told himself, as beads on a bronze wire and then the answer was obvious. A man could make more beads, smaller ones, and try to thread them until they filled the wire perfectly, but that would be a laborious task. The simple way to make the beads fit was to shorten the wire, a task that would be easy for any smith. And if the wire were shortened, the big circle would be smaller and the beads would all touch. 'Slaol must be brought closer to the earth?' Saban suggested diffidently.

'Well done,' Camaban said warmly. 'So what does that tell you?'

Saban thought long and hard, then shrugged. 'I don't know.'

'We tell stories about how Slaol and Lahanna loved each other and then became enemies, but those are just stories. They leave something out. Us. Why are we here? We know that the gods made us, but why? Why do we make things? You make a bow – to kill. You make a pot – to hold things. You make a brooch – to fasten a cloak. So we were made for a purpose, but what was that purpose?' He waited for an answer, but neither Haragg nor Saban spoke. 'And why are we flawed?' Camaban asked. 'Would you make a bow that was weak? Or a pot that was cracked? We were not made flawed! The gods would not have made us flawed any more than a potter would make a bowl that was cracked or a smith would make a knife that was blunt, yet we are sick, we are maimed and we are twisted. The gods made us perfect, and we are flawed. Why?' He paused before offering the answer: 'Because we offended Slaol.'

'We did?' Saban asked. He was accustomed to the story that Lahanna had offended Slaol by trying to dim his brightness, but Camaban was now blaming mankind.

'We offended him by worshipping the lesser gods as fervently as we worshipped him,' Camaban said. 'We insulted him, and so he moved away, and now we must draw him back by worshipping him as he is supposed to be worshipped, by giving him his proper place above all the other gods, and by building him a temple that will show him we have understood his pattern. Then he will come back, and when he returns there will be no more winter.'

'No more winter?' Saban asked in astonishment.

'Winter is Slaol's punishment,' Camaban explained. 'We offended him and so he punishes us each and every year. How? By moving away from us. How do we know that? Because the farther you stand from a fire, the less heat you feel. In summer, when Slaol is near us, we feel his heat, but in winter, when things die, his heat goes. It goes because he is far from us, so if we can bring him back then there will be no more winter.' He turned and faced the sun. 'There will be no more winter,' he said again, 'and no more sickness, and no more grief, and no more children crying in the night.' There were tears in his eyes, and Saban remembered the night when Camaban's mother had died and the crooked child had howled like a wolf cub.

'And no more girls will leap into the flames,' Haragg said quietly.

'And you' – Camaban ignored Haragg's words as he turned to Saban – 'will not be a warrior.' He took the yew bow from Saban's shoulder and, with an effort that made him grimace, snapped the stave across his knee. He flung the broken bow across the cliff top so that it fell into the sea. 'You will be a builder, Saban, and you will help Haragg move the temple from Sarmennyn to Ratharryn and so bring the god back to us.'

'If my brother permits it,' Haragg said, speaking of Scathel.

'In time,' Camaban said confidently, 'Scathel will join us, because he will understand that we have seen the truth.' He dropped to his knees and bowed to the sun. 'We have seen the truth,' he said humbly, 'and we shall change the world.'

Saban felt the excitement. They would change the world. At that moment, poised above the sea, he knew that they could.

Aurenna, in the time between her elevation to a goddess and her death in the sun's fire, was expected to tour the country and hear the people's prayers that she would carry to her husband. She left Kereval's settlement escorted by four spearmen to guard her, two women to attend her, three priests to guide her and a dozen slaves to serve her, as well as by a crowd of other folk who just wanted to follow the footsteps of the sun bride.

Kereval ruled a land greater in size than Ratharryn's holdings, though it was more thinly settled for Sarmennyn's soil was hard; it was Aurenna's duty to show herself to all the tribe and to the dead in their communal mounds. Each night a hut was cleared of its folk and animals so that the sun bride could sleep in privacy and each morning there was a huddle of petitioners waiting outside the hut.

Women begged her to grant them sons, parents pleaded with her to heal their children, warriors asked her to bless their spears and fishermen bowed as she touched their boats and nets. The priests led her from temple to temple and from grave mound to grave mound. They opened the graves, shoving their vast entrance stones aside so that Aurenna could stoop into their cave-like interiors and talk to the dead whose bones lay jumbled in the damp shadows.

Camaban and Saban also accompanied her, following the golden girl to the sheltered valleys on Sarmennyn's south coast where the people farmed and took their long wooden fishing boats out to sea, and then up into the high, bare land of the north where cattle, sheep and the making of stone axes gave a poor living to scattered homesteads. And wherever they went Camaban inspected the temples, looking for the one he wanted moved to Ratharryn. The people, recognising him as a sorcerer, bowed. 'Can you make magic?' Saban asked him one day.

'I turned you into a slave, didn't I?' Camaban retorted.

Saban looked at the scar on his hand. 'That was cruel,' he said.

'Don't be absurd,' Camaban said wearily. 'How else was I to keep you alive? Lengar wanted to kill you, which was entirely the sensible thing to do, but I hoped you might prove useful to me. So I fed him a nonsensical tale about the gods taking revenge on those who killed their half-brothers, then gave him the idea of enslaving you. He liked that. And I wanted you to meet Haragg.'

'I like him,' Saban said warmly.

'You like most people,' Camaban said scornfully. 'Haragg is quite clever,' he went on, 'but you can't trust all his ideas. He's absurdly influenced by his daughter's death! He distrusts ritual, but there's nothing wrong with ritual. It shows the gods that we recognise their power. If we took notice of Haragg's ideas we wouldn't burn Aurenna to death and what is the point of the girl's existence if it isn't to burn?'

Saban looked ahead to where Aurenna walked between her attendant priests. He hated Camaban at that moment, but he said nothing, and Camaban, who knew exactly what his brother was thinking, laughed.

That afternoon they came to another temple, this one a simple circle of five stones that was typical of the shrines in the northern part of Sarmennyn. A few, very few, had as many as a dozen stones, but none of the boulders was as large as those that stood within Cathallo's walls. Sarmennyn's stones were rarely taller than a man nor any thicker than a man's waist, but nearly all of them were squared into trim pillars.

Camaban liked none of the shrines they saw. 'We want a temple that will astonish,' he told Saban. 'We have to find a temple that will tell Slaol we have made a great effort on his behalf. What's the achievement in moving four or five little rocks to Ratharryn?'

Saban reckoned that moving just one stone would be an achievement, and he had begun to doubt that Camaban would ever find the temple he wanted. 'Why don't you just pick any temple?' he asked one night. 'Slaol will know how much effort we made to move it.'

'If I wanted the job done quickly and carelessly,' Camaban said, 'I would have let you find a temple rather than waste my own time searching. Don't be absurd, Saban.' They were eating in a crowded hut where Aurenna's attendants had been greeted with gifts of fish, meat, pelts and pots of liquor. One pot of the liquor could steal a man's brains and legs, though Camaban always seemed unaffected. He drank it like water, belched, drank more, and never slurred his words nor staggered; in the morning, when Saban's head was throbbing and sour, Camaban would be full of energy.

That night they were in the hut of a clan chief, the lord of all his kin whose huts were huddled in the lee of a mountain. The chief was a toothless old man who, in honour of Aurenna's coming, wore a circle of gold about his scrawny neck. His wives had stirred a foul mess of seaweed and shellfish over a smoky fire and when the meal was eaten one of his sons, who looked as old and toothless as his father, took down the polished shell of a sea-turtle that hung from a rafter and used it to beat out a rhythm while he chanted an apparently endless song about his father's exploit in crossing to the land across the western sea where he had slaughtered many enemies, taken many slaves and brought home much gold. 'What it probably means,' Camaban said to Saban, 'is that the old fool wandered up the beach for three days and came back with a couple of striped pebbles and a gull's feather.'

Folk came from the other huts while the chant continued. More and more packed themselves in until Camaban and Saban were crammed against the hut's low stone wall. The people must have heard the tale many times, for they often joined in the chant and the old man nodded happily whenever such a chorus sounded, but then, quite suddenly, the drumbeat and the chanting ended. The old man opened his eyes and looked indignant at the silence until he saw that Aurenna, who had eaten in the privacy of her own hut, had just entered. The clan chief smiled and indicated that the sun bride could sit beside him, but Aurenna shook her head, peered about the hut, then stepped delicately through the press of bodies to sit beside Saban. She nodded to the chanter, indicating he could begin again, and the man tapped his turtle-shell, closed his eyes and picked up his story's thread.

Saban was acutely conscious of Aurenna's proximity. He had spoken to her a few times while they walked Sarmennyn's rough paths, but she had never sought his company and her arrival at his side made him clumsy, shy and tongue-tied. It hurt him even to look at Aurenna for the thought of what must happen to her in a brief time. Her fate and Derrewyn's had become tangled in his mind so that it seemed to him that Derrewyn's soul had entered Aurenna's body and now must be snatched from him again. He closed his eyes and bent his head, trying to will away the thoughts of Derrewyn's rape and Aurenna's impending death.

Then Aurenna leaned close to him so that he would hear her voice above the chanter's song. 'Have you found your temple?' she asked.

'No,' he said, shaking with nervousness.

'Why not?' Aurenna asked. 'You must have seen a new temple every day?'

'They're too small,' Saban answered, blushing. He did not look at her for fear that he would stammer.

'And how will you move your temple?' Aurenna asked. 'Will you have the god make it fly to Ratharryn?'

Saban shrugged. 'I don't know.'

'You should talk to Lewydd,' she said, indicating one of her guardian spearmen who was squatting beside the hut's central post. 'He says he knows how it can be done.'

'If Scathel ever lets us take a temple,' Saban said gloomily.

'I shall defeat Scathel,' Aurenna said confidently.

Saban dared to look into her eyes then. They were dark, though the flicker of firelight was reflected in them, and he suddenly wanted to weep because she was going to die. 'You'll defeat Scathel?' he asked.

'I hate him,' she said softly. 'He spat at me when I was first taken to my temple. That's why I wouldn't let him put you in the pit. So when I go to the fire I shall tell my husband that he is to let you take a temple to Ratharryn.' She looked away from Saban as another man took the turtle-shell drum and started another song, this one in praise of the sun bride herself. Aurenna listened intently as a compliment to the singer as he began by describing the sun god's loneliness and his yearning for a human bride, but when he moved on to describe the sun bride's beauty Aurenna seemed to lose interest for she leaned close to Saban again. 'Is it true that in Ratharryn you do not send the god a bride?'

'No.'

'Nor in Cathallo?'

'No.'

Aurenna sighed, then gazed at the fire. Saban stared at her, while her guards watched him. 'Tomorrow' – Aurenna swayed close to Saban again – 'I must start back towards Kereval's settlement, but you should climb the hill behind this place.'

'Why?'

'Because there is a temple there,' she said. 'The folk here told me of it. It is Scathel's new temple, the one he built when he was recovering from his madness. He says he will dedicate it when the treasures are returned.'

Saban smiled, thinking how angry Scathel would be if he knew that his own new temple might go to Ratharryn. 'We shall look at it,' Saban promised her, though he would rather have stayed with Aurenna – to what purpose, he could not tell. She would be dead soon, dead and gone to her glory in the blazing sky.

Next morning, as a thick fog rolled in from the sea, Aurenna began her southward journey, but Camaban and Saban went north, climbing the hill through the fog's thick whiteness. 'It will be a waste of time,' Camaban grumbled, 'just another tawdry ring of stones,' but he still led Saban up the steep grass and across scree-covered slopes until at last they emerged from the cloud into glorious sunlight. They were now above the fog that lay all about them like a white and silent sea in which the mountain's peak was an island of splintered rock, as tangled and jagged as if a god had hammered the summit in a rage. Saban saw now why all the pillars of Sarmennyn's temples were alike for the rock, shattering from the peak, fell in naturally square shafts and all a man needed to make a temple was to carry the split rock down the mountainside.

There was no temple in sight, but Camaban guessed it lay somewhere in the thick fog beneath and so he sat on a stone ledge to wait. Saban paced up and down, then asked Camaban, 'Why would we want Scathel's temple if Scathel is an enemy?'

'He's no enemy of mine.'

Saban sneered at that. 'Then what is he?'

'He's a man like you, brother,' Camaban said, 'a man who hates things to change. But he is a good servant of

Slaol and in time he will be our friend.' He turned and looked eastwards where the peaks of other mountains stood like a line of islands above the whiteness. 'Scathel wants Slaol's glory, and that is good. But what do you want, brother? And don't say Aurenna,' he added, 'for she'll be dead soon.'

Saban blushed. 'Who says I do want her?'

'Your face says so. You stare at her like a thirsty calf gazing at an udder.'

'She's beautiful,' Saban said.

'So was Derrewyn, but what does beauty matter? In a dark hut at night, how can you tell? Never mind, tell me what you want.'

'A wife,' Saban said, 'children. Good crops. Plentiful deer.'

Camaban laughed. 'You sound just like our father.'

'And what's wrong with that?' Saban asked defiantly.

'Nothing is wrong with that,' Camaban said wearily, 'but what a little ambition it is! You want a wife? Then find one! Children? They come whether you want them or not, and half will break your heart and the other half will die. Crops and deer? They're there now.'

'So what do you want?' Saban asked, stung by his brother's scorn.

'I told you,' Camaban said calmly. 'I want everything to change, and then nothing will change, for we shall reach the point of balance. The sun won't wander and there will be no more winter and no more sickness and no more tears. But to do that we must make Slaol a proper temple, and that is what I want. A temple that does Slaol honour.' With those words he suddenly fell silent and stared, wide-eyed, into the fog beneath, and Saban turned to see what had attracted his brother's attention.

At first he could only see fog, but then, slowly, as the land appears when the night drains, a shape emerged in the whiteness.

And what a shape. It was a temple, but unlike any Saban had ever seen. Instead of one circle of stones it had two, one set inside the other, and at first Saban could only see the dark tips of those stones in the vapour. He tried to count the pillars, but there were too many, and at the double circle's farther side, looking towards the place on the skyline where the winter sun would set, there was an entrance made from five pairs of stone pillars that had other stones laid crosswise on their tops to make a row of five doorways for the dying sun. Saban stared, and for a magical time the whole temple seemed to float in the vapour and then the fog drained from the high valley to leave the stones rooted in the dark earth.

Camaban was standing now, his mouth open. 'Scathel was not mad,' he said quietly, then he gave a cry and leaped off the rocks and hurried down the hill, scattering dark-fleeced sheep as he went. Saban followed more slowly, then edged between the twin rings of stone to find Camaban crouched at the temple's north-eastern side where he was peering into the tunnel made by the lintelled stones. 'Slaol's gates,' Camaban said in wonder.

The temple was built in a high hanging valley that overlooked the low country to the south and, at midwinter, when the sun was on that far horizon, it would shine across the sea and land to pierce the gates of stone. 'All else would be dark,' Camaban said softly, 'all would be shadowed by the stones, but in the shadow's centre would be a shaft of light! It's a temple of shadows!' He hurried to the stone opposite the entrance and there, facing the sun's gateway, he spread his arms and flattened himself against the rock as though the light of the dying sun was pinning him to the boulder. 'Scathel is magnificent!' he cried. 'Magnificent!'

The pillars, naturally square, were not large. Those in the sun's gate were a little taller than Camaban, but the rest were shorter than a man and some were no higher than a toddling child. All the rocks had been prised or lifted from the shattered mountain top and slid down the steep slope to this flat patch of high hanging land where they had been shallowly rooted in the thin soil. Saban pushed against one stone and it rocked dangerously. The stone against which Camaban stood was actually two pillars, both too thin, but they had been joined together by carving a groove in one long side and sculpting a tongue in the other so that the two stones fitted like a man fits to a woman. 'Two halves of the circle,' Camaban said reverently, noticing the jointed stones. 'The sun side' – he gestured to the south, indicating the stones over which the sun would travel in its daily path – 'and the night side, and they're joined here, and the joint must be sealed with blood at the sun's dying.'

'How do you know?' Saban asked. He had been counting the stones, and had already numbered more than seventy.

'How else?' Camaban asked curtly. 'It's obvious.' He whirled around in his excitement. 'The Sea Temple for midsummer and the Temple of Shadows for the winter! Scathel is marvellous! But this one will be ours. It will be ours!' He began walking around the circle, cracking his staff against the stones until he reached the lintelled gate where he stooped to gaze through the tunnel of five stone arches. 'A doorway for Slaol,' he said in wonder, then straightened and wiped the nearest stone. The fog's moisture had left the rocks with a strange blue-green sheen that began to fade to black as the spring sun and the sea wind dried them. Camaban, to Saban's horror, tried to push one of the lintels as if hoping to topple it, but it would not move. 'How do they fix it?' he asked.

'How would I know?'

'I don't suppose you would,' Camaban said carelessly, then frowned. 'Did I tell you Sannas is dead?'

'No.' Saban was oddly shocked, not because he had any fondness for the old woman, but because as long as he had lived she had been a part of his world, and not just any part, but a forbidding presence. 'How?' he asked.

'How would I know?' Camaban retorted. 'She just is. A trader brought the news, and she was an enemy of Slaol so it's good news.' He turned to gaze again at the temple. Now, freed of the fog's moisture, it was a black double ring in a black valley crouched in the mountain's black-rocked grip. It was wide and splendid, a mad priest's tribute to his god, and Camaban had tears in his eyes. 'It is our temple,' he said reverently, 'and it will banish winter.'

Somehow they had to persuade Scathel to let them take it, then carry it halfway across the world to Ratharryn.

The thick fog that had shrouded the Temple of Shadows gave way to days of warm sun and calm winds. Old folk marvelled at that early summer, saying they could not remember its like, while Kereval claimed that the weather's kindness was a sign of the sun god's approval of his new bride. Some of the fishermen, who kept a small salt-reeking hut beside the river where they made offerings to a weather god called Malkin, made dire prophecies of storms, but day after day their pessimism was confounded. Kereval's favourite sorceress, a blind woman who uttered her wisdom while in the throes of violent fits, also predicted storms, but the skies stayed stubbornly clear and the winds light.

Kereval's feared warriors made their summer raids into the neighbouring territories to bring back slaves and livestock; traders came from the land across the western sea bringing gold; and the growing crops greened the land. All was well in Sarmennyn, or should have been, except that when Camaban and Saban returned to Kereval's settlement they found the folk sullen.

It was Scathel's return that had soured Sarmennyn. The high priest raged and preached against Kereval's agreement with Ratharryn, claiming that Lengar would never return the treasures unless he was forced and so, while Camaban and Saban were travelling with Aurenna, the high priest had dug a monstrous hole in front of Kereval's hut and placed above it a lattice of stout branches so that the pit could serve as a prison-cage for Saban. There Scathel could torture Saban, confident that every mutilation would be magically visited on Lengar, but Scathel's hopes were frustrated by Kereval who refused to give his permission. Kereval stubbornly insisted that Lengar would return the treasures and the chief liked to point to the bright sky and ask what better omen the tribe could wish. 'The god loves his bride already,' Kereval claimed, 'and when she goes to him, he will reward us. There is no need for the brother magic to be used.'

Yet Scathel constantly preached the need for Saban's eyes to be gouged out and for his hands to be lopped off. He toured the huts inside the settlement and visited the homesteads that lay within a half-day's journey and he harangued Sarmennyn's people, and the folk listened to him. 'Ratharryn will never take a temple from us!' Scathel ranted, 'Never! The temples are ours, built by our ancestors, made from our stone! If Ratharryn wants a temple, let them pile their own dung and bow to it!'

'If your brother were to send us some of the gold, it would help,' Kereval told Camaban wistfully, but Camaban shook his head and said that that had never been part of the agreement. The gold would come, he said, when the temple was moved, though he took care not to say that it was Scathel's own shrine he wanted for the tribe's passions were already running too high. Kereval did his best to calm the growing anger. 'Folk will calm down when they see the sun bride go in her glory,' the worried chief assured Saban.

Day after day Saban would visit the sun-bride's temple and watch the shadow of the tall outlying stone. He feared that shadow, for it crept ever closer to the centre stone, and when the shadow touched the stone Aurenna must go to the flames. Aurenna herself avoided the temple, as if by ignoring the shadow she might lengthen her life; instead, in those days as she waited for her wedding, she was drawn to Haragg. 'When you go to your husband,' he would tell her, 'you must persuade him to stop the waste. He must reject the brides!' But Haragg could no more persuade the tribe to abandon their yearly sacrifice than Kereval could persuade them that Lengar would keep faith, so Aurenna would have to die. As the days grew longer she spent more time with Haragg and Saban, and Haragg left them together for he understood that Aurenna was attracted to the tall, dark-haired young man who had come out of the heartland with a missing finger and a single blue tattoo on his chest. Other young men boasted of their killing scars, but instead of boasting Saban told Aurenna stories. At first he told her the same stories his own mother had told him, like the tale of Dickel, the brother of Gar-lanna, who had tried to steal the earth's first harvest and how Garlanna had turned him into a squirrel as punishment. Aurenna liked the stories and was ever hungry for more.

The two were never alone for the sun bride was always guarded. She could go nowhere except into the privacy of her own hut without being dogged by the four spearmen and so Saban became used to her guardians and even befriended one of them. Lewydd was a fisherman's son and he had inherited his father's squat build. His chest was broad and his arms hugely strong. 'From the time I could walk,' he told Saban, 'my father made me pull nets. Pull nets and paddle! That makes a man strong.' It was Lewydd who had devised a way of transporting a temple's stones to Ratharryn. 'You must take them by boat,' he said. Lewydd was three years older than Saban and had already gone on two slave-raids deep into the eastern territories. 'Almost all of the journey to Ratharryn can be done on water,' he claimed.

'Ratharryn is far from the sea,' Saban pointed out.

'Not by sea, by river!' Lewydd said. 'You would ride the sea to the river that will carry us to the far edge of Drewenna, and there we would need to carry the boats and the stones to the rivers of Ratharryn. But it can be done.'

The boats at Sarmennyn, like the river craft at Ratharryn, were made from the trunks of old, big trees. There were few woods in Sarmennyn, so the priests would mark certain trees that must be preserved until they grew large enough for the boat-builders and when the trunk was tall enough the tree would be cut down and hollowed out. Lewydd took Saban to sea one day, but Saban hid his head in his hands when the great waves hissed towards him and Lewydd, laughing, turned the boat around and let it run back into the river's calm.

Aurenna liked to cross the river in one of the hollowed-out boats. She and her spearmen would walk in the woods on the eastern bank and inevitably she would seek out a great grey-green boulder that was flecked with sparkling chips and small pink marks, and Aurenna would sit on the rock and watch the river run by. When Saban accompanied her she would ask him to tell her more stories and once he told her how Arryn, god of their valley, had chased Mai, the river goddess, and how she had tried to hinder him by turning great stretches of the land into marsh, and how Arryn had felled trees to make paths across the bog and so cornered her at the spring where she rose from the earth. Mai had threatened to turn him to stone, but Arryn had whispered to Lakka, the god of the air, and Lakka had sent a fog so that Mai could not see Arryn, who sprang on her and made her his wife. Still, Saban told her, a mist would rise from Mai's river on cold mornings to remind Arryn that he had only found happiness through trickery.

'Men use trickery,' Aurenna commented.

'Gods too,' Saban said.

'No,' she insisted. 'The gods are pure.' Saban did not argue with her for she was a goddess and he was a mere man.

Sometimes, as Saban talked, he worked. He had found a yew tree in the woods and he had cut a limb and trimmed away the bark and most of the heartwood, and then shaped a great long bow to replace the one Camaban had hurled into the sea. He tipped the bow with notched horn, greased the wood with bull's fat, and Lewydd found him sinews with which to string it and Aurenna cut some strands of her golden hair that he wove into the sinews so that the bowstring glittered like the sunlight. 'There,' she said, laughing, 'you have a goddess's hair on the bow. It can't miss!'

On the day he first strung the bow he seared an arrow clean across the river and deep into the farther woods. Aurenna wanted to try the weapon, but did not have enough strength to pull the string even halfway. Lewydd could draw it fully, but he was used to the Outfolk's short bow and his arrow spun clumsily away to tumble into the stream.

'Tell me another story,' Aurenna commanded Saban and so he told her the tale of Keri, goddess of the woods, who had been loved by Fallag, the god of stone, but Keri had spurned him and so Fallag forever shaped himself into axes that could cut down Keri's trees. And a day or two later, bereft of stories about the gods, Saban told Aurenna about Derrewyn and how he had hoped to marry her, and how Lengar had come from the darkness and loosed an arrow that had changed his life. Aurenna listened to the tale, staring at the river swirling by, and then she looked at him. 'Lengar killed his own father?'

'Yes.'

She shuddered, then frowned for a long while. 'Will Lengar return the treasures?' she asked, breaking the silence.

'Kereval thinks so.'

'Do you?'

Saban did not answer for a long time. 'Only if he is made to,' he confessed at last.

Aurenna flinched at that answer, plainly distressed. 'Erek will force him,' she said.

'Or Scathel will.'

'Who wants to put you in the pit.'

Saban shrugged. 'He will do worse than that.' And then he thought of what must happen to Aurenna within a few days and his heart was suddenly too full and he could not speak. He looked at her, marvelling at the shine of her hair and the curve of her cheek and the sweetness of her pale face, and he was astonished by her serenity. Soon she must burn, but she faced that fate with a placidity that disturbed Saban as much as it impressed him. He ascribed her calmness to her divinity, for he could find no other explanation.

'I shall talk to Erek,' Aurenna said softly, 'and persuade him to make Lengar keep his agreement.'

'Lengar will say that Erek sent him the gold and that he is entitled to keep it.'

'But surely he wants a temple?' Aurenna asked.

Saban shook his head. 'It's Camaban who wants the temple moved. Lengar told me he doesn't believe it's possible. Lengar wants power. He wants to rule a great land and have hundreds of folk bring him tribute. It's Camaban who dreams of bringing the god to earth, not Lengar.'

'So Erek must kill Lengar?'

'I wish he would,' Saban said forcefully.

'I will ask him,' Aurenna said gently.

Saban stared at the river. It was much wider than Mai's river, and it swirled dark where the sea tides pulled and tugged at the current. 'Are you not terrified?' he asked. He had not meant to ask her, but just blurted out the question.

'Of course,' Aurenna said. It was the first time they had spoken of her marriage and now, also for the first time, Saban saw tears in her eyes. 'I don't want to burn for the god,' she said quietly so that the spearmen could not hear her. 'Everyone says it is quick! The fire is so big, so fierce, that there isn't time to feel anything except Erek's embrace, and after that I shall be in bliss. That's what the priests tell me, but I sometimes wish I could live to see the treasures returned.' She paused and gave Saban a wan smile. 'Live to see my own children.'

'Has any sun bride ever lived?' Saban asked.

'One did,' Aurenna answered. 'She leaped through the flames and fell into the sea, and somehow she did not die but came to a beach near the cliff. So they brought her up and pushed her into the fire. But it was a very slow death because the fire was low by then.' She shuddered. 'I have no choice, Saban. I must jump into Erek's fire.'

'You could –' Saban started.

'No!' she said sharply, stopping him before he could say more. 'How can I not do what Erek wants? What would I be if I ran away?' She frowned, thinking. 'From the moment when I can first remember thinking for myself I knew I was meant to be someone special. Not important, not wealthy, but special. The gods want me, Saban, and I must want the same thing that they want. I sometimes dare hope that Erek will spare me and that I can do his work here on earth, but if he wants me at his side then I should be the happiest person ever born.'

He stared down at the rock on which they sat. It glinted in the evening light as though shards of moonshine were trapped in the pale green stone, while the flecks of red made it seem as if blood were imprisoned within the rock. He thought of Derrewyn. He thought of her often, and that worried him, for he did not know how to reconcile those thoughts with his yearnings for Aurenna. Camaban had told him Derrewyn was pregnant and he wondered if she had given birth yet. He wondered if she was reconciled to Lengar. He wondered if she remembered their time before Hengall's death.

'What are you thinking?' Aurenna asked.

'Nothing,' Saban said, 'nothing.'

Next evening Saban joined the priests as they went to

see how far the stone's shadow had crept in Aurenna's temple. Scathel spat at him, then stooped to see that the shadow was still two finger's breadths from the central stone. Saban wanted to take a stone maul and hammer away the pillar's edge, but instead he prayed and knew, even as he pleaded with Slaol, that his prayers were in vain. He watched for omens, but found nothing good. He saw a blackbird fledgling fly and thought it a good augury, but a sparrowhawk stooped and there was a flurry of feathers and a spray of blood.

Midsummer was a day or so away and still the sun shone bright, though the fishermen, laying their offerings of bladderwrack and oarweed before Malkin's shrine, swore that the storm god was stirring. Camaban climbed a hill that was brilliant with milkwort and crimson-spiked orchids and claimed he saw a brownish line on the western horizon, though that far threat did not cause nearly so much excitement as the return of five young men who had been among the war party that had accompanied Lengar to Ratharryn. The five spearmen had made a long journey, skirting hostile tribes by staying in the woods, and all were weak and tired when they reached the settlement.

That night Kereval ordered a feast of welcome, and when the five young warriors had eaten, the folk of the tribe gathered to hear their news. They assembled outside Kereval's great hut, alongside the pit that Scathel had dug for Saban; the tribe's men squatted nearest the storytellers while the women stood behind. They already knew of Lengar's success in taking Ratharryn from his father, but now the five young men spoke of a year of battles that had occurred in the high land between Ratharryn and Cathallo. They said that the forces of Ratharryn, stiffened by the warrior band from Sarmennyn, had inflicted a series of defeats on Cathallo. Eight men from Sarmennyn had died in the skirmishes and another score were injured, and a few men of Ratharryn had suffered, but Cathallo's casualties, the young men said, were innumerable. 'Their great sorceress had died in the winter,' one of the warriors explained, 'and that omen took their hearts away.'

'What of Kital,' Saban asked, 'their chief?'

'Kital of Cathallo died,' the spearman answered. 'He was slaughtered by Vakkal in one of the battles.' The listeners thumped their spear butts on the dry ground to show their pleasure at hearing that a hero of Sarmennyn had killed the enemy's chieftain. 'His successor sent us lavish gifts in hope of peace.'

'Were the gifts accepted?' Kereval wanted to know.

'In return for a settlement called Maden.'

'Where are the gifts?' Scathel asked.

'Half of them have been put aside,' the warrior answered, 'and will be brought to Sarmennyn.'

There was more pleasure at this, but Scathel silenced the approbation by standing to his full height. 'And what of our gold?' he demanded of the five warriors. 'Did Lengar of Ratharryn send any of our gold with you?'

'No,' the young man's leader confessed, 'but he showed it to us.'

'He showed it to you! How kind of him!' Scathel spoke derisively. The high priest had honoured the feast by dressing in a great woollen cloak that had been threaded with hundreds of gull feathers so that he seemed swathed in white and grey. His lank hair was bound with a leather band into which more feathers had been placed, while round his neck he had hung a chain of small bones. 'Erek's gold is being displayed in Ratharryn!' he said scornfully. 'All of it?'

This last question had been snapped in anger and the tone brought an expectant silence to the listening crowd. The five men looked abashed. 'Not all of it,' their leader confessed after a while. 'There were only three of the great pieces.'

'And some of the smaller pieces were gone too,' another of the warriors added.

'Gone where?' Scathel asked in a furious voice.

'Before we arrived,' the first man said, 'those pieces had been given away by Hengall.'

'Given to whom?' Kereval asked, shocked.

'To Cathallo.'

'And you defeated Cathallo?' Scathel roared. 'Did you not demand the return of the gold?'

'They claim the gold has vanished,' the young man said miserably.

'Vanished?' Scathel shouted. 'Vanished!' He turned on Kereval in a blind fury. The chief, Scathel said, had been stupidly trusting. He had believed Lengar's promises, but already part of the precious gold had been scattered like bird dung. And how much more of the gold would be given away? The crowd was all on Scathel's side now. 'Lengar will feel safe soon,' Scathel yelled. 'He has forced his enemy to plead for peace and soon he will not need our men! He'll slaughter them, then keep the gold. But we have him!' He pointed at Saban. 'I can make Lengar of Ratharryn scream for mercy. I can make him sweat at night, I can crease him with pain, I can make boils erupt on his skin, I can blind him! One eye first, and then the second eye, and then his hands, and after that his feet and,

248

last before his life, his manhood. You think Lengar will not pray for eagles to fly our gold back to us as those wounds are torn into his rotting flesh?' The men cheered this speech, thumping their spear butts on the ground.

Kereval held up his hand for silence. 'Did Lengar promise to give us the treasure?' he asked the five warriors.

'He said he would exchange it for our temple,' their leader answered.

'You have chosen a temple?' Kereval asked Camaban.

Camaban looked surprised to be addressed, as though he had been paying no attention to the heated discussion. 'I'm sure we shall find one,' he said casually.

'But if you do find it,' Scathel jeered at Camaban, 'and if you move it, will your brother return our gold?'

Camaban nodded to the priest. 'He has agreed to do that.'

'He agreed,' Scathel said. 'He agreed! But he never told us that part of our gold was already given away! What else is he hiding from us? What else?' And with that question the gaunt priest suddenly crouched and put his head in his hands so that his long hair trailed in the dust. He mewed for a while, writhing in apparent pain, and the crowd held their breath, knowing that he was speaking with Erek. Saban glanced anxiously at Camaban, wondering why his brother did not put on a similar display, but Camaban just yawned again.

Scathel threw his head back and howled at the clear evening sky. The howl shrank into a mewing whimper and the priest's eyes rolled up so that only their whites showed. 'The god speaks,' he gasped in a hoarse voice, 'he speaks!' Saban fought off terror, suspecting only too well what message the god would bring. He looked at Camaban again, but Camaban had picked up a stray kitten and was unconcernedly plucking fleas from its fur. 'We must use blood!' Scathel shrieked, and with those words he flung a hand towards Saban. 'Seize him!'

A dozen warriors competed to hold Saban who had no time to defend himself. Haragg tried to pull some of the men off, but the trader was knocked down by a spear butt. Cagan roared and charged to his father's rescue and it took six men to tackle the mute giant and hold him face down beside the pit. Saban struggled, but the spearmen held him tight against the wall of Kereval's hut. They ignored the chief's protests for the news that part of Erek's gold had been given away had enraged them.

The high priest shrugged off the gull-feather cloak. He was naked now. 'Erek,' he shouted, 'what I do to this man, do to his brother!'

Saban could do nothing except watch Scathel walk towards him. There was triumph on the priest's face, triumph and excitement, and Saban realised that Scathel was enjoying this cruelty. Camaban was ignoring the confrontation, tickling the kitten's throat while Scathel took a flint blade from one of his priests. 'Take Lengar's eye!' Scathel shouted at the god, then reached out with his left hand and grabbed a handful of Saban's hair. The spearmen held him tighter, and all Saban could do was try to turn away as the flint blade came closer.

'No!' Aurenna's voice called.

The knife quivered like a great shadow at the edge of Saban's sight.

'No!' Aurenna said again. 'Not while I live!'

Scathel hissed and turned on her.

'Not while I live,' she repeated calmly. She had walked

250

through the crowd and now faced Scathel boldly. 'Put the knife down.'

'What is he to you?' Scathel demanded.

'He tells me stories,' Aurenna said. She stared Scathel in the eye, and Saban, who thought the priest was tall, saw that the sun bride was very nearly the same height. She faced him in her white and gold splendour and her back was straight and her face as calm as ever. 'And when I go to my husband,' she told the priest, 'he will send a sign about the gold.'

Scathel's face twisted. He was being given orders by a girl, but the girl was a goddess and he could do nothing except obey and so he forced himself to bow his head and back away. 'Put him in the pit,' he ordered the two spearmen.

But again Aurenna intervened. 'No!' she said. 'He still has tales to tell me.'

'He must go into the pit!' Scathel insisted.

'Not till I leave,' Aurenna said and she stared into Scathel's eyes until the priest gave way. He signalled for the spearmen to let go of Saban's arms.

And next evening the pillar in the sun bride's temple had no shadow for there were thick clouds in the west. But the priests decided the time had come anyway.

In the dawn they would leave for the Sea Temple, and in the evening they would send Aurenna to the fire.

That night the wind rose, tugging at the thatch and thrashing at the trees. Saban lay in his pelt, swathed in misery, and he could have sworn he did not sleep at all, yet even so he did not see or hear Camaban stir in the night's heart and slip silently from the hut.

Camaban went to Malkin's shrine and there prayed to

the weather god. He prayed for a long time as the wind fretted at the settlement's palisade and the small waves of the river were flecked with white. Camaban bowed to the god, kissing the idol's blackened feet, then he went back to Haragg's hut and wrapped himself in a cloak of bear's fur. He listened to Cagan snore, heard Saban whimper in his sleep and he closed his eyes and thought of the temple up in the hills, the Temple of Shadows: he saw it moved as if by magic to the green hill beside Ratharryn, and he saw the sun god poised above the hill, huge and bright and all-embracing, and Camaban began to weep for he knew he could make the world happy if only the fools did not thwart him. And there were so many fools. But then he, too, slept.

Saban was the first to stir in the dawn. He crawled to the hut entrance and saw that the good weather had ended. The wind was whipping the tree tops and grey-black clouds were hurrying low above the hills. 'Is it raining?' Camaban asked.

'No.'

'Did you sleep well?'

'No.'

'I did!' Camaban claimed. 'All night!'

Saban could not stand his brother's cheerfulness and so he went out into the settlement where the newly woken tribe readied themselves for the day and night that lay ahead. They would take bags of food and skins of water to the Sea Temple for the ceremony would last most of the day, and once the bride had gone to the flames they would dance about the temple until the fire had cooled enough for Aurenna's charred bones to be retrieved and pounded into dust.

Kereval, swathed in a cloak of beaver fur and carrying

252

a massive spear with a polished bronze head, ordered his spearmen to open the settlement gate. The warriors had smeared their faces with red ochre and bound their long hair in strips of hide. Today no one would fish. Today nearly all the tribe would go to the Sea Temple. From all across Sarmennyn the folk would gather to send the sun bride on her journey. Haragg watched the preparations and then, unable to endure the sight, abruptly turned away. 'Come hunting with me,' he told Saban.

'Your brother won't let me.' Saban said, nodding to the spearmen who watched him on Scathel's orders. Today Saban would become the high priest's hostage. He wondered why he had not fled eastwards in the night, and he knew it was because of Aurenna. He loved her and he could not leave her, even if by staying he could do nothing to help her.

Haragg and Cagan crossed the river in a log boat and vanished among the trees. A moment later Scathel emerged from Kereval's large hut. The high priest wore his feather cloak that ruffled and shivered in the wind. His hair had been stiffened with red mud, while around his neck hung a chain of sea-monster teeth. At his waist was a belt at which two knives were scabbarded. Leckan, the next most senior priest, was wearing a cape made from tanned human skin and the faces of the two men whose hides had been flayed hung down his back with their long hair trailing. Another priest had antlers on his head. They danced from the hut, and the waiting tribe began to shuffle from side to side. A drummer began to beat a skin and the shuffle took rhythm as someone began to sing. Camaban joined the dance. He was wearing a cloak of deerskin and had smeared his face with strips of soot.

Scathel pointed at Saban. 'Take him!' he ordered, and a dozen of the red-painted warriors closed on Saban with their spears. They herded him to the pit's edge, but before they could throw him into its depths Aurenna appeared.

Her white face was drawn and shadowed, but her tall body was swathed in the fresh woollen robe and the replacement gold glinted at her breast and neck. Her hair had been combed straight, though the wind immediately lifted it as she walked slowly towards the dancing priests. She did not look at Saban, but kept her eyes on the ground, and then, when Scathel summoned her, she turned obediently towards the gate. The crowd sighed and the dancers moved to join the procession that would take her to the Sea Temple.

Scathel nodded to the spearmen guarding Saban and two of them pulled the cloak from his shoulders while a third drew a knife and slashed Saban's tunic from neck to hem, then tugged the garment away so that he was naked. 'Jump,' the spearman ordered.

Saban looked round a last time. Camaban was not looking at him and Aurenna had gone beyond the gate, then one of the impatient spearmen threatened him and so, resigned, he jumped into the prison pit. It was deep and the impact of the fall was painful, and when he stood he saw that he could not reach to the pit's top. The great trellis of branches was placed over his prison and was fixed in place with wooden pegs that were banged into the earth.

Then there was just the sigh of the wind and the sound of the drumming that faded as the tribe left the settlement. One of the two spearmen who had been left to guard Saban dropped a skin of water through the trellis, then went away, and Saban huddled in a corner with his arms about his knees and his head dropped on to a forearm.

Aurenna would die. And he would be tortured, blinded and maimed. Because the gold had gone to Ratharryn.

In Ratharryn the priests had also determined that this day was midsummer and so, as dusk approached, the tribe lit the fires and prepared themselves for the bull-dancing and the flame-jumping. Derrewyn ignored the excitement. She was hunched in a corner of Lengar's hut, hidden from the men by a leather curtain. She was naked. Lengar insisted on it, for he enjoyed humiliating her, calling her the whore of Cathallo. She was Lengar's wife, forced to marry him in Slaol's temple, but in the last moons any of Lengar's friends could summon Derrewyn and she must go to them or else risk a beating, and there were scars on her face, shoulders and arms where they had all drunkenly thrashed her. Jegar had beat her the worst because she mocked him most. She mocked them all, for that had been her best defence. Now she crouched by the curtain, listened to the three men talk and felt the baby stir in her belly. She knew it was Lengar's baby, and she was certain it would be a son. It would be born in two or maybe three moons. The men took less interest in her now that she was pregnant, but still they insulted her. None, however, detected the seething anger that burned within her. They believed they had defeated her.

The three men in the hut, Lengar, Jegar and Vakkal, were talking of Cathallo. Vakkal was the war leader from Sarmennyn who had helped Lengar gain the chieftainship;

he now boasted blue scars like the warriors of Ratharryn and spoke in Ratharryn's tongue. He was another of the men who had been given permission to summon Derrewyn whenever he wished, the privilege of Lengar's friends. Now he listened as Lengar declared Cathallo was ripe for defeat. The tribe had never recovered from Sannas's death and with her had gone the sorcery that Lengar believed had kept Cathallo safe. So in the late summer, Lengar said, Ratharryn should attack Cathallo again, only this time they would leave their enemy's settlement burned. They would pull down its great temple, level the Sacred Mound and piss on the grave mounds of Cathallo's ancestors.

'Are you listening, whore?' Jegar called. Derrewyn did not answer. 'Sullen bitch,' Jegar said, and Derrewyn heard the slurring in his voice and knew he was drinking the Outfolk liquor.

Tonight, Vakkal was saying, they would be burning the sun bride in Sarmennyn.

'Maybe we should burn Derrewyn,' Jegar suggested.

'Slaol wouldn't want her,' Lengar said. 'Give Slaol a whore and he'll turn his back on us.'

'He will not thank us,' Vakkal said, 'if we do not watch his setting tonight.' The fires were already burning in Ratharryn's fields and the bull men were waiting to dance among the wooden poles of Slaol's temple.

'We must go,' Lengar said. 'Stay here, whore!' he called to Derrewyn beyond the curtain and he left one of his young warriors in the hut to guard the treasures that were hidden beneath the floor and under the great piles of precious hides. 'If the whore gives you trouble,' Lengar told the young spearman, 'hit her.'

The spearman settled beside the fire. He was very young, though he already possessed two blue scars to represent the two warriors of Cathallo whom he had slaughtered at a battle on the heights above Maden. Like many of the young men in the tribe he revered Lengar because the new chief had made Ratharryn's spearmen feared and his followers wealthy. The youth dreamed of owning many cattle and wives. He dreamed of a great hut all of his own and of heroic songs sung about his exploits.

A sound made him turn his head and he saw that Derrewyn had appeared at the edge of the curtain. She was kneeling and when the warrior looked at her she dropped her head submissively. She had combed her long hair and hung an amber pendant round her neck, but otherwise she was naked. She kept her eyes lowered and made a whimpering sound as she shuffled forward on her knees. The spearman instinctively looked at the door to see if anyone was watching, but no one was there. Only the very old and the sick were left in Ratharryn; the rest of the folk were at Slaol's temple where the bull men were covering the girls in Slaol's honour.

The spearman watched Derrewyn approach. The fire made the shadows of her small breasts livid and lit her swollen belly. Then she looked up at him and there was an immense sadness in her big eyes. She mewed pitifully, then crept forward into the heat of the fire. The warrior frowned. 'You must go back,' he said nervously.

'Hold me,' she begged him. 'I'm lonely. Hold me.'

'You must go back!' he insisted. He was frightened that her glistening pregnant belly might burst if he used force to push her back behind the curtain.

'Hold me,' she said again, and she edged his spear

257

aside and put her left arm round his neck. 'Please hold me.'

'No,' he said, 'no,' but he was too scared of her to push her away and so he let her pull his head towards hers. He smelt her hair. 'You must go back,' he said, and Derrewyn put her right hand between her thighs where the short bronze-bladed knife was clamped and she ripped the weapon upwards, straight into his belly, and the spearman's eyes widened, then he gasped as she twisted the blade in his guts and jerked it on upwards, through the band of muscle under his lungs and into the tangle of blood tubes about his heart so that she felt the warm gush of his life surge over her wrist and thighs. He tried to push her away, but his strength was gone; she heard the rattle in his throat and saw his eyes turn cloudy and Derrewyn felt the first real joy she had known since Lengar's return. It was as though Sannas's restless spirit had come to fill her and that thought made her go very still, but then the dead man's weight fell onto her and she wrenched the bloody knife free and tilted him sideways so that his head fell in the fire. His hair, greasy because he had wiped his fingers in its strands after eating, crackled and flared bright in the gloom.

Derrewyn was already across the hut. She went to the pile of furs that was Lengar's bed, hauled the pelts aside and began scraping at the soil with the bloody blade. She tore the earth open, delving down until the knife struck leather and then she scrabbled the soil clear and hauled the bag into the firelight.

Inside the bag was one of Sarmennyn's great lozenges and two of their small ones. She had hoped all the gold might be there, but Lengar must have divided the treasure and hidden the other pieces elsewhere in the hut. For a moment she considered tearing the hut apart, upsetting the pelts and scratching at the earth, but these three pieces, surely, would be enough.

She dressed in one of Lengar's tunics, tied leather shoes onto her feet and seized Lengar's precious bronze sword which hung from one of the hut's poles. She took the bag with the three gold pieces and went to the hut's door where she paused. It was still not quite dark, but she could see no one and so she gathered the folds of the tunic and ducked under the lintel.

There were spearmen guarding both the causeways that led through Ratharryn's great embankment, so Derrewyn ran to the ditch halfway between the entrances. There had been rain that summer and the bottom of the ditch was marshy, but she splashed through and then climbed the vast bank. She went slowly so she would meld with the shadows and either the gate guards did not see her or else Lahanna was looking after Derrewyn this night for she reached the embankment's crest undetected. She stopped there for a moment and turned to see that the sun was glinting brilliant through a slit in the dark clouds that otherwise obscured the south-western horizon. The tribe was dancing around the temple poles, while far off, up on the higher land, the new Sky Temple stood deserted again.

She hissed at the sun like a cat. Lengar worshipped Slaol, so Slaol was Derrewyn's enemy, and she crouched above the skulls that topped the embankment and spat at the sun that had turned all the bruised clouds red and gold. Then, quite suddenly, his brightness vanished.

And Derrewyn vanished with him. She slid down the outer bank and through the dark trees until she reached the river where she turned northwards, and as she passed the island where she had first lain with Saban she remembered him, but there was no trace of fondness in the memory. Fondness had been banished from her, along with kindness and laughter and pity, all washed from her by tears. She had become Cathallo's whore and now she would work Cathallo's revenge.

The short midsummer night fell and still she went north.

Later, much later, she heard the hounds baying behind her, but she had taken to the river and hounds cannot follow a spirit across water so Derrewyn knew she was free. She still had to slip past the spearmen who garrisoned Maden and cross the swamps, but she felt confident and strong because Lahanna was shining above her and in her hand she held some of the precious power of the sun god that she would give to Lahanna.

She had escaped, she carried Lengar's child, and now she would make war.

In Sarmennyn it began to rain in the afternoon. The wind was rising, the rain fell heavier and beyond the trellis of branches Saban could see that the sky had become a turbulent grey shot through with black. The wind was flicking the thatch from the huts and the rain began to flood the pit.

When the first thunder sounded Saban put his head back and cried to the god of thunder and then he scrabbled at the dripping wet sides of the pit until he had prised out a sharp-edged stone that he used to make a step in the soil. He hacked a second step, a third, and then tried to climb the steps, but his bare feet slipped on the wet soil and he constantly fell back into the rising water.

He sobbed with frustration, found the stone again and tried to enlarge the steps. The water had risen to his ankles. Rain was thrashing on the trellis and dripping onto his face, the wind was a constant howl and the noise was so loud that he did not hear the splintering as the trellis was lifted clean away from the pit. He only knew he was rescued when a wet cloak was lowered to him and Haragg's voice shouted at him to take hold.

Saban saw Haragg and Cagan in the gloom above him. He gripped the cloak and Cagan lifted him like a child, swinging him up and out of the pit so that he sprawled on the grass. He lay there, wet and shaking, staring into the eye of the storm that had come from the sea to batter and thrash the coast. The trees tossed in the screeching gale while whole armloads of thatch were being torn from the huts and blown beyond the river. There was no sign of the men left to guard Saban.

'We must go,' Haragg said, lifting Saban from the grass, but Saban shook off the trader's hand. Instead he went to Kereval's hut and pushed past the curtain, half expecting to find his guards inside, but the hut was empty and he dried himself by rolling on a great pelt, then pulled on a deerskin tunic.

Haragg had followed him into the hut. 'We must go,' he said again.

'Go where?'

'Far off. There is madness here. We must get you away from Scathel.'

'This is Erek's madness,' Saban said as he helped himself to boots and a cloak and one of Kereval's bronze-bladed

261

spears. 'We must go to the Sea Temple,' he told Haragg.

'To see her die?' Haragg asked.

'To see what sign Erek is sending,' Saban said, and he pushed past the leather curtain into the howling rain. One of the spearmen was now out in the settlement's centre where he was peering into the empty pit. As he turned to shout to his fellow guard he saw Saban and ran at him with his spear levelled. 'You must go into the hole!' he shouted, though his words were snatched away in the wind's fury.

Saban hefted his spear. The guard shook his head, as though to indicate that he had no intention of stabbing Saban, but merely wanted him to go voluntarily to Scathel's pit. Instead Saban began walking to the gate and the guard lunged to head him off and Saban knocked the spear aside. Suddenly he was overcome by all the frustrations of the last few weeks, by the helplessness of watching Aurenna go so placidly to her death, and he drove his own spear back at the guard like a swinging axe so that the blade sliced across the guard's face. Blood started into the wind and was whipped away in a red spray, and Saban, screaming hate, plunged the spear into the man's belly and went on thrusting so that the guard fell back into the mud and Saban had to put his booted foot onto the dying man's belly to tug the blade free.

Then he ran, and Haragg and Cagan followed him.

Saban was not running for fear of the dying man's spirit, but because the long day was already close to dark, though he guessed that darkness was brought by the storm clouds rather than by Slaol's setting. And this, he reckoned, was a storm like that which had brought the gold to Ratharryn, a storm caused by a war among the gods. Saban staggered in the wind's hard blast. The cloak was almost torn from him, flapping at his shoulders like a monstrous bat's wing and he untied the lace at his throat and watched the leather whip away across a land running with water. He struggled on into the rain, near blinded and deafened by the wind.

He came to the hills above the sea and he watched in awe as the ocean tried to break the land to pieces. The waves were ragged, white-crested and large as hills, and their spray burst on rocks then leapt to the black clouds before flying inland on the gale. On Saban went with his head down, stung by salt, buffeting into the wind, and the sky seemed darker than ever. Haragg and Cagan walked with him. There would surely be no last sight of Slaol this day, and perhaps, Saban thought, there would be no sight of Slaol ever again. Perhaps this was the world's ending, and he cried aloud for that thought.

A stab of lightning hissed to the far sea, making all the world white and black, and then a crash of thunder sounded overhead and Saban whimpered in fear of the gods. He was climbing a low hill and another jagged bolt tore from the sky as he reached the crest and in its wicked light he saw the Sea Temple beneath him. At first he thought it was deserted, but then he saw that the crowd of folk had scattered into the fields where they huddled for shelter in tumbled rocks. Only a few men were still in the temple circle and their presence drove Saban on. Haragg and Cagan stayed on the hill crest, sheltering among its boulders.

A great sea tore itself into oblivion at the foot of the cliff and the spray whipped over the cliff's summit to drench the temple stones. On the ledge just below the cliff top, where there should have been a raging fire, there was nothing but wisps of steam or smoke. Priests and spearmen crouched in the stone ring and, as Saban ran closer, he saw Aurenna's white robe among them.

She still lived.

Spearmen carried wood to the cliff's edge and dropped the damp timber on to the failing fire. Scathel was standing and shouting, his robe stripped of its feathers by the wind's rage, and if he saw Saban's arrival he took no notice. Kereval looked aghast, fearing what this omen meant.

Camaban saw Saban, and it was then that Camaban performed the rites. He dragged Aurenna to the beginning of the avenue that led to the fire and he drew a knife from his belt and cut off the pieces of gold that Kereval had bought to replace the lost treasures of Erek. Aurenna seemed in a trance. Scathel pushed against the wind to bellow a protest at Camaban, but Camaban shouted back and it was Scathel who stepped away, and then Saban was beside his brother. 'She must go to the fire!' Camaban shouted.

'There is no fire!'

'She must go to the fire, fool!' Camaban shouted, and he seized the neck of Aurenna's drenched white robe and slashed at it with his knife.

Saban grabbed his brother's hand to stop him, but Camaban shook him off. 'This is how it is done!' Camaban called above the seething fury of the gale. 'And it must be done properly! Don't you understand? It must be done properly!'

And suddenly Saban did understand. Aurenna must do her duty and walk to the fire, and if there was no fire then that was not of her doing. So Saban stepped away and watched as his brother slit down Aurenna's long robe. The heavy wool flapped wildly as it was cut away and then

Camaban tugged at the soaking cloth and tugged again so that it fell to Aurenna's feet and she was naked.

She was naked because that was how a bride went to her husband and now was the time for Aurenna to go to Slaol. Camaban shrieked at her, 'Walk! Walk!' And Aurenna did walk, though it was hard because the elements were fighting against her slender body, but still, and still as if in a trance, she forced herself forward, and Camaban followed a pace behind, urging her on as the horrified priests watched from the temple's stone ring.

Some smoke or steam still came over the cliff top to be snatched into instant nothingness. Saban walked alongside Aurenna, but keeping outside the stones marking the sacred avenue, and the wind seemed fiercer still as she neared the edge. Her feet slipped on the wet turf, her soaked hair streamed behind her, but she obediently bent forward and thrust into the storm. 'Go on!' Camaban screamed at her. 'Go on!'

At the cliff's edge Saban saw that there was still a remnant of fire lurking in the timber. The pile of wood had been huge, and it would have been lit at midday and fed with fuel so that the heat grew ever more intense, but the wind and spray and rain had cowed the fire, had beaten it down and reduced it to wet, black and charred logs, but at its heart, deep down, some embers still fought against the tempest.

'There!' Camaban shouted exultantly. 'There!' And Saban and Aurenna both lifted their heads to see that the south-western horizon was not all black, but was slit with one small wound of red. The sun god was there. He was watching and his blood was showing against the clouds. 'Now jump!' Camaban screamed at Aurenna.

A hammer of thunder deafened the world. Lightning flickered along the cliffs. 'Jump!' Camaban shouted again, and Aurenna screamed with fear or perhaps with triumph as she stepped off the cliff's edge to fall among the rain- and sea-soaked remnants of the fire. She staggered as she landed, her balance upset by the gale and the black timbers that shattered under her feet, and then she fell against the cliff face and Saban saw a last eddy of smoke and suddenly there was no fire. Aurenna had done as she was supposed to do, and the god had rejected her.

Saban jumped down to the ledge. He pulled off his tunic and forced it over Aurenna's head. She seemed incapable of raising her arms and so he dragged the tunic down her body to cover her from the rain. It was then she looked up into his face and he put his bare arms around her and held her tight, and she, exhausted, sobbed on his shoulder above the storm-flayed sea.

But she lived. She had done what she was supposed to do, and disaster had come to Sarmennyn.

The tempest began to lose its force. The sea still pounded on the cliffs and shattered white into the darkening air, but the storm settled into mere gusts, and the rain fell instead of flew.

Saban helped Aurenna to the cliff top. She had pushed her arms into the tunic's sleeves and now clung to him as if in a dream. 'She walked!' Camaban was shouting at the priests.

Haragg had come down from the hill and he added his voice to Camaban's. 'She walked!'

Kereval looked heartbroken. The fate of the sun bride was reckoned to foretell the tribe's fortune in the coming year and no one had ever seen a bride walk to the fire, then walk away.

Scathel shrieked in agony and in his fury he seized a spear from one of the warriors and advanced on Camaban. 'It was you!' he shouted. 'It was your doing! You brought the storm! You were seen in Malkin's shrine last night! You brought the storm!' With that a dozen of the warriors joined the high priest and advanced on Camaban with murder in their faces.

Saban had dropped his spear to help Aurenna and now she clung to him so he could do nothing to save his brother – but Camaban needed no help.

He simply lifted one hand.

In the hand was a golden lozenge. The large lozenge that had come from Sannas's hut.

Scathel stopped. He stared at the scrap of gold, then held up a hand to stop the spearmen.

'You want me to throw the treasure into the sea?' Camaban asked. He opened his other hand to show eleven of the small lozenges. 'I don't mind!' He laughed suddenly, a mad laughter. 'What is Erek's gold to me? What is it to you?' he asked in a shriek. 'You let it go, Scathel! You could not even guard your treasures! So let it go again! Give it back to the sea.' And he turned and made as if to hurl the treasures into the lessening wind.

'No!' Scathel pleaded.

Camaban turned back. 'Why not? You lost it, Scathel! You miserable piece of dried-up lizard dung, you lost Erek's gold! And I have brought some back.' He held the scraps of gold high in the air. 'I am a sorcerer, Scathel of

267

Sarmennyn,' he said in a strong voice, 'I am a sorcerer and you are dirt beneath my feet. I made the spirits of the air and the spirits of the wind travel to Cathallo to rescue this gold, gold which has come to Sarmennyn even though you would break the agreement your chief made with my brother. You, Scathel of Sarmennyn, you have defied Erek! He wants his temple moved and his glory restored, and what does Scathel of Sarmennyn do? He stands in the god's way like a drooling hog before a stag. You oppose Erek! So why should I give you this gold that Erek took from you? It will go to the sea.' He stood on the cliff above the broken fire and once again threatened to hurl the gold into the seething waves.

'No!' Scathel shouted. He was gazing at the gold as though it were Erek himself. Tears were running down his gaunt face and a look of pure wonder was in his eyes. He dropped to his knees. 'Please, no!' he begged Camaban.

'You will move a temple to Ratharryn?' Camaban asked.

'I will move a temple to Ratharryn,' Scathel said humbly, still kneeling.

Camaban pointed northwards. 'In your madness, Scathel,' he said, 'in the mountains, you built a double ring of stone. That is the temple I want.'

'Then you shall have it,' Scathel said.

'It is agreed?' Camaban asked Kereval.

'It is agreed,' Kereval said.

Camaban still held the large lozenge high. 'Erek rejected the bride because you rejected his ambition! Erek wants his temple at Ratharryn!' Folk had crept out of shelter and were listening to Camaban who stood tall and terrible on the dark cliff's edge where the wind lifted his long black hair and rattled the bones tied to its ends. 'Nothing is done for nothing,' he shouted. 'Losing your gold was a tragedy, but a tragedy with meaning, and what does it mean? It means Erek would increase his power! He would spread his light to the world's centre! He will reclaim his proper bride, the earth itself! He will bring us life and happiness, but only if you do what he wishes. And if you move his temple to Ratharryn then you will all be like gods.' He slumped, exhausted. 'You will all be like gods . . .' he said again.

'Thank you for saving her,' Saban said, an arm about Aurenna.

'Don't be absurd,' Camaban said wearily. Then he walked forward and knelt in front of Scathel. He laid the gold, all twelve pieces of it, on the grass between them, and the two men embraced as though they were long-lost brothers. Both wept and both swore to do the sun god's bidding.

So Aurenna lived, Camaban had won and Ratharryn would have its temple.

Scathel did not know what to do with Aurenna: she had walked the path to the fire and lived, and no bride had ever done that. Scathel's first instinct was to kill her, while Kereval wanted to take her as his own bride, but Camaban, whose authority now stood almost unchallenged in Sarmennyn, decided she must go free. 'Erek permitted her to live,' he told the tribe, 'and that means he must have a use for her. If we kill her or if we force her to a marriage, then we defy Erek.'

And so Aurenna walked north to where her own folk lived and she stayed there through the winter, but in the spring she came south again and brought two of her brothers with her.

The three came down the river on a boat made from willow branches that had been bent into a bowl and covered with hides. Aurenna was dressed in deerskins and had her golden hair tied at the nape of her neck. She landed at Kereval's settlement in the evening, and the sinking sun glowed on her face as she walked through the huts where the folk shrank from her. Some believed she was still a goddess, others thought her rejection by Erek had turned her into a malign spirit; all feared her power.

She stooped at the entrance of Haragg's hut. Saban was alone inside, chipping flints into arrow-heads. He liked the task, for it was satisfying to see the sharp slivers emerge from the knobs of rough stone, but then the light by which he was working was blotted out and he looked up, irritated, and did not recognise Aurenna for she was merely a shape against the light outside. 'Haragg is not here,' he said.

'I came to see you,' Aurenna answered, and that was when Saban recognised her and his heart was suddenly too full for him to speak. He had dreamed of seeing her again but had feared he never would; now she had come. She bent to enter the hut and sat opposite him while her two brothers squatted beyond the door. 'I have prayed to Erek,' she said gravely, 'and he has told me to help you move the temple. It is my fate.'

'Your fate? To move stone?' Saban almost smiled.

'To be with you,' Aurenna said and gazed at him anxiously as though he might refuse her help.

Saban did not know what to say. 'To be with me?' he asked nervously, wondering exactly what she meant.

'If you will have me,' she said, and blushed, though it was too dim in the hut for Saban to see it. 'I prayed to Erek all last winter,' Aurenna went on in a small voice, 'and I asked him why he had not taken me. Why had he shamed my family? And I spoke with our priest and he gave me a cup of liquid to drink and I dreamed the wild dream and Erek told me that I am to be the mother of the guardian of his new temple at Ratharryn.'

'You are to be a mother?' Saban asked, hardly daring to believe what she so calmly proposed.

'If you will have me,' she said humbly.

'I have dreamed of little else,' Saban confessed.

Aurenna smiled. 'Good,' she said, 'then I will be with you and my brothers can move your stones.' She explained that the brothers, Caddan and Makin, were accustomed to bringing great lumps of rock from the splintered mountain tops to the lower land where the families broke the boulders and made the axe-heads. 'And I hear,' she went on earnestly, 'that you are finding the task of moving the stones difficult?'

It was not Saban who was finding the task difficult, but Haragg, for Kereval had placed the trader in charge of moving the temple and the big man seemed perplexed by the problems. He had spent all the previous summer and autumn travelling back and forth between Scathel's temple and the chief's settlement and he had still not decided how the stones were to be shifted or, indeed, whether they could be moved at all. He worried at the problem, listened to suggestions, then fell into indecision. Lewydd and Saban were sure they knew how it could be done, but Haragg was nervous of taking their advice. 'It can be done,' Saban now told Aurenna, 'but only when Haragg decides to trust Lewydd and me.'

'I shall tell him to trust you,' Aurenna said. 'I shall tell him of my dream, and he will obey the god.'

Aurenna's return unsettled the priests for they feared her power might rival theirs, so Saban made her a hut on the other river bank, closer to the sea, and there he and Aurenna lived and folk came from all across Sarmennyn, and even from the lands touching Sarmennyn's borders, for her touch. Fishermen brought their boats for her blessing and barren women came to be granted the gift of children. Aurenna disclaimed any power, yet still they came and some even built their own huts close to hers until the place became known as Aurenna's settlement. Lewydd, the spearman who was a fisherman's son, also came to live there, bringing a wife, and Aurenna's brothers made their homes next to his and took themselves wives. Haragg and Cagan came also and Haragg bowed to Aurenna and seemed relieved when she instructed him that Erek had decreed that Saban and Lewydd were to move the temple stones. She told Haragg, 'My brothers will move the stones down the mountains, Saban will make boats to carry the stones and Lewydd will take the boats to Ratharryn.'

Haragg accepted Aurenna's word and thereafter joined Camaban who was travelling all through Sarmennyn and preaching his vision, for the task of moving the stones would need the help of the tribe and so the folk must be convinced. At the beginning of time, Camaban said, the gods had danced together and the folk of Earth had lived in their happy shadow, but men and women had begun to love the moon goddess and the earth goddess more than Erek himself and so Erek had broken the dance. Yet if Erek could be brought back then the old happiness would be restored. There would be no more winter, no more sickness and no more orphans crying in the dark. Haragg preached the same theme and the promises were received with astonishment and hope. In just one year the tribe's sullen opposition to moving a temple was turned into enthusiastic support.

It was one thing to persuade Kereval's people to move the stones, but it was another to make sure Lengar accepted the temple and so Scathel, who was now Camaban's sworn ally, went to Ratharryn in the spring. 'Tell Lengar that the temple we are sending him is a war temple,' Camaban instructed the high priest.

'But it isn't!' Scathel protested.

'But if he believes it is a war temple,' Camaban explained patiently, 'then he will be eager to receive it. Tell him that if he exchanges the gold for the stones then it will grant his spearmen invincibility. Tell him it will make him the greatest warrior of all the world. Tell him that songs of his prowess will ring through the years for ever.'

So Scathel went and told Lengar the lies and Lengar was so awed by the tall, gaunt priest and by his promises of invincibility that he actually yielded a half-dozen more of the small lozenges, though he said nothing of the ones Derrewyn had stolen.

When Scathel returned from Ratharryn he brought Galeth's son, Mereth, to be Saban's helper. Mereth was a year younger than Saban, and he had inherited his father's strength and knowledge. He could shape wood, lift stone, raise a temple pole or chip flint, and do all those things with dexterity, speed and skill. Like his father he had huge hands and a generous heart, though when he came to Sarmennyn that heart was burdened with news for Saban's mother had died.

Saban wept for her, listening as Mereth described how they had carried her corpse to the Death Place. 'We broke pots for her in Lahanna's temple,' Mereth said. 'Lengar wants to pull that temple down.'

'He wants to destroy Lahanna's temple?' Saban was amazed.

'Cathallo worships Lahanna, so Ratharryn isn't allowed to any more,' Mereth explained, then added that Derrewyn had rallied the people of Cathallo.

And that too was news to Saban. Derrewyn had escaped to Cathallo and taken a child in her belly. Saban pressed

274

Mereth for whatever detail he could reveal, though Mereth knew little more than he had already told. Saban felt a fierce pleasure at the news and that, in turn, made him feel guilty about Aurenna. 'Derrewyn must have had the baby by now?' he suggested.

'I heard nothing,' Mereth said.

Mereth and Saban made sledges and boats, while Caddan and Makin, Aurenna's brothers, went to the mountain to move the stones of Scathel's temple from their high valley. They used sledges, each one twice the length of a man's height and half as broad, made of two stout oak runners spanned by baulks of timber. Saban made a dozen sledges that first year, and Lewydd carried them up the river from Aurenna's settlement on a boat made of two hulls joined by timber beams. The river twisted through the woods past Kereval's settlement and into the bleaker country where the trees were sparse and windbent, then wound northwards until it became too shallow for Lewydd's boat, but by then it was under the shadow of the mountain where the temple stood.

Aurenna's brothers needed scores of men to move the stones, but the folk of Sarmennyn had been inspired by Camaban and Haragg and there was no shortage of helpers. The women sang as the men dragged the sledges up the mountain. The first of the temple's stones were rocked loose from their sockets, then lowered onto the sledges. Aurenna's brothers began with the smaller stones for they could be lifted by a mere dozen men and two such stones could be placed on one sledge. A dozen men dragged the first sledge to the high valley's lip and there the sledge tipped over the edge and it needed thirty men, not to pull it, but to stop it from running loose down the steep slope.

It took a whole day to guide the first two stones down the slope, and another full day to drag the sledge from the mountain's foot to the river's bank, and it would take another two years to bring the whole temple down the hill, and in all that time only one sledge ran out of control to thunder down the slope, tip and shatter so that its pillar broke into a thousand pieces. The largest stones, which needed thirty or forty men to lift, were stored beside the river on their sledges while the smaller pillars, which could be manhandled by a dozen men, were left on the grass.

It was Lewydd who would carry the stones to Ratharryn, for the temple would float for most of its journey and he was a seaman. Lewydd devised the boats. In the first year, after the first few stones had been brought down the mountain, he loaded two of the smaller stones onto the same boat that had carried the sledges upstream. He manned the two hulls with a dozen paddlers, then set off downriver. The boat moved fast, carried by the current, and Lewydd was confident enough to take the stones to where the river widened into the sea. He wanted to discover how the boat rode the larger waves, but no sooner had the first green sea broken on the bows than the weight of the stones pushed the two hulls outward and the boat split into two and the pillars sank. Haragg cried aloud, claiming the work was being done all wrong, but Camaban assured the men watching from the cliffs that Dilan, the sea god, had exacted his price and that no more stones would be lost. A heifer was sacrificed on the beach and its blood allowed to run into the water and a moment later three porpoises were seen offshore and Scathel declared that Dilan had accepted the sacrifice.

'Three hulls, not two,' Lewydd told Saban. Lewydd and

his crew had swum safely ashore and the young seaman had decided it was not Dilan who had taken the stones, but the inadequacy of the boat. 'I want three hulls for each boat,' he explained, 'side by side. And I want ten boats, more if you can find the trees.'

'Thirty hulls!' Saban exclaimed, wondering if there were enough trees in Sarmennyn's scanty forests to provide so many. He had thought of using some of the tribe's existing boats, but Camaban insisted that the boats must be new and dedicated solely to Erek's glory and that once they had carried the stones eastwards they must be burned.

That summer the new sun bride burned, going to her death in a blaze of glory. The folk of Sarmennyn had never seen Erek so red, so swollen and so majestic as he was that midsummer night, and the bride died without a cry. Aurenna did not go to the Sea Temple for the ceremony, but stayed in her hut. She was pregnant.

The child was born early the next year. It was a boy and Aurenna called him Leir, which means 'One Who Was Saved', and she named him that because she had been saved from the fire. 'I never really thought I would die,' Aurenna confessed to Saban one winter evening after Leir's birth. They were sitting on their stone, the pink-flecked greenish boulder that lay on the river bank close to their hut, and sharing a bear's pelt to keep warm.

'I thought you would die,' Saban admitted.

She smiled. 'I used to pray to Erek every day, and some-how I knew he would let me live.'

'Why?'

She shook her head, almost as if Saban's question were irrelevant. 'I just did,' she said, 'though I hardly dared believe the hope. Of course I wanted to be his bride,' she added hastily, frowning, 'but I also wanted to serve him. When I was a goddess I had dreams, and in the dreams Erek told me the time of change was coming. That the time of his loneliness was ending.'

Saban was always uncomfortable when she talked of having been a goddess. He was not certain he really believed her, but he admitted to himself that he had not grown up in Sarmennyn and so he was not accustomed to the notion of a girl being changed into a goddess, or, indeed, changing back again. 'I prayed you would live,' he said.

'I still get the dreams,' Aurenna said, ignoring his words. 'I think they tell me the future, only it's like looking into a mist. It's how you told me you first saw Scathel's temple, as a shape in the mist, and that's how my dreams are, but I think they'll become clearer.' She paused. 'I hope they'll become clearer,' she went on, 'but at least I still hear Erek in my head and I sometimes think I am really married to him, that perhaps I am the bride he left on earth to do his work.'

'To move a temple?' Saban asked, suddenly jealous of Erek.

'To end winter,' Aurenna said, 'and bring an end to grief. That is why your brother came to Sarmennyn and why he saved you from Lengar. You and I, Saban, are Erek's servants.'

That winter Saban and Mereth roamed the southern woods of Sarmennyn and found the tallest, straightest oaks and elms, taller even than the highest temple poles at Ratharryn, and they touched their foreheads to the trunks, begging forgiveness of the trees' spirits, and then they cut the trees, trimmed them of branches and used a team of oxen to drag the trunks to Aurenna's settlement. There they shaped the massive trees into double-prowed hulls. They fashioned the outside of the hulls first, then turned the trunks over and hollowed them with adzes made of flint, stone or bronze. A dozen men worked on the river bank, singing as they swung the blades and piled the ground with wood chips. Saban loved the work for he was used to shaping timber and he took pleasure in watching the clean white-golden wood take its shape. Aurenna and the other women worked close by, singing as they slit hides into the thongs that would be used to bind the cross-beams to the hulls and the stones to the beams. Saban was happy in those days. He had been accepted as the head man of Aurenna's settlement and everyone there shared a purpose and took pleasure in watching the work progress. They were good times, filled with laughter and honest work.

When the first three hulls were finished Lewydd carved an eye on each bow so that the god who protected boats would look out for storms and rocks, and then he laid the three boats side by side. Each craft was as long as three men, and the width of the three boats together was half the length of the hulls, which Saban now joined together with two huge beams of oak as thick about as a man's waist. The beams were squared with flint and bronze and their lower halves fitted into slots chipped from the three hulls' gunwales. Once the timbers were jointed to the hulls, they were lashed tight with the long strips of hide. It was a monstrous thing, that first boat, and the fishermen shook their heads and said it would never float, but it did. Twenty men heaved it off the bank onto the mud at low tide and the incoming tide lifted the triple hull easily. They called that boat *Molot*, which meant monster, and Lewydd was certain it would take the weight of the greatest stone and still survive the sea's malevolence.

Camaban travelled to Ratharryn at winter's end and returned to Sarmennyn just as the *Molot* was finished. He admired the great boat, glanced at the other hulls that were being shaped, then squatted outside Saban's hut to give him news from home. Lengar, he said, was more powerful than ever, but Melak of Drewenna had died and there had been a struggle for the chieftainship between Melak's son and a warrior named Stakis. Stakis had won. 'Which is not what we wanted,' Camaban said. He took a bowl of gruel from Aurenna and nodded his thanks.

'What's so bad about Stakis?' Saban asked.

'We have to float the stones through his territory, of course,' Camaban explained, 'and he might not prove a friend to us. Still, he's agreed to meet us.'

'Us?'

'All of us,' Camaban said vaguely, waving a hand that could have encompassed the whole world. 'A meeting of the tribes. Us, Ratharryn and Drewenna. One moon before midsummer. The problem is' – he paused to scoop up some of the gruel – 'the problem' – he went on with his mouth full – 'is that Stakis doesn't like Lengar. I can't blame him. Our brother has to keep his spearmen busy, so he's been raiding Drewenna's cattle.'

'He doesn't fight Cathallo?'

'All the time, only they hide behind their marshes and their new chief is a good warrior. He's one of Kital's sons, Rallin.'

'Derrewyn's cousin,' Saban said, remembering the name.

'Derrewyn's pup, more like,' Camaban said vengefully.

'She calls herself a sorceress now and lives in Sannas's old hut where she wails to Lahanna, and Rallin won't take a piss without her permission. It's strange, isn't it' – he paused to eat more gruel – 'how Cathallo likes being ruled by a woman? First Sannas, now Derrewyn! A sorceress indeed! She grubs about with herbs and makes threats. That isn't sorcery.'

'Did she have Lengar's baby?' Saban asked. He had a sudden image of a dark face framed by black hair, of Derrewyn laughing, then of the same face crying and screaming. He shuddered.

'The baby died,' Camaban said carelessly, then sneered. 'What kind of sorceress can't keep her own child alive?' He put the empty bowl down. 'Lengar wants you to bring Aurenna to the meeting of the tribes.'

'Why?'

'Because I told him she's beautiful.' Camaban said, 'which is good reason to leave her here.'

'Lengar wouldn't touch her,' Saban said.

'He touches every woman he wants,' Camaban said, 'and no one dares deny him for fear of his spearmen. Our brother, Saban, is a tyrant.'

Kereval, Scathel, Haragg, Camaban and a dozen other elders and priests travelled to the meeting of the tribes. Seven boats were needed to carry the delegation, and Saban went with Lewydd in a fishing boat that was driven by eight paddlers. The weather was blustery, and the seas promised to be big, but Lewydd was unworried. 'Dilan will preserve us,' he promised Saban, who faced his first proper sea voyage with trepidation.

The fleet left in a summer dawn, paddling down the river until they reached the sea where they waited in the shelter of a headland. 'The tides,' Lewydd said, explaining the pause.

'What of them?'

'The tides don't just rise and fall, but are like winds in the water. They flow up and down the coast, but unlike the winds they keep to a rhythm. We shall go east with the water-wind, and when it turns against us we rest until it helps us again.' Lewydd had sacrificed a piglet in Malkin's temple, then splashed the animal's blood on the boat's prow, and now he dropped the carcass over the side. The crews of the other six boats did the same.

When the tide turned Saban did not detect it, but Lewydd was satisfied and his eight paddlers gave a shout and drove the boat out to sea. They went well away from the coast before turning east and now the wind was behind them and so Lewydd ordered a sail raised. The sail was made of two ox hides that were hung on a short spar suspended at the top of a stubby mast, and once the wind caught the leather it seemed to Saban that the boat flew, though still the waves came faster. The great seas would heap up behind and Saban feared the boat must be over-whelmed, but then the stern would lift and the paddlers would redouble their efforts and for a heart-stopping moment the wave would carry the boat forward in a great seething surge before the crest passed under the hull and the boat would lurch back and the sail would crack like a whip. The other crews raced them, driving their paddles hard so that the spray flicked up in the sun. They chanted as they worked, rivalling each other in music as well as in speed, though sometimes the chanting paused as men used sea-shells to scoop water from their boats.

Late in the morning the seven boats turned into the

land. The tide, Lewydd explained, was turning, and though it was possible for paddles and sail to drive them against that current, their progress would be small and the effort great, so the boats sought shelter in a small bay. They did not go ashore, but rather anchored with a great stone through which a hole had been chipped and to which a long line of twisted strips of hide was attached. The seven boats rested through the afternoon. Most of the crews slept, but Saban stayed awake and saw men with spears and bows appear on the cliffs of the small cove. The men stared down at the boats, but made no attempt to interfere.

The crews woke towards evening and made a meal of dried fish and water and then the stones were hauled up from the sea's bed, the sails were hoisted and the paddles were plunged into the sea again. Slaol set in a blaze of red that was broken by streaky clouds and all the heaving sea behind flickered with the taint of blood until the last colour drained away and the grey gave way to black and they were sailing in the night. There was no moon at first, and the land was dark, but the sky had never seemed to hold so many stars. Lewydd showed Saban how he was following a star in the group that the Outfolk called the Mooncalf and the people of Ratharryn knew as the Stag. The star moved across the sky, but Lewydd, like all fishermen, knew its motion, just as he recognised the dark outlines of the low hills on the northern bank which, to Saban, were mere blurs. Later, when Saban woke from a half-sleep, he saw that there was land on both sides because the great sea was narrowing. A near full moon had risen and Saban could see the other boats stretched on either side with Lahanna's light flashing rhythmically from their paddles.

He slept again, not waking until the dawn. The paddlers

were driving their boats towards the blaze of the rising sun. Great sheets of gleaming mud lay on either side, and folk walked on the mud's ripples and stared at the boats. 'They're hunting shellfish,' Lewydd said, then lifted his spear because a dozen boats had come from the southern shore. 'Show them your bow,' Lewydd said, and Saban dutifully held up the weapon. All the men in Sarmennyn's boats now brandished spears or bows and the stranger's boats sheered away. 'Probably just fishermen,' Lewydd said.

The sea narrowed between the wide muddy flats on which intricate fish traps, woven from hundreds of small branches, made dark patterns. Saban, looking over the side, saw the sea-bed writhing. 'Eels,' Lewydd said, 'just eels. Good eating!' But there was no time to fish, for the tide was again turning and the paddlers were chanting hard as they drove the boat towards the mouth of a river which slid into the sea between glistening banks. Lewydd said it was the River Sul, the same name that was used in Ratharryn. Birds rose from the mudbanks, protesting at the boats' intrusion, and the sky was filled with white wings and raucous cries.

They waited for the tide to turn again, then let it carry them far up Sul's river. That night they slept ashore and next morning, freed now of the tide's influence, they paddled the boats upstream, gliding beneath vast trees that sometimes arched overhead to make a green tunnel. 'This is all Drewenna's land,' Lewydd said.

'You've been here before?'

'When I hunted your young men on their ordeals,' Lewydd answered with a grin.

'Maybe I saw you,' Saban said, 'but you didn't see me.'

'Or maybe we did see you,' Lewydd said, 'and decided a little runt like you wasn't worth keeping.' He laughed, then lowered his spear shaft over the side to test the river's depth. 'This is the way we shall bring the stones,' he said.

'Only three days' journey?' Saban asked, pleased that the voyage had been so swift.

'The stones will take much longer,' Lewydd warned him. 'Their weight will make the boats slow, and we shall have to wait for good weather. Six days, seven? And more to bring the stones upriver. We shall be fortunate to make one voyage a year.'

'Only one?'

'If we are not to starve,' Lewydd said, meaning that the paddlers could not abandon their fishing or farming for too long. 'Perhaps, in a good year, we might make two voyages.' He poled with his spear shaft, not to test the depth but to push the boat forward. The seven craft were driving against the river's strong current now and most of the crews had abandoned their paddles and were standing and using their spears as Lewydd was doing. Every now and then, through the trees, they could see fields of wheat and barley, or pastures with cows. Pigs rooted on the river bank where herons nested high in the trees. Kingfishers whipped bright from either bank. 'And from here to Ratharryn?' Lewydd asked. 'I don't know how long that will take.' He explained how they could follow the Sul until it was too shallow for the boats to float any more, and there the stones and the boats would have to be hauled onto the bank and dragged on sledges to another river, perhaps a day's journey away. That river flowed into the Mai and once on that river the boats could be turned upstream until they came to Ratharryn.

'More sledges?' Saban asked.

'Ratharryn's folk will build them. Or Drewenna's,' Lewydd said, which was why the new chieftain of Drewenna had called this meeting of the tribes. The stones must pass through his land and their passage would require his help and doubtless Stakis wanted a rich reward for letting the boulders go safely past his spearmen.

The river was narrowing beneath the green trees and each of the boats now carried a leafy branch in its bows to show that the men of Sarmennyn came in peace, yet even so the few folk who saw them hid or ran away. 'Have you been to Sul?' Saban asked Lewydd.

'Never,' Lewydd said, 'though we sometimes raided close to it.' He explained that Sul's settlement was too large and too well guarded and so Sarmennyn's raiders always skirted the place.

The settlement was famous, for it was the home of a goddess, Sul, who welled hot water up from the ground and so had given her name to the river which curled around the cleft in the rocks where her marvellous spring bubbled. Drewenna ruled the settlement and guarded it fiercely, for Sul attracted scores of people seeking healing and those supplicants had to bring gifts if they were to gain access to the waters. Saban had heard many stories of Sul; his mother had told him how a monster had once lived there, a massive beast, larger than an aurochs, with a skin hard as bone and a great horn reaching from its forehead and massive hoofs heavier than stones. Anyone trying to reach the hot water had to pass the monster, and no one ever could, not even the great hero Yassana, who was the son of Slaol and from whose loins all Ratharryn's people had sprung, but then Sul had sung a lullaby and the monster had laid its heavy head in her lap and she had poured a liquid in its ear and the monster had turned to stone, trapping her. The monster and the goddess were still there, and at night, Saban's mother had said, you could hear her sad lullaby coming from the rocks where the hot water flowed.

The famous settlement lay on the river's northern bank. Fields spread downstream, hacked out of the forests that had once grown in the fertile valley, and a score of boats were hauled up on the bank, beyond which Saban could see smoke rising from thatched roofs. The hills were close on either side, steep hills, but looking lush and green after Sarmennyn's wind-scoured slopes.

The folk at Sul had heard the boats were coming upriver and a group of dancers waited at the landing to welcome Kereval and his men. Scathel was first ashore. The priest was naked and carried a great curved bone, a sea-monster's rib, and he crouched in the mud and smelt the air for danger, then turned three times before declaring the place safe.

Stakis, a scarred young warrior who was Drewenna's new chief, welcomed the Outfolk and Saban found himself translating the flowery words. Stakis embraced Saban, saying he was pleased to meet the brother of the mighty Lengar, though Saban sensed that the pleasure was feigned. Indeed, it was rumoured that Stakis had only won the chieftainship of Drewenna because he was reckoned strong enough to resist Ratharryn's insistent demands, while Melak's son, who had expected to succeed his father, had been thought too feeble. Lengar had not yet arrived, though a plume of smoke showing in the clear sky above the eastern hills was a signal that his party had been sighted.

Dancers escorted the visitors from Sarmennyn to some new huts specially raised for the meeting of the tribes and beyond the huts, on the grassland to the north of the settlement, there was a throng of shelters for the folk who had come to witness the meeting. There were jugglers in the crowd and men who had tame wild beasts: wolves, pine martens and a young bear. A larger bear, a great old male with a scarred pelt and claws the colour of scorched wood, was imprisoned in a wooden pen and Stakis promised that when Lengar's men arrived he would arrange a fight between the bear and his best dogs. A score of female slaves waited in the huts. 'They are yours,' Stakis said, 'yours to enjoy.'

Lengar arrived that evening. Drums announced his coming and the whole crowd walked eastwards to greet his procession. Six women dancers came first, all naked to the waist and sweeping the ground with ash branches, while behind them came a dozen naked priests, their skin whitened by chalk and their heads crowned with antlers. Neel, whom Saban remembered as the youngest of Ratharryn's priests, now wore the large antlers denoting he was the high priest.

Behind the priests came a score of warriors and it was those men who caused the crowd to gasp for, despite the day's heat, they wore cloaks made from fox pelts and high-crowned fox fur hats plumed with swan's feathers. They had bronze-headed spears and bronze swords and all looked alike, which made them oddly formidable.

And in their midst were Ratharryn's warlords, their battle captains, led by their renowned chief. Lengar was heavier and full-bearded now, so that he looked like his father, but his horned eyes were as sharp and cunning as ever. He wore his leather tunic on which the bronze plates gleamed, while on his head was a bronze helm like none Saban had ever seen before. He smiled slyly when he saw Saban, then walked on to greet Stakis. Drewenna's dancers circled the newcomers, kicking up a fine dust with their feet. Behind the warriors came a score of slaves, some bearing heavy sacks that Saban guessed must contain gifts for Stakis.

Lengar crossed to Saban when the greetings were done. 'My little brother,' he said, 'no longer a slave.'

'No thanks to you,' Saban said. He had neither embraced nor kissed his brother; he had not even offered his hand, but Lengar did not seem to expect a fond greeting.

'It is thanks to me, Saban, that you live at all,' Lengar said. Then he shrugged: 'But we can be friends now. Your wife is here?'

'She could not travel.'

Lengar's yellow eyes narrowed. 'Why not?'

'She is pregnant,' Saban lied.

'So? She loses a pup and you have the pleasure of whelping another on her.' Lengar scowled. 'I hear she is beautiful.'

'So men say.'

'You should have brought her. I ordered you too, didn't I? Have you forgotten I am your chief?' His anger was rising, but he shook his head as though forcing it down. 'Your woman can wait for another time,' he said, then tapped the blue tattoo on Saban's bare chest. 'Only one killing scar, little brother? And only one son, I hear? I have seven that I acknowledge, but there are plenty of others.' He plucked Saban's tunic, guiding him towards the huts set aside for Ratharryn's people. 'This temple,' he asked in a low voice, 'is it really a war temple?'

'It is Sarmennyn's great war temple,' Saban said. 'Their secret temple.'

Lengar seemed impressed. 'And it will bring us victory?'

'It will make you the greatest warlord of all time,' Saban said.

Lengar looked pleased. 'And what will Sarmennyn's folk do if I take their temple and keep their gold?'

'They might do nothing,' Saban said, 'but Slaol will doubtless punish you.'

'Punish me!' Lengar bridled, stepping away. 'You sound like Camaban! Where is he?'

'Gone to look at the goddess's shrine.' Saban nodded towards the high wooden palisade that surrounded the settlement and the goddess's spring, and when he turned back he saw that Jegar was approaching.

Saban was astonished at the upwelling of hatred he felt at the sight of Jegar and for an instant all the ancient misery about Derrewyn swamped him. It must have shown on his face, for Lengar looked pleased at his reaction. 'You do remember Jegar, little brother?' he asked.

'I remember him,' Saban said, staring into the eyes of his enemy. Jegar was wealthy now, for he was swathed in a cloak of fine otter fur and had a gold chain about his neck and a dozen gold rings on his fingers, but the fingers of his right hand, Saban saw, were still curled uselessly. His hair was streaked with red ochre and his beard was plaited.

'Only one killing scar, Saban?' Jegar said scornfully.

'I could have another if I chose,' Saban said defiantly.

'One more!' Jegar pretended to be impressed, then shrugged off the otter cloak to reveal a chest smothered in tattoos. Each blue scar was a row of dots hammered into the skin with a bone comb. 'Every scar is a man's spirit,' Jegar boasted, 'and every dot of every scar is a woman on her back.' He placed a finger against one blue mark. 'And I remember that woman well. She fought! She screamed!' He looked slyly at Saban. 'Do you remember her?' Saban said nothing and Jegar smiled. 'And as she wept afterwards, she promised me that you would have your revenge.'

'I keep promises made on my behalf,' Saban said stiffly.

Jegar whooped with laughter and Lengar punched Saban softly in the chest. 'You will leave Jegar alone,' he said, 'for tomorrow he will speak for me.' He gestured towards the big cleared space, marked by a ring of slender wooden poles, where the negotiations between the three tribes would take place.

'You won't speak for yourself?' Saban asked, shocked.

'They tell me there is a bull aurochs in the forest north of here,' Lengar said carelessly, 'and I have a mind to hunt it. Jegar knows what to tell Stakis.'

'Stakis will be insulted,' Saban protested.

'Good. He is Drewenna, and I am Ratharryn. He deserves insult.' Lengar began to walk away, then turned back. 'I am sorry you did not bring your woman, Saban. I would have liked to discover if she is as beautiful as everyone says.'

'I am sure she is,' Jegar said, challenging Saban. 'Your last one was beautiful. Did you know she is now a sorceress in Cathallo? She makes spells against us, but you see that we both still live. And both live well.' He paused. 'I look forward to meeting your woman, Saban.' He smiled, then walked after Lengar, both men laughing.

The bear killed seven dogs, then died itself. Three men

were murdered in fights caused by the fierce liquor that Stakis provided and the priests, fearing blood feuds, killed their killers, and then night fell and Lahanna looked down from a star-bright sky as, one by one, the drunken warriors slept and peace came to the valley.

Camaban did not go to the tribal meeting. Instead he sequestered himself with Neel, the new high priest at Ratharryn, and instructed him how the temple was to be built. Camaban had brought slivers of wood, shaped by Saban to represent the stones, and he stuck them in the soil to build the double ring with its entrance corridor that would face towards the place where the midsummer sun rose. 'In Sarmennyn the doors of the sun faced the setting sun,' Camaban explained, 'but in Ratharryn they must face its rising.'

'Why?' Neel asked.

'Because we wish to greet the sun, not say farewell.'

Neel stared at the small timber chips. 'Why don't you come and build it for us?' he asked petulantly. He was uncomfortable with Camaban, for he remembered him as a crippled child, pathetic and filthy, and Neel could not reconcile that memory with the confident sorcerer who now gave him orders. 'I'm not a builder,' he complained.

'You are a toad,' Camaban said, 'who tells my brother what he wants to hear instead of what the gods really say, but if you do as I tell you then the gods will endure your stench. And why should I come to Ratharryn? You have builders enough without wasting my time.' Camaban wanted to visit the land across the western sea for he had heard that their priests and sorcerers knew things that were still hidden to folk on the mainland, and he was ever bored by the practical business of moving or raising stones. 'It won't be difficult to build,' he claimed, and he showed Neel how the stones were to be planted according to height: the tallest by the gates of the sun and the smallest on the opposite side. Then he produced a leather bag containing a long string of sinew. 'Look after that,' he said.

'What is it?'

'The temple's measurement. Secure the sinew at the centre of the Old Temple, then make a circle with the other end. That circle marks the outer edge of the outer ring of stone. The inner ring is one pace inside.'

Neel nodded. 'What do we do with the present temple?'

'Leave it,' Camaban said dismissively. 'It does no harm.' Then he made Neel repeat all his instructions, and then repeat them all again, for he wanted to know that the new temple would be built exactly as it had been made in the high hanging valley in Sarmennyn.

As Camaban and Neel talked the three tribes met. Lengar, as he had promised, went hunting, taking a dozen men, some slaves and a score of dogs, and so it was Jegar, swathed in his thick otter skin cloak despite the day's heat, who brought Ratharryn's men to the meeting place.

Gifts were exchanged. Stakis was generous with his guests, and no wonder, for he intended to exact a high price for the privilege of moving Sarmennyn's stones across his territory. He heaped Kereval with fleeces, pelts, flints, pots and a bag of precious amber. He gave him combs, pins and a fine axe with a polished head of greenish stone, and in return he received a turtle shell, two bronze axes, eight decorated pots of liquor and a necklace of pointed teeth that had come from a strange sea creature.

Stakis presented Jegar with exactly the same gifts he had given to Kereval, and if he was offended that it was Jegar who received them instead of Lengar, he hid his anger. When his gifts were given, and after Jegar had made a flowery speech of thanks, Stakis resumed his seat at the southern side of the circle and two of Ratharryn's warriors carried Lengar's gifts to Drewenna's new chief. They brought the offerings on a willow-plaited hurdle covered with a hide, and they placed the hurdle in front of Stakis then removed the leather cover to reveal a whole basket of bronze spearheads. Then they fetched a second hurdle and this, when it was uncovered, carried a bronze sword, a bundle of bows and more than a dozen stone axes. The watching men were impressed, for Lengar's gifts far outweighed anyone's expectations, but they were still not all given for the two warriors now carried a third hurdle which proved to hold six bronze axes, two aurochs horns and a pile of badger pelts and wolf furs. Stakis was delighted, especially by the largest of the aurochs horns that he took onto his lap, then watched, wide-eyed, as a fourth hurdle, even heavier than the others, was brought from Lengar's huts. This last hurdle, though, was put on the ground in front of Jegar and its hide cover remained in place, suggesting that the final gift would only be given when Stakis yielded what Ratharryn wanted.

Saban thought that for a man who had been reluctant to give gifts his brother had been remarkably generous. Scathel, for once, looked pleased – indeed he was beaming, for how could the new chief of Drewenna now obstruct the passage of the stones? And the sooner the stones were in Ratharryn the sooner Erek's gold would be returned to Sarmennyn. But Stakis, despite his gratitude for Lengar's gifts, wanted more. He wanted Ratharryn's help in hunting down the man who had been his rival for Drewenna's chieftainship. Melak's son was said to be an outcast in the woods, but he had taken three score of warriors with him, and those men constantly raided Stakis's holdings. 'Bring me Kellan's head in a basket,' Stakis said, 'and you may move every stone in Sarmennyn across my land.'

Haragg sidled across to Jegar and urged him to accept the offer, but Jegar seemed confused. He wanted to know where Kellan was, exactly how many men he had and what were their weapons? And why could Stakis not hunt his rival down?

Stakis explained that he had tried, but Kellan constantly retreated before him into southern Ratharryn. 'If your men come westwards,' he said, 'and mine go eastwards, we shall trap him.'

It seemed a simple enough proposition, yet still Jegar worried at it. How could Stakis be certain that Kellan had not gone south and west to the people of Duran? Had Stakis talked with Duran's chief?

'Of course,' Stakis said, 'and he has not seen Kellan.'

'We have not seen him either,' Jegar claimed. 'We could search for him, but if a man has no wish to be found, then the woods can hide him for ever. My friend, Saban' – here he offered Saban a mocking smile – 'wishes to move the stones soon. Maybe he can bring some this very summer! But if he must wait while we search every tree and beat every bush then the stones will never arrive. Besides, Kellan may be dead!'

'He lives,' Stakis said. 'But it is enough for me,' he conceded, 'that you will agree to hunt Kellan down. Give me that promise, Jegar, and I will allow the stones through my territory.'

'With no further payment?' Jegar asked, leaving the matter of Kellan undecided.

'A man deserves payment for the movement of goods across his land,' Stakis said, turning to Sarmennyn's emissaries. 'You must pay me a piece of bronze sufficient to make one spearhead for every stone you bring into Drewenna, and for every ten stones you will pay me one further spearhead.'

'We will give you a bronze spearhead for every ten stones,' Saban offered. He had no right to speak for Kereval, but he knew Stakis's price was exorbitant. He translated his words to Sarmennyn's chieftain, who nodded his approval.

'How many stones are there?' Stakis asked.

'Ten times seven,' Saban answered, 'and two.'

There were gasps from Drewenna's men. They had thought that perhaps Sarmennyn was giving two or three dozen stones, but not twice that many. 'I shall want a spearhead of bronze for every stone,' Stakis insisted.

'Let me talk to Kereval,' Saban said, then leaned over to the chief and changed to the Outfolk tongue. 'He wants too much.'

'I will give him ten spearheads,' Kereval said, 'no more.' He looked across the circle at the gifts. 'He already has a basket of spearheads! Will all his men be armed with metal spears?'

'For every ten stones,' Saban said to Stakis, 'we shall give you one spearhead. No more.'

Jegar was watching this altercation with amusement.

Before Stakis could respond to Saban's offer a horn sounded in the wooded hills just to the north of the meeting place. Stakis frowned at the noise, but Jegar smiled soothingly. 'Lengar is hunting,' he explained.

'No aurochs will be this close to Sul,' Stakis said, staring at the trees.

'It has been driven, perhaps?' Jegar suggested. 'As you wish us to drive Kellan onto your bronze spears?'

'Which you will do?' Stakis asked eagerly. Just then the horn sounded a second time and Jegar leaned forward and plucked the hide cover from the fourth hurdle. This one did not have gifts, but weapons. Men always came to a meeting unarmed, but Ratharryn's warriors now ran forward and picked up spears and bows and suddenly a host of spearmen were running from the trees and the first arrows were whipping overhead to fall among Stakis's men.

'Back!' Jegar shouted at Saban. 'Back to your huts. We have no quarrel with Sarmennyn!' He had thrown off his cloak and Saban saw that a bronze sword was in his crippled right hand. It was lashed there with leather strips, explaining why he had sat so uncomfortably swathed in the otter skin cloak that had hidden the weapon. 'Go back!' Jegar shouted.

Lengar had not been hunting at all, but had met the rest of his spearmen in the forests north of Sul, and now he attacked the unarmed men of Drewenna, and with him was Kellan and his renegade warriors. Stakis had been betrayed, tricked and surprised, and now he would die.

Saban ran to the huts with the rest of Sarmennyn's unarmed warriors. He snatched up his bow and a quiver of arrows, but Kereval put a hand on Saban's arm. 'This is not our fight,' the chief said.

It was no fight at all, but a slaughter. Some of Stakis's men had fled to the river where they tried to launch boats, but a group of Lengar's archers assailed them from higher up the bank and those men only stopped loosing arrows when Ratharryn's spearmen reached the river and killed the few survivors. Dogs howled, women screamed and the dying moaned. Stakis himself, with most of his followers, had fled towards to the settlement of Sul with Jegar and Lengar hard on his heels. A few, very few, of Drewenna's men ran towards their assailants, slipping between the attacking parties to reach the trees and when Lengar saw those men escaping he shouted at Jegar to hunt them down. Lengar then jumped, caught the top of the palisade that ringed the settlement and lithely hauled himself over. A flood of his spearmen struggled to follow, then one thought to split the palisade with an axe and yet more men widened the gap and flooded through to the thatched huts surrounding the sacred spring. Kellan and his men joined the slaughter inside the broken wall.

The men from Sarmennyn watched uneasily from their huts where Camaban had joined them. 'It is Lengar's business,' he said, 'not ours. Lengar has no quarrel with Sarmennyn.'

'It's shameful,' Saban said angrily. He could hear dying men calling on their gods, he could see women weeping over the dead and the river swirling with streamers of blood. Some of the attackers were dancing in glee while others stood guard over the gifts that Jegar had so treacherously given to Stakis. 'It's shameful!' Saban said again.

'If your folk break a truce,' Scathel said scornfully, 'then it is not our concern, though it is to our benefit. Kellan will doubtless let us carry stones through his land without any payment at all.'

Jegar had vanished into the trees with a dozen spearmen, pursuing the last of Drewenna's fugitives. Saban remembered the promise Derrewyn had made on his behalf and he remembered his own oaths of vengeance and so he picked up a spear. 'What are you doing?' Lewydd challenged him and, when Saban tried to pull away, Lewydd gripped his arm. 'It is not your fight,' Lewydd insisted.

'It is my fight!' Saban said.

'It isn't wise to pick a fight with wolves,' Camaban said.

'I made a promise,' Saban said and he threw Lewydd's hand off his arm to run towards the woods. Lewydd picked up his own spear and followed.

Dead and dying men lay among the trees. Like all those who had attended the meeting of the tribes, Stakis's warriors had worn their finery and Jegar's men were now stripping them of necklaces, amulets and clothes. They looked up in alarm as Saban and Lewydd appeared, but most recognised Saban and none feared Lewydd for the grey-tattooed Outfolk were not their enemy this day.

Saban climbed the hill, looking for Jegar, then heard a scream to his right and ran through the trees to see his enemy hacking with a sword at a dying man. The sword was strapped to Jegar's maimed hand, but he still wielded it with sickening force. 'Jegar!' Saban shouted, hefting his spear. It would have been easier to have loosed an arrow from the golden string of his bow, but that would have been the coward's way. 'Jegar!' he called again.

Jegar turned, his eyes bright with excitement, then he saw the hunting spear in Saban's hand and it dawned on him that Saban was not an ally here, but a foe. At first he looked astonished, then he laughed. He stooped, picked up his own heavy war spear and straightened to face Saban with both weapons. 'Sixty-three men have I slaughtered,' he said, 'and some had more killing scars than I did.'

'I have killed two that I know of,' Saban said, 'but now it will be three, and sixty-three spirits in the afterlife will be in my debt and Derrewyn will thank me.'

'Derrewyn!' Jegar said scornfully. 'A whore. You'd die for a whore?' He suddenly ran at Saban, lunging with the spear, and laughed as Saban stepped clumsily aside. 'Go home, Saban,' Jegar said, lowering his spear's blade. 'What pride could I take in killing a bullock like you?'

Saban thrust with his spear, but the blade was contemptuously knocked away. Then Jegar lunged again, almost casually; Saban hit the spear aside and saw the sword coming fast from his other side and had to leap back to escape the fast swing. Then the spear came again, then the sword, and he was scrambling desperately back through the leaf mould, mesmerised by the flashing blades that Jegar used with such confident skill. Fighting was Jegar's life and he practised with weapons every day so he had long learned to compensate for his crippled hand. Jegar stabbed the spear again, then abruptly checked his attack to shake his head. 'You're not worth killing,' he said scornfully. Some of his men had come up the hill to watch the fight, and Jegar waved them back. 'It's our argument,' he said, 'but it's over.'

'It isn't over,' Saban said, and he lunged with the spear, dragging it back as soon as Jegar began to parry and then ramming it forward again, aiming at Jegar's throat, but

Jegar swayed to one side and struck the spear down with his sword.

'Do you really want to die, Saban?' Jegar asked. 'Because you won't. If you fight me, I won't kill you. Instead I shall make you kneel to me and I'll piss on your head as I did before.'

'I shall piss on your corpse,' Saban said.

'Fool,' Jegar said. He thrust the spear blade forward with a serpent's speed, driving Saban backwards, then he thrust again, and Saban leapt up onto a rock so he was higher than Jegar, but Jegar swung the sword at his legs, forcing Saban to retreat higher still. Jegar laughed when he saw the fear on Saban's face, stepped forward to stab with the spear, and Slaol struck him.

The beam of sunlight came down through a myriad shifting green leaves. It was a spear of light that slid through the branches to strike and dazzle Jegar's eyes. The brilliance lasted only for a heartbeat, but Jegar flinched and jerked his head away and in that heartbeat Saban jumped down from the rock and rammed his spear straight into Jegar's throat. He screamed as he did it, and the scream was for Derrewyn's torment and for his own victory and for the joy he felt as he saw his enemy's blood misting bright.

Jegar fell. He had dropped his spear and was clawing at his throat where his breath bubbled with dark blood. He twitched, and his knees came up to his belly and his eyes rolled as Saban twisted the bronze blade, then twisted it again, so that yet more blood ran into the leaves. He dragged the spear free and Jegar looked up at him with disbelief and Saban drove the blade down into his enemy's belly.

Jegar shivered, then was still. Saban, eyes wide and breath heaving, stared at his enemy, scarce daring to believe Jegar was dead. He had thought himself out-matched, and so he had been, but Slaol had intervened. He pulled the spear from Jegar's corpse, then turned to look at Ratharryn's shocked warriors. 'Go and tell Lengar that Derrewyn is avenged,' he told them. He spat on Jegar's corpse.

Jegar's men backed away and Saban stooped to untie the leather thongs that strapped the sword to Jegar's dead hand. 'How long will you stay at Sul?' he asked Lewydd, who had stayed close to Saban throughout the brief fight.

'Not long,' Lewydd said. 'We must be home by mid-summer. Why?'

'I shall be back here in four days,' Saban said, 'and I would travel to Sarmennyn with you. Wait for me.'

'Four days,' Lewydd said, then flinched when he saw what Saban was doing. 'Where are you going?' he asked.

'I shall be back in four days,' Saban repeated, and would say no more. Then he picked up his burden and walked uphill.

The killing at Sul was over.

Saban was tired, hungry and sore. He had walked for the best part of a night and a day, first travelling eastwards from Sul, then following a well-worn traders' path that led northwards through unending woods. Now, on the second evening after leaving Sul, he was climbing a long gentle hill that had been cleared of trees, though any crops that had ever grown on the slope had long vanished to be replaced by bracken. There were no pigs, the only beast that ate the bracken, and no other living thing in sight. Even the air, on this warm and oppressive evening, was empty of birds, and when he stopped to listen he could hear nothing, not even a wind in the bracken, and he knew that this was how the world must have been before the gods made animals and man. The clouds about the low sun were bruised and swollen, shadowing all the land behind him.

Saban had left his bow, his quiver and his spear with Lewydd and he carried only Jegar's bloodstained tunic with its weighty burden. He was dirty, and his hair hung lank. Ever since he had left Sul he had been wondering why he was making this journey and he had found no good answers except for the dictates of instinct and duty. He had a debt, and life was full of debts that must be honoured if fate was to be kind. Everyone knew that. A fisherman was given a good catch so he must offer something back to the gods. A harvest was plump so part must be sacrificed. A favour engendered another favour and a curse was as dangerous to the person who pronounced it as to the person it was aimed against. Every good thing and bad thing in the world was balanced, which was why folk were so attentive to omens – though some men, like Lengar, ignored the imbalance. They simply piled evil on evil and so defied the gods, but Saban could not be so carefree. It worried him that a part of his life was out of balance and so he had walked this long path to the bracken-covered hill where nothing stirred and nothing sounded. More woods crested the hill and he feared to walk in their darkening shadows as night fell, and his fear increased when he reached the trees for there, at the edge of the forest and standing on either side of the path like guardians, were two thin poles that carried human heads.

They were mere skulls now for the birds had pecked the eyes and flesh away, though one of the skulls was still hung with remnants of hair attached to a yellowing scalp. The eyeholes stared a bleak warning down the hill. Turn now, the eyeholes said, just turn and go.

Saban walked on.

He sang as he walked. He had little breath for singing, but he did not want an arrow to hiss out of the leaves so it was better to announce his presence to the spearmen who guarded this territory. He sang the story of Dickel, the squirrel god. It was a child's song with a jaunty tune and told how Dickel had wanted to trick the fox into giving him his big jaw and sharp teeth, but the fox had turned around when Dickel made his spell and the squirrel got the fox's bushy red tail instead. 'Twitch-tail, twitch-tail,' Saban sang, remembering his mother singing the same words to him, and then there was a sound behind him, a footfall in the leaves, and he stopped.

'Who are you, twitch-tail?' a mocking voice asked.

'My name is Saban, son of Hengall,' Saban answered. He heard a sharp intake of breath and knew that the man behind him was considering his death. He had announced that he was Lengar's brother and in this land that was enough to condemn him and so he spoke again. 'I bring a gift,' he said, lifting the blood-crusted bundle in his hand.

'A gift for whom?' the man asked.

'Your sorceress.'

'If she does not like the gift,' the man said, 'she will kill you.'

'If she does not like this gift,' Saban said, 'then I deserve to die.' He turned to see there was not one man, but three, all with kill scars on their chests, all with bows and spears, and all with the bitter and suspicious faces of men who fight an unending battle, but fight it with passion. They guarded a frontier that was protected by the skulls and Saban wondered if the whole of Cathallo's territory was ringed by the heads of its enemies.

The men hesitated and Saban knew they were still tempted to kill him, but he was unarmed and he showed no fear, so they grudgingly let him live. Two escorted him eastwards while the third man ran ahead to tell the settlement that an intruder was coming. The two men hurried Saban for night was looming, but the summer twilight was long and there was still a thin light lingering in the sky when they reached Cathallo.

Rallin, the new chief, waited for Saban on the edge of

the settlement. A dozen warriors stood with him while the tribe had gathered behind to see this brother of Lengar who had dared come to their home. Rallin was no older than Saban, but he looked formidable for he was a tall man with broad shoulders and an unsmiling face on which a wound scar streaked from his beard to skirt his left eye. 'Saban of Ratharryn,' he greeted Saban dourly.

'Saban of Sarmennyn now,' Saban said, bowing respectfully.

Rallin ignored Saban's words. 'We kill men of Ratharryn in this place,' he said. 'We kill them wherever we find them and we strike off their heads and put them on poles.' The crowd murmured, some calling that Saban's head should be added to the cull.

'Is it really Saban?' Another voice spoke, and Saban turned to see Morthor, the high priest with his empty eye-sockets, standing among the crowd. His beard was white now.

'It is good to see you, Morthor,' Saban said, then wished he had not used those words.

But Morthor smiled. 'It is good to hear you,' he answered, then he turned his sightless eyes towards Rallin. 'Saban is a good man.'

'He is from Ratharryn,' Rallin said flatly.

'Ratharryn did this to me,' Saban answered, holding up his left hand with its missing finger. 'Ratharryn enslaved me and cast me out. I do not come from Ratharryn.'

'But you were whelped in Ratharryn,' Rallin insisted obstinately.

'If a calf is born in your hut, Rallin,' Saban asked, 'does that make it your son?'

Rallin considered that for a heartbeat. 'Then why do you come here?' he demanded.

306

'To bring Morthor's daughter a gift,' Saban answered.

'What gift?' Rallin demanded.

'This,' Saban said. He lifted the bundle but refused to unwrap it, and then a scream like a vixen's shriek sounded and Rallin turned to stare towards the great embankment of the shrine.

A pale slim figure stood alone in the temple's dark. She beckoned, and Rallin, obedient to the summons, stood aside and Saban walked towards the woman who waited for him where the paired stones of the western avenue met the temple's embankment. It was Derrewyn and Lahanna was shining on her to make her beautiful. She wore a simple deerskin tunic that fell to her ankles and which appeared almost white in the moonlight, while round her neck was a chain of bones. But as Saban drew nearer he saw that her beauty was the moon's reflection, little more, for she was thinner now and her face was angrier and lined and bitter. Her black hair was scraped back into a tight knot, while her mouth, which had once been so quick to smile, was a thin-lipped slit. In her right hand was the thigh bone that Sannas had once carried and Derrewyn raised it as Saban reached the avenue's last pair of stones. 'You dared to come here?' she asked.

'To bring you a gift,' Saban answered.

She looked at the bundle, then gave an abrupt nod and Saban untied the tunic and shook its contents onto the bare moonlit ground between them.

'Jegar,' Derrewyn said, recognising the head despite the blood which matted its beard and smeared its skin.

'It is Jegar,' Saban said. 'I cut off his head with his own sword.'

Derrewyn stared at it, then grimaced. 'For me?'

'Why else would I bring you the head?'

She looked at him, and it seemed that a mask dropped away for she gave him a tired smile. 'Is it Saban of Sarmennyn now?'

'It is.'

'And you have a wife? A lover of Slaol?'

Saban ignored the sourness of the question. 'All the Outfolk love Slaol,' he said.

'Yet now you come to me,' Derrewyn said, the mask of anger back in its place, 'you crawl to me with a gift! Why? Because you need protection from Lengar?'

'No,' Saban protested.

'But you do,' Derrewyn said. 'You killed his friend, and you think he won't return that favour? Touch one of those maggots of Ratharryn, and the rest pursue you.' She frowned at him. 'You think Lengar won't kill you? You think he won't take your wife as he took me? You've hurt him!'

'I came to bring you this,' Saban said, gesturing at Jegar's head, 'and nothing more.' In truth he had thought little of Lengar's reaction to Jegar's death. His brother would be filled with rage, of that Saban was sure, and he would probably want revenge, but Saban believed he would be safe in Sarmennyn.

'So you brought me your gift, nothing more,' Derrewyn said. 'What were you hoping for, Saban? My gratitude?' She hoisted her deerskin skirts, lifting them almost to her waist. 'Is that what you want?'

Saban turned away to look across the dark fields. 'I wanted you to know that I had not forgotten.'

Derrewyn dropped the skirts. 'Forgotten what?' she asked sourly.

'That we were lovers,' Saban said, 'and that I knew happiness with you. And since that time to this there has not been one day in which I have not thought of you.'

Derrewyn gazed at him for a long time, then sighed. 'I knew you had not forgotten,' she said, 'and I always hoped you would come back.' She shrugged. 'And now you are here. So? Will you stay? Will you help us fight your brother?'

'I shall go back to Sarmennyn,' Saban said.

Derrewyn sneered. 'To move your famous temple? The temple that will draw great Slaol to Ratharryn! Scorching the sky as he comes to do your bidding? Do you really believe he will come?'

'Yes,' Saban said, 'I do.'

'But to do what?' This time Derrewyn spoke without scorn.

'What Camaban promises,' Saban said. 'There will be no more winter, no more disease, no more sadness.'

Derrewyn stared at him, then put her head back and laughed, and her mockery echoed from the farther side of the great chalk embankment, which shone white in the twilight. 'No more winter! No more sadness! You hear that, Sannas? You hear it? Ratharryn will banish winter!' She had been dancing as she mocked, but now she stopped and pointed the thigh bone at Saban. 'But I don't need to tell Sannas that, do I? She knows what Camaban wants because he stole her life.' She did not wait for an answer, but spat and strode forward to pick up Jegar's head by its bloody crown. 'Come with me, Saban of Sarmennyn,' she said, 'and we shall find out whether you will conquer winter with your rattling stones from the west. If only you could! We could all be happy again! We could be young and happy, with no pains in our bones.'

She led him into the shrine. There was no one else there, just the rising moon shining on the huge boulders in which tiny flecks of starlight seemed to be embedded. Derrewyn took Saban to Sannas's old hut, which was still the only building inside the embankment, and there she tossed Jegar's head beside the entrance before pulling up her tunic and tugging it over her head. She dropped the bone necklace on the tunic. 'You too,' she said, indicating that he should take off his own tunic. 'I'm not going to rape you, Saban, I merely want to talk with the goddess. She likes us naked, just as your priests go naked so that nothing lies between them and their gods.' She ducked under the door.

Saban took off his tunic and boots, then followed her into the hut. Someone, presumably Derrewyn, had placed a baby's skull above the door. It had been a very young baby when it died for the crevice in the skull's dome still gaped. The interior of the hut had not changed. There were the same bundles hanging in the shadowed roof and the same jumbled piles of furs and baskets of bones and pots of herbs and ointments.

Derrewyn sat cross-legged on one side of the fire and indicated that Saban should sit opposite. She fed the fire, making it burn bright to flicker ominous shadows among the bat wings and antlers suspended from the roof pole. The flames lit her body and Saban saw she had become cruelly thin. 'I'm not beautiful any more, am I?' she asked.

'Yes,' Saban said.

She smiled at that. 'You tell lies, just like your brothers.' She reached into a big pot and brought out some dried herbs, which she threw onto the fire. She threw more, handful after handful, so that the small pale leaves first flared brilliant, and then began to choke the flames. The light dimmed and the hut began to fill with a thick smoke. 'Breathe the smoke,' Derrewyn ordered him, and Saban leaned forward and took in a breath. He almost choked and his head span, but he forced himself to take another breath and found there was something sweet and sickly in the harsh smoke's touch.

Derrewyn closed her eyes and swayed from side to side. She was breathing through her nose, but every now and then she let a sigh escape, and then, quite suddenly, she began to weep. Her thin shoulders heaved, her face screwed up and the tears flowed. It was as though her heart was broken. She moaned and gasped and sobbed, and the tears trickled down her face, and then she doubled forward as though she would retch, and Saban feared she would put her head into the smouldering fire, but then, just as suddenly, she arched her body back and stared into the peaked roof as she gasped for breath. 'What do you see?' she asked him.

'I see nothing,' Saban said. He felt light-headed, as though he had drunk too much liquor, but he saw nothing. No dreams, no visions, no apparitions. He had feared he would see Sannas, back from the dead, but there was nothing but shadow and smoke and Derrewyn's white body with its protruding ribs.

'I see death,' Derrewyn whispered. The tears still ran down her cheeks. 'There will be so much death,' she whispered. 'You are making a temple of death.'

'No,' Saban protested.

'Camaban's temple,' Derrewyn said, her voice no more

311

than the sigh of a small wind brushing a temple's poles, 'the winter shrine, the Temple of Shadows.' She rocked from side to side. 'The blood will steam from its stones like mist.'

'No!'

'And the sun bride will die there,' Derrewyn crooned.

'No.'

'Your sun bride.' Derrewyn was staring at Saban now, but not seeing him for her eyes had rolled up so that only the whites showed. 'She will die there, blood on stone.'

'No!' Saban shouted and his vehemence startled her from her trance.

Her eyes focused and she looked surprised. 'I only tell what I see,' she said calmly, 'and what Sannas gives me to see, and she sees Camaban clearly for he stole her life.'

'He stole her life?' Saban asked, puzzled.

'He was seen, Saban,' Derrewyn said tiredly. 'A child saw a limping man leave the shrine at dawn, and that same morning Sannas was found dead.' She shrugged. 'So Sannas cannot go to her ancestors, not till Camaban releases her, and I cannot kill Camaban, for I would kill Sannas with him and share her fate.' She looked heart-broken, then shook her head. 'I want to go to Lahanna, Saban. I want to be in the sky. There's no happiness here on earth.'

'There will be,' Saban said firmly. 'We shall bring Slaol back and there will be no more winter and no more sickness.'

Derrewyn smiled ruefully. 'No more winter,' she said wistfully, 'and all by restoring the pattern.' She enjoyed Saban's surprise. 'We hear all that happens in Sarmennyn,' she said. 'The traders come and talk to us. We know about your temple and about your hopes. But how do you know the pattern is broken?'

'It just is,' Saban said.

'You are like mice,' she said scornfully, 'who think the wheat is grown for their benefit and that by saying prayers they can prevent the harvest.' She stared at the dull glow of the fire and Saban gazed at her. He was trying to reconcile this bitter sorceress with the girl he had known, and perhaps she was thinking the same thing for she suddenly looked up at him. 'Don't you sometimes wish everything was as it used to be?' she asked.

'Yes,' Saban said, 'all the time.'

She smiled at the fervour in his voice. 'Me too,' she said softly. 'We were happy, weren't we, you and I? But we were also children. It really wasn't so long ago, but now you move temples and I tell Rallin what to do.'

'What do you tell him?'

'To kill anything from Ratharryn, of course. To kill and kill again. They attack us all the time, but the marshes protect us and if they try to go round the marshes we meet them in the forests and kill them one by one.' Her voice was full of vengeance. 'And who started the killing? Lengar! And who does Lengar worship? Slaol! He went to Sarmennyn and learned to worship Slaol above all the gods and ever since there has been no end to the killing. Slaol has been unleashed, Saban, and he brings blood.'

'He is our father,' Saban protested, 'and loves us.'

'Loves us!' Derrewyn snapped. 'He is cruel, Saban, and why should a cruel god take away our winter? Or spare us sadness?' She shuddered. 'When you worship Slaol as

313

just one of many gods then he is held in check – all is in balance. But you have put him at the head of the gods and now he will use his whip on you.'

'No,' Saban said.

'And I will oppose him,' Derrewyn said, 'for that is my task. I am now Slaol's enemy, Saban, because his cruelty will have to be curbed.'

'He is not cruel,' Saban insisted.

'Tell that to the girls he burns each year in Sarmennyn,' Derrewyn said tartly, 'though he spared your Aurenna, didn't he?' She smiled. 'I do know her name, Saban. Is she a good woman?'

'Yes.'

'Kind?'

'Yes.'

'And beautiful?' Derrewyn asked pointedly.

'Yes.'

'But she was shown to Slaol, wasn't she? Given to him!' She hissed those three words. 'You think he will forget? She has been marked, Saban, marked by a god. Camaban was marked! He has a moon on his belly. Do not trust people marked by the gods.'

'Aurenna was not marked,' Saban protested.

Derrewyn smiled. 'Her beauty marks her, Saban. I know, for I was once beautiful.'

'You still are,' Saban said and he meant it, but she just laughed at him.

'You would do better to make a hundred temples to a hundred gods, or make one temple to a thousand gods, but to make that temple? It would be better to make no temples at all. Better to take the stones and drop them in the sea.' She shook her head, as though she knew her

314

advice was in vain. 'Fetch me the necklace I dropped outside,' she ordered him.

Saban obeyed, scooping up the rattling bones on their string of sinew. They were, he realised with a shock, the bones of a small baby, all tiny ribs and fragile fingers. He handed it across the smouldering remnants of the fire and Derrewyn bit through the sinew and took a single small vertebra out of the string. She reached behind her for a red-coloured pot with a wide mouth that was sealed with beeswax. She used a knife to lever off the wax stopper and immediately a terrible stench pervaded the hut, overpowering even the remnants of the pungent smoke, but Derrewyn, whose head was directly above the evil smell, did not seem to mind. She pushed the small bone into the pot, then brought it out and Saban saw it was smeared with a sticky pale gum.

She put the pot aside and dragged a flat basket towards her and rooted amongst its contents, finally bringing out two halves of a hazelnut's shell. She placed the bone inside the shell and, frowning with concentration, closed the shell and wrapped it in a length of sinew. She wound the thread repeatedly about the nut, then took a leather lace and made the sinew-wrapped nut into an amulet that Saban could wear about his neck. She held it to him. 'Put it on.'

'What is it?' Saban asked, taking the amulet nervously.

'A charm,' she said dismissively, covering the stinking pot with a scrap of leather.

'What sort of charm?'

'Lengar gave me a son,' she said calmly, 'and the bone inside the shell is a bone of that child, and the ointment is what is left of its flesh.'

Saban shuddered. 'A bone of your own child?'

'Lengar's child,' Derrewyn said, 'and I killed it as you'd kill a louse. It was born, Saban, it cried for milk and I cut its throat.' She stared at Saban, her gaze unblinking. He shuddered again and tried to imagine the hate that had been put into her soul. 'But I shall have another child one day,' she went on. 'I shall have a daughter and I shall raise her to be a sorceress like me. I will wait till Lahanna tells me the time is right and then I shall lie with Rallin and breed a girl to guide this tribe when I am dead.' She sighed, then nodded at the nutshell amulet. 'Tell Lengar that his life is trapped inside that shell and that if he threatens you, if he attacks you or if he even offends you, just destroy the amulet. Beat it flat with a stone or burn it and he will die. Tell him that.'

Saban hung the hazel shell about his neck next to the amber pendant that had been his mother's gift. 'You hate him,' he said, 'so why don't you crush the charm?'

Derrewyn smiled. 'It was my child too, Saban.'

'So . . .' Saban began, but could not go on.

'Crush the amulet,' she said, 'and you will hurt me too. Maybe not kill me, for it is my magic and I can make charms to counter it, but it will hurt. It will hurt. No!' She had seen that he was about to take the amulet off. 'You will need it, Saban. You brought me a gift and now you must take mine. You gave me Jegar's life so I give you your brother's life for, believe me, he wants yours.' She rubbed her eyes, then crawled past him into the open air. Saban followed.

Derrewyn pulled the deerskin tunic over her head then stooped to look at Jegar's head. She turned it over and spat into its eyes. 'I shall plant this on a stake outside this hut,' she said, 'and one day, perhaps, put Lengar's head beside it.'

Saban dressed. 'I will go at dawn,' he said, 'with your permission.'

'With my help,' Derrewyn said. 'I'll send spearmen to take you safely away.' She kicked Jegar's head inside the hut. 'We shall meet again, Saban,' she said, and then, abruptly, she turned and hugged him, burying her face in his tunic and holding him with an astonishing strength. He felt her shudder and he put his arms about her.

She immediately pulled away. 'I will give you food,' she said coldly, 'and a place to sleep. And in the morning you can go.'

In the morning, he went.

Lengar had already gone back to Ratharryn when Saban returned to Sul. 'He thought you'd run away,' Lewydd told Saban.

'You didn't tell him I was coming back?'

'I told him nothing. Why should I? But the sooner you're home in Sarmennyn, the better. He wants you dead.'

Saban touched the shape of the nutshell beneath his tunic, but said nothing of it. Would it work? Would he even need it? If he stayed in distant Sarmennyn he would never need face Lengar again and so he was glad when, on the day after his return from Cathallo, Kereval at last tore himself away from the hot spring in which he had been soaking himself, claiming that it cured the aches in his bones. The westwards sea journey home was much harder for the wind was against the boats and though the tides still carried them for half of the time, the voyage took much paddling and a whole day longer than the outward journey. At last, though, the boats turned about the headland and the crews sang as the tide carried them upriver to Kereval's settlement.

Next day Saban picked woad from a hillside and Aurenna infused it in water and, when the dye was ready, she placed a second killing tattoo on Saban's chest. She hammered the marks in with a comb, driving the dye deep, and while she worked Saban told her all that had happened in Sul and how he had taken Jegar's head to Derrewyn. Afterwards, while the blood dried on his chest, he and Aurenna sat by the river and she fingered the nutshell. 'Tell me about Derrewyn,' she said.

'She is thin now,' Saban said, 'and bitter.'

'Who can blame her?' Aurenna asked. She frowned at the nutshell. 'I don't like it. Loosing a curse can hurt the person who releases it.'

'It might keep me alive,' Saban said, taking it from her. 'I shall keep it till Lengar dies, then bury it.' He hung it about his neck. He dared not show it to Camaban for he feared his brother might use the charm to hurt Derrewyn, and so he kept it hidden. He also feared that Camaban would question him about his journey to Cathallo and call him a fool for having made it, but Camaban was preoccupied with finding a trader who could carry him to the island across the western sea. He eventually found some men who were making the voyage with a cargo of flints and so Camaban left Sarmennyn.

'I shall learn their priests' secrets,' he told Saban, 'and come back when it is time.'

'When is that?'

'Whenever I come back, of course,' Camaban said, stepping into the boat. One of the traders handed him a paddle, but Camaban contemptuously swatted it aside. 'I don't paddle,' he said, 'I sit and you paddle. Now take me.' He gripped the boat's gunwales and was carried downstream to the sea.

Ten boats for carrying the temple's pillars were now ready, all of them triple-hulled and tight-lashed, and they were towed upstream to where long grass grew around the growing piles of temple stones. The smaller stones, those about the height of a man, could be loaded two to a boat, but the largest needed a boat to themselves and Saban began by loading one of those huge boulders. At high tide one of the boats was hauled in to the river's edge and its stern was tied firmly to the bank. Saban levered up one end of the boulder, which still rested on its sledge, and slid a beam beneath it. He levered up the other end so three more beams could be placed under the stone, then forty men grasped the beams, heaved up and staggered towards the boat. The men had only a few paces to carry the vast weight, yet they became nervous when they stepped into the water and a dozen more men were needed to steady the stone. The men sweated, but inched onwards until the great stone was poised above the square timbers that spanned the three hulls. They lowered the stone and the boat settled so deep in the water that one hull grounded on the river-bed. Lewydd and a dozen men tugged the boat free and Saban saw how little freeboard the hull had, but Lewydd reckoned they would survive the journey to Ratharryn if Malkin, the weather god, was kind. He and a dozen men boarded the boat and paddled it downriver, followed on the bank by a horde of excited men.

It took three days to load the ten boats. Five of the craft carried large stones while the other five had a pair of smaller stones apiece, and once the stones were lashed to their beams the boats were all floated downstream. There were two places where the river ran shallow and men had to haul the boats across those places as though they were sledges, but in two days all the boats were safe at Aurenna's settlement where they were tethered to trees. At low tide the great hulls rested in the mud while at high they floated free to tug restlessly at their moorings.

They were waiting for the weather. It was already late in the summer, but Lewydd prayed at Malkin's shrine each morning then climbed the hills behind the settlement to peer westwards. He was waiting for the wind to die and the sea to settle, but the wind seemed relentless in those late summer days and the grey waves roared endlessly from the west to shatter white on the rocky coast.

The harvest was cut and then the rains started, blasting from the ocean in teeming downpours so that Saban had to empty the moored boats of rainwater every day. The skies stayed dark and he began to despair of ever moving the stones, but Lewydd never abandoned hope and his optimism was justified for one morning Saban woke to a strange calm. The day was warm, the winds had settled and the fishermen reckoned the fine weather would last. It often happened like this, they said, that, late in the year, just before the autumn brought howling gales, Malkin would send long days of blissful calm and so the ten boats were loaded with skins of fresh water and sacks of dried fish and baskets of the flat bread that was made on hot stones, and then Scathel splashed each boat with the blood of a freshly killed bullock and, at midday, with a dozen paddlers manning each craft, the first of the temple's stones went to sea.

There were plenty of men in the tribe who said the crews would never be seen again. In the heft of the sea, they claimed, the boats would swamp and the weight of the stones would drag them down to where the grey monsters of the deep waited. Saban and Aurenna walked to the coast and watched the ten boats, escorted by two slim fishing craft, turn around the headland and paddle out to sea. The pessimists were wrong. The ten boats rode the small waves easily and then the leather sails were hoisted above the stones, the paddles dug deep, and the small fleet rode the gentle wind and long tide eastwards.

Now all Saban could do was wait for Lewydd's return. He waited as the days shortened and as the wind rose and the air turned chill. Some days Saban and Aurenna would walk to the southern headland from where they would stare from the cliff's top to search for Lewydd's boats, but though they could see fishing boats with men standing and throwing their small nets, and though they saw plenty of traders' boats loaded with goods, they saw none of the triple-hulled boats that had carried the stones. Day by day the wind drove the sea harder, smashing water white on rock and lashing the wave crests to foam, and still Lewydd did not return. There were days when the fishermen would not go out because the water and the wind were too angry and on those days Saban feared for Lewydd.

The first frost came and after that the first snow. Aurenna was pregnant again and some mornings she woke weeping, though she always denied that her tears were for Lewydd. 'He lives,' she insisted, 'he lives.'

'Then why are you crying?'

'Because it is winter,' she said, 'and Erek dies in the winter and I am so close to him that I feel his pain.' She flinched when Saban touched her cheek. There were times when he felt she was distancing herself from him, moving closer to Erek. She would sit on her stone beside the river, her hands outstretched on either side, and claim to be listening to her god, and Saban, who heard no voices in his head, was jealous.

'Spring will come,' he said.

'As always,' Aurenna said and turned away.

Saban and Mereth made more boats. They found the last big oaks in the nearer forests and from those trunks they could make just five more craft. If Lewydd returned and brought his boats with him they would have fifteen boats, and fifteen boats could carry all the stones eastward in four voyages. But if Lewydd did not return then the temple could not be moved and, as day followed day, and as winter's grip locked the land hard, there was neither news nor sight of Lewydd.

Lewydd's long absence began to unsettle the folk of Sarmennyn. Rumours spread. One story claimed that the ten boats had foundered and their crews had been drowned, dragged down by the stones because Erek did not want them moved. Other folk claimed that Lewydd and his men had been slaughtered by the folk of Drewenna who, instead of providing the sledges as their new chief had promised after the massacre at Sul, had decided to take the stones for themselves. The rumours fed on themselves and, for the first time since Aurenna had walked from the fire, there were murmurs that Camaban and Kereval were wrong. Haragg tried to keep the tribe's faith, but more and more folk muttered that the temple should never have been given away. Over a hundred of the tribe's young men were gone with the boats and the tribe feared they would never see those men again. They had left widows and orphans, they had left Sarmennyn dangerously weak in spearmen, and because so many of the missing were fishermen, it meant there would be hunger in Sarmennyn that winter, and it was all the fault of those who had said the temple should be moved. Scathel, Haragg and Kereval tried to stanch the anger, advising the people to wait for news, but still the rumours flourished and turned to a sudden rage one winter evening when a crowd of resentful folk left Kereval's settlement and crossed the river with burning torches to walk south to Aurenna's settlement.

Scathel took a boat down the river to warn Saban that men were coming to burn the settlement and destroy the new boats. Kereval had tried to stop them, the high priest said, but Kereval was ailing and his authority was weakening.

Haragg spat angrily. 'Who leads them?' he asked his brother. Scathel named some of the men who were coming and Haragg shook with anger. 'They are worms,' he said derisively, and seized a spear.

'Let me talk to them,' Saban said.

'Talking won't stop them,' Haragg retorted as he stalked down the path, spear in hand. Cagan went with him. Saban ordered Mereth to take the women of the settlement into the trees then he ran after Haragg, catching the huge man just as he confronted the firelit crowd on the narrow forest path. Haragg lifted his spear. 'You are fighting against Erek,' he shouted, but before he could say another word an arrow whipped from the crowd to strike his chest and Haragg staggered back to fall against an oak. Cagan bellowed in distress, plucked up his father's spear and charged at the crowd. He was met by more arrows and a shower of stones, but the arrows might as well have been loosed at an aurochs. The giant deaf-mute flailed the spear clumsily, driving men back, and Saban ran to help him, but then Cagan was tripped; he fell, and the crowd surged over the huge man and their spears were rising and falling as he writhed beneath the blades. Saban seized Haragg's arm, hauled the trader to his feet and dragged him away so he would not see his son's death. 'Cagan!' Haragg called.

'Run!' Saban shouted. An arrow hissed past his ear and another thumped into a tree.

The crowd was following, their blood roused by Cagan's death. A spear was thrown and it skidded along the path, nearly striking Saban's ankle, then he saw Aurenna standing in the path's centre. 'Go back!' Saban shouted at her, but she waved him aside. Her golden hair hung free and her deerskin tunic swelled over her pregnant belly. 'Go!' Saban said. 'They've killed Cagan. Go!' He tried to pull her away, but Aurenna shook off his hand, refusing to be moved. She waited calmly, as placid as she had been when she had waited to endure the sun-bride's fire, and then, when the rampaging crowd came into sight, she walked slowly forward to meet them.

She did not raise her hands, she did not speak, but just stood there and the attackers checked. They had killed a man, but now they were faced by a bride of Erek, a woman who was either a goddess or a sorceress, a woman of power, and none had the courage to attack her, though one man did step out of the crowd to confront her. His name was Kargan and he was a nephew of Kereval and a famous warrior in Sarmennyn. He wore ravens' wings in

324

his hair and had ravens' feathers tied to the shaft of his spear which was longer and heavier than any other in Sarmennyn. He had a long jaw and brooding eyes and thick grey scars that boasted of the souls he had slaughtered in battle, but he reverently bowed his head to Aurenna. 'We have no quarrel with you, lady,' he said.

'Then with whom, Kargan?' Aurenna asked gently.

'With the folk who stole our young men,' Kargan said. 'With the fools who would move a temple across a world!'

'Who stole your young men, Kargan?' Aurenna asked.

'You know who, lady.'

Aurenna smiled. 'Our young men will return tomorrow,' she said. 'They will come in their boats and their song will be heard in the river. There will be joy tomorrow, so why cause more sadness tonight?' She paused, waiting, but no one spoke. 'Go back,' she instructed the crowd, 'for our men will come home tomorrow. Erek has promised it.' Then, with a last calm smile, she turned and walked away.

Kargan hesitated, but Aurenna's certainty had taken the anger from the crowd and they obeyed her. Saban watched them go, then followed Aurenna. 'And when the boats do not come tomorrow,' he asked her, 'how will we stop them killing us?'

'But the boats will come,' Aurenna said. 'Erek told me in a dream.' She was quite confident, even astonished that Saban might doubt her dream. 'The dream mists have cleared,' she told him happily, 'and I see Erek's future.' She smiled at him, then led Haragg to her hut where she soothed the trader's grief. He was breathing hard for the arrow had struck deep and pink blood was dribbling from his mouth, but Aurenna assured him he would live and gave him a potion to drink and then pulled the arrow's shaft free.

Next morning, after Cagan's body had been burned on a pyre, almost all the tribe walked south to the headland where the river met the sea, and there they waited above the grey waters. The white birds wheeled and their cries were like the wailing of drowned spirits. Saban was on the cliff top with Scathel and Mereth, and Kargan had come with the folk who had followed him the previous night, but Aurenna did not go. 'The boats will come,' she had told Saban that morning, 'and I do not need to see them.' She stayed with Haragg.

The morning passed and all that came was a squall. The rain hissed on the sea and the cold wind whipped it into the faces of the watching crowd. Scathel was praying, Saban was hunched in the lee of a rock and Kargan was pacing up and down the cliff top thumping the pale grass with his heavy spear. The sun was hidden by cloud.

Kargan finally faced Saban. 'You and your brother have brought a madness to Sarmennyn,' he said flatly.

'I brought you nothing,' Saban retorted. 'Your madness came when you lost the gold.'

'The gold was stolen!' Kargan shouted.

'Not by us.'

'And a temple cannot be moved!'

'The temple must be moved,' Saban said wearily, 'or you and I will never have happiness again.'

'Happiness?' Kargan spat. 'You think the gods want our happiness?'

'If you want to know what the gods want,' Saban said, 'then ask Scathel. He's a priest,' and he gestured towards the gaunt man who had been praying at the cliff's edge, but Scathel was no longer holding his arms to the sky. Instead he was staring eastwards, staring into the grey, shifting veils of rain and suddenly he shouted. He shouted again, pointed his staff and all the watching people turned to see where the high priest looked.

And they saw boats.

They saw a fleet of boats: a fleet racing home against rain and wind as it was carried on the last of the tide's surging ebb. Lewydd had split the great hulls apart so that each triple boat was now three, and the beams that had supported the stones were stored inside the hulls driven by cold men eager to be home. The crowd, which the night before had murdered Cagan and had been ready to slaughter everyone in Aurenna's settlement, now cheered. Lewydd, standing in the leading boat, waved his paddle. Saban was counting the boats and saw they were all there, every one. They came from the sullen waves into the lee of the headland in the river's mouth where the exhausted paddlers waited for the tide to turn.

The evening tide brought the fleet upriver and, just as Aurenna had promised, the crews sang as they guided their big boats into her settlement. They sang the song of Dilan, the sea god, and they drove their paddles in time to the song's rhythm and the crowd, which had followed them upstream, sang with them.

Lewydd jumped ashore and was greeted with embraces, but he fought through the crowd to put his arms about Saban. 'We did it,' he exulted, 'we did it!'

Saban had made a great fire in the open space beside the half-finished boats. The women had pounded roots and grain, and Saban had ordered venison roasted on the fire. The boats' crews were given dry pelts and Kargan returned from Kereval's settlement with pots of liquor and still more people so that it seemed to Saban that all of Sarmennyn was crowded around his home to hear Lewydd's tale. He told it well and the listeners groaned or gasped or cheered as he described how the boats had carried the stones to the River Sul at summer's end. There had been no difficulty in the voyage, he said. The boats rode the seas well, the stones stayed secure and the river was safely reached, but then their troubles began.

The supporters of Stakis, who had been defeated by Lengar, still roamed Drewenna and some of those men demanded tribute that Lewydd did not have. So he stayed at the Sul's mouth where he made himself a palisade and waited for men to come from Kellan, the new chief of Drewenna, and drive the vagabonds away.

Kellan's spearmen escorted the boats up the Sul, but when they reached the shallow headwaters where the boats could no longer float there were no sledges waiting. Kellan had promised to make the sledges, but he had broken the promise and so Lewydd walked to Ratharryn and there argued and pleaded with Lengar, who, finally, agreed to persuade Kellan. By then, however, the autumn winds were cold and the rain was falling and it took long days of tiresome work to fell the trees and trim the trunks and make the great sledges onto which the stones, and then the boats, were laid.

Oxen hauled the boats and the sledges over the hills to the east-flowing river where the boats were relaunched and the stones reloaded, and Lewydd then took the fleet east until they came to Mai's river up which he poled the stones to Ratharryn.

And there he had left the stones. He had split his big

boats into their three hulls and had retraced his steps, dragging the boats across the watershed and relaunching them in the Sul, but when he reached that river's mouth the winter had struck cold and hard and he had not dared come home across the bitterly turbulent sea and so he had waited at the Sul's mouth until the weather relented.

Now he and all his men were home. The first stones were in Ratharryn. And Saban wept because Cagan was dead and burned, but also because there would be joy on earth. The temple was being moved.

Aurenna's second child was a girl, and Aurenna called her Lallic, which meant 'the Chosen One' in the Outfolk tongue. Saban was not happy with the name at first, for it seemed to impose a destiny on the child before fate had had a chance to decide her life, but Aurenna insisted and Saban became used to it. Aurenna never again conceived, but her son and her daughter grew healthy and strong. They lived by the river and Leir could swim almost before he could walk. He learned to paddle a boat, draw a bow and spear fish in the river shallows. And as the brother and sister grew they watched the stones go past their hut towards the sea.

It took five years to move them all. Lewydd had hoped to do it in less, but he would take his cumbersome fleet to sea in nothing less than perfect weather, and one year no stones were moved at all and the year after it was only possible to make one voyage, but when the boats did set out the gods were kind and no more stones were lost and not one man was drowned.

Lewydd brought news back from Ratharryn, telling how the temple was being remade and how the war between Lengar and Cathallo went on. 'Neither side can win,' Lewydd said, 'and neither side will give in, but your brother believes that the temple will bring him good fortune. He still thinks it's a war temple.'

One year he brought news that Derrewyn had given birth to a child.

'A daughter,' Saban said.

'You heard?' Lewydd asked.

Saban shook his head. 'I guessed. And she's well?'

Lewydd shrugged. 'I don't know. I just heard that your brother's priests put a curse on mother and child.'

That night Saban went to the sun-bride's temple in Kereval's settlement and buried his mother's amber pendant beside one of the stones. He bowed to Slaol and asked the god to lift Ratharryn's curses from Derrewyn and her daughter. His mother, he knew, would forgive him, though whether Aurenna would be as understanding he did not know: when she asked him what had happened to the amulet he pretended its sinew had broken and that the amber had fallen in the river.

It was in springtime of the fifth year that the very last stones of the Temple of Shadows were brought down the river. There were only eleven of the dark pillars left and all were hoisted on to their triple-hulled boats and floated downstream to a mooring off Aurenna's settlement. Lewydd was eager to carry the final cargo eastwards, but both Scathel and Kereval wanted to accompany the stones because, with the safe delivery of the last boulders, Sarmennyn's side of the bargain would be fulfilled and Lengar must yield the rest of Erek's treasure. Scathel and Kereval wanted to be present when the treasures were restored to their tribe and they insisted that a small army of thirty spearmen travel with them and it took time to collect the food that those men would need.

No sooner had the extra boats been provisioned than the wind turned sharply into the east to bring cold squalls and short, steep seas. Lewydd refused to risk the boats and so they waited in the river, bucking on their moorings under the impact of the gusting wind and changing tides. Day after day the wind stayed cold and when at last it turned into the west it blew too hard and still Lewydd would not take the fleet to sea.

So they waited, and one day towards the end of spring, on a day in which the wind howled at the tree tops and broke white in shattering spume against the cliffs, a boat appeared in the west, coming from the land across the sea. The boat was manned by a dozen paddlers who fought the storm. They shrieked at it, bailed their boat, paddled again, cursed the wind god and prayed to the sea god and somehow brought their fragile boat safe past the foam-shredded headland and into the river. They drove their hull upriver against the tide's ebb, too angry to wait for the flood, and they chanted as they paddled, boasting of their victory over the storm.

The boat brought Camaban back to Sarmennyn.

He alone had showed no fear at sea. He alone had not bailed, paddled, cursed, nor chanted, but had sat silent and serene, and now, as the boat grounded at Aurenna's settlement, he stepped ashore with apparent unconcern. He staggered slightly, still expecting the world to pitch and rock, then walked to Aurenna's hut.

At first Saban did not recognise his brother. Camaban was still as thin as a sapling and gaunt as a flint blade, but his face was now terrifying for he had scarred his cheeks and forehead with deep vertical cuts into which he had rubbed soot so that his face was barred black. He had plaited his long hair into a hundred narrow braids that writhed like vipers and were hung with a child's knuckle bones. Leir and Lallic shrank from the stranger who sat by Saban's fire and said nothing and who did not even respond when Aurenna offered him food.

He sat there all night, saying nothing, eating nothing, awake.

In the morning Aurenna revived the fire and heated stones to put in the broth and still Camaban did not speak. The wind fidgeted the thatch, plucked at the moored boats and drove rain across the settlement where the crew of Camaban's boat had found shelter.

Saban offered his brother food, but Camaban just stared into the fire. A single tear once ran down a black scar, but that could have been the wind-whirled smoke irritating an eye.

It was not till mid-morning that he stirred. He frowned first, pushed hair from his face, then blinked as if he had just been woken from a dream. 'They have a great temple in the land across the sea,' he said abruptly.

Aurenna stared at Camaban in a trance, but Saban frowned, fearing that his brother would demand that this new temple be fetched by boat.

'A great temple,' Camaban said with awe in his voice, 'a temple of the dead.'

'A temple to Lahanna?' Saban asked, for Lahanna had ever been reckoned the guardian of the dead.

Camaban shook his head. A louse crawled from his hair down into his beard, which was braided like his hair and decorated with more small knuckle bones. He smelt of brine. 'It is a temple to Slaol,' he whispered, 'to the dead who are united with Slaol!' He smiled suddenly, and to Saban's children the smile looked so wolfish that they shrank from their strange uncle. Camaban made the shape of a low mound with his hands. 'The temple is a hill, Saban,' he said enthusiastically, 'circled by stone and hollowed out, with a stone house of the dead in its heart. And on the day of Slaol's death the sun pours down a rock-lined shaft into the very centre of the house. I sat there. I sat among the spiders and the bones and Slaol talked to me.' He frowned, still gazing into the fire. 'Of course it's not built to Lahanna!' he said irritably. 'She has stolen our dead, and we must reclaim them.'

'Lahanna has stolen the dead?' Saban asked, puzzled by the concept.

'Of course!' Camaban shouted, turning his eerily striped face to Saban. 'Why did I never see it before? What happens when we die? We go the sky, of course, to live with the gods, but we go to Lahanna! She has stolen our dead. We are like children without parents.' He shuddered. 'I met a man once who believed the dead go to nothing, that they are lost in the chasm between the stars, and I laughed at him. But maybe he is right! When I sat in that house of the dead with the bones all about me I heard the corpses of Ratharryn calling to me. They want to be rescued, Saban, they want to be reunited with Slaol! We have to save them! We have to bring them back to the light!'

'You have to eat,' Aurenna said.

'I must go,' Camaban said. He looked again at Saban. 'Have they started building the temple at Ratharryn?'

'So Lewydd says,' Saban confirmed.

'We have to change it,' Camaban said. 'It needs a death house. You and I will rebuild it. No mound, of course. The people across the sea are wrong about that. But it must be a place to pull the dead back from Lahanna.'

334

'You can rebuild it,' Saban said, 'but I shall stay here.'

'You will go!' Camaban shouted, and Aurenna scurried to comfort Lallic who had begun to weep. Camaban pointed a bony finger at Saban. 'How many stones must still be delivered?'

'Eleven,' Saban said. 'Just those you see on the river.'

'And you shall go with them,' Camaban said, 'because it is your duty to Slaol. Carry the stones to Ratharryn, and I shall meet you there.' He frowned. 'Is Haragg here?'

Saban jerked his head to show that the big man was in his hut. 'His son died,' he told Camaban.

'Best thing for him,' Camaban said harshly.

'And Haragg himself was wounded,' Saban went on, 'but he recovered, though he still mourns Cagan.'

'Then he must be given work,' Camaban said, then stood and ducked out into the wind and rain. 'It is your duty to go to Ratharryn, Saban! I spared Aurenna's life for you! I spared your life! I didn't do it so you could rot on this river bank, I did it for Slaol and you will repay him by building his temple.' He went to Haragg's hut and pounded a fist on the mossy thatch. 'Haragg!' he shouted. 'I need you.'

Haragg came from the door with a startled expression. He was completely bald now and unnaturally thin, so that he looked old before his time. The arrow's strike had left him sick for a long time and there had been days when Saban was sure the breath would die in the big man's throat, but Haragg had survived. Yet it seemed to Saban that he was wounded in his spirit far more grievously than in his body. Haragg now stared at Camaban and, for a heartbeat, did not recognise the man with a striped face, then he smiled. 'You've come back!' he said.

'Of course I've come back!' Camaban snapped. 'I always said I would, didn't I? Don't just gaze at me, Haragg, come! You and I have much to discuss and far to travel.'

Haragg hesitated an instant, then abruptly nodded and, without even looking back at his hut, let alone fetching anything he might need, followed Camaban towards the trees.

'Where are you going?' Saban called after them.

'To Ratharryn, of course!' Camaban said.

'You're walking?' Saban asked.

'I never wish to see another boat,' Camaban said fervently, 'so long as I live,' and with that he walked on. To make his new temple even greater. To tie Slaol to the living and the dead to Slaol. To make a dream.

'Camaban is right,' Aurenna said that evening.

'He is?'

'Erek saved us,' she said, 'so we must travel where he wishes. It is our duty.'

Saban rocked back and forth on his heels. It was night, the children were sleeping and the fire was burning low to fill the hut with smoke. The wind had dropped and the rain had ended, though the eaves of the thatch still dripped. 'Camaban said nothing of you going to Ratharryn,' Saban said.

'Erek wants me there,' Aurenna retorted.

Saban groaned inwardly for he knew he must now argue with the god. 'My brother Lengar would want nothing more than for me to take you to Ratharryn. He will see you, lust after you and then take you. I shall fight for you, of course, but his warriors will cut me down and you will be forced onto his pelts and raped.'

'Erek will not permit it,' Aurenna said placidly.

'Besides,' Saban said petulantly, 'I don't want to go to Ratharryn. I'm happy here!'

'But your work here is done,' Aurenna pointed out. 'There are no more boats to be made and no more stones to be fetched down the mountain. Erek's work moves to Ratharryn and he saved our lives, so that is where we shall go.' She smiled. 'We shall go to Ratharryn and we shall wind the world back to its beginning.'

It was an argument Saban could not win for Erek was against him, and so Aurenna readied herself and the children for the voyage. Yet the sea winds would not abate and still the great waves broke white and ragged on the headland and day after day passed until the summer brought bramble blossom and bryony, bindweed and speedwell, and still Lewydd would not risk the journey. 'The gods,' Lewydd said one night, 'they are holding us back.'

'It's the missing stones,' Aurenna said. 'The two that we lost in the river and the one that broke on the mountain. If we don't replace those stones the temple will never be complete.'

Saban said nothing, though he did glance at Lewydd to see how he would respond to the thought of fetching more stones from the mountains.

Aurenna closed her eyes and swayed back and forth. 'It is a temple to Erek,' she said softly, 'but it is being built to draw him back to Modron' – Modron was the Outfolk name for Garlanna – 'so we should send one stone for her. One great stone to replace the three that were lost.'

'We could fetch one more stone from the mountain,' Lewydd said grudgingly.

'Not from the mountain,' Aurenna said, 'but from here.' In the morning she showed Lewydd the greenish boulder beside the river where she and Saban liked to sit, the great stone with shining flecks and pink sparkles embedded in its heart. The mother stone, Aurenna called it, for it lay in mother earth's dark grip while the rest of the boulders had been plucked from the hanging valley in Erek's sky.

It was vast, that mother stone, twice the weight of the heaviest of the temple's pillars, and it lay deeply embedded in the grassy bank. Saban stared at the stone for two days, trying to work out how to shift it, then he and Mereth went into the woods and found six tall trees that they chopped down. They trimmed the trunks into smooth poles, then cut them into eighteen shorter lengths.

Next day they lifted the mother stone from the earth with levers of oak. Saban dug deep on either side of the stone, scraping holes like badgers' setts far under the rock, and the levers were thrust down into the earth and then, with six men on either side, the front end of the rock was heaved up. It came reluctantly, and men had to scrabble the earth away from beneath the boulder to free it from the soil's grip, but at last it lifted and Mereth could thrust one of the short rollers under the stone.

For three days they levered and lifted until the stone was resting on the eighteen rollers, and now Lewydd could bring one of the empty triple-hulled boats in to the bank. He tethered the craft with its bows facing the stone, then waited for the tide to drop so that the boat was stranded on the mud. Once the boat was in place, Saban's men levered the rock forward while others stood in the riverbank's mud and tugged on ropes to drag the mother stone along the rollers. The boulder was almost three times the height of a man, but slender, and it rolled willingly enough. Men dragged the rollers as they emerged behind the rock and placed them in front of it, and so, hand's breadth by hand's breadth, the great slab was dragged and pushed until one end of it jutted out from the bank to overhang the stranded boat.

'Careful now!' Saban called. One of the rollers had been placed on the boat and two men held it in place as a dozen others manned levers at the back of the stone. 'Heave again!' Saban called, and the great slab edged forward and then began to tip down. 'Let it tip! Let it tip!' Saban shouted, and watched as the stone's forward edge swung down to rest on the boat. The three hulls creaked alarmingly under the stone's weight. More rollers were placed on the boat and the men levered again and, as the rain speckled the river and the women watched and the tide rose, the vast tongue of stone was pushed onto the boat. The mother stone was so long that it almost filled the boat's whole length.

'Now to see if it floats,' Lewydd said, and he, Saban and Aurenna waited on the river bank as night fell and the tide went on rising. They lit a fire and by its light they saw the dark incoming water swirl about the boat's three hulls. Higher and higher the water came until Saban was sure that it must rise above the boat's gunwales and so flood the hulls, but then the mud under the boat yielded a sucking sound and the three hulls were shifting in the current. 'I never thought we'd move that stone,' Lewydd said wonderingly.

'We've still got to shift it to Ratharryn,' Saban said.

'Erek will help,' Aurenna claimed confidently.

'The boat floats low,' Lewydd said, worried, and explained that at sea the waves inevitably slopped over the hull's gunwales to flood the boats. The outer hulls, where the paddlers knelt, could be bailed easily enough, but the mother stone was so long there was scarce room for a man to crouch in the central hull.

'Put a small boy there,' Saban suggested, and in the morning they discovered there was just room for a boy to crouch in front of the stone, and another behind it, and Lewydd reckoned that if the two boys kept scooping out the seawater then the heavily laden boat might survive the voyage. 'So long,' he added, 'as the weather is kind.'

But the weather stayed hard. The boats waited, the warriors were ready to travel, but the winds heaped up the seas and brought yet more stinging rain. Another moon passed, the summer was slipping away and Saban began to fear he could never leave. Or hope he could never leave, for he did not really want to go back to Ratharryn. Home was Sarmennyn, beside this river, where he had thought he would live out his life, watch his children grow and become a member of Kereval's tribe. He would put Sarmennyn's scars on his face and rub ash into them so that they showed grey. Only now Camaban and Aurenna insisted he go back to the heartland and Saban did not want to go, so he welcomed the bad weather that kept him beside Sarmennyn's river where he and Mereth whiled away the wasting time by shaping and hollowing a trunk that had been rejected as too short to be turned into one of the hulls for carrying the stones, but which would make a fine fishing craft. They planned to give the boat to Lewydd as a reward for moving the temple.

Mereth had taken a wife from the women of Sarmennyn and he too was wondering whether to go or stay. 'I'd like to see my father again,' he said, 'and Rai wants to see Ratharryn.' Rai was his wife.

Saban tipped a bag of beach sand into the new boat, then rubbed it up and down with a stone, smoothing the wood. 'It will be good to see Galeth again,' Saban said, and he thought it would also be good to visit his father's grave, but he could think of no other reason to take him back to his childhood home. He touched the nutshell under his jerkin, then rocked back on his heels and wondered why he was so reluctant to return. Of course there was fear of Lengar, but Saban possessed the nutshell charm and he believed it would work, so why was he frightened of going home? If the temple was built then Slaol would return and all would be well, and he glanced out into the river where the stones floated on their boats. When those stones reached the Sky Temple the dream would be completed, and then what? Would everything change? Would Slaol scorch through the sky to obliterate winter and sickness? Or would the world change slowly? Would anything happen at all?

'You look worried,' Mereth said.

'No,' Saban said, though he was. He was worried by his unbelief. Camaban believed, Scathel believed and Aurenna believed, indeed most of Kereval's people were sure that they were changing the world, but Saban was not certain he shared their faith. Perhaps, he decided, it was because he alone had known Camaban as the crooked child, as the outcast stutterer, the despised son. Or perhaps it was because he had fallen in love with this river and its banks. 'I was thinking,' he said, 'maybe I could share this boat with Lewydd? Become a fisherman?'

341

'All you'll ever catch is a cold,' Mereth said. He shaved a trace of wood so that the rising curve of the prow looked perfect. 'No,' he said, 'I reckon you and I are going home, Saban, and we might as well get used to it. It's what our wives want and what wives want they seem to get.'

The summer passed and the winds did not abate and Saban doubted the stones would leave the river that year, but then, just as it had in the very first year, the approaching autumn brought a spell of calm seas and gentle winds. Lewydd waited two days, spoke to the fishermen, prayed at Malkin's shrine and then declared the small fleet could leave. Food and water were put back into the boats, the warriors took their places, and Mereth and Saban settled their families in two of the long, single-hulled craft that would escort the stones eastwards. Scathel sacrificed a heifer and splashed its blood on the tightly lashed stones, Kereval kissed his many wives and it was time to go.

The heavily laden boats went downstream to the lee of the headland in the river's mouth with the paddlers chanting a song to Erek. The folk left behind stood on the river bank and listened to the strong voices fade. They listened until there was no sound but the running of the river and the sigh of the wind. Sarmennyn had kept faith. It had sent its temple to Ratharryn and all the folk could do now was wait for the return of their chief, their high priest and their treasures.

The weather was placid, and it needed to be, for the boat holding the mother stone was clumsy and slow. When Saban had first made this voyage it had seemed swift, but then he had been in a single-hulled boat that had cut through the water like a knife slicing flesh, but the big, triple-hulled boats seemed to batter their way through the waves. The tide carried them and the paddlers worked themselves to weariness, but it was still an agonisingly slow voyage. Saban and his family shared one of the boats carrying Kereval's warriors and that was frustrating for the boat could have leapt ahead of the fleet, but instead had to stay with the lumbering stone-carriers. The mother stone was the slowest, and the two small boys in the centre hull had to bail water constantly. If the boat sinks, Scathel had warned the boys, they would be blamed and would be allowed to drown, and the warning kept them hard at work scooping with their sea-shells. Aurenna clutched Lallic, while Leir had a leash about his waist so that when he fell overboard he could be hauled back like a fish. The sun shone, proof that Erek approved their voyage.

They anchored at each tide's turning and set off when the water flowed east again. It did not matter whether that turning came by day or night; that they slept between the tides and, as often as not, travelled beneath the stars. The moon was a sickle, low in the sky, so there seemed little danger of Lahanna's jealousy thwarting the journey. Day after day, night after night, the stones crept eastwards until at last, after nine days and nights, the sun rose to show the green hills close on either bank, with the great shining mud flats slowly drying as the river shrank. They paddled hard, racing to keep with the dying tide and competing with each other as the banks came closer and at last Sul's mouth came into view. The paddlers drove the boats up into the narrower stream, between the high mud flats, past fish and eel traps, to where a small settlement of fishermen had their huts near the palisade Lewydd had made on the very first journey of the stones, and there at last they could rest. Scathel gave a stone axe-head to the chief of the settlement in return for a scrawny goat that he sacrificed to Erek as thanks that the most dangerous part of the journey was done. The fisherfolk watched bemused as the Outfolk warriors danced to the setting sun. In times past there would have been nothing but enmity between the two groups, but the settlement gave their allegiance to Drewenna and the river folk had become used to the voyaging stones.

Lewydd sent one of the fishermen with a message to Kellan, Drewenna's chief, asking of him to send men to haul the sledges which waited at the end of the first river journey, and next morning they started up the Sul with the incoming tide. That first day was easy enough, but after then the tide was of small help and they had to pole the boats upstream. It took three days to reach Sul where Kereval decreed they would rest for two days. Aurenna and Saban took the children to splash in the hot spring that bubbled over the rocks to make a pool amidst ferns and moss. The rocks above the pool were strewn with scraps of wool where petitioners had left their prayers for the goddess and all that day a succession of the lame, the crippled and the sick came to the shrine to beg Sul's help. Aurenna washed her hair in the spring and Saban combed it out for her and the folk of Sul watched in amazement for she was so tall, so clean and so calm. One man asked Saban whether she was a goddess, while another offered him seven oxen, two axe-heads, a bronze spear and three of his daughters if Aurenna would be his wife.

They spent that night in one of the huts Stakis had made for the meeting of the tribes. Saban lit a fire on which they cooked trout and then he watched Aurenna until she became tired of his gaze. 'What is it?' she asked.

'Are you a goddess?' Saban asked.

'Saban!' she said reproachfully.

'I think you are a goddess.'

'No,' she replied with a smile, 'but Erek does want me for something special. That is why we travel.' She knew he was worried for her and so she reached over and touched his hand. 'And Erek will preserve us. You'll see.'

Saban woke in the dawn to discover that a party of Ratharryn's warriors had come to the shrine during the night. The leader of the warrior band was Gundur, one of Lengar's closest companions and the man who had dragged Saban from his hut on the morning that he had been enslaved to Haragg. Gundur had come from south of the river, from Drewenna, and Saban saw how Gundur and his men strutted through Sul's huts. This was Kellan's territory, but the spearmen of Ratharryn were lords here. Saban ate with Gundur's men and listened as they told of Lengar's wars: how he had seized a herd of Cathallo's oxen; how he had raided deep into the land of the people to the east of Ratharryn; and how he had forced a heavy tribute from the people who lived by the sea at the mouth of the River Mai. Now, Gundur said, even as they spoke, Lengar was at Drewenna. He had gone there, Gundur explained, to fetch Kellan's spearmen. 'The harvest is in,' Gundur said, 'so what better time to attack Cathallo? We'll finish them for ever. You can join us, Saban. Share the plunder, eh?' Gundur smiled as he offered the invitation. He seemed friendly, hinting that the old enmity between Saban and Lengar was long past.

'What brings you to Sul?' Saban asked.

'You,' Gundur said. 'Lengar heard the last of the stones had come and sent us to find out if it were true.'

'It is true,' Saban said, gesturing at the boats, 'and you should tell Lengar that Kereval of Sarmennyn has come with them to receive the treasures.'

'I shall tell him,' Gundur promised, then turned to watch as Aurenna walked from the huts to the river. She carried a water-skin that she stooped to fill, then carried back, and Gundur watched her every step. 'Who is that?' he asked in an awed voice.

'My wife,' Saban said coldly.

'I shall tell Lengar you're both here. He'll be pleased.' Gundur stood. He hesitated a heartbeat and Saban wondered if he was about to mention Jegar's death, which had taken place so close to where they had eaten, but Gundur merely asked if Saban intended to carry the stones up river that same day.

'We do,' Saban said.

'Then we shall see you in Ratharryn,' Gundur said, and he led his men south while Saban and his family went back to the stones and continued the weary journey of poling the heavy boats against the river's flow. So now Lengar knew that Aurenna had come to the heartland, and knew she was beautiful; Saban surreptitiously touched the nutshell that hung at his neck.

The journey became much easier when they were half a day out of Sul for now the river was shallow enough for men to wade and so haul the boats, and next day they came to a place where a smaller river joined the Sul from the south and Lewydd turned the boats into that narrower stream. The current was less strong, almost placid, and they made easy progress, coming that evening to the place where the water was at last too shallow to carry the boats and where the great sledges waited. Next day men arrived

346

from Drewenna and they heaved the eleven small stones off the boats and on to the sledges, then hauled the boats themselves on to even larger sledges.

The mother stone alone remained and it took a whole day to align the boat with a sledge on the shore and to cut more rollers, and next day, using oxen to drag the boulder, they slid the mother stone from boat to sledge. They hauled the boat ashore the following day, by which time the first stones were already being dragged eastwards.

It took three days to cross the low watershed. They followed a grassy track that climbed gently and then fell, just as gently, to the bank of the river which flowed eastwards. Here the boats were lifted from the sledges and relaunched and the stones were carried back aboard. For five years Lewydd and his men had been doing this. Five years of lifting and levering, heaving and sweating, and now the great task was almost finished. It took three days to carry all the stones off their sledges and on to the boats, but at last the job was done and it would never need to be done again.

Next morning they floated the boats down the river and the men sang as they rode the current. They did not hurry and the only effort that was ever needed was an occasional shove of a pole to drive a boat around an obstruction. The sun shone, filtering through the last green leaves as the river slowly twisted between banks thick with feathery willow-herb. Corncrakes sounded harsh from the fields and woodpeckers stuttered in the trees. The sun shone. When they passed Cheol, Ratharryn's southernmost settlement, the folk lined the river bank to dance and sing a welcome to the stones. 'Tomorrow!' Saban called to them. 'We shall be at Ratharryn tomorrow! Tell them we're coming!'

Once past Cheol the river entered the trees again. The current was faster now, so fast that those men who had elected to walk along the bank had to half run to keep up with the fleet. There was an air of excitement now. The great work was so close to its finish and Saban wanted to shout his triumph at the sun. It had all been done for Slaol, and surely Lengar's enmity would fade in the glory of Slaol's approval. Saban was not sure how that approval would be shown, but his doubts about Camaban's dream were fading. It was the journey itself that had restored his faith for he had seen for himself just how much effort had been needed to move the boats and the stones and he could not believe that five such hard years were for no purpose. Slaol must respond! Just as a short lever of wood could move a great stone, so little men could shift a vast god. Camaban was surely right.

'Don't let the current take them!' Lewydd was shouting and Saban came out of his happy reverie to see that the river had almost reached its confluence with the bigger River Mai and that it was time to drag the boats into the bank and tether them there for the night. Next morning they would have to haul the stones upriver against the Mai's current to Ratharryn, so they would spend this last night of the journey amidst the trees which grew on the narrowing spit of land between the two rivers.

They tied the boats to the bank, then made fires. It was a warm, dry night, so there was no need for shelters, but they did make a cordon of fires from river bank to river bank to deter the malevolent spirits, and Kereval's warriors were set to watch beside the fires and feed the flames through the darkness. The rest of the travellers gathered and sang songs until tiredness overwhelmed them and then they wrapped themselves in cloaks and slept beneath the trees. Saban listened to the river noises until the dreams came. He dreamed of his mother, seeing her try to hammer a peg into their hut's pole, and when he asked her why she did it, she had no answer.

And suddenly the dream was full of new noises, of screaming and terror, and he woke, realising it was no dream at all, and he sat up to hear shouts from beyond the fire cordon and a strange ripping sound overhead. Then something thumped into a tree and he realised it was an arrow and the ripping sound was the noise of other arrows flickering through the leaves. He seized his bow and his quiver of arrows and ran to the fire cordon. Immediately two arrows whipped from the dark close to him and he understood the flames made him into a target, so he hid himself behind some bushes where Mereth and Kereval both sheltered. 'What's happening?' Saban asked.

Neither man knew. Two of Kereval's warriors were wounded, but no one had seen the enemy or even knew what enemy it was, but then Kargan, Kereval's nephew, came running and shouting for his uncle and his voice provoked another flight of arrows from the dark.

'They're stealing one of the stones,' Kargan said.

'They're stealing a stone?' Saban could not believe what he heard.

'They're towing one of the boats upstream!' Kargan said.

Scathel had overheard. 'We have to follow,' he said.

'What about the women and the children?' Kereval demanded. 'We can't leave them alone.'

'Why would they want to steal a stone?' Mereth asked.

'For its power?' Saban suggested.

The noises in the wood were fading and no more arrows

flickered from the dark. 'We should follow them,' Scathel demanded again, but when Saban and Kargan crept into the darkness beyond the fire cordon, they found nothing. The enemy had gone, and in the morning, when a mist was drifting over the rivers, they discovered that one of the triple-hulled boats had been dragged away. It had carried one of the smaller stones, but now it was gone. One of the two wounded men died that morning.

And Saban saw that the moon stayed in the sky after the dawn and he recalled that he had dreamed of his mother and she had ever been a worshipper of Lahanna. The goddess, he feared, was striking back, but then he found some of the arrows and saw they were fledged with ravens' feathers. Black feathers, like those the men of Ratharryn used, but he said nothing of his suspicions for the great work was almost done.

The last part of their journey was up the Mai. The sun shone warmly, but the mood was sombre and the memory of the arrows in the night chilling. The men watched the wooded banks warily as they towed the boats through the waist-deep water with the spearman's corpse laid on the long mother stone. Scathel had insisted that the corpse be carried to Ratharryn for he wanted to place the treasures against the dead man's skin so that the departed spirit would know that his journey and death had not been wasted.

Saban walked up the river bank holding Leir's hand. Aurenna carried Lallic and listened as Saban talked of the hills they passed. That one was where a great bear had been killed, and that one was where Rannos, the god of lightning, had struck a thief dead, and this one, he said, pointing to a wooded hill on the left, is where our Death Place lies. 'The Death Place?' Leir asked.

'We don't burn our dead in Ratharryn,' Saban explained, 'but lay them in a small temple so the birds and beasts can eat their flesh. Then we bury the bones, or perhaps put them in a mound.'

Leir made a face. 'I'd rather be burned than eaten.'

'So long as you go to the ancestors,' Saban said, 'what does it matter?'

They rounded the corner of the hill and on the river bank ahead was a great crowd of people who began to sing in welcome as the first of the boats came in view. 'Which one is Lengar?' Aurenna asked.

'I don't see him,' Saban said, and as he drew closer he saw that Lengar was not there. Mereth's younger half-brothers were there and so were Saban's sisters, and a host of others he remembered, and when he came near they ran to him and reached out to touch him as though he had a sorcerer's power. When they had last seen Saban he had been little more than a boy, but now he was a man, tall and bearded and straight-backed, with a hardened face and a son of his own. They stared at Aurenna in amazement, awed by her golden hair and gentle face that was so miraculously untouched by the scars of any disease. Lengar, folk told Saban, was still at Drewenna, and then the crowd parted to let Galeth through. He was old now, old and white-haired, and one eye was milky white and his back was bent and his beard thin. He first embraced Mereth, his eldest son, then clasped Saban. 'You have come back for good?' Galeth asked Saban.

'I don't know, uncle.'

'You should stay,' Galeth said softly, 'stay and be chief.'

'You already have a chief.'

'We have a tyrant,' Galeth said fiercely, his hands on Saban's shoulders. 'We have a man who loves war more than peace, a man who thinks every woman is his own.' He looked at Aurenna. 'Take her away, Saban,' he added, 'and don't bring her back until you have become chief here.'

'Has Lengar built the temple?'

'It is being built,' Galeth said, 'but Camaban came in the spring and he and Lengar argued. Camaban came with Haragg, and they both said the temple must be changed, but Lengar insisted it must be finished just as it is for it will give him power, and so Camaban and his companion went away.' Galeth looked at Aurenna again. 'Take her away, Saban! Take her away! He'll see her and he will take her for himself!'

'I want to see the temple first,' Saban said and he led Aurenna up the hill on a wide path that had been worn into the turf by the passage of the sledges carrying the stones from the river. Kereval and his men followed, wanting to see how their temple looked in its new home.

'Lengar assures us it is a great war temple,' Galeth said, hobbling beside Saban. 'He believes Slaol is not just the god of the sun, but the god of war too! We already have a god of war, I told him, but Lengar says Slaol is the great god of war and of slaughter. He believes he will finish his temple, Saban, then rule all the world.'

Saban smiled. 'The world may not agree.'

'What Lengar wants, Lengar takes,' Galeth said grimly, giving Aurenna another anxious glance.

Saban touched the nutshell. 'We shall be safe, uncle,' he said, 'we shall be safe.'

The path led north at first, climbing between harvested fields and skirting the high trees where the Death Place was hidden, then turned westwards and now Saban could see the great earthen wall of Ratharryn off to his right. He showed the embankment to Leir, telling him that that was the place where he had grown up. On either side now were the ancestors' grave mounds and Saban dropped to his knees and bent his head to the grass in thanks for their protection over the years.

Once past the mounds the path turned south to drop into a small valley, then joined the sacred path that Gilan had ordered made when the first stones came from Cathallo. The hill bulged, serving like the double bend in Cathallo's sacred path to hide the temple until the last moment of the approach, and Saban felt a growing excitement as he climbed between the ditch and chalk banks. He had last seen the Temple of Shadows in the high valley at Sarmennyn, but now he would see it again, though wondrously moved across a whole wide land and a cold green sea. He took hold of Aurenna's hand and she smiled at him, sharing his anticipation.

The first they saw of the temple was the sole remaining sun stone that stood high in the sacred path, and after it the twin pillars at the shrine's gateway of the sun came into view, and then at last they breasted the hill's slope and the temple was in front of them.

It was more than half built. The entrance corridor of lintelled stones was finished and the double circle of pillars was almost two-thirds complete, standing around the temple's centre and flanked by the four moon stones.

Saban guessed that only thirty more stones needed to be placed and he saw that the holes for those pillars had already been dug, while off to one side of the temple, beyond the ditch and banks, a pile of Sarmennyn's stones waited to be placed. All that was needed now was for those pillars to be carried across the entrance causeway and for the last stones to be brought up from the river and the temple would be finished. But already it was near enough complete so that a man could see how the shrine would look when the last stone was planted. Saban stopped by the lichen-covered sun stone and gazed at what he and Lewydd and so many others had achieved over the last five years. 'Well?' Galeth asked.

Saban said nothing. He had been waiting for this moment, and he was remembering the awe he had felt when he had first seen the double ring emerging from Sarmennyn's fog, yet somehow, here at Ratharryn, there was no awe. He had thought he would be overwhelmed by the temple, that he might even fall to his knees in spontaneous worship, yet somehow the two rings looked smaller here and their stones appeared shrunken. In Sarmennyn, cradled by the dark valley and poised above the gulf of air, the stones had snatched an awesome power from the windy sky as they had stared across a whole land to where the sun died in a distant sea. In Sarmennyn the stones had formed a snare to capture a god, but here the dark pillars were dwarfed by the wide grassland. Dwarfed, too, by the seven taller and paler stones from Cathallo.

'Well?' Galeth asked again.

Saban did not want to answer the query. 'We were attacked last night,' he said instead.

Galeth touched his groin. 'By outcasts?'

'We don't know who attacked us,' Saban said, remembering the black-fledged arrows.

'The outcasts have become bold,' Galeth said. He laid a hand on Saban's arm and lowered his voice. 'People have fled.'

'From the outcasts?'

'From Lengar!' Galeth leaned closer. 'There are rumours, Saban, that the spirits of the dead have gathered to kill Lengar. Folk are frightened!'

'We saw no dead last night,' Saban said, then went to stand between the entrance pillars that had come from Cathallo. He had to look steeply up to the tops of those stones, while the tallest stones of the new rings were not much higher than Saban himself and most were much shorter. 'What did Camaban say of the temple?' he asked Galeth.

'He wanted it remade,' Galeth said, then shook his head. 'I do not know what else he wanted, but he did not seem pleased and Lengar shouted at him and they argued and Camaban and his companion walked away.'

'This is how it was in Sarmennyn,' Saban said, still gazing at the stones.

'You're disappointed?' Aurenna asked.

'It's not my disappointment that matters,' Saban said, 'but what Slaol thinks.' He was looking beyond the temple now, to the southern grave mounds that clustered so thick on the brow of the hill. There were new mounds there, their chalk flanks white in the sun, and he supposed one of those newer graves belonged to his father. 'Where is Camaban now?' he asked Galeth.

'We haven't seen him all summer,' the old man said.

'He wanted me here to finish the temple,' Saban said.

'No!' Galeth insisted hotly. 'You must go away, Saban. Take your woman, go!' He turned to Aurenna. 'Don't let him keep you here. I beg you.'

Aurenna smiled. 'We are supposed to be here. Erek' – she corrected herself – 'Slaol wants us to be here.'

'Camaban insisted we come,' Saban added.

'But Camaban is gone,' Galeth said. 'He has not been here in four moons. You should follow him.'

'Where to?' Saban asked. He led Aurenna around the temple's margin, following the low bank that lay outside the ditch until he came to the place where he had sat on the grass with Derrewyn on that far-off day after his ordeals. She had made a daisy chain, he remembered, and he was suddenly overcome with sadness for it seemed that five years of work had been for nothing. The temple had been moved, but Slaol would never be drawn to these little stones. Most were scarce as tall as a child! The temple was supposed to call the god to earth, but this little pattern of stones would pass under Slaol's gaze like an ant beneath a hawk's eye. No wonder, Saban thought, that Camaban had fled, for all their labour had been for nothing. 'Maybe we should just go home,' he said to Aurenna.

'But Camaban insisted –' she began.

'Camaban has gone!' Saban said harshly. 'He is gone, and we have no need to stay if he is gone. We shall go home to Sarmennyn.' The music of Sarmennyn had become his music, the tales of its tribe his tales, its language his tongue, and he felt no kinship with this frightened place with its shabby temple. He turned and walked to where Kereval was standing beside the sun stone. 'With your permission,' Saban said to the chief, 'I would return home with you.'

'I would be sad if you did not,' Kereval said, smiling. The chief was white-haired now, and stooped, but he had lived long enough to see his bargain fulfilled and so he was happy.

Scathel intervened, 'But we do not go back until the gold and the other treasures are returned.'

'My brother knows that,' Saban said and just then a warning shout made him turn round to see that six horsemen had appeared among the grave mounds to the south. All carried spears and had short Outfolk bows across their shoulders and all six were warriors who, long before, had marched to Ratharryn to help Lengar snatch the chieftainship. Their leader was Vakkal whose face had the grey ashen scars of Sarmennyn, but whose arms now boasted the blue scars of Ratharryn. He was a tall man with a harsh face and a short black beard that had a badger's streak of white. He wore a leather tunic that was armoured with bronze strips, had a bronze sword at his waist and fox tails woven into his long plaited hair. He dismounted when he came to Kereval, then dropped to his knees in submission. 'Lengar sends his greetings,' Vakkal told the chief.

'He follows you?' Kereval asked.

'He will come tomorrow,' Vakkal said, then stood aside as his five Outfolk warriors came to greet their chief. Saban saw how the folk of Ratharryn made way for the men, how they scuttled apart as if it was suddenly bad luck to be close to a spearman. Vakkal was gazing at Aurenna who, made uncomfortable by his stare, went to stand beside Saban. 'I don't know you,' Vakkal challenged Saban.

'We met once,' Saban said, 'when you first came to Ratharryn.'

Vakkal smiled, though no pleasure showed in his eyes. 'You are Saban,' he said, 'Jegar's killer.'

'And my friend!' Kereval said loudly.

'We are all friends,' Vakkal said, still looking at Saban.

'Does Lengar bring us the gold?' Scathel demanded.

'He does,' Vakkal said, at last looking away from Saban. 'He brings the gold, and until he comes he asks only that you and your men be his honoured guests.' He turned and gestured towards Ratharryn. 'He says you are welcome to his home and that a feast will be made for you.'

'And we are to receive the gold?' Kereval asked eagerly.

'All of it,' Vakkal promised with a sincere smile, 'all of it.'

Kereval fell to his knees in gratitude. He had sent a temple and kept faith with his god and the treasures would now be returned to his tribe. 'Tomorrow,' he said happily, 'tomorrow we shall take our gold and we can go home.'

Home, Saban thought, home. Tomorrow. It would all be over and he could go home.

Ratharryn had grown. There were more than twice as many huts as when Saban had left, indeed there were so many that they now filled more than half the space inside the encircling wall, while a whole new settlement had been built beyond the embankment on the higher ground close to the wooden temple of Slaol. Yet the most startling change was that Lahanna's temple had been replaced by a great round thatched building. 'It used to be the temple,' Galeth told Saban, 'only now it is Lengar's hall.'

'His hall?' Saban was shocked. It seemed a terrible thing to transform a temple into a hall.

'Derrewyn worships Lahanna in Cathallo,' Galeth explained, 'so Lengar decided to insult the goddess. He pulled down most of the poles, roofed it, and he now feasts here.' Galeth had led Saban through the soaring hut's doorway into a cavernous interior much higher and larger than Kereval's great building at Sarmennyn. A dozen of the Old Temple posts were left, only they now supported a high thatched roof that soared towards a hole at the peak where smoke could escape, though that vent was barely visible because the roof beams were hung with a multitude of spears and smoke-darkened skulls. 'The spears and heads of his enemies,' Galeth told Saban in a hushed voice. 'I do not like this place.'

Saban hated it and Lahanna, he thought, would surely want revenge for the desecration of her shrine. The hall was so large that all Kereval's men, well over a hundred of them, could sleep on its rush- and bracken-strewn floor, and all ate there that night, feasting on pork, trout, pike, bread, sorrel, mushrooms, pears and blackberries. Saban and Aurenna ate in Galeth's hut where they listened to tales of Lengar's chieftainship. They heard stories of endless raids, of the slaughter of strangers, the enrichment of the warriors and the enslavement of countless folk from neighbouring tribes, yet through it all, Galeth said, Cathallo had resisted. 'All who hate Ratharryn,' he said, 'befriend Cathallo.' So Cathallo and Ratharryn still fought, though it was Ratharryn who raided the deepest. No boy could now become a man in Ratharryn until he had brought back a head to add to the skulls in Lengar's great hut. 'It is not enough to survive the forest these days,' Galeth said, 'a boy must also show his bravery in battle, and if he is thought a coward then he must spend a whole year dressed as a woman. He must squat to piss and fetch water with the slaves. Even their own mothers despise them!' He shook his head and made a keening noise.

'Yet Lengar is building the temple?' Aurenna asked, puzzled that a man who so loved war should make a temple that was supposed to bring a time of peace and happiness.

'It is a war temple!' Galeth said. 'He claims Kenn and Slaol are one!'

'Kenn?' Aurenna asked.

'The god of war,' Saban explained.

'Slaol is Kenn, and Kenn is Slaol,' Galeth said, shaking his head. 'But Lengar also says a great leader must have a great temple and he likes to boast that he has stolen a temple clean across the world.'

'Stolen?' Aurenna asked with a frown. 'He is exchanging it for gold!'

'He is building it for his own glory,' Galeth said, 'though there are rumours that the temple will never be finished.'

'What rumours?' Saban asked.

The old man rocked back and forth. The fire lit his gaunt face and threw his shadow on the underside of the roof's thatch. 'There have been omens,' he said quietly. 'There are more outcasts than ever among the trees and they grow bold. Lengar led all his spearmen against them, but all they found were corpses hanging in trees. They say the outcasts are led by a dead chieftain and none of our spearmen dare confront them now, not unless a priest goes with them to make charms and spells.' Galeth's wife Lidda, who was toothless and bent now, cried aloud and groped under her pelt to touch her groin. 'Healthy children have died,' Galeth continued, 'and lightning struck Arryn and Mai's temple. One of its posts is all blackened and split!'

Lidda sighed. 'Corpses were seen walking beyond the Sky Temple,' she moaned, 'and they cast no shadows.'

'It isn't a Sky Temple now,' Saban said bitterly. The airy lightness of the first stones had been stolen by Sarmennyn's squat ring. It was not even a Temple of Shadows, but something belittled and inadequate.

'An ash was cut in the forests and it cried like a dying child!' Galeth said. 'Though I did not hear it myself,' he added. 'Axes are blunt before they are used.'

'The moon rose the colour of blood,' Lidda carried on

the lament, 'and a badger killed a dog. A child was born with six fingers.'

'Some say' – Galeth lowered his voice and glanced warily at Aurenna – 'that the Outfolk temple has brought ill fortune. And when Camaban came here in the spring he said the temple should be remade, that it was all wrong.'

'And Lengar disagreed?' Saban asked.

'Lengar says Camaban has gone mad,' Galeth said, 'and that Slaol's enemies are trying to prevent the temple's completion. He called Camaban an enemy of Slaol! So Camaban went away.'

'And the priests?' Saban asked. 'What do they say?'

'They say nothing. They fear Lengar. He killed one!'

'He killed a priest?' Saban asked, shocked.

'The priest tried to stop him turning Lahanna's temple into a hut, so Lengar killed him.'

'And Neel?' Saban asked. 'What did he do?'

'Neel!' Galeth spat at the mention of the high priest's name. 'He's nothing but a dog at Lengar's heels.' Galeth turned to Aurenna. 'You must go, lady, before Lengar returns.'

'Lengar will not touch me,' Aurenna said, using the language of Ratharryn that she had learned from Saban.

'We are here with warriors of Sarmennyn,' Saban explained, 'and they will protect her.' He touched the nutshell beneath his tunic.

Galeth looked dubious at that assertion. 'When my brother was chief,' he told Aurenna, 'we were happy.'

'We were happy,' Lidda echoed.

'We lived in peace,' Galeth said, 'or tried to. There was hunger, of course, there is always hunger, but my brother knew how to share food. But it has all changed, all changed.'

Next morning, under a cloudless sky and a warm sun, a hundred men slid the mother stone ashore and levered it onto a sledge that was harnessed to sixteen oxen. The beasts dragged the stone away from the river while Galeth took Saban and Aurenna to the Sky Temple and asked where the stone should be placed. It was Aurenna who decreed that it should stand on its own within the double ring and opposite the lintelled gateway of the sun. That way, she said, the rising sun at midsummer would touch the mother stone as a symbol of the earth and sun united. There was no one else to make the decision so Galeth ordered a dozen men to make a hole where Aurenna had indicated.

Galeth watched as the turf was peeled back and the antler picks prised at the chalk beneath. 'I can't dig any more,' he told Saban. 'My joints ache. I can't even swing an axe now.'

'You've worked hard enough,' Saban said.

'If a man can't work, a man shouldn't eat, eh?' Galeth said, then turned to watch the oxen hauling the mother stone, which was so long that it overhung its sledge at both ends. Three of the smaller stones were following, their sledges being dragged by men. 'All slaves,' Galeth told Saban. 'Our spearmen raid constantly for slaves and food. We trade in slaves now and it makes Lengar rich.'

A horn sounded to the south. The noise was booming, but made tremulous by the warm autumn air. Saban looked enquiringly at Galeth, who nodded. 'Your brother,' he said wearily.

Saban crossed the banks and ditch, going to Aurenna. He put an arm about her and placed his other hand on his son's shoulder. The horn sounded again, and then there was a long silence. Saban watched the near crest that was broken by the humps of the graves. Farther off, blurred by the warm air, the distant horizon was dark with trees.

They waited, but still nothing showed on the crest. A wind lifted Aurenna's long hair and rippled the grass, turning it pale and then dark again. Lallic was wriggling in her mother's arms and Aurenna soothed the child. The men digging the hole for the mother stone had dropped their antler picks and were staring south. Even the oxen dragging the boulder were standing still, their heads low and their flanks bleeding from the goads. A hawk slid across the sacred path, its black shadow flicking sharp against the chalk banks.

'Is a bad man coming?' Leir asked his father.

Saban smiled. 'It is your uncle,' he said, ruffling his son's hair, 'and you must treat him with respect.'

The ox-horn sounded again, much louder and closer, and Leir, startled by the blast, jumped under Saban's hand, though still nothing showed at the hill's crest. Then the ox-horn sounded a fourth time and a single man ran to the top of one of the grave mounds. He carried a long pole from which hung a standard of fox brushes and wolf tails. The standard bearer wore a cloak of an untrimmed wolf pelt and the wolf's mask was perched on his head like a second face. He stood silhouetted against the sky and shook the standard and a heartbeat later the whole crest filled with men.

They had come in a long line, and if they meant to impress, they did. One moment the crest was empty, the next it was thronged with a battle-line of spearmen, so many spearmen that Saban knew that he must be staring at the combined armies of Ratharryn and Drewenna. Their

364

spears made a ragged hedge and their sudden shout frightened Lallic. It was a display of awesome power, only this
army was not arrayed before an enemy, but in front of
Lengar's own home. Lengar must have known Cathallo
would hear of this horde, and he wanted them to fear its
power.

Lengar himself, tall and cloaked, spear in hand and with
a sword at his belt, appeared at the centre of his army. A
dozen men, his war chiefs, surrounded him, while next to
him, looking short and plump, was Kellan, chief of Drewenna and Lengar's lackey. Lengar stood for an instant then
beckoned his escorts forward.

'How are they all fed?' Aurenna wondered aloud.

'In summer it's easy enough,' Saban said. 'There are
deer and pigs. More pigs than you can imagine. It is a
fat country. In winter,' he went on, 'you raid your
neighbours.'

Lengar saw Saban and swerved towards him. The chief
of Ratharryn was wearing his long leather tunic that was
sewn with bronze strips, a woollen cloak hung from his
shoulders and he carried a massive spear with a polished
bronze blade. Strips of fox fur hung from the spear shaft
and more were wound about his legs and arms. Eagle
feathers had been woven into his hair that had been oiled
so that it lay slicked back close to his skull, reminding
Saban of that far-off day when the stranger had died and
Lengar had pursued him down to the settlement. The kill
scars now stretched to cover the backs of Lengar's hands
and fingers, while the tattooed horns at his eyes gave his
face a terrifying intensity. Saban felt Leir give an involuntary shudder and he patted the boy's head reassuringly.

Lengar halted a few paces away. For a heartbeat or two

he stared at Saban, then spoke derisively. 'My little brother. I thought you would never dare come home.'

'Why should a man fear to come home?' Saban asked.

But Lengar was not listening to Saban. He was staring at Aurenna. She was still as tall and slender and straight-backed as on the day Saban had first met her, still a woman who could have drawn chieftains across the sea, and she met Lengar's gaze calmly, while Lengar looked truly astonished as if he did not really believe his eyes. He kept staring at Aurenna, he stared from her head down to her feet, then back up again. 'Is this Aurenna?' he asked.

'My wife, Aurenna,' Saban said, his arm still about her shoulders.

'Gundur told the truth,' Lengar said quietly.

'About what?' Saban asked.

Lengar still gazed at Aurenna. 'About your woman, of course,' he answered brusquely. His war chiefs stood behind him like leashed hounds, all of them tall men with long spears, long cloaks, long plaited hair and long beards, and they too stared hungrily at the tall, fair-haired woman from Sarmennyn. Lengar at last forced himself to look away from Aurenna. 'Your son?' he asked Saban, nodding towards Leir.

'He is called Leir, son of Saban, son of Hengall.'

'And that child is a daughter?' Lengar nodded at Lallic who was in Aurenna's arms.

'She is called Lallic,' Saban said.

Lengar smiled derisively. 'Only one son, Saban? I have seven!' He looked back at Aurenna. 'I could give you many sons.'

'I am content with your brother's son,' Aurenna said.

'My half-brother's son,' Lengar said scornfully, 'and if

366

the boy dies your life would have been in vain. What use is a woman who whelps only one son? Would you keep a sow that littered only one piglet? And sons do die.' He still gazed at Aurenna, indeed he seemed incapable of looking anywhere else. He looked her up and down again, not bothering to hide his admiration. 'Do you remember, Saban,' he asked, keeping his eyes on Aurenna, 'how our father would always tell us to marry wide-rumped girls? Women are just like cattle, he used to say. The thin ones are not worth keeping. Yet you chose this woman. Perhaps you would have more sons if you followed Hengall's advice?'

'I will take no other wife,' Saban said.

'You will do what you are told, brother,' Lengar said, 'now that you are in Ratharryn.' He turned and pointed his spear to a new mound on the low crest. 'That is Jegar's mound. You think I have forgotten him?'

'A man should remember his friends,' Saban said.

The spear was now pointing at Saban. 'You owe Jegar's family a death price. It will be many oxen, many pigs. I have promised them.'

'And you keep your promises?' Saban asked.

'You will keep this promise,' Lengar said, 'or I will take something from you, brother, of great value.' He looked at Aurenna and forced a smile. 'But we must not quarrel. This is a happy day! You have returned, you have brought the last stones and the temple will be completed!'

'And you will return the treasures to our tribe,' Aurenna said.

Lengar's face twitched. He did not like being told what to do by a woman, but he nodded his assent. 'I shall return the treasures,' he said curtly. 'Is Kereval here?'

'He is in the settlement,' Saban said.

'Then we should not keep him waiting. Come!' Lengar held out his arm for Aurenna, but she refused to leave Saban's side and Lengar pretended not to notice.

The spearmen streamed past Saban and Aurenna. 'I think that we should go now,' Saban said. 'Just walk away.'

Aurenna shook her head. 'We are supposed to be here,' she said.

'Only because Camaban told us to come!' Saban protested. 'And he's gone! He's fled! We should follow him.'

'Erek, Slaol, told us to be here. With or without Camaban, this is where I am supposed to be.' She turned to gaze at the stunted stones of the unfinished temple. 'Slaol has been speaking to me ever more clearly in my dreams,' she said softly, 'and he wants me here. That is why he spared my life, to bring me here.' Saban wanted to argue, but it was hopeless fighting against a god. He did not speak to any god in his dreams. Aurenna turned and frowned at the mass of spearmen walking towards the settlement. 'Why does your brother need so many men?' she asked.

'Because he will attack Cathallo,' Saban said. 'We have arrived in time to see a war.'

They walked back to the settlement. Small boys were driving pigs out of the woods to a patch of land near Slaol's old temple where the beasts were being butchered. Women and children slashed the flesh from the bones while dogs crouched and prowled, hoping for offal, but it was being pounded in mortars, mixed with barley and stuffed into the pigs' intestines, which would be baked in hot ashes. The squeals of the dying animals were constant and the pungent blood sufficient to trickle down the slope in small bright rivulets that were lapped by the hungry dogs. Inside

368

the settlement the stench was worse for there women were mixing pots of the glutinous poison that would coat the warriors' spears for their attack on Cathallo. Other women were readying for the night's feast. Swans were being plucked, pork roasted and grain pulverized on quern stones. The tannin pits, filled with dung and urine, added their smell. Men tied flint arrow-heads to shafts and beat the edge of spear blades to make them sharp.

Aurenna went to Galeth's hut to feed the children while Saban wandered about the settlement in search of old friends. At Arryn and Mai's temple, where he marvelled at the lightning-riven post that was split and blackened, he met Geil, his father's oldest widow, who was laying a little bunch of feathery willow-herbs at the temple's entrance, and she embraced Saban, and then began to cry. 'You should not have returned,' she sobbed, 'for he kills everything he does not like.'

'It was worth coming back,' Saban said, 'just to see you.'

'I won't last this next winter,' the old woman said, dabbing her tears with the ends of her white hair. 'Your father was a good man.' She stared at the flowers she had laid by the entrance markers. 'And all our sons die,' she added sadly, then sniffed and hobbled away towards her hut.

Saban walked into the temple and laid his forehead against a post that he and Galeth had raised many years before. He had not even been a man then. He closed his eyes and had a sudden vision of Derrewyn coming from the stream naked and with water dripping from her hair. Had Mai the river goddess sent that vision? And what did it mean? He prayed to Mai that she would keep his family safe, then rapped on the post to draw the goddess's attention to that prayer when a shout made him turn round. 'Saban!' It was Lengar's voice. 'Saban!'

Lengar was striding through the huts with two spearmen who were evidently his guards. 'Saban!' Lengar shouted again, then saw his brother in the temple and hurried towards him. The folk close to the shrine edged aside.

Lengar was in a rage, his right hand resting on the wooden hilt of the bronze-bladed sword that hung at his waist. 'Why did you not tell me that one of the stones was stolen in the night?' he demanded.

Saban shrugged. 'By men with black-fledged arrows,' he said. 'Why should I tell you what you already know?'

Lengar seemed taken aback. 'Are you saying –'

'You know what I'm saying,' Saban interrupted.

Lengar shouted him down. 'I have an agreement with Sarmennyn!' he bellowed. 'And the agreement was that they should bring me a temple. Not part of one!'

'It was your men who took the stone,' Saban said accusingly.

'My men!' Lengar sneered. 'My men did nothing! You lost the stone!' He punched Saban's chest. 'You lost it, Saban!'

The two spearmen watched Saban warily in case he responded to his brother's anger with a rage of his own, but Saban just shook his head wearily. 'You think you've been cheated because one stone is missing?' he asked. 'One stone from so many?'

'If I chop off your prick, brother, will you miss it? Yet it is such a little scrap of flesh,' Lengar spat. 'Tell me, when these men attacked you with black-fledged arrows, did you kill one? Did you take a prisoner?'

'No.'

'So how do you know who they were?'

'I don't,' Saban confessed, but only Ratharryn used black-fledged arrows. Cathallo mixed the blue feathers of jays with their raven black while Drewenna tipped their arrows with a mix of black and white.

'You don't know,' Lengar jeered, 'because you didn't fight them, did you?' He plucked aside the upper hem of Saban's tunic. 'Just two scars, Saban? Still a coward?'

'One scar is for Jegar,' Saban said defiantly, 'and he did not find me a coward.'

But Lengar did not rise to that bait. Instead he had found the nutshell on its leather thong and, before Saban could stop him, he had pulled it out from under the tunic. 'Cathallo puts its spells inside hazel shells,' he said in a dangerously soft voice. He lifted his gaze to look into Saban's eyes. 'What charm is this?'

'A life.'

'Whose?'

'It is the bone of someone's bone,' Saban said, 'and flesh of their flesh.'

Lengar paused, considering that answer, then gave the leather thong a sharp tug, jerking Saban forward, but succeeding in breaking the nut free. 'I asked whose life it is,' he said.

'Yours, brother,' Saban said.

Lengar smiled. 'Did you think, little brother, that this nutshell would keep your woman safe?'

'Slaol will keep Aurenna safe.'

'But this charm, little brother,' Lengar said, holding the shell in front of Saban's eyes, 'is not of Slaol. It is of Lahanna. Did you crawl back to Derrewyn?'

'I did not crawl to her,' Saban said. 'I went to her with a gift.'

'A gift to my enemy?'

'I gave her Jegar's head,' Saban said. He knew it was dangerous to provoke Lengar, especially as he had no weapon, but he could not help himself.

Lengar stepped back and shouted for Neel, the high priest. 'Neel! Come here! Neel!'

The priest ducked from his hut. He limped because of the arrow that had pierced his thigh on the night that Lengar had killed Hengall. His hair was spiked with dried mud, a ringlet of bones circled his neck and his belt was hung with pouches in which he kept his herbs and charms. He bobbed in front of Lengar, who gave him the nutshell. 'This is a charm on my life,' Lengar said, 'a thing of Derrewyn's. Tell me how it is done.'

Neel glanced nervously at Saban, then took a small flint blade from a pouch and cut the sinews which bound the nut. He split the two halves, then sniffed the contents. He made a face at the stench, then poked at the tiny bone with a finger. 'It must be from Derrewyn's child,' he decided.

'My child, too,' Lengar said.

'She killed it,' Neel said, 'and used its bones and flesh to curse you.'

'A curse of Lahanna's?'

'She would use no other god,' Neel confirmed.

Lengar took the shell back and carefully placed its two halves together. 'Will it work?' he asked the priest.

Neel hesitated. 'Lahanna has no power here,' he said nervously.

'So you constantly assure me,' Lengar said. 'Now we can

test your belief.' He looked at Saban. 'To kill me, little brother, what did you have to do? Crush it?'

Saban said nothing. Lengar laughed. 'One day I shall feed your flesh to the pigs and use your skull as a pisspot.' His words were defiant, but there was nervousness on his face as he placed the nut between the heels of his hands and slowly applied pressure. He paused, evidently wondering whether his defiance of the goddess was sensible, but Lengar had not made Ratharryn feared by being cautious. A man must take risks if he was to achieve greatness and Lengar was willing to wager his life if the reward were large enough, and so he squeezed again. It took more strength than he expected, but at last the shell gave way and the charm was crushed. He held the sticky scraps between his hands and held his breath, waiting. Nothing happened.

He laughed softly, then carefully scooped the remnants of the charm onto one palm. He gave the scraps to Neel. 'Put them in the closest fire,' he ordered, then watched as the priest went obediently to the nearest cooking fire and tossed the charm into the flames. There was a small burst of brighter fire and a hiss of fat, and still Lengar lived.

'Why should I care for Lahanna's curse?' Lengar demanded loudly. 'I live in her temple, and she does nothing. We are Slaol's people! Kenn's people!' He shouted this, making folk stare at him nervously as he brushed his hands together. 'So much for Derrewyn's curse,' he said to Saban. 'Or am I dead?'

Neel laughed at this jest. 'You are not dead!' the high priest cried.

Lengar patted his body. 'I seem to be alive!'

'You are alive!' the priest cackled.

'But Derrewyn is hurting, yes?' Lengar asked the priest.

'Oh, yes,' Neel said, 'yes! She is hurting!' He writhed to show the pain that would be racking Derrewyn. 'She hurts!'

'And Saban is disappointed,' Lengar said pityingly, then gave his brother a stare so chilling that Saban expected the sword to be drawn and buried in his belly. Instead, surprisingly, Lengar smiled. 'I shall make you an offer, little brother. I have cause to kill you, but what merit is there in slaughtering a coward? So you can crawl back to Sarmennyn, but if I ever see your face again I shall cut it off.'

'I want nothing more than to go to Sarmennyn,' Saban said.

'But you shall go without your wife,' Lengar said. 'Lest you be disappointed, brother, I shall buy her from you. Her price is the cost of Jegar's life.'

'Aurenna is not for sale,' Saban said, 'and her people are Sarmennyn's people. You think they will let her go to slake your appetite?'

Lengar sneered at that question. 'I think, little brother, that by tonight your wife will be mine, and that you will bring her to me.' He prodded Saban with a finger. 'You hear that? You will bring her to me. You forget, Saban, that this is Ratharryn where I rule and where the gods love me.' He half turned away, then twisted back, smiling. 'Or you could rule? All you have to do is kill me.' He waited a heartbeat, as if expecting Saban to attack him, then reached out and patted Saban's cheek before leading his grinning spearmen away.

And Saban ran to find Aurenna and was relieved to find

her safe. 'We must go,' he told her, but Aurenna scoffed at his terror.

'I am supposed to be here,' she said. 'Erek wants me here. We are here to do a great thing.'

The nutshell had failed, Aurenna was lost in her dream of the sun god and Saban was trapped.

That night Lengar gave a great feast for the men of Sarmennyn. It was a lavish feast of oysters, swan, trout, pork and venison. His slaves served it in the feasting hall and Lengar supplied generous pots of intoxicating liquor.

Lengar's own men, like the warriors from Drewenna, feasted outside, for there was not room inside the feasting hall for so many and, besides, the men outside prepared themselves for battle and so had gathered first at Slaol's old temple where they sacrificed a heifer and dedicated themselves to slaughter, then they took their liquor pots and drank deep for they believed the fiery drink gave a man courage. The women gathered at Arryn and Mai's temple where they prayed for the men.

Aurenna and Saban ate with Kereval and his men. Scathel complained that a woman should be in a feasting hall, but Kereval soothed the querulous priest. 'She is one of ours,' he said, 'one of ours, and it is only for this night. Besides,' he added, 'is not Aurenna's fate bound up with the treasures' return?'

Lengar came to the hall after dark. The cavernous building was lit by two great fires that sent their smoke up to the skulls that shimmered red in the flame-light. Smoke looped and curled about the skulls before gusting out of the hole in the roof's peak. The food had been plentiful, the liquor potent and Kereval's men were in a fine mood when Lengar arrived escorted by six spearmen. Ratharryn's chief was dressed for battle, with bronze glinting on his tunic and eagle feathers hanging from his spear blade. He beat the spear shaft against the hut's door post for silence.

'Men of Sarmennyn!' he shouted, using the Outfolk tongue. 'You have come here for your gold! For your treasures! And I have them!'

There were murmurs of appreciation. Lengar let the murmurs go on, then smiled. 'But I only agreed to return the treasures when you had brought me a temple.'

'We have brought it!' Scathel shouted.

'You have brought most of it,' Lengar said, 'but one stone is missing. One stone was stolen from you.'

The murmurs turned angry now, so angry that the spearmen behind Lengar moved to protect their chief, but Lengar waved them back. 'Will the temple have power if one stone is missing?' Lengar asked. 'When we bury an enemy's corpse we chop off a hand, or remove the foot, so it is incomplete. Why? So the dead man's spirit will not have power. And now my temple is incomplete. Perhaps Erek will not recognise it?'

'He will know it!' Scathel insisted. The gaunt priest was standing, taut with anger. 'He has watched us move it! He has seen our work!'

'But suppose he is angry because a stone is missing?' Lengar suggested, then shook his head sadly. 'I have thought deeply on this and I have talked with my priests and together we have found an answer that will allow you take the gold back to your country. Is that not why you came? To take the gold home and to be happy there?'

He paused. Scathel was puzzled and said nothing, so Kereval stood. 'What is your answer?' the chief asked courteously.

Lengar smiled. 'I must attract Erek to his temple. To a temple that is not complete. And how better to draw him to us than with his bride?' He pointed at Aurenna. 'Give me that woman,' he said, 'and I will give you your gold. I will give you more besides! I will send you back richer than you were before the gold was stolen from you – this night! I will give you the gold, but only if my brother brings me his bride.' He pointed his spear at Saban, smiling. 'You must bring me Aurenna.'

'No!' Saban shouted. He knew now why Lengar had sent men to steal the stone and he knew also that no one would believe his tale. 'No!' he shouted again.

'Send her to me,' Lengar said to Kereval, 'and I will bring you the treasures,' and with that he went back outside, unhooking a leather curtain that dropped over the doorway.

'No!' Saban shouted a third time.

'Yes!' Scathel shouted even louder. 'Yes! Why else did Erek spare her at the Sea Temple? No bride has ever been rejected, not once in all our tribe's time! There was a purpose in that rejection and now we know the purpose.'

'He doesn't want her for Erek,' Saban shouted, 'but for himself!' Lewydd was standing beside Saban now, adding his voice to the protest, and some of Lewydd's paddlers, the men who had worked for five years to bring the stones across the sea and land, thumped the floor rushes in Saban's support, but the warriors, the men who had come to escort the treasures home, were not looking at Saban, nor at Aurenna. They just stared at the floor.

Scathel spat. 'For five years,' he shouted, 'we have enslaved ourselves to regain our treasures. We have spent blood and toil. We have done what most men said could not be done, and now we are to be denied our reward?' He pointed a bony finger at Saban. 'Why did Erek spare her life? What was his purpose, if not for this moment?'

'That is a good question,' Kereval said quietly.

'This isn't being done for Erek, but for my brother's lust!' Saban shouted, but his protest was howled down by the warriors. It was the treasures that mattered to them, nothing else.

Aurenna stood with Lallic cradled in one arm. She touched Saban's hand. 'It doesn't matter,' she said softly, 'look.' She gazed up, past the fire-tinged skulls to where the smoke vanished through the roof hole.

'What of it?' Saban asked.

Aurenna gave him one of her gentle smiles. 'It is night,' she said softly, 'and a curse of Lahanna's will not work in the sun, will it?' She knew Lengar had destroyed Derrewyn's charm and she had grimaced when she heard the tale. 'It will go badly for him,' she had said quietly then, and now she tried to reassure Saban. 'He has risked the gods, and the gods do not like being defied.'

'Drag her out!' Scathel shouted, impatient with the delay, and Kargan, the leader of Kereval's spearmen, beckoned to his closest companions.

'Leave her!' Kereval ordered.

Aurenna still looked into Saban's face. 'All will be well,' she said, and she walked towards the hall's doorway with

Lallic in her arms. Lewydd picked up Leir as Saban caught up with Aurenna and took her arm and tried to haul her back. She frowned at him. 'You cannot stop me now,' she said, pulling away from him.

'I would rather kill you than give you to him,' Saban said. He had never forgiven himself for Derrewyn's fate and now he was to let Aurenna just walk to his brother's bed?

'Erek wants me here,' Aurenna said.

'Erek wants you raped?' Saban shouted.

'I trust Erek,' Aurenna said placidly. 'Is not my whole life his gift? So how can anything be bad? I won't be raped. Erek will not permit it.'

Kereval moved to intercept them, but the chief had nothing to say. He was fond of both Saban and Aurenna, but his tribe had made sacrifices to regain the gold and now they must sacrifice further. He wanted to say he was sorry, but the words would not come and so he just turned away. Scathel was right, the chief thought. Aurenna had always been supposed to die for Erek and she had gained years of life from her escape at the Sea Temple, so perhaps nothing was as tragic as it seemed. The god's purpose had been hidden, even mysterious, but now it was made plain. Fate was inexorable.

There was silence in the feasting hall as Aurenna lifted the curtain. She stooped under the leather and Lewydd and Saban followed her into the night to see Lengar waiting a few yards away. He was flanked by his bronze-hung warriors who ringed the feasting hut, spears and bows in hand. Some had flaming torches to light the moonless dark. They jeered drunkenly at Saban, who looked into the sky. 'There's no moon!' he said.

'All will be well,' Aurenna said quietly. 'I know it. Erek has not deserted me.'

'Bring her to me,' Lengar said.

Saban hesitated, but Aurenna pulled him forward and walked calmly towards the tall figure of Lengar, whose face showed triumph.

'I said you would bring her, Saban,' Lengar said. 'What a sheep you are.' He jerked his head and four of his men prised Aurenna away from Saban with their spears. They pushed her towards Lengar, while other men, their breath reeking of liquor, seized Lewydd and Saban and forced them away through the cordon of warriors. Saban looked back to see that Aurenna was standing between two guards just behind Lengar.

Yet for the moment Lengar ignored her. Instead he gazed towards the feasting hall and raised his spear. 'Now!' he shouted gleefully, 'now!' and some of the warriors with the torches hurled them onto the feasting hall roof while others jammed their flaming straw-wrapped sticks into the hall's wide eaves. The flames caught the steep thatch with a sickening speed and after only a few heartbeats the first frightened men tried to escape the fire, but as soon as they appeared at the hall door they were met by arrows that threw them back with brutal force. Burning thatch was dropping into the hall, which was thickening with smoke. The weather had been dry and the hall caught the flame like a puffball. More torches were thrown onto the steep roof, now a patchwork of flame and darkness, but the fires spread, joined, blazed bright, and men were screaming beneath the hanging skulls. Some men tried to break through the walls, but arrows spitted them. One man did break free, but he was struck by a half-dozen arrows, then chopped to the ground with a bronze axe.

Aurenna watched, a hand over her mouth, her eyes aghast and her daughter held tight against her body so that Lallic could not see the carnage. The walls were burning now. The long hair of a dead man who was trapped in a gap of the wall suddenly flared. Part of the roof collapsed, spewing a stream of sparks into the night. Skulls fell as burning straw whirled up towards the stars. Lengar's warriors watched enthralled. Some among the spectators were Kereval's own men, the warriors who had followed Vakkal to Ratharryn and who now gave their allegiance to its dark chief, and those Outlanders cheered with the rest. They could see through the burning gaps where flaming men staggered in whirls of fire. A boy, one of the two who had bailed the mother stone's boat dry, screamed frantically. Saban could smell roasting flesh. The screams slowly died, though here and there a dark figure jerked in the smoke and fire, but soon there was no movement at all except for the collapse of rafters and the gouts of spark and fire and smoke. The whole roof caved in, leaving only the twelve temple posts standing. Flames licked up the thick posts. A smoking skull rolled across the grass. Lewydd had put Leir down and was struggling in the arms of two spearmen, but he suddenly collapsed, sinking to his knees and burying his head in his hands. Saban crouched beside him. 'I am sorry,' he said, putting an arm on his friend's shoulders. He held Leir close to him. 'Lengar was never going to give the gold back,' Saban said to Lewydd. 'I should have known. I should have known.'

'Are those two still alive?' Lengar's voice spoke behind Saban. 'Strangle them. No, push them into the flames.'

The spearmen reached for Saban and Lewydd. The moon had just risen in the west, coming from behind the trees on the high land. It was almost full, vast, flattened and red, a swollen moon, monstrous in the murderous night, but its light was drowned by the leaping flames. Yet in Lahanna's light, where it sifted across the dark trees, Saban suddenly saw shapes on the embankment's crest. He saw shadows moving among the white skulls that protected the settlement against the spirits, and the shadows were crossing the earth wall; he twisted to the east, struggling against the spearmen who tried to haul him upright, and he saw more shapes moving there, but no one else in Ratharryn saw the shadows for they were staring into the inferno where over a hundred men of Sarmennyn had choked on smoke and now burned under a layer of scorched skulls and blazing thatch.

The spearmen at last managed to haul Saban and Lewydd to their feet and just then the first arrows flickered in the flame-light. A man fell close by, a shaft dark in his throat. Saban rammed his elbow hard back, heard his captor's breath rush out and wrenched himself free. More arrows thumped home as Saban crouched and wrapped Leir in his arms. He could hear little over the roar of the fire, but he saw the arrows whip through the firelight. Lewydd was free now, his captor struck by one of the missiles. Lengar's spearmen were slowed by the liquor they had drunk and they had still not seen the attackers who had come down from the embankment's crest into the shadows where they were now loosing arrow after arrow. The flint heads drove into flesh. Some struck the huts and a few wasted themselves in the fire.

Saban pulled at Lewydd. 'Come!' He picked up Leir and

ran towards Aurenna who had still not realised the danger. Lengar's drunken men were only just awakening to the attack, and did not yet know where it came from. Saban reached Aurenna, but one of her guards saw him and moved to intercept him, opening his mouth to shout a warning to Lengar, and an arrow slapped straight into his gullet. The man staggered back, choking and with blood pouring down his beard, then fell to the ground. Lengar turned anyway and Saban hit him with his free hand. It was a desperate, wild blow, but it struck Lengar's cheek, knocking him down and Saban grabbed Aurenna with his bruised hand and tugged her into the shadows between the huts where women screamed and dogs howled. 'Run!' Saban shouted at her. 'Run!'

But there was nowhere to run. Enemies had crossed the embankment's northern side and were already at the tanning pits, and their arrows plunged into the thatch close to Saban who, frantic, twisted aside to Galeth's hut. He pushed Aurenna and Lallic inside, then Leir, and afterwards ducked in himself. 'A weapon!' he said to Galeth, who had refused to witness the murderous blaze.

He took Galeth's old spear, the great heavy spear, and gave another to Lewydd.

There was screaming outside. Spearman ran past as Saban pushed into the moonlight. No one noticed him now. He and Lewydd were simply two more spearmen in the chaotic night where a handful of folk tried to extinguish the many small fires that had been started on the thatch of the huts where burning straw had blown from the flaming hall, but most of the panicked and inebriated throng were seeking an enemy and when Ratharryn's warriors did discover the archers and ran towards them, those attackers retreated back across the embankment into the dark beyond.

'Who are they?' Lewydd shouted at Saban.

'Cathallo?' Saban guessed. He could think of no other enemy, but surmised that Rallin, knowing he was to be attacked next day, had sent his bowmen through the night to sting and humiliate Lengar's men.

The archers had all vanished now. They had come, they had wounded and killed, and now they had gone, but the panic did not subside. Some of Ratharryn's warriors attacked Drewenna's men, mistaking them for the enemy, and Drewenna's spearmen fought back as Lengar strode among them, shouting at them to stop. Saban stalked him.

The fighting slowly died. Men and women beat out burning thatch with cloaks and pelts, or else dragged the burning straw clean off their hut roofs. Wounded men crawled or just lay bleeding. The twelve temple poles stood charred and smoking above the red hot fire that still consumed the feasting hall. Lengar parted two fighting warriors, then turned when one of the temple poles fell to scatter bright fire across the settlement and, in the sudden livid light, he saw Saban and saw the spear in his brother's hand. He smiled. 'You want to be chief, little brother? You want to kill me?'

'Let me kill him,' Lewydd said vengefully. 'Let me!'

'No.' Saban pushed Lewydd aside and walked forward.

Lengar tossed aside his own spear and drew his sword. He looked bored, as though the chore of killing Saban would be a small thing. Saban should have been cautioned by his brother's confidence, but he was too furious to be wary. He simply wanted to kill his brother, and Lengar knew it, just as he knew that Saban's fury would make him clumsy and easy to kill. 'Come on, little brother,' he taunted Saban.

Saban hefted the spear, took a breath and readied himself to make a wild charge fuelled by rage, but then a man screamed and pointed to the settlement's southern entrance and both Lengar and Saban turned that way: Both stared open-mouthed. And both, for an instant, forgot their quarrel.

For a dead man walked the night.

PART THREE

The Temple of
the Dead

A dead man walked in the moonlight and the folk of
Ratharryn gave a great moan because of the horrors that
were being brought on their tribe.

The walking corpse was stark naked and skeletally thin.
His eyes were black holes in a pale mask, his skin was
ghostly white, his ribs were edged with black and his lank
hair was grey. Scraps of his skin and hair dropped and
floated away in the air as if he were decomposing even as
he walked. The moon was higher now, higher and smaller
and paler and brighter, and a spearman near Lengar suddenly screamed in terror, 'He has no shadow! He has no
shadow!' Warriors who had been drunkenly fighting now
fled or else dropped to the ground and hid their faces.
Lengar alone dared advance towards the dead thing that
cast no shadow, and even Lengar shook.

Then Saban, who had been rooted to the ground with
fear, saw that the wraith did have a mooncast shadow. He
saw, too, that every time the corpse put his weight onto
his left foot he gave a small lurch. And the dropping grey-
white scraps were not flesh flaking, but ash drifting in
the small wind. The man had soaked himself in the river,
drenched himself in ashes and blackened his eyes and ribs

with soot, and as the ashes dried they sifted and fell away from his hair and skin.

'Camaban!' Lengar snarled. He too had recognised the limp and he spoke the name angrily, ashamed of having been afraid of the ghostly figure.

'Brother!' Camaban said. He opened his arms to Lengar who answered the gesture by raising his sword. 'Brother!' Camaban said again, chidingly. 'Would you kill me? How are we to defeat Cathallo if you kill me? How will we defeat Cathallo without sorcery?' He capered some clumsy dance steps as he shrieked at the moon: 'Sorcery! Trickery! Spells in the dark and charms in the moonlight!' He howled and shuddered as though the gods were commanding his body, then, when the fit passed, he frowned quizzically at Lengar. 'You do not need my help to thwart Derrewyn's curses?'

Lengar kept his sword blade extended. 'Your help?' he asked.

'I have come,' Camaban said loudly enough so that the warriors who had fled to the huts could hear him, 'to defeat Cathallo. I have come to grind Cathallo into powder. I have come to unleash the gods against Cathallo, but first, brother, you and I must make peace. We must embrace.' And again he stepped towards Lengar who backed away and glanced towards Saban. 'There will be time for his death,' Camaban said, 'but first make peace with me. I regret our quarrel. It is not right that we should be enemies.'

Lengar checked Camaban with his sword. 'You have come to defeat Cathallo?'

'Ratharryn will never be great so long as Cathallo thrives,' Camaban cried, 'and how I do wish for Ratharryn to be great again.' He gently pushed Lengar's sword aside. 'There is no need for us to quarrel, brother. So long as you and I fight, so long will Cathallo be unconquered. So embrace me, brother, in the cause of victory. And then I shall fall at your feet to show your folk that I was wrong and you were right.'

The thought of defeating Cathallo was more than enough to persuade Lengar to end his quarrel with Camaban and so he opened his arms to allow Camaban to step into his embrace.

Saban, who was standing close to his two brothers, remembered the day Hengall had made peace with Cathallo by embracing Kital, but then he realized that Camaban had not come to make peace. As he placed his right arm about Lengar's neck there was a dull glint of black in his hand and Saban saw there was a knife there, a flint knife with a black blade short enough to have been concealed in Camaban's palm, and the knife came from behind Lengar's head and sliced into his neck so that the blood spurted sudden and warm and dark. Lengar tried to pull away, but Camaban held him with surprising strength. He smiled through his black and white mask and forced the flint blade deeper, sawing it back and forth so that the stone's feathered edge cut through taut muscle and pulsing arteries. Lengar's blood poured down to wash the ashes from Camaban's thin body. Lengar was choking now and blood was welling and spilling from his gullet, and still Camaban would not let him go. The knife sawed again, and then at last Camaban released his grip so that Lengar fell to his knees. Camaban kicked him in the mouth, forcing Lengar's head back, and then he slashed the short knife one more time to cut his brother's throat wide open.

Lengar collapsed. For a few heartbeats he twitched and the blood pulsed from his slit throat, but the pulses grew weaker and finally stopped. Saban stared. He hardly dared believe that Lengar was dead and Aurenna was safe. Lahanna's moon shone, glossing the puddle of black blood beside Lengar's oiled hair.

Camaban stooped and picked up Lengar's bronze sword. Lengar's warriors had watched their chief's death in disbelief, but now some growled angrily and advanced on Camaban who raised the sword to check them. 'I am a sorcerer!' he screamed. 'I can put worms in your bellies, turn your bowels to slime and make your children die in agony.' The warriors stopped. They would carry their spears against human enemies, but sorcery shrank their courage to nothing.

Camaban turned back to Lengar's corpse and hacked at it again and again with the sword, finally slashing off its head with a series of clumsy strokes. Only then did he turn and look at Saban.

'He would not rebuild the temple,' Camaban explained in a calm voice. 'I told him to, but he would not. It's all wrong, you see. The stones from Sarmennyn aren't tall enough. It's my fault, entirely my fault. I chose that temple, but it's wrong. Haragg has always told me we learn as we grow and I have learned, but Lengar simply wouldn't listen. So I decided to come back and start again.' He threw down the sword. 'Who is to be chief here, Saban, you or I?'

'Chief?' Saban asked, surprised by the question.

'I think I should be chief,' Camaban said. 'I am, after all, older than you and a great deal cleverer. Don't you agree?'

'You want to be chief?' Saban asked, still dazed by the night's events.

'Yes,' Camaban said, 'I do. I want other things as well. No more winter, no more sickness, no more children crying in the night. That is what I want.' He had come close to Saban as he spoke. 'I want union with the gods,' he went on softly, 'and endless summer.' He embraced Saban and Saban could smell Lengar's blood on his brother's skin. He felt Camaban's arms wind round his neck, then stiffened as the black knife touched his neck. 'Is Aurenna here?' Camaban asked quietly.

'Yes.'

'Good,' Camaban said, then he held the knife against Saban's skin as he whispered. 'What I want, brother, is to build a temple like no other in the land. A temple to bring the gods together. To bring the dead back to Slaol. A temple to make the world anew. That is what I want.' Camaban teased Saban by suddenly pressing the flint's sharp edge against his skin, then just as suddenly took it away and stepped back. 'It will be a temple that will stand for ever,' he said, 'and you, my brother' – he pointed the knife at Saban – 'will build it.' Camaban turned to stare at the remaining timber posts and vivid flames of Lengar's burning hall. He sniffed the stench of roasted flesh. 'Who was in the hall?'

'Your friends from Sarmennyn.'

'Kereval? Scathel?'

'Both of them, and near a hundred others. Only Lewydd still lives.'

'Lengar was always thorough in his slaughter,' Camaban said with evident admiration, then turned to look at the spearmen. 'I am Camaban!' he shouted. 'Son of Hengall, son of Lock, who was whelped of an Outfolk bitch taken in a raid! Slaol has sent me here. He sent me to be your chief! Me! The cripple! The crooked child! And if any man disputes that, let him fight me now, and I shall stroke that man's eyeballs with nettles, turn his belly into a cauldron of burning piss and bury his skull in the shit pits! Does any man challenge me?' No one moved, no one even spoke, they just stared at the naked, ash-covered figure who ranted at them. 'Slaol speaks to me!' Camaban declared. 'He has always spoken to me! And Slaol now wants this tribe to do his bidding, and his will is mine! Mine!'

A warrior pointed beyond Camaban towards the settlement's northern entrance and Saban turned to see a crowd of men coming through the embankment. They carried bows, and Saban understood that these were the men who had attacked Ratharryn earlier to panic the warriors gloating over the fiery massacre of Kereval and his men. The attackers had not come from Cathallo after all, but were the forest outlaws whom rumour said were led by a dead man – by Camaban. The newcomers were wild-bearded and wild-haired, fugitives from Lengar's rule who had taken refuge in the trees where, during the summer, Camaban had spoken with them, inspired them and recruited them. Now they were coming home, led by Haragg whose bald pate shone in the moonlight. The big man carried a spear and had smeared his face with black strips of soot.

'Those men are mine too!' Camaban shouted, pointing at the outlaws. 'They are my friends and they are now reinstated to the tribe.' He raised his arms and glared defiantly at Ratharryn's appalled warriors. 'Does any man challenge me?' he demanded again.

None did, for they feared him and his sorcery. They went silent to their huts as the funeral pyre of Sarmennyn burned itself out during the night.

'Would you have turned their bellies into burning piss?' Saban asked his brother that night.

'I learned one true thing from Sannas,' Camaban replied wearily, 'which is that sorcery is in our fears, that our fears are in our minds and only the gods are real. But I am now chief in my father's place and you, Saban, will build me a temple.'

The men of Drewenna went home in the morning. Their chief declared that Camaban was mad and that he wanted no part of Camaban's madness, so his warriors took up their spears and trailed away across the grasslands.

The spearmen of Ratharryn complained that their best chance of defeating Cathallo was gone with Drewenna's defection and Rallin, they said, would soon attack Ratharryn. Camaban might be a sorcerer, they grumbled, but he was no war leader. Cathallo had sorcerers of its own whose magic would surely counter Camaban's spells, so Ratharryn's men foresaw nothing but shame and defeat.

'Of course they do,' Camaban said when Saban warned him of the tribe's sour mood. It was the morning after Camaban's return and the new chief had summoned the tribe's priests and prominent men to advise him. They sat cross-legged in Mai and Arryn's temple, close to the smoking remains of the feast hall from which eleven charred posts protruded. 'Spearmen are superstitious,' Camaban explained. 'They also carry their brains between their legs, which is why they must be kept busy. How many sons does Lengar have?'

'Seven,' Neel the high priest answered.

'Then let the spearmen start by killing them,' Camaban decreed.

Lewydd protested. 'They are children,' he said, 'and we didn't come here to soak the land in blood!'

Camaban frowned. 'We came here to do Slaol's will, and it is not Slaol's will that Lengar's children should live. If you find a nest of vipers do you kill the adults and let the snakelings live?' He shrugged. 'I like it no more than you, my friend, but Slaol spoke to me in a dream.'

Lewydd looked to Haragg, expecting the big man's support, but Haragg said that the boys' deaths were probably necessary if the new chief were to be safe. 'It has nothing to do with the gods,' he said.

'It has everything to do with the gods,' Neel snapped. Neel had been an avid supporter of Lengar, but overnight he had transferred his loyalty to Camaban. 'Slaol spoke to me also in a dream last night,' he claimed, 'and Camaban's decision is the wise one.'

'I am relieved,' Camaban said drily, then looked at Gundur, whom men said was the best of Ratharryn's warriors. 'See to the boys' deaths,' Camaban ordered and moments later the mothers screamed as Lengar's sons were dragged away. They were taken to the ditch inside the embankment and there killed and their bodies given to pigs. 'It was Slaol's will,' Neel said enthusiastically to Camaban.

'It is also Slaol's will that Haragg should be the new high priest here.'

Neel twitched as though he had been struck, then opened his mouth to protest, but no words came. He stared

398

at Camaban, then at Haragg who looked equally startled. Haragg recovered first. 'I stopped being a priest years ago,' he said mildly.

'And I am high priest!' Neel complained shrilly.

'You are nothing,' Camaban said calmly. 'You are less than nothing. You are slime beneath a stone and you will go to the trees or else I shall bury you alive in the dung pits.' He pointed a bony finger towards the southern causeway, indicating that Neel was outlawed. 'Go,' he said. Neel dared say nothing more; he just obeyed. 'He was a weak man,' Camaban said when Neel had gone, 'and I would have my high priest strong.'

'I am not a priest,' Haragg insisted. 'I am not even of your tribe.'

'You are of Slaol's tribe,' Camaban said, 'and you will be our high priest.'

Haragg took a deep breath and stared over the embankment's crest and thought of far places, sea cliffs, wild forests, strange tribes and all the world's untravelled paths. 'I am not a priest,' he protested again.

'What is it you want?' Camaban asked him.

'A land where folk do good,' Haragg said, frowning as he considered his words, 'where they live as the gods meant us to live. A land without war, without unkindness.'

'You talk like a priest,' Camaban said.

'Men are weak,' Haragg said, 'and the demands of the gods are strong.'

'Then make us stronger!' Camaban insisted. 'How are we to bring the gods to earth if we are weak? Stay, Haragg, help us make the temple, help us be worthy! I would have you as my priest and Aurenna as my priestess.'

'Aurenna!' Saban exclaimed.

Camaban turned brooding eyes on Saban. 'You think Slaol spared Aurenna's life so she could whelp your children? You want her to be a sow? A ewe with swollen udders? It was for that we stirred the thunder in Sarmennyn?' He shook his head. 'It is not enough to keep men busy,' he went on, 'we must also inspire them, and who better than Aurenna? She has visions and is beloved of Slaol.'

'Slaol must want something of her,' Haragg agreed. 'Why else did he spare her?'

'And he spared you,' Camaban said forcefully, 'on the night your son died. You think there was no purpose in that? So be a father to my tribe. Be my high priest.'

Haragg was silent for a while, his implacable face unreadable, but then he gave a reluctant nod. 'If it is Slaol's will,' he said.

'It is,' Camaban said confidently.

Haragg sighed. 'Then I will be high priest here.'

'Good!' Camaban smiled, though the smile hardly detracted from the grimness of his thin face. He had washed most of the ash from his hair and had twisted its long braids round and round his head before pinning them with long bone spikes, but his face still had the ineradicable black barred tattoos. 'Haragg will be high priest, Aurenna will be a priestess, Gundur will lead our spearmen and Saban will make the temple. What will you do, Lewydd?'

Lewydd glanced at the smoking remnants of the feasting hall. 'Bury my folk,' he said grimly, 'and then go home.'

'Then you must take these with you,' Camaban said, and he gave Lewydd a leather bag which, when it was opened, proved to hold the golden lozenges of Sarmennyn. 'There are three missing,' Camaban explained. 'Last night

I learned that they were stolen by Derrewyn, but we shall retrieve those pieces and return them to you.' Camaban leaned over and patted Lewydd's shoulder. 'Take your treasure home,' he said, 'and become chief of Sarmennyn. Grow fat, grow wealthy, grow wise, and do not forget us.'

Saban suddenly laughed, and Camaban looked enquiringly at him. Saban shrugged. 'For years now,' he said, 'everything we have done has been driven by that gold. And now it is over.'

'It is not over,' Camaban said, 'it is just beginning. The gold dazzled us and so we sought our destiny in Sarmennyn, but it never lay there. It lies in Cathallo.'

'In Cathallo?' Saban asked, astonished.

'How can I make a temple worthy of Slaol if I don't have boulders?' Camaban asked. 'And who has boulders? Cathallo.'

'Cathallo will give you stones,' Saban said, 'or exchange them.'

'They will not,' Camaban replied fiercely. 'I met Derrewyn this summer. Did you know she has a daughter? Merrel is the wretched infant's name. Derrewyn lay with Rallin because she wanted the chief's child and she will raise it, she tells me, to be a sorceress like herself. A sorceress! She rubs bones together, mutters over snail shells, pounds toadflax and butter into paste, stares into pisspots and thinks she's influencing the gods. But I still went to her this summer. I went in secret, in the dark of night, and I bowed to her. I abased myself. Give me stones, I begged her, and I will bring peace between Ratharryn and Cathallo, but she would not give me so much as a pebble.' He was bitter at the humiliating memory. 'Sannas once told me she prayed to the wolf god when she walked where wolves ran, but why? Why even give him a prayer? For why should the wolf god listen? It is the nature of wolves to kill, not to spare. By begging of Derrewyn I was making Sannas's mistake. I was praying to the wrong god.'

'Give her Lengar's head,' Saban suggested, 'and she might give you every stone in Cathallo.'

'She will give us nothing,' Gundur said, his hands still bloody from the killing of Lengar's sons.

Camaban looked at the warrior. 'If I attack Cathallo tomorrow, can I win?'

Gundur hesitated, then glanced at Vakkal, the Outfolk war leader whose allegiance was now to Ratharryn, and both men shrugged. 'No,' Gundur admitted.

'Then if we cannot get what we want by war, we must try peace,' Camaban said. He turned to Saban. 'Take our brother's head to Derrewyn,' he said, 'and offer her peace. Say all we want of them is some stones.'

'Praying to the wolf god?' Haragg suggested.

'Threatening the wolf god,' Camaban insisted. 'Tell her she must give us stones or I will give them war as they have never seen it.'

So Saban took his elder brother's head, put it in a bag and next morning walked north.

Saban carried no weapons, for he went in peace, but he was still nervous as he crossed the streams beside Maden and climbed the hills into Cathallo's skull-marked territory. No one accosted him, though more than once he had the sensation that he was being watched and he flinched at the thought of an arrow flicking through the leaves to strike his back.

It was evening when he crossed the small river to climb the hill that led to the small temple and the sacred way. He had not gone more than thirty paces from the river when a dozen spearmen came from the scattered woods behind, ran through the stream and formed a silent escort on either side of him. They had not only tracked him through the woods, but seemed to expect him, for none challenged his right to be there, but just led him between the paired stones of the sacred path, about the double bend and so into the shrine where, outside Sannas's old hut, a fire burned bright in the gathering twilight and three people waited for him. Rallin, chief of Cathallo, was there, and to one side of him was Derrewyn and on the other her father, the blinded Morthor. Behind that group were the warriors of Cathallo, blue-stained for war and with spears in their hands.

Rallin stood to greet Saban. 'You bring us news,' he said flatly.

Morthor also stood. His skin was chalked white and his empty eye-sockets had been rimmed with red ochre. 'Is that you, Saban?'

'It is.'

Morthor smiled. 'You are well?'

'He crawls in his brother's shadow like a worm,' Derrewyn said, staying seated. She was thinner than ever and her pale skin was stretched taut across her cheekbones, making her dark eyes look very large. Her hair was gathered at the nape of her neck, but Saban saw she had discarded the necklace of her dead child's bones. Perhaps that was because she now had another child, the daughter who lay in her arms and who was a dark-haired girl no older than Lallic. 'Saban has come, father,' Derrewyn went on, 'to tell us that Lengar is dead, that Camaban is chief and that Ratharryn threatens war if we do not meekly allow them to take stones from our hills.'

'Is it true?' Rallin asked.

'Of course it is true!' Derrewyn hissed at him. 'I felt Lengar's death here!' She slapped her belly, making Merrel cry aloud. With surprising gentleness, Derrewyn stroked her daughter's forehead and crooned a few words to soothe the girl. 'I felt his death when the nutshell was broken. Did you bring me his head, Saban?'

He held out the bag. 'Here.'

'It will match Jegar's,' she said, gesturing for Saban to drop the bag. He obeyed, spilling Lengar's bloody head onto the grass, then he looked at her hut and saw that Jegar's skull was displayed on a pole beside its door.

Rallin and Morthor sat, and Saban followed their example. 'So why are you here, Saban?' Rallin asked.

'What Derrewyn says is true,' Saban said. 'Camaban is now chief of Ratharryn and he does not want war with you. He wants peace and he wishes to take stones from your hills. That is all I came to say.'

'Lengar is truly dead?' blind Morthor asked.

'Truly dead,' Saban confirmed.

'Lahanna did that!' Morthor said, and raised his eye-sockets to the sky. 'If I could weep,' he added, 'I would shed tears of joy.'

Derrewyn ignored her father's pleasure. 'And why do you want stones?' she asked.

'We wish to build a temple,' Saban said. 'It will be a great temple to bring us peace. That is all we want, peace.'

'We have a great temple here,' Rallin said, 'and your people can come and worship.'

'Your temple has not brought the land peace,' Saban said.

'And yours will?' Derrewyn asked sourly.

'It will bring peace and happiness,' Saban said.

'Peace and happiness!' Derrewyn laughed. 'You sound like a child, Saban! And Camaban has already been here. He crawled to me in the summer and begged for stones, and I will give you now the same answer I gave him then. You may have your stones, Saban of Ratharryn, when you return Sannas's spirit to her ancestors.'

'Sannas's spirit?' Saban asked.

'Who stole her last breath?' Derrewyn demanded fiercely. 'Camaban did! And she can have no peace while Camaban holds her breath in his belly. So bring me Camaban's head, Saban, and I will exchange it for a stone.'

Saban looked at Rallin, hoping for a kinder answer. 'We have no quarrel with Cathallo,' Saban said.

'No quarrel!' Derrewyn screamed, startling her child again. 'Ratharryn brought Outfolk to the heartland, and worse, you brought an Outfolk temple. How long before you march the brides to the fire? And for what? For Slaol! Slaol who deserted us, Slaol who brought the Outfolk vermin to our land, Slaol who gives us winter, Slaol who would destroy us if we did not have Lahanna and Garlanna to protect us. No quarrel? I have a quarrel.' She suddenly pushed her crying daughter into the arms of a slave, then stripped the cloak from her upper body to show Saban the three lozenges, the one great and the two small, hanging between her small breasts. 'It burns!' she said, tapping the large piece of gold. 'It burns me night and day, but it

405

reminds me of Slaol's evil.' She wailed, swaying from side to side. 'Yet Lahanna has promised us victory. She has promised that we shall destroy you. We shall cage up your Slaol and burn your corpses to fill his nostrils with filth.' She stood, leaving the cloak on the ground, and brandished the human thigh bone that Sannas had once wielded. 'You shall have no stones,' she declared, 'and you shall have no peace.'

Saban tried a last time. 'I would that my children grew up in a land of peace,' he said.

'I want the same,' Rallin answered, glancing at Merrel who lay in the slave's arms, 'but there cannot be peace so long as Camaban has Sannas's spirit.'

'Our ancestors are unhappy,' Morthor explained. 'They want Sannas to join them. Send us Camaban, Saban, and we shall give you stones.'

'Or tell Camaban to make war on us,' Derrewyn sneered. 'You think he is a warrior? Let him come to our spears! And tell him, Saban, that when he comes we shall tear the flesh from his bones piece by piece and we shall make him scream for three days and three nights and at their end I will take his soul and the soul of Sannas.' She spat into the fire, then plucked the cloak from the ground to cover her nakedness. 'I thank you for Lengar's head,' she said coldly, 'but have nothing to give you in return.' She took her daughter back, then stalked to her hut and ducked inside.

Saban looked at Rallin. 'Do women make the law here?'

'Lahanna does,' Rallin said curtly. He stood, and pulled Morthor to his feet. 'You should leave now,' he told Saban.

'There will be war if I leave.'

'There will be war whether you leave or stay,' Rallin

said. 'We have known nothing but war with Ratharryn since your father died. Do you think we can so quickly make peace?' Rallin shook his head. 'Go,' he said, 'just go.'

So Saban went.

And the war would go on.

Camaban did not seem surprised or disappointed that Saban's mission had failed. 'They want war,' he said. Camaban was at the Sky Temple where Saban found him brooding over the twin rings of Sarmennyn's stones. 'Cathallo thinks that with Lengar dead we shall be easy prey to their spears,' Camaban went on. 'They think I cannot lead men into battle.'

'They said as much,' Saban confessed.

'Good!' Camaban said happily. 'I like an enemy who underestimates me, it makes his humiliation so much easier.' He raised his voice so that Gundur and Vakkal, the war leaders of Ratharryn who were among his entourage, could hear him. 'Men think war is the application of force, but it isn't. War is the application of thought. Cleverness. And I think we should march tomorrow, straight across the marshes, over the hills and into Cathallo.'

Gundur half smiled. 'We have tried that before,' he said softly, 'and failed.'

'You've tried everything and failed,' Camaban retorted.

'And we hear Cathallo is filled with spearmen,' Vakkal put in. 'They expected to meet our forces and the men of Drewenna and so they gathered their allies.'

'But they will know Drewenna has deserted us,' Cama-

407

ban said, 'and will hardly believe we dare to attack them. What better time to do so?'

'They're probably planning to attack us,' Gundur said gloomily.

'You always think of difficulties!' Camaban shouted at them, astonishing both men. 'How can you win a war if all you do is worry about losing one? Are you women?' He limped towards the warriors. 'We shall leave tomorrow morning, we shall attack in the next dawn and we shall win. Slaol has promised it. Understand? Slaol has promised it!'

Gundur bowed his head, though he was plainly unhappy with Camaban's decision. 'We shall march tomorrow,' he reluctantly agreed, then plucked Vakkal's elbow and walked back to the settlement to warn his spearmen.

Camaban watched the two warriors walk away, then laughed. 'We'd better win now or those two will want my head.'

'It will be hard to win,' Saban said carefully, 'for Cathallo seems to know everything we do. They must have spies here and they will know you're coming.'

'What choice do I have?' Camaban demanded. 'I have to fight now, and not just to take the stones, either, or to persuade Gundur and Vakkal not to hack me down like a dog. If I am to be chief here then I must show myself a greater leader than Lengar. It's easier to be cleverer than Lengar, but men don't admire cleverness. They admire power. So by defeating Cathallo I achieve something Lengar never did. The problem, of course, is what to do with all these spearmen once we've won peace. Warriors do not like peace.'

'You think you will have peace?' Saban asked.

'I think, brother, that Slaol will give us victory,' Camaban said, 'and I think you will build me a temple and that your first job will be to pull out these stones.' He gestured at the pillars that had been brought across the sea to be sunk in Ratharryn's turf. 'They looked so splendid in Sarmennyn,' Camaban went on, frowning. 'Do you remember? And you could feel the presence of Slaol. Brooding. Always there! Trapped in stone. Not here, though. Dead, that's what they are here, dead!' He pushed at a stone, trying to topple it, but it was too well sunk in the ground. 'They'll all have to come out, all of them! How many men will you need to haul out the stones?'

'Thirty?' Saban guessed. 'Forty?'

'You'll need more than that,' Camaban said confidently. 'And you're going to need men and oxen to drag the new stones from Cathallo.' He fell silent, staring at the unfinished circles of stone. 'I wish I did not have to fight,' he finally said, then turned to his brother. 'Have you ever seen a battle between whole tribes?'

'No.'

'You should. Before it begins every man is a hero, but as soon as the arrows begin to fly half of them find they've got sprained ankles or upset bellies.' He smiled. 'I think you will prove a hero, Saban.'

'I thought I was to be a builder?'

'A warrior first, a builder after,' Camaban said. 'I would not go to battle without you, brother.'

It had been a long time since Saban saw warriors ready themselves for battle, but next dawn he watched as men stripped themselves naked and daubed their bodies with a paste made from water and woad, then dipped their spear blades and arrow-heads in a viscous mix of faeces and

409

herb-juice. When the sun was at its height the spearmen danced about Mai and Arryn's temple and a captive from Cathallo, who had been kept under guard ever since the last skirmish between the tribes, was dragged to the temple and slaughtered. Camaban was curious about that rite which Gundur told him had begun with Cathallo killing their captives before battle and so Lengar had ordered it done at Ratharryn as revenge. Haragg protested at the killing, but Gundur assured him it was no sacrifice and so the high priest held the skull pole as Gundur, naked and smeared blue, and with his hair blowing wild, took a bronze knife and slowly slit the man from crotch to breastbone. Ratharryn's spearmen then dipped their right hands in the blood of the victim whose long dying scream had been a message to the gods that the tribe was going to battle.

Saban did not dip his hand, nor did he dance about the temple poles as the drummers beat out a quick rhythm on their goatskin hoops. Instead he squatted beside Aurenna who had watched the captive's death unmoved. 'You will win the battle,' she said. 'I saw the victory in a dream.'

'You have a lot of dreams these days,' he said sourly.

'Because I am here,' Aurenna said, 'where Slaol wants me to be.'

'I wish we were going home with Lewydd,' Saban said. He had helped Lewydd drag the burned and shrunken bodies of Kereval and his men from the ashes of the hall. The corpses were to be buried high on the grassy slope above Slaol's old temple and Lewydd would then take the gold back to Sarmennyn.

'This is now my home,' Aurenna said. She watched the warriors crouch one by one over the eviscerated corpse.

'All this was meant to be,' she said happily. 'We did not know what Slaol intended when we came from Sarmennyn. We thought we were just bringing stones! But instead he wants us here to make his glory.'

'So the last years were all wasted?' Saban asked bitterly. He had given the best years of his life to moving the stones from Sarmennyn, only to have them rejected as soon as the task was done.

Aurenna shook her head. 'The years were not wasted,' she said calmly. 'They were given to Slaol, as proof that we could do great things for him, but now we must do more. Scathel's temple was a place for killing, a temple like the Sea Temple, and our new shrine must be a temple of life.'

Saban shuddered. 'Derrewyn once prophesied that our temple would steam with blood. She said the sun bride would die there. She said you would die there.'

Aurenna laughed softly. 'Saban! Saban! Derrewyn is an enemy. She would hardly speak well of what we do. And there will be no blood. Haragg hates sacrifice! He detests it!' She touched his arm. 'Trust us,' she urged him. 'Slaol is inside us! I can feel him like a child in my belly.'

Haragg was to accompany the war band. It was expected of the high priest, though Saban was surprised Haragg was so enthusiastic. 'I have never liked killing,' the dour high priest confessed, 'but war is different. If you had not offered them peace, Saban, I would be unhappy, but they have been given their chance and refused it, so now we must do Slaol's duty.' Haragg was carrying the tribe's skull pole that he took to Arryn and Mai's temple where the warriors assembled. Camaban had donned one of Lengar's old tunics with bronze strips sewn to its breast and at his side

411

hung Lengar's bronze sword. He had dipped his hand in the corpse's blood, then smeared the blood on his tattooed face so that, with his black hair loose, he looked like a thing from a nightmare. He gestured for Haragg to lower the skull, then placed his bloody hand on the yellowed dome and shouted, 'I swear on our ancestors' souls that we shall destroy Cathallo!'

Over two hundred warriors watched that solemn oath. Most were veterans of Lengar's wars, a few were youngsters who had passed their ordeals but had not been tattooed as men for they had not yet killed in battle, while the wildest spearmen were the outlaws who had come from the forests with Camaban. 'We march now and we shall reach Cathallo in tomorrow's dawn,' Camaban cried, 'and that is when we shall attack. And Slaol has spoken with me. He has always spoken with me. Even when I was a child he came to me, but now he speaks more clearly and he tells me we shall win a great victory! We shall conquer Cathallo! We shall kill many spearmen and take many prisoners. We shall end, for all time, the threat of Cathallo and your children will grow in a land at peace!'

They cheered him and the tribe's women added their shouts of approval, then the drummers beat on their skins and the war band followed Camaban north into the woods. They walked all afternoon and it was almost dark by the time they reached the marshes about Maden, but their path across the wet land was lit by a white high moon that glossed the streams and shone on the ghostly white skulls that Cathallo had planted at the edge of the wooded hills to deter Ratharryn's spearmen. Camaban plucked a skull from its pole and threw it to the ground, then the rest of the war band followed him into the forest. Camaban's outlaws, who were at home among the dark trees, went ahead as scouts, but found no enemy.

It was slow going in the woods for the leaves obscured Lahanna's light and the spearmen travelled cautiously. They stopped when they reached the highest ground and there waited through the chill night. Gundur and Vakkal were nervous, for Cathallo had never before allowed Ratharryn's warriors to cross the marshes unchallenged: they were now deep in the enemy's territory and they feared an ambush, but no arrows or spears came from the dark. In the past, Gundur said, Cathallo had forced Ratharryn's warriors to fight their way into these hills where they were constantly ambushed by archers, but now the woods were empty, tempting every warrior to believe that Cathallo was ignorant of their coming. As dawn approached a mist sifted through the trees. Fox cubs scattered across a clearing as the advance resumed, and men took the presence of the cubs as a good omen for the beasts would surely never have left their dens if Cathallo's warriors were lurking among the trees, but then, just as spirits were rising in hopes of an easy victory, a terrible roar made the men crouch and even Camaban's striped face showed sudden fear. There was a trampling in the bushes, not quick like a deer's movement, nor deliberate like a man's, but something huge and ponderous that sounded out of the mist to make the whole war band shudder.

The dreadful sound came closer. Saban had put an arrow on his bow's string, though he doubted any flint head could damage some sorcery from Cathallo, and then a monster appeared with a massive head crowned by spreading horns that twisted forward. Saban pulled the bowstring back, but did not release the arrow. It was no sorcery, nor a monster, but a bull aurochs twice the size of the largest ox Saban had ever seen: a creature of huge muscle, black hide, sharp horns and beady eyes. It stopped when it saw the men, swished its dung-encrusted tail, then pawed at the ground with a huge hoof before bellowing its challenge again. It raised its head and spittle streamed from a cavernous mouth. Its small eyes looked red in the misty light. For a heartbeat Saban thought the animal was going to charge the war band, then it swung away and pounded northwards. 'An omen!' Camaban said. 'Follow it!'

Saban had never seen Camaban so excited. His brother's usual sardonic confidence had been replaced by a childish verve, born of a nervousness that made him boisterous and loud. In these same circumstances, Saban suspected, Lengar would have been silent, but the warriors still followed Camaban willingly enough. He might be dressed as a warrior, but the spearmen believed he was a sorcerer who could defeat Cathallo with spells rather than spears and the absence of any enemy in the woods had convinced them that his spells were working.

The sun rose just after they reached the edge of the trees. The mist was white and damp, muffling the world. The men, who had been so confident in the night, were now assailed by nervousness. They had never pierced so deep into Cathallo's territory and that achievement should have encouraged them, but the mist was frightening them for, once they passed beyond the trees, it seemed as though they walked through a white nothingness. At times the sun would show as a pale disc in the vapour, but then it would vanish again as the wet fog drifted thick again. Some men loosed arrows at shadows just beyond the eye's reach, but no arrows came back and no wounded enemy cried aloud.

'We should go back,' Gundur said.

'Back?' Camaban asked. The blood on his face had dried to a cracking crust.

Gundur gestured into the fog, suggesting that it was hopeless to continue, but just then a man at the left of the ragged war band came to an ancient grave mound, one that had been built as a long ridge instead of a round heap, and Camaban headed for it and gathered his spearmen in the tomb's forecourt, which was cradled by a crescent of vast stones. 'I know where we are,' Camaban told them. 'Cathallo lies that way' – he pointed into the mist – 'and it is not far.'

'Too far in this fog,' Gundur said, and the spearmen growled their agreement.

'Then we shall let the fog thin a little,' Camaban said, 'and harm the enemy while we wait.'

He ordered a dozen men to heave aside two of the smaller stones from the crescent of great boulders and, when the slabs were gone, a dark tunnel lined with yet more stones was revealed. Camaban crawled into the tunnel, muttered a charm to protect his soul from the dead, and then began to hurl out bones and skulls. These were Cathallo's ancestors, the spirits who would guard their descendants in any battle, and Camaban ordered the bones to be made into a pile at the foot of the tomb's stone façade and then, one by one, the warriors climbed to the top of the ridge and pissed onto their enemies. The gesture restored their spirits so that they laughed and began to boast as they had the previous night.

Saban was the last man to climb the mound. His bladder

was empty and he feared the scorn of the war band, but then he looked north and saw another person climb out of the fog. The figure was a long way off and for a moment he felt terror, thinking it was a spirit who walked on the fog's surface, then he understood it was someone who had just climbed the chalk-white Sacred Mound and was staring southwards. The figure stared at Saban, who stared back. Was it Derrewyn? He thought it was her and he felt a sudden pang that she should be his enemy now. To his right, much farther off, the hills where the great stones lay emerged from the mist, but here there was just Derrewyn and Saban staring at each other across the silent white valley.

'What is it?' Camaban called up to him.

'Come here,' Saban said, and Camaban went round to the ridge's flank and scrambled up its steep turf slope.

The far figure dropped her cloak and began raising and lowering her arms. 'Curses,' Camaban said, and he spat towards her.

'Is it Derrewyn?' Saban asked.

'Who else?' Camaban asked. Derrewyn was standing on Lahanna's hill, summoning the goddess to hurt Cathallo's enemies.

Saban touched his groin. 'So they know we're coming?'

'They brought the fog,' Camaban said, 'hoping we would get lost in it. But we are not lost. I know the way from here.' He raised a fist to the distant figure, then dragged Saban down from the mound. 'We follow a path north,' he said, 'and the path goes through a wood, then crosses the stream before joining the sacred way.' And the sacred way would lead them into Cathallo's shrine.

The drenching of the bones had restored the war band's

spirits so they were now eager to follow Camaban north. He went fast, following a path that had been beaten into the grassland by countless feet. The path led gently downhill through a thick stand of oaks and, as the spearmen threaded the trees, a wind rustled the leaves and the same wind swirled the mist and thinned it so that Ratharryn's leading warriors could see the sacred path across the small valley and there, waiting in a strong line by the grey boulders, was Cathallo's army.

Rallin, Cathallo's chief, was waiting for them. He was ready. All Cathallo's warriors were there, and not just Cathallo's men, but also their allies, the spearmen from the tribes that hated Ratharryn because of Lengar's raids. The enemy host filled the avenue and they gave a great shout as they saw Camaban's men come from the oaks and then the mists thickened again and the two armies were hidden from each other.

'They outnumber us,' Gundur said nervously.

'They are as nervous as we are,' Camaban said, 'but we have Slaol.'

'They let us come this far because they would crush us here,' Gundur explained, 'then follow our survivors back across the hills and slaughter us one by one.'

'What they want,' Camaban agreed, 'is a battle to end the war.'

'They do,' Gundur said, 'and they will win it. We should retreat!' He spoke fiercely and Vakkal nodded his agreement.

'Slaol does not want us to retreat,' Camaban said. His eyes were bright with excitement. 'All our enemies are gathered,' he said, 'and Slaol wants us destroy them.'

'They are too many,' Gundur insisted.

'There are never too many enemies to kill,' Camaban said. The spirit of Slaol was inside him and he was certain of victory, and so he shook his head at Gundur's advice and drew his sword. 'We shall fight,' he shouted, then his whole body shuddered as the god filled him with power. 'We shall fight for Slaol,' he screamed, 'and we shall win!'

The mist shredded slowly, swirled by a fitful wind and reluctantly yielding to Slaol's rising power. Two swans flew above the stream, their wing beats suddenly the loudest noise in a valley edged by two armies. The aurochs had long disappeared, gone, Saban assumed, into the deeper forests to the west, yet he clung to the belief that the beast's appearance had been a good omen. Now every spearman in the opposing armies watched the swans, hoping they would turn towards their side, but the birds flew steadily on between the two forces to vanish in the eastern mists. 'They have gone to the rising sun!' Camaban shouted. 'It means Slaol is with us.'

He could have been speaking to himself, for no one on Ratharryn's side reacted to his shout. They were staring across the shallow valley to where the forces of Cathallo made a formidable line armed with spears, axes, bows, maces, clubs, adzes and swords. That battle-line began near the small temple on the hill, followed the path of paired stones westwards and then went on towards the Sacred Mound. On the low hills behind the battle-line were groups of women and children who had come to watch their menfolk crush Ratharryn.

'Four hundred men?' Mereth had been counting and now spoke softly to Saban.

'Not all men,' Saban said, 'some are scarce boys.'

'A boy can kill you with an arrow,' Mereth muttered. He was armed with one of his father's precious bronze axes and looked formidable, for he had inherited Galeth's height and broad chest, but Mereth was nervous, as was Saban. The men of both armies were nervous, all except the hardened warriors who dreamed of these moments. Those were the men about whom songs were sung, of whom tales were told in the long winter nights; they were the heroes of slaughter, fighters like Vakkal the Outlander who now strutted ahead of Camaban's force to shout insults across the valley. He called the enemy worm dung, claimed their mothers were goitred goats, reviled them as children who wet their pelts at night and invited any two of them to come and fight him on the stream bank. Similar taunts and invitations were being shouted by Cathallo's leading warriors. Hung with feathers and fox tails, their skins thick with kill marks, they strutted in bronze. Saban had once dreamed of being such a warrior, but he had become a maker instead of a destroyer and a man who felt caution, if not outright fear, at the sight of an enemy.

'Spread out,' Gundur shouted at Ratharryn's men. Gundur had not wanted to fight this morning, fearing that Cathallo and its allies were too numerous, but Camaban had taken him aside and Gundur's confidence had been miraculously restored by whatever Camaban had told him, and he now tugged men into line. 'Spread out!' he shouted. 'Make a line! Don't bunch like children! Spread out!'

The war band reluctantly scattered along the edge of the oaks to make a line which, like the enemy's line, was not

420

continuous. Men stayed close to their kin or friends and there were wide gaps between the groups. The priests of both sides were out in front now, shaking bones and shrieking curses at the enemy. Haragg carried Ratharryn's skull pole so that the ancestors could see what was being done in the thinning mist and Morthor, Cathallo's blind high priest, carried a similar pole. He shook it so threateningly that Cathallo's skull toppled clean off its staff, raising a cheer from Ratharryn's men who reckoned the fall of the skull was an ominous sign for the enemy. Derrewyn was still on the Sacred Mound where, attended by a half-dozen spearmen, she was spitting more curses at Camaban. 'I want the sorceress killed!' Camaban shouted at his army. 'A gift of gold to the man who brings me the bitch's head! I shall fill her skull with gold and give it all to the man who kills her!'

'He thinks we'll win?' Mereth asked sourly.

'Slaol is with us,' Saban said, and the sun had indeed broken through the remnants of mist to green the valley and spark shimmering light from the stream between the armies.

'Slaol had better be with us,' Mereth muttered. The enemy outnumbered Ratharryn's men by two to one.

'I want their chief dead!' Camaban was calling to his men. 'Him and his children! Find his children and kill them! If his wives are pregnant, kill them too! And kill the sorceress's whelp, kill it! Kill her, kill her child, kill them all!'

Rallin was walking along his own line, doubtless encouraging his own spearmen to a similar slaughter. The priests of both sides had advanced to the stream's banks, almost within spitting distance of each other, and there they hissed insults and spat curses at each other, leapt in the air, shook as though they were in the grip of the gods and shrieked as they summoned the invisible spirits to come and eviscerate the enemy. Haragg alone had not gone to the stream. Instead he was standing a few paces in front of the line and holding the skull pole towards the sun.

The braver warriors had gone close to the priests to shout more insults, but neither battle-line moved forward. Groups of men danced in a frenzy as they summoned the courage to advance, others sang war hymns or chanted the names of their gods. The mist was all gone now and the day was growing warmer. Mereth stepped back into the wood which stood just behind Camaban's line and began picking blackberries, but Camaban, returning from the left wing of his forces, pulled him out of the bushes and back into the line. Camaban said, 'Every man who has a bow is to go back into the trees and make his way to the centre of the line. You hear me?' He walked on, repeating the instruction, and the archers slipped back into the trees and, unseen by the enemy, ran to the centre of Ratharryn's loose line. Saban alone disobeyed, reluctant to abandon Mereth's companionship.

A drum began to beat from Cathallo's line and the heavy pounding gave Rallin's men courage so that small groups of them darted forward to taunt Camaban's forces. The most courageous splashed through the stream, then stood baring their blue-smeared bodies as if inviting Ratharryn's bowmen to loose their arrows. Vakkal and some of his Outlander spearmen ran to challenge those bolder enemies who quickly retreated, provoking jeers from Ratharryn's men. The priests stood in the centre of these rushes and counter-rushes, ignoring and being ignored by the spear-men.

Scattered archers ran from Cathallo's line to loose their arrows across the valley. Most fell short, though a few hissed overhead to rattle through the leaves in the wood. Small boys ran to retrieve the arrows and carry them to Ratharryn's own archers, a handful of whom advanced from the centre of the line to drive the enemy bowmen back. No one had been injured yet, let alone killed, and though the insults flew thick, neither army seemed inclined to cross the stream and begin the bloodletting. Rallin was walking up and down his line again, exhorting and shouting, and women were carrying pots of liquor to their men.

'We're going to let them come to us,' Camaban was walking behind his line again. 'We stay here,' he said, 'and let them attack us.' He sounded cheerful. 'When they advance, just stand still and wait for them.'

The whole of Cathallo's line was chanting now, the strong voices joining in the battle verse of Lahanna. 'They're working themselves up to it, aren't they?' Mereth observed, his lips stained with blackberry juice.

'I'd rather be making boats in Sarmennyn,' Saban said.

'I'd rather be making boats anywhere,' Mereth said. He did not have even one kill scar on his chest. 'I reckon if they come over that stream,' he went on, 'I'm going to run back and keep running till I reach the sea.'

'They're just as frightened of us,' Saban said.

'That might be true,' Mereth observed, 'but there's two scared fellows over there for every one of us.'

A great shout sounded from Cathallo's line and Saban saw that a large group of warriors had started towards the stream. They came from the centre of Rallin's line and they called Lahanna's name as they advanced, but after a few paces they looked left and right and saw that the rest of their line had stayed rooted and so they themselves stopped and were content to shout insults at Camaban who had returned to the centre of Ratharryn's line. Derrewyn, Saban saw, had come down from the Sacred Mound and was now striding along the front of Cathallo's reluctant battle-line. Her long black hair was unbound and, like the pale cloak she wore, was lifted by the small wind. Saban could see she was shouting, and he could imagine that she was reviling her men's courage, insulting Ratharryn and urging the spearmen forward. More liquor pots were brought to Rallin's men. The drummer was beating his goatskin drum with redoubled force and men were shuffling in a grotesque dance as they summoned their nerves. The priests of both sides, their throats sore from so much shouting, huddled together by the stream where they drank from cupped hands, then talked with each other.

'This isn't how Lengar would have fought,' a man near Saban grumbled.

'How would he have done it?' Saban asked.

'Your brother was always one for attacking,' the man said. 'None of this waiting. Just scream loud, then run at the enemy in a howling rush.' He spat. 'They always broke.'

Saban wondered if that was what Gundur was now planning for he had assembled his best warriors at the line's centre where Ratharryn's skull pole was displayed. The gathered men had been Lengar's best, the spearmen with the most kill scars who had foxes' brushes woven into their hair and dangling from their spear shafts. Gundur was haranguing them, though Saban was too far away to hear what he said. Vakkal and his picked Outfolk warriors joined them, and just behind that fearsome group were Camaban's massed archers.

The sun climbed. Rallin and Derrewyn walked up and down their line, and still neither side attacked, though some bowmen from Cathallo became bold and dared to cross the stream to loose some arrows. They struck one man in the leg and the enemy cheered that wound, then Camaban sent a half-dozen of his own archers forward to chase the enemy away and it was Ratharryn's turn to jeer.

'Maybe there won't be a battle,' Mereth said cheerfully. 'Perhaps we just stand here all day, shout ourselves hoarse, then go home and boast about how brave we've all been. That would suit me.'

'Or perhaps Rallin expected us to attack like Lengar,' Saban suggested.

'He thought we'd charge?'

'Probably,' Saban guessed, 'and now that we're not doing what he expected, he has to come to us if he's to win.'

Rallin had evidently reached the same conclusion for he and Derrewyn now exhorted their army to advance, claiming that the vermin of Ratharryn were too timid to attack and too stubborn to retreat without a fight, and so were just waiting to be slaughtered. Rallin shouted that glory waited for Cathallo and that any man killed this day would go straight to Lahanna's bliss in the sky. The first men into Ratharryn's line, Cathallo's chief promised, could take their pick of the enemy's women and herds, and that encouragement was emboldening his men. The liquor was also having its effect and the drumbeat was filling the sky and the women who watched from the hills were shouting at their men to go forward and kill. The noise was constant, shouting and screaming, drum and chanting, singing and foot-stamping. Rallin's war captains had spread along the line and kept dragging men forward and their example and Rallin's promises at last succeeded in urging the whole excited mass into motion.

'Just stand and wait!' Camaban shouted. 'Stand and wait!'

'The gods help us,' Mereth said, touching his groin.

The enemy came slowly. None was willing to be the first to reach Ratharryn's line and so they edged forward, calling encouragement to each other, and the archers were the only ones who ran ahead, but even they took care not to get too far in front. Rallin was at his line's centre where he did succeed in quickening his best warriors. He wanted the rest of his army to see those heroes smash through the centre of Ratharryn's line and start the slaughter which would turn into massacre when Camaban's men broke and fled. The warriors shouted their war cries, shook their spears and still none of Ratharryn's men stepped forward to meet the attack.

'Stand and wait!' Camaban called. 'Slaol will give us victory!'

The enemy archers had reached the far bank of the stream now and they hesitated for a heartbeat amid the thick willow-herb before jumping into the water. 'Watch for the arrows!' a man shouted close to Saban.

The first arrows were loosed and Saban watched them flicker in the sky. None came at him, though in other places men skipped aside when they saw an arrow diving straight towards them. Cathallo's archers were spread all along the line and so their arrows were few in any one place, though they did succeed in hitting a handful of men and those injuries encouraged the spearmen advancing behind the bowmen. They splashed through the stream, avoiding the priests who still talked placidly. 'Are you going to use that bow?' Mereth asked Saban, and Saban took an arrow from his quiver and laid it on the string, but he did not pull the string back. There had been a time when all he had dreamed of being was a hero of his tribe's songs, but he felt no bloodlust here. He could not hate Derrewyn or her people and so he just stared at the advancing enemy and wondered how Camaban planned to repel such an onslaught.

'Let them come!' Camaban called.

None of Ratharryn's archers had replied to the enemy's arrows, which emboldened Rallin's bowmen who stepped even closer so that now their arrows were driven flat and fast, too fast to avoid, and men shouted as they were hit, staggered and fell backwards, and the sight of the wounded men provoked Rallin's group of experienced warriors to break into a run and scream a challenge as they raced up the gentle slope.

'Now!' Camaban cried, and his own prime spearmen stepped aside to let the massed archers release a stinging cloud of arrows straight into the face of Rallin's charge. A dozen of the enemy were down, one with an arrow through an eye, and the rest of Cathallo's spearmen stopped, astonished at the sudden hail of flint-headed shafts, then another black-fledged flight whipped into them, then a third, and it was then that Gundur shouted Ratharryn's war shout and his picked warriors, fox tails flying, screamed and charged. Camaban's bowmen were scattering now, going left and right to drive the enemy archers back. Ratharryn's men had seemed to be waiting placidly and their sudden counter-strike, swift as a viper's attack, stunned the enemy.

Gundur and Vakkal led the charge into Rallin's injured men. Vakkal, swan feathers bright in his hair, hacked with a long-handled axe while Gundur used a heavy spear with sickening efficiency. For a brief while the centre of the field was a tangle of men stabbing and hacking, but Camaban's archers had hurt the enemy grievously and now Ratharryn's picked warriors broke through Rallin's centre. They killed Cathallo's greatest heroes in the stream where Rallin tried to rally them until Vakkal hurled his axe and the heavy blade struck Rallin on the head and the enemy chieftain fell among the willow-herb. Gundur screamed and splashed through the stream to stab his spear down into Rallin's chest, then Camaban was past him, swinging his sword in huge slashes that were as much a danger to his own side as to the enemy. Camaban's wild appearance, his striped face, bone-hung hair and bloody skin, terrified Cathallo's men who stepped back and stepped back again, and then stepped back faster as the fox-tailed warriors attacked in a howling rush.

'Now!' Camaban shouted at the rest of his line. 'Come and kill them! Come and kill them! Their lives are yours!' And the men of Ratharryn, as astonished as the enemy by the success of their line's centre, and seeing that Cathallo's men were fear-racked and retreating, gave a great shout and charged towards the stream. 'Kill them!' Camaban howled. 'Kill them!' His howling rallied his victorious centre, which he led in a wild screaming charge that turned into a pursuit of an enemy which still outnumbered Camaban's forces, but which had been panicked by their chief's death. Ratharryn's men whooped their victory as they cut the fleeing enemy down from behind. Axes and maces crushed skulls, shattered bones, came back bloody. Men killed in a frenzy of released fear, shrieking and stabbing, slashing and battering, and the panic became a rout when Cathallo's skull pole was taken by Vakkal. He hacked blind Morthor down with a sword, seized the pole and smashed the skull with his blade, and the sight of the skull's destruction caused a great wailing in the enemy's disordered ranks. Cathallo's women fled towards the great shrine and the fugitive spearmen followed in panic. It was chaos now, with Camaban's men hunting and herding the fleeing mass. Cathallo was beaten, Cathallo was running and Ratharryn's men were drenching their weapons with slaughter.

Saban alone did not pursue the enemy. Mereth had taken his great axe to the wild killing that soaked the avenue between the sacred stones, but Saban had been watching Derrewyn who had been at her line's western end when Gundur and Vakkal struck Rallin's men, staring appalled as her tribe collapsed. Saban saw two of Cathallo's warriors try and pull her back towards the settlement, but Derrewyn must have known that was where Camaban's army would aim their pursuit and so she ran a few paces west and, when she saw the screaming charge of Cathallo's men cross the stream and converge on the sacred avenue, she headed for the trees that had stood behind Camaban's battle-line. There was nowhere else to hide. Saban thought she must reach the trees safely, but then two of Ratharryn's archers saw her hurrying southwards and loosed their arrows. One of the missiles thumped into Derrewyn's leg, making her stumble, but her two spearmen picked her up and half carried her into the trees as the archers, eager for Camaban's reward of gold, ran after her.

Saban followed the archers into the wood. He could not see Derrewyn or her pursuers, but then he heard a bowstring being released and Derrewyn screaming an insult. Saban twisted towards the noise, plunging through a thicket of hazels into a small clearing where he saw that one of the Cathallo spearmen was lying dead with a black-fledged arrow through his throat. Derrewyn, her face pale and drawn with pain, was sitting against the moss-covered bole of an oak while her last protector faced the two bowmen of Ratharryn. They were grinning, pleased at the ease of their expected victory, but frowned as Saban burst into the clearing. 'We found her,' one of the archers said emphatically.

'You found her,' Saban agreed, 'so the reward is all yours. I don't want it.' He knew neither of the young men, who were scarce more than boys. He smiled at the nearest man, then placed an arrow on his bowstring. 'Do you have a knife?' he asked them.

'A knife?' one of them asked.

'You'll have to cut off the sorceress's head,' Saban explained, drawing back the arrow and aiming its long flint head at the enemy spearman. 'Remember the reward for her death? It is her skull filled with gold, so you must take my brother her head if you want to become wealthy.' He glanced at Derrewyn who was watching him with an expressionless face. 'But do you know how to ward off her dying curse?' Saban asked the two archers.

'Her curse?' the closest man asked in a worried tone.

'She is a sorceress,' Saban said ominously.

'Do you know?' the archer asked.

Saban smiled. 'You kill the curse like this,' he said, then turned fast so that his arrow was pointing at the nearest archer. He loosed it, saw the blood spurt bright in the green shadows, then threw the bow aside as he leaped the body of the dying man to drive the second bowman down into the leaf mould. He hammered the man in the face, grunted as his opponent punched back, then he saw the man's eyes widen in agony and heard the crunch of rib bones as Derrewyn's spearman thrust his bronze blade into the bowman's chest.

Saban stood. His heart was beating fast and sweat was stinging his eyes. 'I thought that I would go through this whole battle without killing anyone.'

The first bowman, who had Saban's arrow through his throat, heaved against the pain and then lay still. 'You didn't want to kill?' Derrewyn asked scornfully. 'Has your Outfolk woman turned you against killing?'

'I have no quarrel with you,' Saban said. 'I have never had a quarrel with you.'

The surviving spearman was holding his bloody spear threateningly, but Derrewyn waved the weapon down. 'He means no harm,' she told her protector. 'Saban blunders through life meaning no harm, but he causes plenty. Go and guard the end of the wood.' She watched the spearman go, beckoned Saban forward, then crooked her wounded leg and hissed with pain. The arrow had gone clean through the muscle of her right thigh and its flint head stood proud at one side and the raven-black feathers of Ratharryn showed on the other. She broke off the feathered end, grimaced, then snapped off the head. There was not much blood, for the flesh had closed about the shaft.

431

'I can take the rest of the arrow out,' Saban said.

'I can do that for myself,' Derrewyn said. She closed her eyes for a heartbeat and listened to the faint screams that sounded from the north. 'Thank you for killing them,' she said, gesturing at the two dead bowmen. 'Did your brother truly promise a reward for me?'

'For your corpse,' Saban said.

'So now you can become rich by killing me?' she asked with a smile.

Saban returned the smile. 'No,' he said, crouching in front of her. 'I wish none of this had ever happened,' he said. 'I wish everything was as it used to be.'

'Poor Saban,' Derrewyn said. She leaned her head against the tree. 'You should have been chief of Ratharryn, then none of this would ever have happened.'

'If you go south,' Saban said, 'you should be safe.'

'I doubt I will ever be safe,' she said, then began to laugh. 'I should have given Camaban his stones when he asked for them. He came to me last summer, at night, secretly, and begged me for stones.' She grimaced. 'Do you know what he offered me for the stones?'

'Peace?' Saban suggested.

'Peace!' Derrewyn spat the word. 'He offered more than peace, Saban, he offered me himself! He wanted to marry me. He and I, he said, were the two great sorcerers and between us we would rule Ratharryn and Cathallo and make the gods dance like hares in the springtime.'

Saban stared at her, wondering if she spoke the truth, then decided that of course she did. He smiled. 'How my father's sons do love you,' he said.

'You loved me,' Derrewyn said, 'but Lengar raped me and Camaban fears me.'

432

'I still love you,' Saban blurted out, and he was far more surprised at his words than she was. He blushed, and felt ashamed because of Aurenna, but he also knew he had spoken the truth, a truth he had never really acknowledged in all the years. He stared at her and he did not see the gaunt drawn face of Cathallo's sorceress, but the bright girl whose laughter had once enraptured a whole tribe.

'Poor Saban,' Derrewyn said, then flinched as pain lashed up her leg. 'It should have been you and I, Saban, just you and I. We would have had children, we would have lived and died and nothing would ever have changed. But now?' She shrugged. 'Slaol wins, and his cruelty will be loosed on the world.'

'He is not cruel.'

'We shall see, won't we?' Derrewyn asked, then she opened her cloak to show Saban the three gold lozenges hanging from a leather thong about her neck. She raised one of the small gold pieces to her mouth, bit through its sinew, then held the shining scrap out to Saban. 'Take it,' she said.

He smiled. 'I don't need it.'

'Take it!' she insisted and waited until he obeyed. 'Keep it safe.'

'I should give it back to Sarmennyn,' he said.

'For once,' she said wearily, 'don't be a fool, because in time you will want my help. Do you remember Mai's island?'

He nodded. 'Of course I remember it.'

'We lay beneath a willow tree there,' she said, 'and it has a fork in the trunk just higher than a man can reach. Leave the gold piece in that fork and I shall come to your aid.'

'You will help me?' Saban asked, gently amused, for Ratharryn had won this day and Derrewyn was now nothing but a fugitive.

'You will need my help,' she said, 'and I will give it when you ask. I shall become a ghost now, Saban, and I shall haunt Ratharryn.' She paused. 'I suppose Camaban wants my daughter dead too?'

Saban nodded. 'He does.'

'Poor Merrel,' Derrewyn said. 'Camaban won't find her, but what life can I give her now?' She fell silent and Saban saw that she was crying, though he could not tell whether it was from grief or pain. He went and cradled her head in his arms so that she sobbed on his shoulder. 'I do hate your brothers,' she said after a while, and then she took a deep breath and gently pulled away from him. 'I shall live like an outlaw,' she said, 'and I shall make a temple to Lahanna deep in the forests where Camaban will never find it.' She held her hand out to him. 'Help me up.'

He pulled her to her feet. She moaned as she put her weight on her wounded leg, but she waved away Saban's help then called for her spearman. It seemed she would leave without saying any farewell, but then, abruptly, she turned back and kissed Saban. She said nothing, just kissed him a second time then limped southwards through the trees.

Saban watched until the leaves hid her, then closed his eyes because he feared he would weep.

There would be so many tears that day. The avenue of stones was thick with bodies, many with skulls crushed by

434

axes or clubs, and still more with missing heads. But there had been so many heads to take as trophies that, after a while, the bodies were no longer decapitated and some heads had even been discarded by the pursuers. Others of the enemy still lived, though they were horribly wounded. One man, blood dripping from his hair, clung to a stone pillar as Saban trudged past. What songs they would make of this in Ratharryn, Saban thought sourly. Ravens flapped down and dogs came to feast on dead men's flesh. Two small boys who had followed Camaban's men to war were trying to hack a woman's head off. Saban chased them from the corpse, but knew they would find another. The avenue's stones were dripping with gore and he remembered Derrewyn's prophecy that the stones of the new temple at Ratharryn would steam with blood. She was wrong, he told himself, wrong.

The first curls of smoke were writhing from the thatch in the settlement where Camaban's warriors, having fetched what valuables they could from within the huts, were hurling firebrands onto the roofs. While their huts were thus destroyed, the surviving folk of the defeated tribe sought sanctuary in the great shrine. It was there that Saban found Camaban. He was alone on the summit ridge of the huge encircling earthwork where he was systematically kicking the guardian skulls down into the ditch. 'Where have you been?' he demanded.

'Looking for Derrewyn,' Saban said.

'You found her?'

'No,' Saban said.

'She's probably dead,' Camaban said vengefully. 'I pray she is. But I still want to piss on the bitch's corpse.' He kicked a wolf's skull down to the ditch bottom. There was blood on his long hair and on the bones tied to its braids, but it was not his own blood. The bronze sword, which hung from a loop on his belt, was thick with blood. 'I hope Rallin's children have been found by now,' he went on, 'because I want them dead.'

'They're no danger to us,' Saban protested.

'They're Rallin's family and I want them all killed. And Derrewyn's bitch-child with them.' He kicked another skull off the embankment. 'Calls herself a sorceress! Ha! See where her sorcery has left her tribe!' He grinned suddenly. 'I like war.'

'I hate it.'

'That's because you're no good at it, but it isn't difficult. Gundur wanted to retreat because he hadn't thought about the problem, but I knew Rallin would lead with his best men so it was easy enough to lay a trap for them and, to give Gundur his due, he did see how it could work. Gundur fought well. Did you fight well?'

'I killed one man,' Saban said.

'Only one?' Camaban asked, amused. 'I used to be so envious of you when I was a child. You were like Lengar, tall and strong, and I thought you'd be a warrior and I would always be a cripple. But it's the cripple who has conquered Cathallo. Not Lengar, not you, but me!' He laughed, proud of his day's work, then turned to stare at the crowd of Cathallo's people who had gathered about Sannas's old hut. 'Time to frighten them, I think,' Camaban said, and he walked back to the causeway and then into the temple's centre. Less than a dozen of Ratharryn's spearmen had come into the shrine, so Camaban was virtually unguarded, but he showed no fear as he walked to the very centre of the temple, into the space between the twin stone circles that were girdled by the greater ring of boulders, and there he raised his arms to the sky and held them aloft until the frightened crowd had quietened. 'You know me!' he shouted, 'I am Camaban! Camaban the crooked child! Camaban the cripple! Camaban of Ratharryn! And I am now Camaban, chief of Cathallo. Does anyone dispute that?' He stared at the crowd. There were at least two score of men there, most of them still armed, but none of them moved.

'I am more than Camaban,' Camaban shouted, 'for I came here in the night many years ago and I took the soul of Sannas with her last breath! I, Camaban, have Sannas inside me. I am Sannas! I am Sannas!' He screamed this claim, and then, suddenly, began chanting in Sannas's old voice, her exact voice, ancient and dry like old bones, so that if Saban closed his eyes it was as if the old sorceress were still alive. 'I am Sannas come back to earth, come to save you from punishment!' And he began to writhe and dance, to leap and twist, yelping desperately as though the old woman's soul struggled against his own spirit, and the display made terrified children hide their faces in their mothers' clothes. 'I am Sannas!' Camaban screamed. 'And Slaol has conquered me! Slaol has taken me! Slaol has lain between my thighs and I am full with him! But I will fight for you!' He screamed again, and thrashed his head so that his long bloody hair whipped up and down. 'You must obey, you must obey,' he said, still in Sannas's voice.

'Kill them . . .' He was speaking in his own voice now, and he drew his gory sword and advanced on the crowd as he chanted the words. 'Kill them, kill them, kill them.' The crowd backed away.

437

'Take them as slaves!' He had changed to Sannas's voice again. 'They will be good slaves! Whip them if they are not good! Whip them!' He began writhing again, and howling again, and then, very suddenly, went still.

'Slaol talks in me,' he said in his own voice. 'He talks to me and through me. The great god comes to me and he asks why you are not all dead. Why should we not take your babies and dash their heads against the temple stones?' The women cried aloud. 'Why not give your children to Slaol's fire?' Camaban asked. 'Why not give your women to be raped, and bury your men alive in the dung pits? *Why not?*' These last two words were a screech.

'Because I will not let it.' It was Sannas once more. 'My people will obey Ratharryn, they will obey. On your knees, slaves, on your knees!' And the people of Cathallo went on their knees to Camaban. Some held out their hands to him. Women clung to their children and appealed for their lives, but Camaban just turned away, went to the nearest stone and rested his head against it.

Saban let out a great breath that he had not even been aware he had been holding. The folk of Cathallo stayed kneeling, terror on their faces, and that was how Gundur's spearmen found them when they filed through the western entrance.

Gundur went to Camaban. 'Do we kill them?'

'They're slaves,' Camaban said calmly. 'Dead slaves can't work.'

'Kill the old, then?'

'Kill the old,' Camaban agreed, 'but let the others live.' He turned and stared at the kneeling crowd. 'For I am Slaol and these are the slaves who will build me a temple.' He raised his arms to the sun. 'For I am Slaol,' he cried again in triumph, 'and they are going to build my shrine!'

Camaban left Gundur to govern Cathallo. Keep the people alive, he told him, for in the spring their labour would be needed. Gundur also had orders to search the woods for Derrewyn, whose body had never been found, and for her daughter who had also disappeared. Rallin's wives and children had been discovered and their bodies now rotted in a shallow grave. Morthor was buried under a mound and a new high priest had been appointed, but only after the man had kissed Camaban's misshapen foot and sworn to obey him.

So Camaban went home in triumph to Ratharryn where, all winter long, he toyed with wooden blocks. He had asked Saban to make the blocks, insisting that the timber was squared into pillar shapes, and he demanded more and more of them and then disappeared into his hut where he arranged and rearranged the blocks obsessively. At first he made the blocks into twin circles, one nested within the other like the unfinished temple that Saban was now removing, but after a while Camaban rejected the twin circles and instead modelled a temple like the existing shrine to Slaol just beyond Ratharryn's entrance. He devised a forest of pillars, but after staring at the model for days he swept it aside. He tried to remake Slaol and Lahanna's pattern in stone: twelve circles imposed on one greater circle; but when he stooped so that he could see the blocks with an eye close to the ground he saw only muddle and confusion and so he also rejected that arrangement.

It was a cold winter and a hungry one. Lewydd carried Erek's gold home, taking with him a half-dozen of Vakkal's men who wanted to live out their days in Sarmennyn, but that still left a horde of mouths to be fed in Ratharryn and Lengar had never been as careful as his father in storing food which meant the grain pits were low. Camaban did not care for he thought of little except his temple. He was chief of two tribes, yet he performed none of the tasks that his father had done. He allowed other men to lead his war bands, he insisted that Haragg dispense justice and was content to let Saban worry about amassing enough food to see Ratharryn through the winter. Camaban took no wives, bred no children and did not amass treasures, though he did begin to dress in some of the finery that he discovered in Lengar's hut. He wore the thick buckle of gold that the stranger had worn when he came to the Old Temple so many years before, he hung a cloak of wolf pelts edged with fox fur from his shoulders, and he carried a small mace that Lengar had taken from a priest of a defeated tribe. Hengall had carried a mace as a symbol of power, and it amused Camaban to ape his father and mock his memory for, where Hengall's mace had been a bone-crushing lump of rough stone, Camaban's mace was a delicate and precious object. Its wooden handle was circled by bone rings sculpted into the shape of lightning bolts, while its head was a perfectly carved and beautifully polished egg of black-veined brown stone, which must have taken a craftsman days of meticulous work. He had shaped the head smooth, then drilled a circular hole for its handle, and when the work was done the man had made a weapon that was good only for ceremony, for the small mace-head was much too light to inflict damage on anything but the most delicate of skulls. Camaban liked to flourish the mace as proof that stone could be worked as easily as wood. 'We won't use rough boulders like those at Cathallo,' he told Haragg. 'We'll shape them. Sculpt them.' He caressed his mace head. 'Smooth them,' he said.

Saban gathered the tribe's grain into one hut, purchased more from Drewenna and doled it out through the cold days. Warriors hunted, bringing back venison and boar and wolf. No one starved, though many of the old and the sick died. And through that cold winter Saban also took away all the dark pillars that had been brought from Sarmennyn. It was not a hard task. The stones were dug out of their holes, tipped onto the grass and dragged down into the small valley that lay east of the temple. Men dug chalk rubble from the ditch and filled the stone holes so that the centre of the temple was once again smooth and empty. Only the moon stones remained within the ditch, and the three pillars beyond it, but then Saban raised the mother stone close to the temple's centre. It took sixty men, a tripod of oak and seven days to raise the stone that was placed opposite the temple's entrance so that on midsummer's day the sun would shine down the avenue onto the pillar. The mother stone stood tall, much taller than the other pillars from Sarmennyn had stood, and in the low winter sun its shadow lay long and black on the pale turf.

Camaban spent whole days at the temple, brooding mostly and rarely taking any notice of the men who laboured to dismantle the Temple of Shadows. As the days grew shorter and the air colder he went there more often, and after a time he carried spears to the temple and rammed their blades into the hard ground, then peered across the tops of their staffs. He was using the spears to judge how high he wanted his stone pillars, but the spears did not satisfy him and so he ordered Mereth to cut him a dozen longer poles and he asked Saban to dig those into the turf. The poles were long, but light, and the work was done in a day. Camaban spent day after day staring at the poles, seeing patterns in his mind.

In the end there were just two poles left. One was twice the height of a man and the other twice as long again, and they stood in line with the midsummer sun's rising, the taller post behind the mother stone and the shorter pole closer to the shrine's entrance, and as the winter came to its heart, Camaban went each evening to the temple and stared at the thin poles, which seemed to shiver in the icy wind.

Midwinter came. It had ever been a time when cattle bellowed as they were sacrificed to appease the sun's weakness, but Haragg would have no such killings in his temples and so the tribe danced and sang without the smell of fresh blood in their nostrils. Some folk grumbled that the gods would be angered by Haragg's squeamishness, claiming sacrifice was necessary if the new year was not to bring plague, but Camaban supported Haragg and that evening, after the tribe had sung a lament to the dying sun, Camaban preached that the old ways were doomed and that if Ratharryn kept their faith then the new temple would ensure that the sun never died again. They feasted that night on venison and pork, then lit the great fires that would draw Slaol back in the dawn after midwinter's day.

There was snow in that dawn: not much, but enough to coat the higher ground with white in which Camaban left footprints as he walked to the temple. He had insisted that Saban accompany him and the brothers were swathed in furs for it was bitter cold and a sharp wind cut from a pale sky banded with wispy pink clouds. The heavier snow clouds had cleared at midday and the afternoon sun was low enough to cast shadows on the snow from the hummocks made by the filled-in stone holes. Camaban gazed at his twin poles, but shook his head in irritation when Saban asked their purpose. Then he turned to stare at Gilan's four moon stones, the paired pillars and slabs that showed the way to Lahanna's most distant wanderings. 'It is time,' Camaban said, 'to forgive Lahanna.'

'To forgive her?'

'We fought against Cathallo so we could have peace,' Camaban said, 'and Slaol will want peace among the gods. Lahanna rebelled against him, but she has lost the battle. We have won. It is time to forgive her.' He gazed at the distant woods. 'Do you think Derrewyn still lives?'

'Do you want to forgive her?' Saban asked.

'Never,' Camaban said bitterly.

'The winter will kill her,' Saban said.

'It will take more than winter to kill that bitch,' Camaban said grimly. 'And while we work for peace she'll be praying to Lahanna in some dark place, and I do not want Lahanna to oppose us. I want her to join us. It is time that she was drawn back to Slaol, and that is why we shall leave her four stones because they show her that she belongs to Slaol.'

'They do?' Saban asked.

Camaban smiled. 'If you were to stand by either pillar,' he said, pointing to the nearest moon stone pillar, 'and looked at the slab across the circle, you will see where Lahanna wanders?'

443

'Yes,' Saban said, remembering how Gilan had placed the four stones.

'But what if you were to look at the other slab?' Camaban asked.

Saban frowned, not understanding, and so Camaban seized his arm and walked him to the pillar and pointed towards the great slab standing on the circle's far side. 'That's where Lahanna goes, yes?'

'Yes,' Saban agreed.

Camaban turned Saban so that now he looked towards the second slab. 'And what would you see if you looked in that direction?'

Saban was so cold that he found it hard to think, but it was late in the day and the sun was low among the pink clouds and he saw that Slaol would touch the horizon in line with the moon stones. 'You would see Slaol's midwinter death,' he said.

'Exactly! And if you looked the other way? If you were to stand by that pillar,' Camaban pointed diagonally across the circle, 'and looked across the other slab?'

'Slaol's summer rising.'

'Yes!' Camaban shouted. 'So what does that tell you? It tells you that Slaol and Lahanna are linked. They are joined, Saban, like a feather is in the wing or a horn in the skull. Lahanna might rebel, but she must come back. All the world's sadness is because Slaol and Lahanna parted, but our temple will bring them together. The stones tell us that. Her stones are his stones, don't you understand that?'

'Yes,' Saban said, and wondered why he had never realised that the moon stones could as easily point to the limits of Slaol's wanderings as to Lahanna's.

'What you'll do, Saban,' Camaban said enthusiastically, 'is dig me a ditch and bank round the two pillars. They're the watching stones. You'll make me two earth rings, and the priests can stand in the rings and watch Slaol across the slabs. Good!' He began to walk briskly back towards the settlement, but stopped by the sun stone which lay farthest from the shrine. 'And another ditch and bank round this stone.' He slapped the stone. 'Three circles round three stones. Three places where only priests can go. Two places to watch the sun's death and Lahanna's wanderings and one place to watch Slaol rise in glory. Now all we have to decide is what goes in the centre.'

'We have more than that to decide,' Saban said.

'What?'

'Cathallo is short of food.'

Camaban shrugged as if that were a small thing.

'Dead slaves' – Saban grimly echoed Camaban's own words – 'can't work.'

'Gundur will look after them,' Camaban said, irritated by the discussion. He wanted to think of nothing except his temple. 'That's why I sent Gundur to Cathallo. Let him feed them.'

'Gundur is only interested in Cathallo's women,' Saban said. 'He keeps a score of the youngest in his hut, and the rest of the settlement starves. You want the remnants of the tribe to rebel against you? You want them to become outlaws instead of slaves?'

'Then you go and rule Cathallo,' Camaban said carelessly, walking away through the thin snow.

'How can I build your temple if I'm in Cathallo?' Saban shouted after him.

Camaban howled at the sky in frustration, then stopped

and stared at the darkening sky. 'Aurenna,' he said.

'Aurenna?' Saban asked, puzzled.

Camaban turned. 'Cathallo has ever been ruled by women,' he said. 'Sannas first, then Derrewyn, so why not Aurenna?'

'They'll kill her!' Saban protested.

'They will love her, brother. Is she not be beloved of Slaol? Didn't he spare her life? You think the people of Cathallo could kill what Slaol spared?' Camaban danced some clumsy steps, shuffling in the snow. 'Haragg will tell the folk of Cathallo that Aurenna was the sun's bride and in their minds they will think she is Lahanna.'

'She's my wife,' Saban said harshly.

Camaban walked slowly towards Saban. 'We have no wives, brother, we have no husbands, we have no sons, we have no daughters, we have nothing till the temple is built.'

Saban shook his head at such nonsense. 'They will kill her!' he insisted.

'They will love her,' Camaban said again. He limped close to Saban and then, grotesquely, he fell on his knees in the snow and held up his hands. 'Let your wife go to Cathallo, Saban. I beg you! Let her go! Slaol wants it!' He gazed up at Saban. 'Please!'

'Aurenna might not want to go,' Saban said.

'Slaol wants it,' Camaban said again, then frowned. 'We are trying to turn the world back to its beginnings. To end winter. To drive sadness and weariness from the land. Do you know how hard that is? One wrong step and we could be in darkness for ever, but sometimes, suddenly, Slaol tells me what to do. And he has told me to send Aurenna to Cathallo. I beg you, Saban! I beg you! Let her go.'

446

'You want her to rule Cathallo?'

'I want her to draw Lahanna back! Aurenna is the sun's bride. If we are to have joy in the world, Saban, we must have Slaol and Lahanna united again. Aurenna alone can do it. Slaol has told me so and you, my brother, must let her go.' He held out a hand so that Saban could pull him to his feet. 'Please,' Camaban said.

'If Aurenna wishes to go,' Saban said, reckoning his wife would have no wish to be isolated so far from the new temple, but to his surprise Aurenna did not reject the idea. Instead she talked a long time with Camaban and Haragg, and afterwards she went to Slaol's old temple where she submitted herself to the widow's rite by having her long golden hair hacked short with a bronze knife. Haragg burned the hair, the ashes were placed in a pot and the pot was broken against one of the timber poles.

Saban watched horrified as Aurenna walked from the temple with her once beautiful hair ravaged into crude clumps smeared with blood where the knife had grazed her scalp, yet on her face was a look of joy. She knelt to Saban. 'You will let me go?' she asked.

'If you really want to,' he said reluctantly.

'I want to!' she said fervently. 'I want to!'

'But why?' Saban asked. 'And why the widow's rite?'

'My old life is gone,' Aurenna said, climbing to her feet. 'I was given to Slaol, and even though he rejected me I was ever his worshipper. But from today, Saban, I am a priestess of Lahanna.'

'Why?' he asked again, his voice filled with pain.

She smiled calmly. 'In Sarmennyn we used to offer the god a human bride each year, but in a year's time the god demanded another bride. One girl after another, Saban, burning, burning! But the girls didn't satisfy Slaol. How could they? He wants a bride for ever, a bride to match his glory in the sky and that can only be Lahanna.'

'The Outfolk have never worshipped Lahanna,' Saban protested.

'And we were wrong,' Aurenna said. 'Lahanna and Slaol! They are made for each other as a man is made for a woman. Why did Slaol spare me from the fire at the Sea Temple? He must have had a purpose and now I see what it is. He rejected a human bride because he wants Lahanna and my task will be to draw her to his embrace. I shall do it by prayer, by dancing, by kindness.' She smiled at Saban, then cupped his face in her hands. 'We are to do a great thing, you and I. We are to make the marriage of the gods. You will make the shrine and I shall bring the bride to Slaol's bed. You cannot forbid me that task, can you?'

'They will kill you in Cathallo,' Saban growled.

Aurenna shook her head. 'I shall comfort them, and in time they will worship at our new temple and share in its joy.' She smiled. 'It is why I was born.'

She left next day, taking Leir and Lallic with her, and Gundur returned to Ratharryn, but left a score of his warriors behind. Aurenna had those men hunt the forests for boar and deer to feed the settlement.

Saban stayed in Ratharryn. Camaban wanted him there, for Camaban was intent on his temple's design and needed his brother's advice. What was the largest stone that could be raised as a pillar? Could one stone be piled on another? How were the stones to be moved? Could the stone be shaped? The questions did not end, even if Saban had no answers. Winter ended and the spring touched the trees with green and still Camaban brooded.

448

Then one day there were no more questions for the doorway of Camaban's hut stayed curtained and no one, not even Saban or Haragg, was allowed inside. A mist hung across Ratharryn, hiding the skulls on the embankment's crest. There was no wind that day and the world was silent and white. The tribe, sensing that the gods were close about the settlement, kept their voices low.

At sunset Camaban screamed, 'I have found it!'

And the wind blew the mists away.

Haragg and Saban were summoned to Camaban's hut
where a patch of the earthen floor had been swept clean
and smooth. Saban expected to see the finished model,
but instead the wooden blocks had been pushed into a
jumbled heap beside which Camaban squatted with eyes
so bright and skin so sheened with sweat that Saban wondered if his brother had a fever, but the fever was no
sickness, it was excitement. 'We shall build a temple,' Camaban greeted Saban and Haragg, 'like none that is now or
ever will be again. We shall make the gods dance with
joy.' Camaban was naked, his skin reddened by the glare
of the fire which warmed and lit the hut. He waited until
Saban and Haragg had settled, then he placed a single
wooden pillar very close to the centre of the cleared space.
'That is the mother stone,' Camaban said, 'reminding us
that we are of the earth and that the earth is at the heart
of all that exists.' The bones hanging from his hair and
beard clicked together as he rocked back on his heels. 'And
around the mother stone,' he went on, 'we shall build a
death house, only this death house will also be Slaol's
house. It will remind us that death is the passage to life,
and we shall make Slaol's house with stones as tall as any

wooden temple pole.' He took the longest two blocks and placed them just behind the mother stone. 'We shall touch the sky,' he said reverently, then took a smaller piece of wood and put it across the two pillars' tops so that the three stones formed a tall and very narrow archway. 'Slaol's arch,' he said reverently, 'a slit through which the dead can go to him.'

Saban stared at the high arch. 'How tall are the stones?' he asked.

'They are the same height as the tallest of the two poles at the temple,' Camaban answered and Saban flinched as he remembered the height of the slender wands that his brother had planted in the cleared temple. Camaban was demanding that the arch should stand more than four times the height of a man, taller than any stone Saban had ever seen, so tall that he could not imagine how such stones were to be raised, let alone how the capstone was to be lifted onto their summits, but he said nothing. He just watched as Camaban placed eight more pillars to flank the first two, not in a straight line, but curved sharply forward in the shape of an ox's horns to make a bay that wrapped about the mother stone. He put blocks on each pair of pillars so that the sun's house was now made of five archways. The central arch was tallest, but the flanking four would all soar high above the ground. 'These arches' – Camaban tapped the four lower arches – 'point towards the moon stones. They will let the dead escape from Lahanna's grip. Wherever she goes, north or south, east or west, the dead will find a gateway into Slaol's house.'

'And from Slaol's house,' Haragg said, 'the dead will escape through the tallest arch?'

'And thus we shall take the dead from Lahanna and give

them to Slaol,' Camaban agreed, 'and it is Slaol who gives life.'

'Gateways of the moon,' Haragg said approvingly, 'and an archway of the sun.'

'It isn't finished,' Camaban said, and he took thirty blocks of wood and placed them in a wide circle of pillars all around the sun's house. All but one of the stones were the same size, all were neatly squared and all were shorter than any of the central arches, but the last of the pillars, though as tall as the others, was only half as wide. 'These pillars show the days of the moon,' Camaban explained, and Haragg nodded for he understood that the thirty stones represented the twenty nine and a half days in which the moon travelled from nothingness to fullness, 'So Lahanna will see that we recognise her.'

'But Slaol –' Haragg began, meaning to protest that Camaban had surrounded Slaol's house with a ring dedicated to the moon.

Camaban hushed him and picked up thirty more wooden blocks that he laid one by one on top of the ring of pillars until he had completed a circle of lintels. 'We shall make a ring of stone,' he explained, 'to reflect Slaol. Lahanna will carry the ring and will understand that her duty is to be subservient to Slaol.'

'A sky ring,' Saban said quietly. He did not know how it could be done, but he felt a surge of excitement as he stared at the wooden blocks. It would be magnificent, he thought, and then he told himself that these were mere playthings, and the temple was to be made of boulders that Camaban assumed could be moved and shaped as easily as timber.

Camaban took a last block which he placed a long way

from the others, putting it where, on the hillside, the sacred avenue had been dug. 'That,' he said, tapping the final block, 'is our sun stone, and at midsummer its shadow will reach into the sun's house, and at midwinter the sun's light will go through the tall arch and strike the stone. So when Slaol dies his last light will touch the stone that marked his greatest power.'

'And Slaol will remember,' Haragg said.

'He will remember,' Camaban agreed, 'and he will want his power again and so he will fight against winter and thus come closer to us. Closer and closer until his ring' – he touched the sky ring of stones – 'matches Lahanna's twelve seasons. And then Slaol and Lahanna will be wed and we shall have bliss. We shall have bliss.' He fell silent, gazing at his model temple of wood, but in his mind's eye he was seeing it made of stone and standing on the hill's green slope where it would be ringed by the bank and ditch of whitest chalk. A circle of chalk and a ring of stone and a house of arches to call the far gods back to their home.

Saban stared at the wooden blocks. Their shadows made a complex pattern that flickered black and red. Camaban was right, Saban thought. There was nothing like it in all the land, nothing like it under the sky or between the grey seas. Saban had never dreamed of a temple so splendid, so clean, and so difficult to build.

'It can be done?' Camaban asked with a trace of nervousness in his voice.

'If the god wants it done,' Saban answered.

'Slaol wants it done,' Camaban replied confidently. 'Slaol demands that it be done! He wants it done in three years.'

Three years! Saban grimaced at the thought. 'It will take longer than that,' he said mildly, expecting an angry retort.

Camaban dismissed the pessimism with a shake of his head. 'Whatever you need,' he said, 'demand. Men, timber, sledges, oxen, whatever you want.'

'It will need many men,' Saban warned.

'We shall use slaves,' Camaban decreed, 'and when it is done you will be reunited with Aurenna.'

So Saban began the work. He did it gladly for he had been inspired by Camaban's vision and he longed for the day when the gods would be restored to their proper pattern and so bring an end to the world's afflictions. He had Mereth take a team of men to cut oaks in the forests around Maden for it was in that settlement that the oaks would be trimmed, cut and made into sledges. Each sledge would have two broad runners joined by three massive beams on which a stone could rest, and a fourth beam at the front to which oxen would be harnessed. Men might pull some of the smaller stones, but the great stones, the ten tall ones which would make the sun house and the thirty that would hold the sky ring aloft, would need teams of oxen, so oxen had to be counted. And the ox teams would need harness ropes, which meant more oxen had to be killed, their hides tanned and then cut and twisted into strong lines. There were not enough oxen in Ratharryn and Cathallo so Gundur and Vakkal led their warriors on long raids to find more. Saban made other ropes by soaking stripped lime bark in water-filled pits and, when the strands separated, weaving them into long lines that were curled down in a storehouse.

Camaban laid out the temple's plan in the turf where the stones of Sarmennyn had stood. He scribed a circle in the earth with a plough stick attached by a line to a peg at the shrine's centre and the scratched ring showed where the stones of the sky ring would be planted. He marked the places for its thirty pillars, then banged pegs into the ground where his tall sun house would be built. The shrine's centre was now bare of grass for so many feet trampled the space each day while the chalky rubble that had been used to fill the old holes where the stones from Sarmennyn had stood got kicked all across the circle.

Camaban had given Saban six willow wands, each cut to a precise length, and careful instructions how many stones were needed of each length. The longest pole was four times the height of a man, and that merely represented the length of the stone that needed to be above the turf. Saban knew that a stone needed a third of its length sunk in the ground if it were to resist the storms and winds. Camaban was demanding two such massive stones and when Saban visited Cathallo he could only find one boulder that was big enough. The next longest was too short, though if it was buried shallowly it might just stand. It was simple enough to select the shorter stones, for plenty were scattered across the green hills, but time and again Saban wandered back to the monstrous rock that would form one pillar of the sun's high arch.

It was indeed monstrous. It was a piece of stone so huge that it looked like a rib of the earth itself. It was not thick, for its lichened top barely reached to his knee, though much of the rock's bulk was buried in the soil. Yet at its widest it stretched more than four paces and it was over thirteen paces long. Thirteen! If it could be raised, Saban thought, then it would indeed touch the sky, but how to raise it? And how to lift it from the earth and move it to

Ratharryn? He stroked the stone, feeling the sun's warmth in its lichened surface. He could imagine how the smaller stones might be prised from their turf beds and eased onto the beams of an oak sledge, but he doubted there were enough men in all the land to lift this great boulder from the ground.

But however he lifted the stone he knew he would need a sledge that was three times bigger than any he had made before, and he decided the sledge must be made in Cathallo from oak timbers that he would place in a long and narrow hut so that the timber could season. Dry wood was just as strong as green timber, but weighed much less, and Saban reckoned he must make the sledge as light as possible if the big boulder were to be shifted off the hill. He would let the timbers dry for a year or more and in that time he would worry at the problem of how to lift the stone.

He found Aurenna in Cathallo's shrine. She was wearing a strange robe made of deerskin cut with a myriad tiny slits into which she had threaded jays' feathers so that the garment seemed to shiver blue and white whenever a breeze blew. 'The people expect a priestess to be different,' she said, explaining the robe, and Saban thought how beautiful she looked. Her pale skin was still unflawed, her gaze was firm and gentle, while her ravaged hair was growing back so that it now enclosed her face like a soft golden cap. She looked happy, radiantly so, and laughed off Saban's worries that the defeated folk of Cathallo would burn his drying timbers. 'They'll work hard to make our temple a success,' she promised.

'They will?' Saban asked, surprised.

'When the temple is finished,' Aurenna explained, 'they will be free again. I have promised them that.'

'You promised them freedom?' Saban asked. 'And what does Camaban say?'

'Camaban will obey Slaol,' Aurenna said. She walked Saban through the settlement and though she proclaimed a blithe belief in the goodness of Cathallo's people, to Saban they looked sullen and resentful. Their chief was dead, their sorceress had vanished and they lived under the spears of Ratharryn's warriors, and Saban feared they would try to burn the long timbers. He also feared for Aurenna's life, and for the life of his two children, but Aurenna laughed at his worries. She explained how she refused the protection of Ratharryn's warriors and how she walked unguarded in the humiliated settlement. 'They like me,' she said simply, and told Saban how she had fought to keep the shrine unviolated. Haragg had wanted to pull down the temple's boulders and move them to Ratharryn, but Aurenna had persuaded Camaban to leave the stones alone. 'Our job is to entice Lahanna, not to offend her,' she said, and so the temple had remained and the folk of Cathallo took some comfort from that.

They evidently took more comfort from Aurenna. She had proclaimed herself a priestess of Lahanna and though, obedient to Haragg, she would not permit the sacrifice of living things, she had taken care to learn the tribe's ritual prayers. Each night she sang to the moon and in each dawn she turned thrice to lament Lahanna's fading. She consulted Cathallo's priests, rationed the settlement's food so that none starved and, best of all, she was proving to be a healer as effective as either Sannas or Derrewyn. Indeed, she was reckoned better than Derrewyn, for Aurenna loved all children and when the women brought her their sons and daughters Aurenna would soothe away their pain with a kindness and patience that Derrewyn had never shown. A dozen small children lived in Aurenna's hut now, all of them orphans whom she fed, clothed and taught, and the hut had become a meeting place for Cathallo's women. 'I like it here,' Aurenna said as she and Saban walked back to the shrine. 'I am happy here.'

'And I shall be happy with you,' Saban said cheerfully.

'With me?' Aurenna looked alarmed.

Saban smiled. He had not seen his wife since midwinter and he had missed her. 'We shall start moving stones very soon,' he told her. 'The small ones first, then the bigger, so I shall be spending time here. A lot of time.'

Aurenna frowned. 'Not here,' she said, 'not in my hut.' A gaggle of children spilled from the hut, led by Leir. Saban lifted his son, whirled him round and tossed him in the air, but Aurenna, when Leir's feet were safe on the ground, pushed the boy away and took Saban's arm. 'We cannot be together as we used to be. It isn't proper.'

'What isn't proper?' Saban growled.

Aurenna walked a few paces in silence. The children followed, their small faces watching the adults anxiously. 'You and I have become servants of the temple that you will build,' Aurenna said, 'and the temple is Lahanna's bridal shrine.'

'What has that to do with you and me?'

'Lahanna will struggle against the marriage,' Aurenna explained. 'She has tried to rival Slaol, but now we will give her to his keeping for ever and she will resist it. My task is to reassure her. That is why I was sent here.' She paused, frowning. 'Have you heard the rumour that Derrewyn still lives?'

'I heard,' Saban grunted.

'She will be encouraging Lahanna to oppose us, so I am to oppose Derrewyn.' She smiled placidly, as if that explanation must prove satisfying to Saban.

He gazed into the shadowed ditch where the pink and brown blossoms of bee orchids grew so thick. The children crowded round Aurenna who broke off scraps of honey-comb to put into their greedy hands. Saban turned back to look at her and, as ever, was dazzled by her startling beauty. 'I can live here,' he said, gesturing towards Sannas's old hut. 'It's a better place to live than Ratharryn, at least while we're moving the stones.'

'Oh, Saban!' She smiled chidingly. 'Don't you understand anything I've said? I cut my hair! I turned away from my other life! I am now dedicated to Lahanna, only to Lahanna. Not to Slaol, not to you, not to anyone but Lahanna! When the temple is built then we shall come together, for that is the day Lahanna will be coaxed from her loneliness, but till then I have to share the loneliness.'

'We're married!' Saban protested angrily.

'And we shall be married again,' Aurenna said placidly, 'but for now I am Lahanna's priestess and that is my sacrifice.'

'Camaban told you this?' Saban asked bitterly.

'I dreamed it,' Aurenna said firmly. 'Lahanna comes to me in my dreams. She is reluctant, of course, but I am patient with her. I see her as a woman dressed in a long robe that shines! She is so beautiful, Saban! So beautiful and hurt. I see her in the sky and I call to her and sometimes she hears me. And when we bring Slaol to the temple she will come to us. I am sure of it.' She smiled, expecting Saban to share her happiness. 'But until that day,' she went on, 'we must be calm, obedient and good.' She turned

459

and asked the question of her children: 'What are we to be?'

'Calm, obedient and good,' they chorused.

She looked back at Saban. 'I cannot stop you coming to the hut,' she said softly, 'but you will drive Lahanna away if you do and the temple will be meaningless, meaningless.'

Saban went to Haragg when he returned to Ratharryn and told the high priest what Aurenna had said. Haragg listened, thought for a while, then shrugged. 'It is the price you pay,' he said, 'and we shall all pay a price for the temple. Your brother is tortured with visions, I am made a priest again and you will lose Aurenna for a while. Nothing good comes easily.'

'So I should not insist on sleeping with her?'

'Get yourself a slave girl,' Haragg said in his grim voice. 'Forget Aurenna. She must share Lahanna's loneliness for now, but you have a temple to build. So get yourself a slave girl and forget your wife. And build, Saban, just build.'

Before Saban could build he had to move the stones from Cathallo. He knew he could not shift them along the direct path to Ratharryn for that crossed the marshes by Maden and climbed the steep hill just south of that settlement, and the big boulders would never pass those obstacles, so he spent that summer searching for a better route. He insisted that Leir should accompany him for it was time, he told Aurenna, that the boy learned how to survive far from any settlement. He and Leir roamed the western country in search of a path that avoided the wet lands and the steepest hills. Their exploration took the best part of the late summer, but eventually Saban discovered a path that would take the stones out of Cathallo towards the setting sun, then round in a great arc so that they would approach the Sky Temple from the west.

Saban enjoyed Leir's company. They kept a sharp eye for outlaws, but saw none, for this western countryside was much hunted by Ratharryn's warriors. Saban taught Leir to use a bow and, on their last day, after Saban had brought down a pricket with a single arrow, he let Leir kill the beast with a spear. The boy was eager enough, but seemed surprised at how much strength was needed to puncture the deer's skin. He managed to avoid the flailing hooves and thrust the bronze blade home and, because it was his son's first kill, Saban smeared the boy's face with the pricket's blood.

'Will the deer come back to life?' Leir asked his father.

'I don't think so,' Saban said with a smile. He tore the hide away from the animal's belly then drew a knife to slit the muscles covering the entrails. 'We'll have eaten most of him!'

'Mother says we'll all come back to life,' Leir said earnestly.

Saban swayed back on his heels. His hands and wrists were covered with blood. 'She says what?'

'She says the graves will empty when the temple is built,' Leir said earnestly. 'Everyone we've ever loved will come back to life. That's what she says.'

Saban wondered if his son had misunderstood Aurenna's words. 'How will we feed them all?' he asked lightly. 'It's hard enough to feed the living, let alone the dead.'

'And no one will ever be ill,' Leir went on, 'and no one will be unhappy again.'

'That's certainly why we're making the temple,' Saban said, going back to the warm carcass and slashing the knife through the flesh to release the deer's coiled guts. He decided Leir must be confused for neither Camaban nor Haragg had ever claimed that the temple would conquer death, but that night, after he and Leir had carried the best of the deer's meat to Ratharryn, Saban asked Camaban about Aurenna's words.

'No more death, eh?' Camaban said. He and Saban were in their father's old hut where Camaban now had a half-dozen female slaves to look after him. The brothers had shared a meal of pork and Camaban now stripped one of the rib bones with his teeth. 'Is that what Aurenna says?'

'So Leir tells me.'

'And he's a clever boy,' Camaban said, glancing at his bloody-faced nephew who slept to one side of the hut. 'I think it's possible,' he said guardedly.

'The dead will come to life?' Saban asked in astonishment.

'Who can tell what will happen when the gods reunite?' Camaban asked, poking in the bowl for another rib. 'Winter will go, of that I'm sure, and death too? Why not?' He frowned, thinking about it. 'Why do we worship?'

'Good harvests, healthy children,' Saban said.

'We worship,' Camaban corrected him, 'because life is not the end. Death is not the end. After death we live, but where? With Lahanna in the night. But Lahanna does not give life, Slaol does, and our temple will take the dead from Lahanna to Slaol. So perhaps Aurenna is right. Have some blackberries, they're the first of the year and very good.' One of his slave girls had brought the berries and now settled beside Camaban. She was a thin young girl

462

from Cathallo with big anxious eyes and a mass of curly black hair. She leaned her head on Camaban's shoulder and he absent-mindedly slipped an arm under her tunic to caress a breast. 'Aurenna's been thinking about these things a long time,' Camaban went on, 'while I've been distracted by the temple. She must think that the gods will reward us for bringing them back together, and that does seem likely, doesn't it? And what greater reward could there be than an end to death?' He put a blackberry into the girl's mouth. 'When will you be ready to move some stones?'

'As soon as the frost hardens the ground.'

'You'll need slaves,' Camaban said, feeding the girl another blackberry. She playfully nipped at his fingers and he pinched her, making her squeal with laughter. 'I'm sending some war parties out this winter to capture more slaves.'

'It isn't slaves I need,' Saban said distractedly. He was jealous of his brother's girl. He had not taken Haragg's advice, though at times he was tempted. 'I need oxen.'

'We'll fetch you oxen,' Camaban promised, 'but you'll need slaves too. You're going to shape the stones, remember? Oxen can't do that!'

'Shape them?' Saban asked so loudly that he woke Leir.

'Of course!' Camaban said. He pointed with his free hand at the wooden blocks of his model temple, which had been Leir's playthings earlier in the evening. 'The stones must be smooth like those blocks. Any tribe can raise rough stones like Cathallo's, but ours will be shaped. They will be beautiful. They will be perfect.'

Saban grimaced at his brother's careless demand. 'Do you know how hard that stone is?' he asked.

'I know the stones must be shaped, and that you are to do it,' Camaban said obstinately, 'and I know that the more time you spend talking about it, the longer it will take.'

Saban and Leir walked back to Cathallo next day. The deer's blood, dry and flaky, was still on the boy's face when he ran to his mother and Aurenna was horrified. She spat on her fingers to wash the blood away, then scolded Saban. 'He doesn't need to know how to kill!' she protested.

'It's the first skill every man needs,' Saban said. 'If you can't kill, you can't eat.'

'Priests don't hunt for their food,' Aurenna said angrily, 'and Leir is to be a priest.'

'He may not want to be.'

'I have dreamed it!' Aurenna insisted defiantly, once again claiming an authority that Saban could not challenge. 'The gods have decided,' she said, then pulled Leir away.

It was after the harvest that Saban moved the first stone off the hillside. It was one of the small stones yet it still needed twenty-four oxen to draw its sledge down the hill. The oxen were in three rows, eight to a row, and behind each line of beasts, like a great bar behind their tails, was a tree trunk to which their harnesses were attached. Each trunk was tied to the sledge by two long lines of twisted ox hide to pull the sledges along. In the first few paces Saban discovered that the oxen at the back were prone to step over the hauling lines whenever the oxen in front faltered and so the stone rested while a dozen small boys were collected from the settlement and taught how to walk between the animals and hold the hauling lines high whenever they slackened. The boys were given sharpened sticks to goad the oxen while a dozen more boys and men ranged ahead of the stone to remove fallen branches or kick down tussocks that might impede the sledge runners. Ten more oxen plodded behind the stone. Some were there to replace any beast that fell ill in its harness, while the others carried fodder and spare hide ropes.

It took a whole day to drag the stone from the hill and through Cathallo's shrine where, as the oxen lumbered by, Aurenna had a choir of women sing a song in praise of Lahanna. Haragg had come from Ratharryn and he beamed as the first stone passed through the boulders. He draped the oxen's horns with chains of violet flowers while Cathallo's priests scattered meadowsweets on the stone. Those priests had been the first to reconcile themselves to Ratharryn's conquest, perhaps because Camaban had taken care to pay them well with bronze, amber and jet.

The oxen's harnesses were great collars of leather, but even on the first day the collars chafed the animals' necks raw and bloody, so Saban had the boys smear pig's fat on the leather. The next day they hauled the stone out of sight of Cathallo. Most of the men and boys went back to the settlement to eat and sleep, but a handful stayed with Saban to guard the stone. They made a fire and shared a meal of dried meat with some pears and blackberries that they had found growing in a nearby wood. Besides Saban there were three men and four boys around the fire; all were from Cathallo and at first they were awkward with Saban, but afterwards, when the meal was eaten and the fire was streaming sparks towards the stars, one of the men turned to Saban. 'You were Derrewyn's friend?' he asked.

'I was.'

'She still lives,' the man said defiantly. He had a scar on

his face from where an arrow had struck his cheek during the battle that had destroyed Cathallo's power.

'I hope she still lives,' Saban answered.

'You hope so?' The man was puzzled.

'As you said, I was her friend. And if she does still live,' Saban said firmly, 'then you would do well to keep silent unless you want more of Ratharryn's spearmen searching the forests for her.'

Another of the men played a short tune on a flute made from the bone of a crane's leg. 'They can search all they like,' he said when he had finished, 'but they will never find her. Nor her child.'

The first man, whose name was Vennar, poked the fire to prompt a thick flurry of sparks, then gave Saban a sidelong glance. 'Are you not afraid to be here with us?'

'If I was afraid,' Saban said, 'I would not be here.'

'You need not be afraid,' Vennar said very quietly. 'Derrewyn says you are not to be killed.'

Saban smiled. All summer he had suspected that Derrewyn was close and that, unknown to Cathallo's conquerors, she kept in touch with her tribe. He was touched, too, that she had ordered his life spared. 'But if you try to stop the stones from reaching Ratharryn,' he said, 'then I shall fight you, and you will have to kill me.'

Vennar shook his head. 'If we do not move the stones,' he said, 'someone else will.'

'Besides,' the flute player added, 'our women would fear Lahanna's anger if you were to die.'

'Lahanna's anger?' Saban asked, puzzled. Ratharryn's vengeance, maybe, but surely not Lahanna's anger?

Vennar frowned. 'Some of our women say that Aurenna is Lahanna herself.'

'She is beautiful,' the second man said wistfully.

'And Slaol would not take her life,' Vennar said. 'Is that not true?'

'She is not Lahanna,' Saban said firmly, fearful what Derrewyn might do if she heard such a tale.

'The women say she is,' Vennar insisted, and Saban could tell from his tone that Vennar was not sure what to believe for he was torn between his old loyalty to Derrewyn and his awe of Aurenna. Saban doubted that Aurenna herself would have encouraged such a rumour, but he wondered if Camaban had. It seemed likely. The folk of Cathallo had lost a sorceress, and what better to replace a sorceress than a goddess? 'Didn't the Outfolk worship her as a goddess?' Vennar demanded.

'She is a woman,' Saban insisted, 'just a woman.'

'So was Sannas,' Vennar said.

'Your brother claims to be Slaol,' the flute player said, 'so why shouldn't Aurenna be Lahanna?' But Saban would not talk of it any more. He slept instead, or rather he wrapped himself in his cloak and watched the brilliant stars that lay so thick beyond the shimmering smoke and he began to wonder if Aurenna was indeed turning into a goddess. Her beauty did not fade, her serenity was never broken and her confidence was unshakeable.

It took eleven days to move the first stone to Ratharryn, and once it was there Vennar and his men took the oxen and the sledge back to Cathallo to load another stone, while Saban stayed at the Sky Temple. The first stone was one of the smallest, destined to form a thirtieth part of the sky ring lifted on its pillars. Camaban had marked the ring on the ground by scratching a pair of concentric circles, and he now insisted that the stone be placed on that band.

'The stone has to be shaped,' Camaban told Saban, 'so that its outer edge curves to match the bigger circle, and its inner edge curves to match the smaller.'

Saban stared at the lump of stone. It was bulbous, protruding far over the two scratched lines, yet Camaban insisted that it be smoothed into a small segment of a wide circle. 'All the thirty stones of the sky ring must be the same length,' Camaban went on enthusiastically, 'but you're not to blunt their ends.' He took a lump of chalk and drew on the stone's slab-like surface. 'One end is to have a tongue and in the other end you'll carve a slot, so that the tongue of one stone fits into the slot of the next stone all around the ring.'

A man might as easily carve the sun, Saban thought, or wipe the sea-bed dry with thistledown, or count the leaves of a forest. And there were not just the sky ring's stones to shape, but the thirty stones that would lift it so high into the air, and the fifteen huge stones of the sun house, which would stand even higher. Camaban had worked out the dimensions of each stone and cut willow-sticks to record the measurements. Saban kept the sticks in a hut he made close to the temple. That hut became his home now. He had slaves to bring him firewood and to fetch water and to cook food, and more slaves to shape the first six stones, which had all arrived by midwinter.

The six grey boulders, like all the stones that came from Cathallo's hills, were slabs. Their top and bottom surfaces were parallel and nearly flat, and all the stones were of much the same thickness, so to make a pillar or a lintel it was only necessary to chip away the slab until its corners were square and its sides matched the lengths of the willow wands in Saban's hut. But the stone was cruelly hard, much harder than the boulders from Sarmennyn, and at first Saban's slaves merely broke their stone hammers on it, so Saban found harder stones. The stone hammers were skull-sized balls that the slaves lifted and dropped, lifted and dropped, and each blow ground away a patch of dust and stone splinters, so that, patch by patch, splinter by splinter, dust-grain by dust-grain, the stones were sculpted.

The slaves learned as they worked. It was quicker, they discovered, to grind shallow trenches down the face of the stone, then to knock away the ridges left between. Some of the stones came with a dull brown line traceable in their grey faces and Saban found that the discoloration betrayed a weakness in the boulders that could sometimes be exploited if it ran where excess stone was to be removed. A dozen hammers dropped together on one side of the brown line could sometimes shear a great lump away, but if that failed Saban would set a fire down the length of the stain, feed the fire till it raged, then feed it again with a trickle of pig's fat which carried the searing heat down to the stone's surface. He would let the fat sizzle and flare until the rock was almost red hot and then his workers would dash cold water onto the fire and as often as not the stone would crack down the line of the stain. Sometimes the boulders were already cracked and the slaves could drive wedges into the split and hammer the rock apart or, on the coldest nights, fill the cracks with water and let it freeze so that the water spirits, trapped in the ice, would break the rock apart to escape. Yet most of the stones had to be shaped by sheer hard work, by repetitive grinding, by continuous blows, and the crash of the hammers and the grating of the grind-stones never stopped. Even in his dreams Saban heard the scrape and crack and screech of stone on stone, and his skin turned as grey as the boulders and his hair and beard were filled with the gritty dust.

Eight stones came the second year, and eleven the third, and Saban had to find more workers to grind and hammer and split and burn the stone, and more workers required still more slaves to bring food and water to the temple, and Camaban now had war parties permanently roaming up and down the land in search of captives. He led some of those war bands himself. He wore a sword now and had a bronze-plated tunic and a close-fitting cap made of bronze panels that had been cunningly riveted into the shape of a bowl. Men reckoned him as great a warrior as Lengar and a better sorcerer than Sannas, because those whom his spears could not defeat, his reputation could scare into submission.

Yet no sorcery could shape the stones and Camaban, between his raiding forays, grew ever more impatient with the slow progress. He would watch the slaves singing as they worked and the sound angered him. 'Work them harder!'

'They are working as hard as they can,' Saban said.

'Then why do they have breath to sing?'

'The song gives the work rhythm,' Saban explained.

'A whip would give them a faster rhythm,' Camaban grumbled.

'There will be no whips,' Saban said. 'If you want them to work faster then send them more food. Send pelts for clothes. They are not our enemies, brother, but the folk who will build our dream.'

Camaban might be dissatisfied with the temple's progress, but that did not stop him from creating yet more

470

work for the builders. He wanted the pillars jointed to their capstones so that the sky ring would never fall. Saban had thought it would be enough to rest the stones on top of their pillars, but Camaban insisted they must be fixed and so each pillar had to have two knobs sculpted into its top. In time the lintels would need holes ground into their undersides to slot over the knobs, but Saban would not do that work until the pillars were raised and he could measure exactly where the holes had to be bored.

And still Camaban refined his temple. He visited Cathallo and talked for hours with Aurenna, so many hours that folk whispered about their being together, but Haragg dismissed the rumours, saying that the two only spoke of the temple. Saban feared those conversations for they invariably hatched some new and impossible demand. In the fourth year of the work Camaban demanded to know if Saban had ever noticed how some of the temple poles in Ratharryn seemed to look the same width all the way up from the ground to the sky.

Saban had been helping lay a trail of firewood down a boulder's flank. He straightened, frowning. 'They look straight and regular because that's the way they grow.'

'No,' Camaban said. 'Aurenna watched a hut being built in Cathallo and she said the centre-post was tapered, but once it was raised it looked straight. I talked to Galeth about it, and he tells me it's an illusion.'

'An illusion? You mean it's magic?' Saban asked.

'Slaol spare me from idiots!' Camaban seized a piece of chalk and swept aside the line of firewood that Saban had so carefully placed. 'Tree trunks are wider at one end than the other,' he said, scratching an exaggeratedly tapered outline on the stone's rough surface. 'But sometimes

Galeth would find a trunk that was just about the same width all the way up, and those, he says, all look wider at the top. It's the ones with narrower tops that look straight, while the straight ones look deformed. So I want you to taper the stones. Make them slightly narrower at the top.' Camaban threw away the chalk and brushed his hands together. 'You don't have to taper them much. Say a hand's width on every side? That way they'll all look regular.'

A moon later Camaban said that Aurenna had dreamed that the faces of the stones had been polished to a shine, and by then Saban was so numb to the immensity of the task that he just nodded. He did not try to tell Camaban how huge was the effort needed to turn each finished stone so its four sides could be ground into a shining surface, instead he just told six of the younger slaves to start polishing one of the finished pillars. They rubbed stone hammers back and forth, back and forth, and sometimes poured scraps of flint, sand and stone dust onto the surface and ground the abrasive mix into the stubborn rock. All summer they pushed the hammers backwards and forwards, tearing their hands to raw shreds as they scraped the flinty dust, and at the summer's end there was a patch of stone the size of a lamb's pelt that was smooth and, when wet, shiny. 'More!' Camaban demanded, 'more! Make it shine!'

'You must give me more workers,' Saban said.

'Why not whip the ones you have?' Camaban asked.

'They must not be whipped,' Haragg said. The high priest limped now, his back was bent and his muscles slack, but there was still a great power in his deep voice. 'They must not be whipped,' he repeated harshly.

472

'Why not?' Camaban wanted to know.

'It is a temple to end the world's woes,' Haragg said. 'You want it to be born in blood and pain?'

'I want it made!' Camaban screamed. For a few heartbeats it seemed as though he would bring his precious mace crashing down onto one of the boulders and Saban flinched in expectation of the smooth head breaking into a thousand shards, but Camaban controlled his anger. 'Slaol wants it built,' he said instead, 'he tells me it can be done, yet nothing happens here! Nothing! You might as well piss on the stones for all the progress you're making.'

'Give Saban more workers,' Haragg suggested, and so Camaban led raiding parties deep into the northern lands and brought back captives who spoke unknown languages, slaves who tattooed their faces red, slaves who worshipped gods Saban had never heard of, but still more slaves were needed for the work was cruelly hard and painfully slow, and Saban had yet to move any of the long boulders that would form the pillars of the sun's house at the temple's centre. He had cut and shaped the big sledge runners, and those timbers had seasoned in Cathallo, but he had not dared try to move the gigantic stones.

He went to Galeth for advice. His uncle was old and feeble now, his scanty hair was white and his beard a mere wisp. Lidda, his woman, was dead and Galeth was blind, but in his blindness he could still envisage stones and levers and sledges. 'Moving a large stone is no different from moving a small one,' he told Saban. 'It's just that everything is larger: the sledge, the levers and the ox team.' Galeth shivered. It was a warm night, but he had a large fire in his hut and had pulled a bearskin about his shoulders.

'Are you sick?' Saban asked.

473

'A summer fever,' Galeth said dismissively.

Saban frowned. 'I can build the sledge,' he said, 'and make levers, but I do not see how to shift the stones onto their sledges. They're too big.'

'Then you must build the sledge under the stone,' Galeth suggested. He paused, his body racked with the shakes. 'It's nothing,' he said, 'nothing, just a summer fever.' He waited until the shivering fit had passed, then described how he would first dig a trench down each of the stone's long sides. Once the trenches had reached the bedrock chalk, he said, the huge runners could be laid down each flank. Then the stone must be levered up, using the sledge runners as fulcrums. 'Do it one end at a time,' Galeth advised, 'and put beams under the stone. That way you won't have to shift the stone onto the sledge, but instead build the sledge under the stone.'

Saban thought about it. It would work, he decided, it would work very well. A ramp would have to be made in front of the sledge, and that ramp would need to be long and shallow so that oxen could haul the boulder up from the bedrock to the turf. How many oxen? Galeth did not know, but guessed Saban would need more beasts than had ever been harnessed to a sledge before. More ropes, more beams to spread the load of the ropes, and more men to guide the oxen. 'But you can do it,' the old man said. He shivered again, then moaned.

'You're sick, uncle.'

'Only fever, boy.' Galeth drew the bear's pelt tighter about his old shoulders. 'But I shall be glad to go to the Death Place,' he said, 'and join my dear Lidda. You will carry me, Saban?'

'Of course I will,' Saban said, 'but it will be years yet!'

'And Camaban tells me I shall live on earth again,' Galeth said, ignoring Saban's optimism, 'but I do not see how that can be.'

'He says what?'

'That I shall come back. That my soul will use the gates of his new temple to return to earth.' The old man sat silent for a while. The flames of his fire made the lines on his face deep shadowed like knife cuts. 'I must have raised twenty temples in my life,' he said, breaking the silence, 'and I saw nothing get better with any one of them. But this one will be different.'

'This one will be different,' Saban agreed.

'I hope so,' the old man said, 'but I cannot help thinking that the folk of Cathallo said the same thing when they made their big shrine.' Galeth chuckled and Saban reflected that his uncle was not nearly as slow-thinking as folk thought. 'Or do you think,' Galeth asked, 'that they moved the stones because they had nothing better to do?' He thought about that, then reached out and touched a deerskin bag in which he kept Lidda's flensed bones. He wanted his own bones added to hers before they were buried. He shivered again, then waved a hand to avert Saban's expression of concern. 'This longest stone,' he said after a while, 'is it slender?'

Saban found a piece of kindling in a pile at the hut's edge and put it into Galeth's hand. 'Just like that,' he said.

Galeth felt the long, thin sliver of wood. 'You know what you should do?'

'Tell me.'

'Put it in the hole sideways,' the old man said, and showed what he meant by bending the long thin piece of wood. 'A long flat rock could snap in two when you try to hoist it,' he explained. He turned the scrap of wood sideways and no amount of pressure could bend or snap it, but when he bent it again flatwise it snapped easily. 'Put it in the hole sideways,' he said again, tossing the scraps aside.

'I will,' Saban promised.

'And carry my corpse to the Death Place. Promise me that.'

'I will carry you, uncle,' Saban promised a second time.

'I shall sleep now,' Galeth said, and Saban backed from the hut and went to Camaban to tell him Galeth was sick. Camaban promised to take him an infusion of herbs, but when Saban went back to his uncle's hut he could not wake the old man. Galeth lay on his back, his mouth open and the hairs of his moustache not moving with any breath. Saban gently tapped Galeth's cheek and the old man's blind eyes opened, but there was no life there. He had died as gently as a feather falls.

The women of the tribe washed Galeth's body, then Mereth, his son, and Saban laid the corpse on a hurdle woven from willow. Next morning the women sang the body to the settlement's entrance before Mereth and Saban carried it on to the Death Place. Haragg walked in front of the corpse while a young priest came behind and played a lament on a bone flute. The body was covered with an ox hide on which Saban had strewn some ivy. Camaban did not come, and the only other mourners were Galeth's two younger sons who were Mereth's half-brothers.

The Death Place lay to the south of Ratharryn, not so very far from the Sky Temple, though it was separated from it by a wide valley and hidden by a wood of beech and hazel trees. The Death Place was itself a temple, dedicated to the ancestors, though it was never used for worship, or for bull dances, or for weddings. It was for the dead and so it was left derelict and overgrown. It stank, especially in the high summer, and as soon as the rank smell soured the funeral party's nostrils the young priest hurried ahead to dispel the spirits which were known to cluster about the temple. He reached the sun gate and shrieked at the unseen souls. Ravens called harshly back, then reluctantly spread their black wings and flew to the nearby trees, though the bolder of the birds settled on the remains of a ring of short timber poles which stood inside the temple's low bank. A fox snarled at the approaching men from among the nettles in the ditch, then ran to the trees. 'Safe now,' the young priest called.

Mereth and Saban carried Galeth through the entrance that faced the rising midsummer sun, then threaded the small spirit stakes, which were scattered throughout the temple. Haragg found an empty space and there the two men laid the hurdle down. Mereth pulled the heavy ox hide from the naked corpse, then he and Saban tipped Galeth onto the rank grass, which grew so thick among the dead. The old man was on his side, mouth agape, and Saban pulled on a stiff shoulder so that his uncle lay staring towards the clouded sky. A slave of Camaban's who had died only two days before lay close by; already her pregnant belly had been torn apart by beasts and her face ravaged by ravens' beaks. A dozen other bodies lay in the Death Place, two of them almost reduced to skeletons. One had weeds growing through its ribcage and the young priest bent over the bones to judge whether the time had come to remove them. The spirits of the dead lingered in this grim place until the last of their flesh was gone, and only then did they rise into the sky to join the ancestors.

Galeth's younger sons had brought a sharpened stake and a stone maul which they gave to Mereth. He squatted beside his father's corpse and banged the spirit stake into the turf until it struck the bedrock chalk, and then he gave it three more sharp taps to tell Garlanna that another soul had passed from her domain. Saban closed his eyes and cuffed away a tear.

'What's this?' Haragg asked and Saban turned to see that the high priest was frowning at the turf beside a half-rotted body. Saban stepped over the corpse to see that a lozenge shape had been scratched into the yellow grass. 'It's Lahanna's symbol,' Haragg said, frowning.

'Does it matter?' Saban asked.

'It is not her temple,' Haragg said, then scratched at the symbol with his foot, obliterating the lozenge shape from the turf. 'Maybe it's just child's play,' he said. 'Do children come here?'

'They're not supposed to,' Saban said, 'but they do. I did.'

'Child's play.' Haragg dismissed the lozenge. 'Have we finished?'

'We're finished,' Saban said.

Mereth looked a last time at his father, then walked from the temple and tossed the ivy that had covered the corpse down the deep hole that led to Garlanna's mansion. He and his half-brothers walked on through the hazels and the beech trees, then Mereth realised that Saban was still lingering by the corpse. 'Aren't you coming?' he shouted back.

'I want to say a prayer here,' Saban said, 'alone.'

So Mereth and the others went and Saban waited amidst

the foul stench. He knew who had carved the lozenge shape in the Death Place's rank soil, so he stood beside his uncle's pale corpse until he heard a rustle in the trees. 'Derrewyn,' he then said, turning towards the noise and surprising himself by the eagerness in his voice.

And Derrewyn surprised him by smiling as she stepped from the trees, then surprised him further for, when he had crossed the low bank and ditch, she put her hands on his shoulders and kissed him. 'You look older,' she said.

'I am older,' Saban said.

'White hairs.' She touched his temples. She was painfully thin and her hair was tangled and dirty. She had been living as an outlaw, harried from woodland to woodland, and her pelts were filthy with mud and dead leaves. Her skin was stretched tight over her cheekbones, reminding Saban of Sannas's skull-face. 'Do I look older?' she asked him.

'As beautiful as ever,' Saban said.

She smiled. 'You lie,' she said gently.

'You shouldn't be here,' Saban told her. 'Camaban's spearmen search for you.' The rumours of Derrewyn's survival had never subsided and Camaban had sent scores of warriors and dogs to scour the forests.

'I see them,' Derrewyn said scornfully. 'Clumsy spearmen blundering through the trees, following their hounds, but no hound can see my spirit. Do you know that Camaban sent me a messenger?'

'He did?' Saban was surprised.

'He released a slave into the forests, carrying in his head Camaban's words. "Come to Ratharryn," he said, "and kneel to me and I shall let you live and worship Lahanna."' Derrewyn laughed at the memory. 'I sent the slave back

479

to Camaban. Or, rather, I left his head on Ratharryn's embankment with its tongue cut out. The rest of him I gave to the dogs. Do you still have the lozenge?'

'Of course.' Saban touched the pouch where he kept the sliver of Sarmennyn's gold.

'Guard it well,' Derrewyn said, then she walked to the Death Place's ditch and stared at the bodies. 'I hear,' she said over her shoulder, 'that your wife has become a goddess?'

'She has never claimed that,' Saban insisted.

'But she will not lie with you.'

'Did you come all this way to tell me that?' Saban asked, nettled.

Derrewyn laughed. 'You do not know where I have come from. Just as you do not know that your wife lies with Camaban.'

'That isn't true!' Saban snapped angrily.

'Isn't it?' Derrewyn asked, turning. 'Yet men say Camaban is Slaol and the women claim Aurenna is Lahanna. Are you not supposed to be bringing them together with your stones? A sacred marriage? Perhaps they rehearse the wedding, Saban?'

Saban touched his groin to avert evil. 'You tell stories,' he said bitterly, 'you have always told stories.'

Derrewyn shrugged. 'If you say so, Saban.' She saw how much she had upset him and so she walked to him and lightly touched his hand. 'I will not argue with you,' she said humbly, 'not on a day that I come begging a favour from you.'

'What you said isn't true!'

'I do tell stories,' Derrewyn said humbly, 'I am sorry.'

Saban took a deep breath. 'A favour?' he asked guardedly.

Derrewyn made an abrupt gesture towards the trees and Saban had the impression of six or seven people back there in the shadowed beeches, but only two emerged from the trees. One was a tall and fair-haired woman in a ragged deerskin tunic half covered with a sheepskin cloak, while the other was a child, perhaps Lallic's age or a year younger. She was a dark-haired girl with wide eyes and a frightened face. She stared at Saban, but clung tight to the woman's hand and tried to hide beneath the skirt of the sheepskin cloak.

'The forests are no place for a child,' Derrewyn said. 'We live hard, Saban. We steal and kill for our food, we drink from streams and we sleep where we can find safety. The child has been weak. We had another child with us, but he died last winter and I fear this girl will also die if she stays with us.'

'You want me to raise a child?' Saban asked.

'Kilda will raise her,' Derrewyn said, nodding at the tall woman. 'Kilda was one of my brother's slaves and she has known Merrel since birth. All I want from you is somewhere safe for Kilda and Merrel.'

Saban stared at the child, though he could see little of her face for it was tucked into the slave's skirt. 'She is your daughter,' he said to Derrewyn.

'She is my daughter,' Derrewyn admitted, 'and Camaban must never know that she lives, so from this day on she will carry another name.' She turned on Merrel. 'You hear that? And take that thumb from your mouth!'

The child abruptly snatched her hand away from her face and stared solemnly at Derrewyn who stooped so that her face was close to the child's. 'Your name will be Hanna, for you are Lahanna's child. Who are you?'

'Hanna,' the girl said in a timid voice.

'And Kilda is your mother, and you will live in a proper hut, Hanna, and have clothes and food and friends. And one day I shall come back for you.' Derrewyn straightened. 'Will you do that for me, Saban?'

Saban nodded. He did not know how he would explain the arrival of Kilda and Hanna, but nor did he care. He was lonely, and the work at the temple seemed endless, and he had missed his own daughter so Derrewyn's child would be welcome.

Derrewyn stooped and hugged her girl. She held the embrace for a long while, then stood, sniffed and walked back into the trees.

Saban was left with Kilda and the child. Kilda's skin was grubby and her hair a greasy tangle, but her face was broad, strong-boned and defiant. 'Come,' he said gruffly.

'What will you do with us?' Kilda asked.

'I shall find you a place to live,' Saban said, leading the two out of the trees and onto the open hillside. Across the low valley he could see the Sky Temple where the slaves ground, hammered and scraped the unyielding stones. Closer, just to the east of the sacred path, there was a huddle of slave huts from which wisps of smoke rose.

'Are you going to pretend we're slaves?' Kilda demanded.

'Everyone will know you are not my relatives,' Saban said, 'and you are not of the tribe, so what else could you be in Ratharryn? Of course you'll be slaves.'

'But if we are slaves,' Kilda said, 'your spearmen will use us.'

'Our slaves are under the protection of the priests,' Saban said. 'We are building a temple and when it is done the slaves will be free. There are no whips, nor are there spearmen watching the work.'

'And your slaves don't run?' Kilda asked.

'Some do,' Saban admitted, 'but most work willingly.' That had been Haragg's achievement. He had talked with the slaves, enthusing them with the temple's promise and though some vanished into the forests most wanted to see the temple built. They would be free when it was done, free to stay or go, and free to enjoy Slaol's blessings. They ruled themselves and carried no mark of slavery like Saban's missing finger.

'And at night?' Kilda asked. 'In the slave huts? You think a woman and a child will be safe?'

Saban knew there was only one sure way to keep Hanna safe. 'You will both live in my hut,' he said, 'and I shall say you are my own slaves. Come.' He led them down into the valley, which stank because it was here the slaves dug their dung pits, then up to the chalk ring where the air was clamorous with the sound of hammers on stone.

He took Kilda and Hanna to his hut and that night he listened as Kilda prayed to Lahanna. She prayed as she used to pray in Cathallo: that Lahanna would protect her worshippers from the spite of Slaol and from the scourge of Ratharryn. If Camaban heard that prayer, Saban thought, then Kilda and Hanna would surely die. He supposed he ought to protest to Kilda, demanding that she change her prayers, but he reckoned the gods were powerful enough to sort one prayer from another without his help.

Next day Camaban came to the temple and wanted to know when Saban would move the longest stones from Cathallo. 'Soon,' Saban said.

'Who is that?' Camaban had seen Kilda in the doorway of Saban's hut.

'My slave,' Saban said curtly.

'She looks as if you found her in the forest,' Camaban said scathingly, for Kilda was still dirty and her long hair was dishevelled. 'But wherever you found her, brother, take her to Cathallo and bring me the big stones.'

Saban did not want to take Kilda to Cathallo. She would surely be recognised there, and Hanna's life would be at risk, but Kilda would not leave him. She feared Ratharryn and trusted only Saban. 'Derrewyn said my safety lies with you,' she insisted.

'And Hanna's safety?'

'Is in Lahanna's hands,' Kilda declared.

So all three went to Cathallo.

'You shouldn't be coming to Cathallo,' Saban grumbled to Kilda. He was carrying Hanna who clung to his neck and watched the world from wide eyes. 'You'll be recognised, and this child will die.'

Kilda spat into the undergrowth. She had stopped at a stream and washed her face and dragged water through her hair, which she had then tied at the nape of her neck. She had a strong, bony face with wide blue eyes and a long nose. She was, Saban thought guiltily, a good-looking woman. 'You think I will be recognized?' Kilda asked defiantly. 'You are right, I will. But what does that matter? You think the people of Cathallo will betray us? What do you know of Cathallo, Saban? You can read its heart? The folk of Cathallo look back to the old days, to Derrewyn, to when Lahanna was properly worshipped. They will welcome us, but they will also keep silent. The child is as safe in Cathallo as if she were in Lahanna's own arms.'

'You hope that,' Saban said sourly, 'but you do not know it.'

'We have been to Cathallo often enough,' Kilda retorted. 'Your brother searched the woods for us, but some nights we even slept in Cathallo and no one betrayed us. We

485

know what happens in Cathallo. One night I will show you.'

'Show me what?'

'Wait,' she said curtly.

Aurenna greeted them gently enough. She gave Kilda a cursory glance, made a fuss of Hanna and ordered a hut prepared for Saban. 'Your woman will share it?' she asked.

'She is my slave, not my woman.'

'And the child?'

'Hers,' Saban said shortly. 'The woman cooks for me while I work here. I shall need a score of men in a few days, more later.'

'You can have all there are after the harvest,' Aurenna said.

'Twenty will do for now,' Saban said.

Saban had decided he would move the very largest stone first. If that great earthbound rock could be shifted then the others must prove easier, and so he summoned the twenty men and ordered them to dig the earth away all around the boulder. The men worked willingly enough, although they refused to believe that such a rock could be lifted. Galeth, however, had told Saban how to do it and Saban now made the task easier by hammering and scraping and burning the vast boulder to reduce its width and so lessen its weight. It took a whole moon, and when the work was done the great boulder had begun to resemble the tall pillar it was destined to become.

Leir liked to come to watch the stone being hammered and Saban welcomed his son, for he had seen too little of the boy in the last years. While the men roughly shaped the stone the children of Cathallo scrambled over its surface, fighting to occupy its long stony plateau. They used ox goads as spears, and sometimes their mock battles became fierce and Saban noted approvingly that Leir did not complain when he was pierced in the arm so deeply that the blood ran to drip from his fingers. Leir just laughed the injury away, snatched up his toy spear and charged after the boy who had wounded him.

Once the stone's weight had been lessened they dug two trenches down its long sides. That took six days, and it took another two to bring the seasoned sledge runners up from the settlement. The huge runners were laid in the trenches, and then, using two dozen men and levers so long that their outer ends had to be hauled downwards with hide ropes, Saban raised one end of the great rock so that a beam could be shoved beneath it. Raising the one end took a whole day, and another was spent lifting the back of the stone and putting three more beams beneath. Saban fastened the beams to the runners, then dug a long smooth ramp up from the bedrock chalk.

He had to wait now, for it was harvest and all the folk of Cathallo were busy in the fields or on the winnowing floors, but those harvest days gave Saban a chance to spend time with Leir. He taught the boy how to draw a bow, geld a calf and stroke fish out of the river. He saw little of his daughter. Lallic was a nervous child, scared of spiders, moths and dogs, and whenever Saban appeared she would hide behind her mother. 'She is frail,' Aurenna claimed.

'Sick?' Saban asked.

'No, just precious. Fragile.' Aurenna patted Lallic fondly. The girl did indeed look fragile to Saban, but she was also beautiful. Her skin was white and clean, her golden eyelashes were long and delicate, and her hair was as bright as her mother's. 'She has been chosen,' Aurenna added.

'Chosen as what?' Saban asked.

'She and Leir are to be the guardians of the new temple,' Aurenna said proudly. 'He will be a priest and she a priestess. They are already dedicated to Slaol and Lahanna.'

Saban thought of his son's enthusiasm in the war games that the children had fought around the stone. 'I think Leir would rather be a warrior.'

'You give him ideas,' Aurenna said disapprovingly, 'but Lahanna has chosen him.'

'Lahanna? Not Slaol?'

'Lahanna rules here,' Aurenna said, 'the true Lahanna, not the false goddess they once worshipped.'

When the harvest was gathered the folk of Cathallo danced in their temple, weaving between the boulders to lay gifts of wheat, barley and fruit at the foot of the ring-stone. There was a feast in the settlement that night, and Saban was intrigued to see that both of his children, and all the orphans who lived with Aurenna, were at the feast, but that Aurenna herself stayed in the temple. Lallic missed her mother and when Saban made a fuss of her she looked as if she wanted to cry.

There was a fire burning in the temple, its glow outlining the skull-topped crest of the embankment, but when Saban walked towards that embankment a priest stopped him. 'There is a curse on it this night.'

'This night?'

'Just this night.' The priest shrugged and gently pulled Saban back towards the feast. 'The gods do not want you there,' he said.

Kilda saw Saban return and, leaving Hanna with another woman, came and took his arm. 'I said I would show you,' she said.

'Show me what?'

'What Derrewyn and I have seen.' She drew him into the shadows then led him north away from the settlement. 'I told you,' she said, 'that no one would betray us.'

'But you have been recognised?'

'Of course.'

'And Hanna? Do folk know who she is?'

'They probably do,' Kilda said carelessly, 'but she has grown since she was here, and I tell people that she is my daughter. They pretend to believe me.' She leapt a ditch then turned eastwards. 'No one will betray Hanna.'

'You are not from Cathallo?' Saban asked. He still knew little about Kilda, but her voice betrayed that she had learned Cathallo's language late. He did know that she was little more than twenty-two summers old, but otherwise she was a stranger to him.

'I was sold into slavery as a child,' she answered. 'My people live beside the eastern sea. Life is hard there and daughters are more valuable if they are sold. We worshipped the sea god, Crommadh, and Crommadh would choose which girls were to be sold.'

'How?'

'They would take us far out on the mud flats and make us race the incoming tide. The fastest were kept to be married and the slowest were sold.' She shrugged. 'The very slowest were drowned.'

'You were slow?'

'I deliberately went slowly,' she said flatly, 'for my father would use me in the night. I wanted to escape him.'

She went south now, approaching the temple. No priest or guard had seen them loop far out into the fields and there was only a sliver of a moon to light the stubble. 'Be quiet now,' Kilda said, 'for if they see us they will kill us.'

'If who sees us?'

'Quiet,' she cautioned him, then the two of them climbed the steep chalk slope of the embankment under the baleful gaze of the wolf skulls. Kilda reached the summit first and lay flat. Saban dropped beside her.

At first he could see nothing in the wide temple. The big fire burned close to Aurenna's hut and its violent flames threw the flickering shadows of the boulders across the black ditch onto the inner slope of chalk. The fire's smoke plume, its underside touched red by the fires in the settlement, sifted towards the stars. 'Your brother came to Cathallo this afternoon,' Kilda whispered into Saban's ear, then pointed to the temple's far side where Saban saw a black shadow detach itself from a boulder.

He knew it was Camaban, for even at that distance and although the man was swathed in a bull-dancer's cloak, he could see that the figure was limping slightly. The great hide hung from his shoulders, the bull's head flopped over his face, while the hoofs and tail of the dead beast flopped or dragged on the ground. The bull-man limped in a clumsy dance, stepping from one side to another, stopping, going on again, peering about him. Then he bellowed and Saban recognized the voice.

'In your tribe,' Kilda whispered, 'the bull is Slaol, yes?'

'Yes.'

'So we are watching Slaol,' Kilda said scornfully.

Then Saban saw Aurenna. Or rather he saw a shimmering white figure come from the shadow of the hut and run lithely across the temple. White scraps floated behind her. 'Swan feathers,' Kilda said, and Saban realized his wife was wearing a cloak like her jay-feather cape, only

490

this one was threaded with swan feathers. It seemed to glow, making her ethereal. She danced away from Camaban who roared in feigned rage and then rushed towards her, but she evaded him easily and ran around the temple's margin.

Saban knew how the dance would end and he buried his face in his arms. He wanted to throw himself down the embankment and kill his brother, but Kilda had placed a hand on his back. 'This is their dream,' she said flatly, 'the dream which drives the temple you build.'

'No,' Saban said.

'The temple is to reunite Slaol and Lahanna,' she said remorselessly, 'and the gods must be shown the way. Lahanna must be taught her duties.'

Saban looked up to see that Camaban had abandoned the chase and was now standing beside the piled harvest which lay by the ringstone. Aurenna was watching him, sometimes skipping aside, then gingerly going nearer before skittishly darting away again, yet always the erratic steps took her closer to the monstrous bull.

This was the dream, Saban realized, and yet the anger was hot in him. If he killed Camaban now, he thought, then the dream would die, for only Camaban had the rage to build the temple. And the temple would reunite Slaol and Lahanna. It would end winter, it would banish the world's troubles. 'Did Derrewyn tell you to bring me here?' he asked Kilda. 'So I would kill my brother?'

'No.' She sounded surprised that he had asked. 'I brought you here to see your brother's dream.'

'And my wife's dream,' he said bitterly.

'Is she your wife?' Kilda asked scornfully. 'I was told she cut her hair like a widow.'

491

Saban looked into the temple again. Aurenna was close to Camaban now, yet still she seemed reluctant to join him; she took some fast steps backwards and then danced to one side, smoothly and gracefully. Then, slowly, she sank to her knees and the dark shape of the bull lumbered forward. Saban closed his eyes, knowing that Aurenna was surrendering to his brother just as Lahanna was supposed to surrender to Slaol when the temple was made. When he opened his eyes again he saw that the feathered cloak had been tossed aside and Aurenna's naked back was slim and white in the firelight. Saban growled, but Kilda held him firm with her hand. 'They are playing at being gods,' she said.

'If I kill them,' Saban said, 'then there will be no temple. Isn't that what Derrewyn wants?'

Kilda shook her head. 'Derrewyn believes the gods will use their temple as they want, not as your brother wants. And what Derrewyn wants of you is her daughter's life. That is why she gave Hanna to you. If you kill them now, won't there be revenge? Will you live? Will your children live? Will Hanna live? Folk think those two are gods.' She nodded towards the temple, but all Saban could see there now was the great humped shape of the bull cloak, and under it, he knew, his wife and brother coupled. He closed his eyes and shuddered, then Kilda took him in her arms and held him close. 'Derrewyn has talked with Lahanna,' she whispered, 'and your task now is to raise Hanna.' She rolled onto him, holding him down with her body, and when he opened his eyes he saw she was smiling and saw she was beautiful.

'I have no wife,' he said.

She kissed him. 'You are doing Lahanna's work,' she said quietly, 'and that is why Derrewyn sent me.'

In the morning there were just ashes in the temple, but the harvest was gathered and the work on the long stones could at last be resumed.

The sledge had been made beneath the longest stone, the ramp was finished, the hide ropes were laid on the grass and now the largest ox team that Saban had ever seen was assembled on the hillside. He had a hundred of the beasts; neither he nor any of the ox herdsmen had ever managed a team so large and at first, when they tried to harness the oxen to the stone, the beasts tangled themselves. It took three days to learn how to lead the ropes to tree-trunks from which more ropes led to the harnessed oxen.

Camaban had gone from Cathallo as secretly as he had come, leaving Saban in a confusion of anger and joy. Anger because Aurenna was his wife; joy because Kilda had become his lover, and Kilda did not talk with the gods, she did not preach how Saban should behave, but loved him with a fierce directness that assuaged years of loneliness. Yet that joy could not overcome the anger in Saban and he felt it when he saw Aurenna climbing the hill to watch the long stone dragged from its place. She wore her jay-feathered cloak so that she glinted white and blue as she led Lallic by the hand. Saban turned from her rather than greet her. Leir was standing beside him, an ox goad in his hand, and the boy looked at Kilda and Hanna who both carried bundles. 'Are you going back to Ratharryn?' Leir asked his father.

'I'm travelling with the stone,' Saban said, 'and I don't know how long it will take, but yes, I'm going back to

Ratharryn.' He cupped his hands. 'Take them forward!' he shouted to the ox herdsmen and a score of men and boys prodded the beasts who lumbered ahead until the traces were all stretched tight.

'I don't want to be a priest,' Leir blurted out. 'I want to be a man.'

It took a few heartbeats for Saban to realize what the boy had said. He had been concentrating on the hide ropes, watching them stretch tighter and wondering if they were thick enough. 'You don't want to be a priest?' he asked.

'I want to be a warrior.'

Saban cupped his hands. 'Now!' he shouted. 'Forward!'

The goads stabbed, the ox blood ran, the beasts fought the turf to find their footing and the ropes began to quiver with tension. 'Go,' Saban shouted, 'go!' and the oxen's heads were down and suddenly the sledge gave a grating lurch. Saban feared the ropes would snap, but instead the stone was moving. It was moving! The great boulder was grinding up from the earth's grip and the watching folk cheered.

'I don't want to be a priest,' Leir said again, misery in his small voice.

'You want to be a warrior,' Saban said. The sledge was coming up the ramp, leaving a smear of crushed chalk behind the broad runners.

'But my mother says I can't take the ordeals because I don't need to.' Leir looked up at his father. 'She says I have to be a priest. Lahanna has ordered it.'

'Every boy should take the ordeals,' Saban said. The sledge had reached the turf now and was sliding steadily through the ox dung and grass.

Saban followed the sledge and Leir ran after him

with tears in his eyes. 'I want to pass the ordeals!' he wailed.

'Then come to Ratharryn,' Saban said, 'and you can take them there.'

Leir stared up at his father. 'I can?' he asked, disbelief in his voice.

'Do you really want to?'

'Yes!'

'Then you will,' Saban said, and he lifted his delighted son and put him on the stone so that Leir rode the moving boulder.

Saban took the cumbersome sledge north around Cathallo's shrine because the team of oxen was much too large to go through the gaps in the temple's embankment. Aurenna paced alongside, followed by the crowd, and when the boulder had gone past the temple she called for Leir to jump down from the sledge and follow her home. Leir looked at her, but stubbornly stayed where he was. 'Leir!' Aurenna called sharply.

'Leir is coming with me,' Saban told her. 'He is coming to Ratharryn. He will live with me there.'

Aurenna looked surprised, then the surprise turned to anger. 'He will live with you?' Her voice was dangerous.

'And he will learn what I learned as a child,' Saban said. 'He will learn how to use an axe, an adze and an awl. He will learn how to make a bow, how to kill a deer and how to wield a spear. He will become a man.'

The oxen bellowed and the air stank of their dung and blood. The stone moved at less than a man's walking pace, but it did move. 'Leir!' Aurenna shouted. 'Come here!'

'Stay where you are,' Saban called to his son and hurried to catch up with the sledge.

'He is to be a priest,' Aurenna shouted. She ran after Saban, jay feathers fluttering from her cloak.

'He will become a man first,' Saban said, 'and if, after he has become a man, he wishes to be a priest, then so be it. But my son will be a man before he is ever a priest.'

'He can't go with you!' Aurenna shrieked. Saban had never seen her angry before, indeed he had not believed there was such fierce emotion inside her, but now she screamed at him and her hair was wild and her face distorted. 'How can he live with you? You have a slave woman in your bed!' She pointed at Kilda and Hanna who were following the sledge along with the folk of Cathallo who were eagerly listening to the argument. Leir was still on the stone from where he gazed at his parents while Lallic hid her small face in Aurenna's skirts. 'You keep a slave whore and her bastard!' Aurenna howled.

'But at least I don't dress in a bull-dancer's cloak to cover her!' Saban snapped. 'She is my whore, not Slaol's whore!'

Aurenna stopped and the anger on her face turned to a cold fury. She drew back her hand to strike Saban across the face, but he seized her wrist. 'You took yourself from my bed, woman, because you claimed a man would frighten Lahanna away. I did what you wanted then, but I will not let you deny my son his manhood. He is my son and he will be a man.'

'He will be a priest!' There were tears in Aurenna's eyes now. 'Lahanna demands it!'

Saban saw that he was hurting her with his grip, so he let her wrist go. 'If the goddess wants him to be a priest,' he said, 'then he will be a priest, but he will be a man first.' He turned on the ox herdsmen who had abandoned their animals to watch the confrontation. 'Watch the hauling lines!' he shouted. 'Don't let them slow down. Leir! Get down, use your goad, work!' He walked away from Aurenna who stood still, crying. Saban was trembling, half fearing a terrible curse, but Aurenna just turned and led Lallic back to her home.

'She will want revenge,' Kilda warned him.

'She will try to take her son back, that is all. But he won't go. He won't go.'

It took twenty-three days to move the long stone to Ratharryn and Saban stayed with the great sledge for most of the journey, but when they were a day or two away from the Sky Temple he hurried ahead with Kilda, Hanna and Leir for he knew that the temple's entrance would need to be widened if the stone was to be hauled through. The ditch by the entrance would have to be filled and the portal stones taken down, and he wanted both jobs done before the long boulder arrived.

The stone arrived two days later and Saban had forty slaves start sculpting it into a pillar. It might have been roughly shaped in Cathallo, but now it must be made smooth, polished and tapering. A dozen other slaves began to dig the socket for the stone, delving deep into the chalk under the soil.

Saban did not go down to the settlement, nor did Camaban come to the temple in the first days after the long stone had arrived, but Saban could smell the trouble in the air like the stench of a tanner's pit. Those folk who did come from the settlement avoided Saban, or else they forced idle conversation and seemed not to notice that Leir was now living with his father. The slaves worked, Saban pretended there was no danger and the stone shrank into its smooth shape.

The first frosts came. The sky looked washed and pale, and then at last Camaban did come to the temple. He came with a score of spearmen, all dressed for battle and led by Vakkal, his spear decorated with the scalps of men he had killed in the battle at Cathallo. Camaban, swathed in his father's bear cloak, had a bronze sword at his waist. His hair was bushy and wild, its tangles threaded with children's bones, which also hung from his beard that now had a badger's streak of white. He signalled for his spearmen to wait by the sun stone, then limped on towards Saban. A single young priest came with him, carrying the skull pole.

There was silence as Camaban crossed the entrance causeway between the two pillars that had been thrown down so that the longer stones could be hauled into the circle. His face was angry. The slaves close to Saban backed away, leaving him alone beside the mother stone where Camaban stopped to look around the temple, the priest with the skull pole two paces behind. 'No stones have been raised.' His voice was mild but he frowned at Saban. 'Why have no stones been raised?'

'They must be shaped first.'

'Those are shaped,' Camaban said, pointing his mace at some of the pillars for the sky circle.

'If they are raised,' Saban said, 'then they will get in the way of the larger stones. Those must be raised first.'

Camaban nodded. 'But where are the longer stones?' His tone was reasonable, as though he had no quarrel with Saban, but that reticence only increased the threat of his presence.

'The first is here,' Saban said, pointing to the monstrous boulder, which lay amidst piles of stone chips and dust. 'Mereth has taken the big sledge back to Cathallo and will be bringing another. But that one' – he nodded at the longest stone – 'will be raised before midwinter.'

Camaban nodded again, apparently satisfied. He drew his sword, walked to the long stone and began to sharpen the blade on the rock's edge. 'I have talked with Aurenna,' he said, his voice still calm, 'and she told me a strange tale.'

'About Leir?' Saban asked, bristling and defensive as he tried to hide his nervousness.

'She told me about Leir, of course she did.' Camaban paused to feel the edge of his blade, found it blunt and began scraping the sword on the stone again. It made a ringing noise. 'But I agree with you about Leir, brother,' he went on, glancing at Saban, 'he should be a man. I don't see him as a priest. He has no dreams like his sister. He is more like you. But I don't think he should live with you. He needs to learn a warrior's ways and a hunter's paths. He can live in Gundur's household.'

Saban nodded cautiously. Gundur was not a cruel man and his sons were growing into honest men. 'He can live in Gundur's hut,' he agreed.

'No,' Camaban said, frowning at a small nick in the sword's edge, 'the strange tale that Aurenna told me was about Derrewyn.' He looked up at Saban. 'She still lives. Did you know that?'

'How would I know?' Saban asked.

'But her child is not with her,' Camaban said. He had straightened from the stone and was staring into Saban's eyes now. 'Her child, it seems, was sent to live in a settlement because Derrewyn feared it would sicken and die in the forests. So she sent it away. To Cathallo, do you think? Or maybe here? To Ratharryn? The tale is whispered in

499

Cathallo's huts, brother, but Aurenna hears all. Have you heard that tale, Saban?'

'No.'

Camaban smiled, then made a gesture with his sword and Saban turned to see that two spearmen had found Hanna and were dragging her from the hut. Kilda was screaming at them, but a third man barred her way as the terrified child was brought to Camaban. Saban moved to take the child from the spearmen, but one of them held his weapon towards Saban while the other gave the child to Camaban who first gripped her, then laid his newly sharpened sword across her throat. 'Her mother, if that woman of yours is her mother,' Camaban said, 'has fair hair. This child is dark.'

Saban touched his own black hair.

Camaban shook his head. 'She is too old to be your child, Saban, not unless you met the mother before we ever began to build the temple.' He tightened the pressure of the sword and Hanna gasped. 'Is she Derrewyn's bastard child, Saban?' Camaban asked.

'No,' Saban said.

Camaban laughed softly. 'You were Derrewyn's lover once,' he said, 'and maybe you still love her? Enough, perhaps, to help her?'

'And you wanted to marry her once, brother,' Saban hissed, 'but that does not mean you would help her now.' Saban saw Camaban's astonishment that he knew of his offer of marriage to Derrewyn, and the astonishment made him smile. 'Would you like me to shout that news aloud, brother?'

Hanna screamed as Camaban twitched with anger. 'Do you threaten me, Saban?' he asked.

'Me?' Saban laughed. 'Threaten you, the sorcerer? But how will you build this temple, brother, if you fight me? You can build a tripod? You can line a hole with timber? You can harness oxen? You know how the stone breaks naturally? You, who boast that you have never held an axe in your life, can build this temple?'

Camaban laughed at the question. 'I can find a hundred men to raise stones!' he said scornfully.

Saban smiled. 'Then let those hundred men tell you how they will raise one stone upon another.' He pointed to the long stone. 'When that pillar is raised, brother, it will stand four times the height of a man. Four times! And how will you lift another stone to rest on its summit? Do you know?' He looked past Camaban and shouted the question even louder. 'Do any of you know?' He called to the spearmen. 'Vakkal? Gundur? Can you tell me? How will you raise a capstone to the summit of that pillar? And not just one capstone, but a whole ring of stones! How will you do it? Answer me!'

No one spoke. They just stared at him. Camaban shrugged. 'A ramp of earth, of course,' he said.

'A ramp of earth?' Saban sneered. 'You have thirty-five capstones to raise, brother, and you'll make thirty-five ramps? How long will that take? And how will you scrape those ramps from this shallow soil? Raise the stones with earth and our great-grandchildren won't see this temple finished.'

'Than how would you do it?' Camaban asked angrily.

'Properly,' Saban answered.

'Tell me!' Camaban shouted.

'No,' Saban said, 'and without me, brother, you will never have a temple. You will have a pile of rocks.' He pointed at Hanna. 'And if you kill that child I will walk away from this temple and I will never look back, never! She is a slave's whelp, but I am fond of her. You think she is Derrewyn's daughter?' Saban spat his scorn onto the long stone. 'Do you think Derrewyn would send her child to a tribe where you ruled? Search the land, brother, haul down every hut, but don't search here for Derrewyn's child.'

Camaban watched him for a time. 'Do you swear this child is not Derrewyn's daughter?'

'I do,' Saban said, and felt a chill run through him for a false oath was not to be taken lightly, yet if he had hesitated, or if he had told the truth, Hanna would have died instantly.

Camaban watched him, then gestured that the priest should step forward and lower the skull to Saban. Camaban still held his sword at Hanna's small throat. 'Put a hand on the skull,' he ordered Saban, 'and swear before the ancestors that this child is not Derrewyn's whelp.'

Saban reached his hand out slowly. This was the most solemn oath he could make, and to lie to the ancestors was to betray his whole tribe, but he placed his fingers on the bone and nodded. 'I swear it,' he said.

'On your daughter's life?' Camaban demanded.

Saban was sweating now. The world seemed to tremble about him, but Hanna was staring at him and he felt himself nod again. 'On Lallic's life,' he said and he knew he had told a terrible lie. He would have to make amends if Lallic were to live and he did not know how he could do that.

Camaban pushed Hanna away and she ran to Saban and clung to him, weeping. He picked her up and held her close.

'Make me a temple, brother,' Camaban said, pushing

502

the sword into his leather belt, 'make me a temple, but hurry!' His voice was rising now. 'You are forever making excuses! The stone is hard, the ground is too wet for sledges, the oxens' hooves are breaking. And nothing gets done!' He screeched the last four words. He was shaking and Saban wondered if his brother was about to roll his eyes and go into a howling trance that could fill the temple with blood and fear, but Camaban just yelped as if he were in pain and then abruptly turned and walked away. 'Make me a temple!' he shouted, and Saban held Hanna tight for she was weeping with fear.

As Camaban crossed the temple causeway, followed by his warriors, Saban leaned on the long stone and let out a great breath. It was a cold day, but he was still sweating. Kilda ran to him and took Hanna into her arms. 'I thought he would kill you both!' she said.

'I have sworn my daughter's life on Hanna's life,' Saban said dully. 'He knew who Hanna was and I swore she was not.' He closed his eyes, shaking. 'I have sworn a false oath.'

Kilda was silent. The slaves watched Saban.

'I have risked Lallic,' Saban said, and the tears ran down his cheeks to make furrows in the white stone dust.

'What will you do?' Kilda asked quietly.

'The gods must forgive me,' Saban said, 'no one else can.'

'If you build the gods a temple,' Kilda said, 'then they will forgive you. So build it, Saban, build it.' She reached out and wiped a tear from his face. 'And how will you raise the capstones?' she asked.

'I don't know,' Saban said, 'I truly don't know.' But if he found out, he thought, then perhaps the gods would forgive him and Lallic would live. Only the temple could save her now, and so he turned on the slaves. 'Work!' he told them. 'Work! The sooner it's done, the sooner we're all free.'

They worked. They hammered, they ground patches of stone to dust, they dug rock and earth, and they polished stone until their arms ached and their nostrils were filled with dust and their eyes stung. The strongest of them worked on the long stone and, as Saban had promised, it was ready before midwinter. The day came when it could not be shaped any more, it had been turned from a rock into a slender, elegant and tapering monolith, and Saban knew he must raise it. He remembered Galeth's advice and proposed raising the stone on edge, for he feared the narrow stone's weight might shear it in two. But first the stone had to be manoeuvred to the edge of its hole and that took six days of levering and sweating and cursing, and then it had to be turned onto one of its long narrow edges and that took a whole day, but at last it stood on its log rollers and Saban could loop ropes about the whole length of the stone and attach the ropes to the sixty oxen that would haul the monstrous rock into its hole.

The hole was the deepest Saban had ever dug. Its depth was almost twice the height of a man and he had protected its ramp and the face opposing the ramp with split tree trunks greased with pig fat. The ropes led from the stone clear across the hole, then across the ditch and banks to where the breath of sixty oxen formed a mist. Saban gave the signal and the ox drivers goaded their beasts and the twisted hide ropes lifted from the ground, went taut, quivered, stretched and then at last the stone lurched forward. 'Slowly now! Slowly!' Saban called. He feared that the slab might topple, but it edged forward safely enough, grinding splinters from the log rollers. Slaves pulled the logs from the back of the pillar as its leading edge began to jut out over the ramp. Then one of the ropes broke and there was a flurry of shouts and a long wait while a new rope was fetched and tied to the harness.

The oxen were goaded again and, finger's breadth by finger's breadth, the huge stone eased forward until half of it was poised above the ramp and the other half was still resting on the rollers, and then the oxen tugged once more and Saban was shouting at the beasts' drivers to halt the animals because the stone was tipping at last. For a heartbeat it seemed to balance on the ramp's edge, then its leading half crashed down onto the timbers. The ground shook with the impact, then the great boulder slid down the ramp to lodge against the hole's face.

Saban left the stone there that night. One end of the pillar jutted into the sky at an angle and the carved knob on its end, which would anchor the capstone of the highest arch, was stark against the winter stars.

Next day he ordered fifty slaves to bring baskets filled with chalk rubble and river stones to the edge of the hole, then he looped ten ropes about the canted stone. He led the ropes up over a tripod, which stood four times the height of a man, and then on to the oxen waiting beyond the ditch. The notch at the tripod's peak, over which the ropes would slide, was smoothed and greased. The ropes themselves were greased. Camaban and Haragg had both come to watch and the high priest could not contain his excitement. 'I don't suppose a greater stone has ever been raised!' Haragg exclaimed.

And if the stone broke now, Saban thought, then the

temple would never be built for there was no slab long enough to replace this first great pillar.

It took the best part of the morning to arrange the ox teams, to anchor the tripod's legs in small pits dug into the soil just inside the bank and to attach the ropes, but at last all was ready and Saban waved at the ox drivers and watched as the ten ropes lifted from the ground. The tripod settled into the earth, it creaked, and the ropes went taut as bronze bars. The men beyond the ditch stabbed the oxen with goads so that blood poured down their hind legs. The ropes seemed to catch in the tripod's peak for there was a jerk and a shudder, but then they slid and there was suddenly a small gap between the pillar and the ramp and the slaves began to cram the gap with the stones fetched from the river.

'Drive them!' Saban shouted. 'Drive them!' And the oxen had their heads down and the trembling tripod creaked as the stone edged up, its front edge gouging the timbers that faced the deep hole, but the higher the stone went the easier the hauling became because the ropes, coming from the tripod's peak, were now pulling at a right angle to the stone. Saban watched, holding his breath, and still the stone was rising and its base was grinding the hole's face and the slaves were desperately hurling baskets of chalk rubble and stones into the ramp so that if the stone did fall back it would not collapse all the way.

'Drive them! Drive them!' Camaban shouted, and the goads prodded, the ropes quivered, the oxen bled and the stone shuddered upwards.

'Slow now! Slow!' Saban cautioned. The pillar was close to its full height and if the oxen pulled too hard now there was a danger they might pull the pillar clean over and out of its socket. 'Just one step more!' Saban called, and the ox teams were goaded a last time and the stone shifted another fraction and then its own weight took over and the pillar thumped upright, its leading edge smashing into the protective timbers with a sickening crash. Saban held his breath, but the stone stayed where it was and he screamed at the slaves to fill the hole's edges and ram down the filling. Camaban was clumsily leaping up and down and Haragg was crying for joy. The first, the tallest stone of the temple was raised.

The ropes were taken away, the hole was filled, and at last Saban could step back and see what he had done.

He saw a marvel to exceed any at Cathallo, a marvel such as no man had ever seen in all the world.

He saw a stone standing as high as a tree.

His heart seemed to swell as he looked at it and there were tears in his eyes. The stone looked gaunt and high and slender against the grey winter sky. It looked, Saban thought, beautiful. It was smooth and shaped and awesome; it suddenly dominated the wide landscape. It towered over the mother stone which he had previously thought so huge. It was magnificent.

'It's splendid,' Camaban said, his eyes wide.

'It is Slaol's work,' Haragg said humbly.

Even the slaves were impressed. It was their work, and they looked at the pillar in wonder. In none of their tribes, in none of their temples, in none of their lands and in none of their dreams was there a stone so large and sculpted and stark. At that moment Saban knew the gods must recognise what Camaban was doing and even Kilda was impressed. 'And you will place another stone on top of that?' she asked Saban that evening.

'We will,' he said, 'for that is just one pillar of an arch.'

'But you still don't know how?'

'Maybe the gods will tell me,' he said. They were alone by the great stone. Night was falling, turning the grey rock black. Saban gazed up the monolith and was overcome again, astonished that he had ever moved it, ever shaped it, ever raised it, and he knew at that instant that he would finish the temple. There were men who said it could not be done, and even Camaban did not know how it could be achieved, but Saban knew he would do it. And he felt a sudden certainty that by building the temple he would appease the gods who would then forgive him the oath he had sworn on Lallic's life. 'I sometimes think,' he told Kilda, 'none of us really knows why we are building this temple. Camaban says he knows, and Aurenna is certain it will bring the gods to a marriage bed, but I do not know what the gods want. Except that they want it built. I think it will surprise us all when it's done.'

'Which is what Derrewyn always said,' Kilda answered.

Midwinter came and the tribe lit their fires and made their feast. The slaves ate by the temple and after midwinter, when the first snow came, they began shaping the second pillar of the long arch. That pillar was the second longest stone, but it was too short for Saban had been unable to find a stone as long as the first, so he had deliberately left the second pillar's foot clubbed and bulbous, just like Camaban's foot before Sannas had broken and straightened it, and he hoped that the heavy clubbed foot would anchor the pillar in the earth. He would sink it in a hole he knew was too shallow, but the hole had to be shallow if the second pillar were to match the height of the first.

He raised that stone in the spring. The tripod was placed and the oxen were harnessed and when the beasts took the stone's weight Saban heard the pillar's clubbed foot scrunching the chalk and timbers, but at last it was standing and the hole could be filled and there were two pillars in the earth now, side by side and so close together at their base that a kitten could scarce wriggle between them, while at their tops the twin pillars tapered and so made a gap through which the winter sun would shine.

'When do you put the top stone on?' Camaban asked.

'In a year's time,' Saban said, 'or maybe two.'

'A year!' Camaban protested.

'The stones must settle,' Saban said. 'We'll be ramming and filling the holes all year.'

'So every pillar must stand a year?' Camaban asked, appalled.

'Two years would be better.'

Camaban became even more impatient then. He was frustrated when oxen were stubborn or ropes broke or, as happened twice, a tripod splintered. He hated it when stones ended up canted and it took days of hard work to haul them straight and ram their bases with rocks and soil.

It took three whole years to shape and raise the ten tall pillars of the sun's house. The raising of the stones was the easiest part; the hardest was the grinding and shaping that still filled the temple with noise and dust. The knobs on the pillars' tops, which would anchor the capstones, proved hardest to carve, for each was twice the width of a man's hand and to make the knobs the slaves had to wear away the rest of the pillar's top, which they did dust grain by dust grain. Saban also had them leave a lip around the stone's edge so that the capstones would be held at their sides as well as by the protruding knobs.

Leir became a man in the year that the last of the sun house's pillars was raised, the same year that six of the sky-ring stones were sunk in the ground. Leir passed his ordeals and gleefully broke the chalk ball of his spirit into fragments. Saban gave him a bronze-headed spear, then hammered the tattoos of manhood into his son's chest. 'Will you go and show yourself to your mother?' he asked his son.

'She will not want to see me.'

'She will be proud of you,' Saban said, firmly, although he doubted that he spoke the truth.

Leir grimaced. 'She will be disappointed in me.'

'Then go to see your sister,' Saban said, 'and tell her I miss her.' He had not seen Lallic since he had taken Leir away from his mother, not since he had sworn her life on the skull pole.

'Lallic sees no one,' Leir said. 'She is frightened. She shivers in the hut and cries if her mother leaves her.'

Saban feared his false oath had settled a dreadful curse on his daughter and he decided he would have to see Haragg, swear the high priest to silence, confess the truth and do whatever penance Haragg commanded.

But it was not to be. For on the night when the ordeals finished, before Saban could find him, Haragg gave a great cry and died. And Camaban went mad.

Camaban howled as he had when his mother had died. He howled in unassuageable grief, claiming that Haragg had been his father. 'He was my father and my mother,' he shouted, 'my only family!' He drove the slave girls from his hut and slashed himself with flints so that his naked body was laced with blood when he emerged into the daylight. He threw himself onto Haragg's corpse, wailing that the high priest was not really dead at all, but sleeping, though when he tried to breathe his own life into Haragg's soul, the corpse stubbornly remained dead. Camaban turned on Saban then. 'If you had finished the temple, brother, he would not have died!' Camaban was quivering, scattering droplets of blood onto Haragg's body, then he snatched up handfuls of turf and hurled them at Saban. 'Go!' he shouted. 'Go! You never really loved me! You never loved me, go!'

Gundur hurried Saban out of Camaban's sight behind a hut. 'He'll kill you if you stay.' The warrior frowned as he listened to Camaban's howls. 'The gods are in him,' Gundur muttered.

'That was Haragg's tragedy,' Saban answered drily.

'His tragedy?'

Saban shrugged. 'Haragg loved being a trader. He loved it. He was curious, you see, and he wandered the land to look for answers, but then he met Camaban and he believed he had found the truth. But he missed the trader's life. He shouldn't have stayed here as high priest, for he was never the same man after.'

Camaban insisted that Haragg's body would not be taken to the Death Place, but must lie in the new temple's death house and so the corpse was carried on a hurdle and placed between the mother stone and the tallest pillars that still awaited their capstone. The whole tribe accompanied the body. Camaban wept all the way. He was still naked, his body a web of crusted blood, and at times he threw himself to the turf and had to be persuaded onwards by Aurenna who had come from Cathallo at the news of Haragg's death. She wore a robe of grey wolf fur into which she had rubbed ashes. Her hair was dishevelled. Lallic, almost grown now, was at her side. She was a wan and thin girl with pale eyes and a frightened expression. She looked startled when Saban approached her. 'I will show you the stones,' he told Lallic, 'and how we shape them.'

'She already knows,' Aurenna snapped. 'Lahanna shows her the stones in her dreams.'

'Does she?' Saban asked Lallic.

'Every night,' the girl answered timidly.

'Lallic!' Aurenna summoned her, then glared at Saban. 'You have taken one child from the goddess. You will not take another.'

The slaves stayed in their huts that day as the women of the tribe danced about the temple's ditch and bank, singing Slaol's lament. The men danced inside the temple, threading their heavy steps between the unfinished boulders and the emptied sledges. Camaban, some of his cuts reopened and bleeding, knelt beside the body and shrieked at the sky while Aurenna and Lallic, the only women who had been allowed to cross the temple causeway, cried loudly on either side of the corpse.

What shocked Saban was that two priests then led an ox into the temple. Haragg had hated the sacrifice of anything living, yet Camaban insisted the dead man's soul needed blood. The beast was hamstrung, then its tail was lifted so that its head dropped and Camaban swung the bronze axe, but his blow merely glanced off one of the horns and gouged into the animal's neck. It bellowed, Camaban struck again, missed again, and when a priest tried to take the axe from him he swung it round in a dangerous arc, just missing the man, then hacked at the animal in a maniacal frenzy. Blood spattered on the mother stone, on the corpse, on Aurenna and Lallic and Camaban, but at last the hobbled beast crumpled and Camaban drove the axe deep into its spine to end its torment. He threw the axe down and dropped to his knees. 'He will live!' he cried, 'he will live again!'

'He will live,' Aurenna echoed, then she put her arms around Camaban and lifted him up. 'Haragg will live,' she said softly, stroking Camaban who was weeping on her shoulder.

The body of the heifer was dragged away and Saban angrily scuffed chalk dust over the blood splashes. 'There was never supposed to be sacrifice here,' he said to Kilda.

'Who said so?' she asked.

'Haragg.'

'And Haragg is dead,' she answered grimly.

513

Haragg was dead and his body stayed in the sun house where it slowly decayed so that the stench of the dead priest was ever in the nostrils of the men digging the holes and shaping the stones. Ravens feasted on the corpse and maggots writhed in his rotting flesh. It took a whole year for the corpse to be reduced to bone, and even then Camaban refused to let it be buried. 'It must stay there,' he decreed, and so the bones remained. Some were taken by animals, but Saban tried to keep the skeleton whole. Camaban recovered his wits during that year and declared that he would replace Haragg, which meant he was now chief and high priest. He insisted that Haragg's bones needed the blood of sacrifices, therefore he brought sheep, goats, oxen, pigs and even birds to the temple and slaughtered them above the dry bones that became stained black with the constant blood. The slaves avoided the bones, though one day Saban was shocked to see Hanna crouching over the drenched skeleton. 'Will he really live again?' she asked Saban.

'So Camaban says,' Saban answered.

Hanna shuddered, imagining the priest's skeleton putting on flesh and skin, then climbing awkwardly to its feet and staggering like a stiff-legged drunk between the high stones. 'And when you die,' she asked Saban, 'will you lie in the temple?'

'When I die,' Saban told her, 'you must bury me where there are no stones. No stones at all.'

Hanna frowned at him, then suddenly laughed. She was growing fast and in a year or two would be accounted a woman. She knew who her real mother was, and knew too that her life depended on never admitting it, so she called Kilda her mother and Saban her father. She sometimes asked Saban if her real mother still lived, and Saban could only say that he hoped so, yet in truth he feared the opposite. Hanna reminded him more and more of the young Derrewyn: she had the same dark good looks, the same vigour, and the young men of Ratharryn were acutely aware of her. Saban reckoned in another year he might have to place a clay phallus and a skull on his hut's roof. Leir was among Hanna's admirers, and she in turn was fascinated by Saban's son who had grown tall, wore his dark hair plaited down his back and now had the first kill marks on his chest. It was rumoured that Camaban wanted Leir to be the next chief, and most thought that a good thing for Leir was already achieving a reputation for boldness. He fought in Gundur's band and was kept busy either defending Ratharryn's wide borders or in the raids that went beyond those hazy frontiers to bring back oxen and slaves. Saban was proud of his son, though he saw little enough of him for Camaban, in the years following Haragg's death, demanded that the work on the temple be hurried.

More slaves were sought, and to feed them and the tribe more war bands ranged in search of pigs, oxen and grain. The temple had become a great mouth to be fed, and still the stones came from Cathallo to be shaped by hammers, sweat and fire, and still Camaban fretted. 'Why does it all take so long?' he constantly demanded.

'Because the stone is hard,' Saban constantly replied.

'Whip the slaves!' Camaban demanded.

'And it will take twice as long,' Saban threatened, and then Camaban would get angry and swear that Saban was his enemy.

When half the pillars of the sky ring were in place

515

Camaban demanded a new refinement. 'The sky ring will be level, won't it?' he asked Saban.

'Level?'

'Flat!' Camaban said angrily, making a smoothing gesture with his hand. 'Flat like the surface of a lake.'

Saban frowned. 'The temple slopes,' he said, pointing to the gentle fall in the ground, 'so if the sky ring's pillars are all the same height then the ring of stone will follow the slope.'

'The ring must be flat!' Camaban insisted. 'It must be flat!' He paused to watch Hanna walk away from the hut and a sly smile crossed his face. 'She looks like Derrewyn.'

'She is young and dark haired,' Saban said carelessly, 'that is all.'

'But your daughter's life says she is not Derrewyn's daughter,' Camaban said, still smiling, 'does it not?'

'You heard my oath,' Saban said, and then to distract Camaban he promised to make the sky ring flat, although he knew that would take still more time. He laid light timbers across the tops of the pillars and on each timber in turn he laid a clay trough; when he filled the trough with water he could see whether or not the adjacent pillars were level. Some pillars stood too tall and slaves had to climb pegged ladders and hammer the pillar tops down. After that, because Saban dared not erect a stone that proved too short, he deliberately made the new pillars slightly too long so that each of them had to be hammered and scraped down until it stood level with its neighbours.

One stone almost broke as they erected it. It slid from its rollers, rammed into the facing timbers and a great crack showed in the stone, running diagonally up its face. Saban ordered it raised anyway and by some miracle it did not break as it swung into place, though the crack was still visible. 'It will serve,' Camaban said, 'it will serve.'

In another two years all the stones had come from Cathallo and half the sky ring's pillars had been placed, but before those pillars could be completed Saban knew he had to drag the sun house capstones into the temple's centre and he did that in the summer. The stones were hauled by scores of slaves who manoeuvred the sledges so that each capstone stood squarely by the twin pillars it would surmount.

Saban had spent days and nights wondering how to lift those capstones. Thirty-five had to be raised into the sky, thirty of them for the sky ring and five on the arches of the sun house, and it had been deep in one winter's night that the answer had come to him.

The answer was timber. A vast amount of timber that had to be cut from the forests and dragged to the temple where, with a team of sixteen slaves, Saban would try to make his idea work.

He began with the tallest arch. The sledge with the arch's capstone lay parallel to the twin pillars and about two paces away from it and Saban ordered the slaves to lay an oblong of timbers all about the sledge so that when they were done it seemed as though the long stone rested on a platform of wood. The slaves now used oak levers to raise one end of the capstone and Saban shoved a long timber underneath it, crosswise to the timbers in the bottom layer. He did the same at the stone's other end, and now the capstone rested on two timbers a forearm's height above the oblong platform.

More timbers were brought and laid all about the two supporting beams until, once again, the stone appeared to be resting on a platform, and then the stone was levered up again and propped on two blocks of wood. A new platform was laid about the blocks, using timbers that lay parallel with the beams of the first layer. The platform was now three layers high and was wide enough and long enough for men to work their levers under the stone with each subsequent raising.

Layer by layer the stone was raised until the boulder had been carried to the very top of the twin pillars and was poised there on a monstrous pile of stacked timbers. Twenty-five layers of wood now supported the capstone, but it still could not be slid across to the pillars for Saban had to measure the twin knobs on the pillars' tops and make chalk marks on the capstone where the corresponding sockets should be bored. It had taken eleven days to raise the stone and another twenty were needed to hammer and grind the holes, and then the stone had to be turned over with levers, and two more layers of wood added beneath it before the slaves could lever it, finger's breadth by finger's breadth, across from the platform and onto two beams that carried the stone until its sockets were poised directly above the twin knobs on the pillar tops.

Three men levered up one end of the capstone and Saban kicked away the beam that had been supporting the stone, and the slaves pulled the lever away so that the stone crashed down onto the pillar. The platform shook, but neither the capstone nor the pillar broke. The second beam was freed, the stone crashed down again and the first, and tallest, of the five great arches was complete.

The platform was dismantled and taken to the second pair of pillars and, as the slaves began to place the first

518

layer of timbers about the second capstone, Saban stepped back and gazed up at the first.

And he felt humbled. He knew, better than anyone, how much labour, how many days of grinding and hammering, and how much sweat and grief had gone into those three stones. He knew that one of the pillars was too short and stood on a grotesquely clubbed foot in a hole that was too shallow, but even so the archway was magnificent. It took his breath away. It soared. And its capstone, a boulder so heavy that sixteen oxen had been needed to drag it from Cathallo, was now lifted into the sky out of man's reach. It would stay there for ever and Saban trembled as he wondered whether any man would ever again lift so great a burden so high into the sky. He turned and looked at the sun which was setting behind pale clouds on the western horizon. Slaol must surely be watching, he thought. Slaol would surely reward this work with Lallic's life and that hope brought tears to Saban's eyes and he dropped to his knees and touched his forehead to the ground.

'It took how many days?' Camaban wanted to know.

'A few days more than a whole moon,' Saban said, 'but the others will be swifter, for the pillars are lower.'

'There are thirty-four more capstones to raise!' Camaban shouted. 'That's three years!' He howled his disappointment, then turned to stare at the slaves who were hammering and grinding the remaining sky-ring pillars smooth. 'Not every stone has to be properly shaped,' Camaban said. 'If they're nearly square, then let them go up. Forget the outer faces, they can be left rough.'

Saban stared at his brother. 'You want me to do what?' he asked. For years Camaban had been demanding perfection, now he was willing to let half-shaped stones be raised?

519

'Do it!' Camaban shouted, then turned on the listening slaves. 'None of you will go home till the work is done, none of you! So work! Work! Work!'

It was possible now to see how the finished temple would look, for the last pillars were being erected and, from the west and north, the circle of pillars already looked complete. The sun house was built, towering above the growing ring of stone, and Saban would often walk a hundred or more paces away and stare at what he had made and feel astonishment. It had taken years, this temple, but it was beautiful. Most of all he loved the pattern of shadows that it cast, regular and straight-sided, unlike any shadows he had ever seen, and he understood how he was watching the broken pattern of the world being mended on this hillside and at those moments he would marvel at his brother's dream. At other times he would stand in the temple's centre and feel shrunken by the pillars and oppressed by their shadows. Even on the sunniest days there was a darkness inside the stones that seemed to loom over him so that he could not rid himself of the fear that one of the capstones would fall. He knew they could not. The capstones were socketed, and the pillars' tops were dished to hold the lintels firm, yet even so, and especially standing beside Haragg's bones in the narrow space between the tallest arch and the mother stone, he felt crushed by the temple's dark heaviness. Yet if he walked away from it, crossed the ditch and turned to look again, the darkness went.

And this temple was not slight, as the stones of Sarmennyn had been slight. It filled its proper place, no longer dwarfed by the sky and the long slope of grass. Visitors, some coming from strange lands across the seas, would often drop to their knees when they first saw the stones, while the slaves now kept their voices low as they worked. 'It's coming alive,' Kilda said to Saban one day.

The last pillar of the sky ring, which was only half as wide as the others because it represented the half-day of the moon's cycle, was erected on midwinter's day. It went up easily and Camaban, who had come to see that final pillar raised, stayed at the temple as the sun sank. It was a fine day, cold but clear, and the south-western sky was delicately banded with thin clouds that turned from white to pink. A flock of starlings, looking like flint arrow-heads, wheeled over the temple. The birds were innumerable and black against the high sky's emptiness, they all shifted together, changing direction as one, and the sight made Camaban smile. It had been a long time since Camaban had smiled with pleasure. 'It's all about pattern,' he said quietly.

The sun sank lower, lengthening the temple's shadows, and Saban began to feel the stones stirring. They looked black now, for he was standing with Camaban beside the sun stone in the sacred avenue and the shadows were imperceptibly reaching towards them. And as the sun went lower the temple seemed to grow in height until its stones were vast and black. Then the sun vanished behind the capstone of the tallest arch and the first shadows of night engulfed the brothers. Behind them, in Ratharryn, the great midwinter fires were being lit and Saban assumed Camaban would go back to preside over the day's feast, but instead he waited, staring expectantly at the shadowed stones. 'Soon,' Camaban said softly, 'very soon.'

A few heartbeats later the lower edge of the highest capstone was touched a livid red and then the sun blazed through the sliver between the tallest pillars and Camaban clapped his hands for pure joy. 'It works!' he cried. 'It works!'

The land all about them was in darkness, for the shadows of the sky ring's pillars locked together to cast a great pall across the sacred avenue, but in the centre of that great stone-cast shadow there was a beam of light. It was the sun's dying light, the last light of the year, and it lanced across the horizon, over the woods, above the grass and through the arch to dazzle Camaban as he stood beside the sun stone. 'Here!' he shouted, thumping his breast as if he were drawing Slaol's attention. 'Here!' he shouted again, then stared, entranced, as the sun slid behind the stones and the shadows of the stones melded into one great blackness that spilt across the grassland. 'Do you see what we have done?' Camaban asked excitedly. 'The dying sun will see the stone that marked his greatest strength, and he will yearn for that strength and so rid himself of his winter weakness. It will work! It will work!' He turned and clasped Saban's shoulders. 'I want it ready for next midwinter.'

'It will be ready,' Saban promised.

Camaban stared into Saban's eyes, then frowned. 'Do you forgive me, brother?'

'Forgive you what?' Saban asked, knowing full well what Camaban was asking.

Camaban grimaced. 'Slaol and Lahanna must be one.' He let go of Saban's shoulders. 'I know it is hard for you, but the gods are hard on us. They are hard! There are nights when I pray that Slaol will let go of his goad, but he makes me bleed. He makes me bleed.'

'And Aurenna gives you joy?' Saban asked.

Camaban flinched, but nodded. 'She gives me joy, and what you have made, brother' – he nodded at the temple – 'will give us all such joy. Finish it. Just finish it.' He walked away.

The entrance pillars were taken to the causeway and put back in their holes, and then all that needed to be done was to raise the last capstones of the sky ring. Saban worried that the newest pillars would not have had time to settle in the ground, but Camaban would endure no delay now. 'It must be done,' he insisted, 'it must be ready.'

But ready for what? Sometimes, when Saban gazed for a long time at the shadowed stones, it seemed to him that they did have their own life. If he was tired and the light was dim the stones appeared to shift like ponderous dancers, though if he raised his head and stared directly at the pillars they would all be still. Yet the gods were in the stones, of that he was sure. The temple was not dedicated, yet the gods had found it. They brooded over the high stones. Some nights he would pray to them; Kilda found him doing so one evening and she sat and waited for him to finish, then asked him what he had begged of the gods.

'What I always pray,' Saban said, 'that they will spare my daughter's life.'

'Your daughter is Hanna now,' Kilda said. 'Mine too.'

'You think Derrewyn is dead?'

'I think she lives,' Kilda said, 'but I think you and I will always be parents to Hanna.'

Saban nodded, yet still he prayed for Lallic. She would be a priestess here, and he was the temple's builder, so, in time, he decided, she would lose her fear of him and come to trust him, for she would surely see that this was a beautiful place, a home for the gods, and know that her father had made it.

And now it was almost finished.

The bull dancers capered at midsummer. The fires scared the malevolent spirits away and in the next dawn, for the very first time, the rising sun threw the shadow of the sun stone through the completed ring of pillars to the temple's heart where Haragg's bones lay.

The last capstones were shaped. One of those stones had its sockets too close together because Camaban had insisted that it would be faster to make the holes before the lintels were raised, and Saban had to order the grinding of a third hole. It would, he prayed, be the last delay.

The harvest was cut. The women danced the threshing floors smooth and the priests husked the first grains. No more slaves came to Cathallo for there was scarce enough work for those already at the temple, but Camaban refused to release them. 'We can feed them till the temple is dedicated,' he said. 'They built it, they should see it finished, and then they will be freed.'

Winter came and folk hoped it would be the very last winter on earth. Kilda had a miscarriage and wept for days afterwards. 'I always wanted a child,' she told Saban, 'but the gods will not give me one.'

'You have Hanna,' Saban said, trying to comfort her just as she had tried to comfort him.

'She is almost grown,' Kilda said, 'and her fate is close.'

'Her fate?'

Kilda shrugged. 'She is Derrewyn's child. She has

Sannas's blood. She has a fate, Saban, and it will come soon.'

It came the very next day. It was a cold day and the temple stones were frosted white. There were just two lintels left to be raised and Saban was starting the platform for the first when Leir walked up from the settlement. He was dressed in the finery of a Ratharryn warrior with foxes' brushes woven into his hair, his chest was blue from tattoos and he carried a spear hung with a rare sea eagle's feathers that had been part of the tribute brought to Ratharryn by an admiring chief from a distant coast. Leir crossed the causeway and gazed at the stones. 'The temple will be ready by midwinter?' he asked his father.

'Easily,' Saban said.

Leir offered a half-smile, then nodded towards the sacred avenue as if suggesting they should walk there. Saban, puzzled, followed his son back across the causeway. 'Camaban says Haragg's body needs blood,' Leir said flatly.

Saban nodded. 'Always.' Only that morning Camaban had come with a trussed swan that had hissed at the stones before having its neck cut. The temple stank of blood, for no sooner had the blood of one sacrifice dried than another beast or bird was brought to Haragg's bones and killed.

'And when it is dedicated,' Leir went on grimly, 'we are promised that all the dead, not just Haragg, will find new life through the stones.'

'Are we?' Saban asked. He had thought that the dead were supposed to be taken from Lahanna's keeping and sent to Slaol's care, but the temple's effects were constantly subject to rumour and tales. Indeed, the closer the dedication came, the less anyone was certain what the temple would achieve. All knew that winter would be banished, but much more was expected. Some folk declared that the dead would walk while others claimed that only the dead who were placed in the temple would have their lives given back.

'And to give the dead life,' Leir went on, 'Camaban wants more blood.' He stopped beside the sun stone and looked back. Some slaves were polishing the standing pillars while a score of women were grubbing the ditch of weeds. 'Those slaves will not be going home when the temple is finished.'

'Some will stay,' Saban said. 'They've all been promised their freedom, but most will want to go home if they can remember where home is.'

Leir shook his head. 'Camaban became drunk last night,' he said, 'and told Gundur that he wants an avenue of heads to lead from the settlement to the temple. It is to be a path of the dead to show how we go from death back into life.' He was looking into Saban's face. 'He says he dreamed it and that Slaol demands it. Gundur's men are to kill the slaves.'

'No!' Saban protested.

'They are to be killed in the temple so their blood soaks the ground, then their heads are to be cut off and placed on the avenue's banks,' Leir said remorselessly, 'and we spearmen are expected to do the killing.'

Saban flinched. He looked at his hut where Kilda was tending a fire and he saw Hanna come through the low doorway with dry firewood. The girl saw Leir, but she must have sensed that he wanted to be alone with his father for she stayed at the hut with Kilda. 'And what do you think of Camaban's idea?' Saban asked Leir.

'If I liked it, father, would I have come to you?' Leir

paused and glanced towards Hanna. 'Camaban wants to kill all the slaves, father, all of them.'

'And what would you have me do about it?'

'Talk to Camaban?'

Saban shook his head. 'You think he listens to me? I might as well talk to a charging boar.' He stroked the sun stone. In time, he supposed, all the temple's stones would lose their pristine greyness and go dark with lichen. 'We could talk to your mother,' he suggested.

'She won't talk to me,' Leir confessed. 'She talks to the gods, not to men.' He sounded bitter. 'And Gundur says there's another reason to kill the slaves. He says that if they are allowed to go to their homes then they will take the secrets of the temple's construction with them and then others will build like it and Slaol will not come to us, but go to them.'

Saban stared at the grey dust that smothered the ground. 'If I tell the slaves to run away,' he said softly, 'then the spearmen will just gather more.'

'You can do nothing?' Leir sounded indignant.

'You can do something,' Saban said. He turned and beckoned to Hanna and as she ran eagerly towards Leir she looked so like her mother that the breath caught in Saban's throat. A dozen spearmen had asked Saban if they could marry Hanna and Saban's rejection of their requests had caused resentment. Hanna, they said, was only a slave, and a slave should be flattered to be courted by a warrior, but there was only one warrior whom Hanna liked and that was Leir. She smiled shyly at him, then looked obediently to Saban and bowed her head as a girl would to her father. 'I want you to take Leir to that island in the river,' Saban told her, 'the island I showed you a year ago.'

Hanna nodded, though she looked puzzled for she had never before been given the freedom to go with a young man into the forest. Saban felt in his pouch and brought out the small patch of worn leather that was folded about the golden lozenge. 'You are to take this,' Saban said to Leir, unwrapping the lozenge, 'and you are to place it in the fork of a willow tree. Hanna will show you which tree.' He put the gold into his son's hand.

Leir frowned at the bright scrap. 'What will this do?'

'It will change things,' Saban said, and hoped it was true for he did not even know if Derrewyn was still alive, yet the gold had always changed things. Its coming to Ratharryn had changed everything, and now he would let the sun-filled metal work its magic again. 'Hanna will tell you what the gold will do,' Saban told his son, 'for it is time that Hanna told you everything.' He kissed the girl on the forehead, for Saban knew that with those last words he had released Derrewyn's daughter from his care. He was giving her and Leir to the truth and he hoped his son would not be aghast when Hanna told him she was the daughter of Ratharryn's bitterest enemy. 'Hanna will tell you everything,' he said. 'Now go.'

He watched them walk towards the river and remembered how he had walked that same path with Derrewyn so many years before. He had thought then that his happiness would never end, and later he had believed his happiness would never return. He saw Hanna reach out and take Leir's hand and Saban's eyes filled with tears. He turned to look at the temple and saw how intricately the light and the shadows mixed on the soaring stones, and he knew his brother had dreamed a wondrous thing, but he understood now how that soaring dream was curdling into madness.

He walked back to the stones. There were only two to raise before the temple would be finished and it would be then, and only then, Saban reckoned, that he would discover why the gods had wanted it made.

The very last stone was placed just three days before midwinter. It was the capstone which rested on the smallest pillar of the outer circle. Saban had worried about that pillar for Camaban had insisted it should be only half as wide as the others because it represented the half-day of the moon's journey and it also left a wider gap in the outer stones through which folk could file into the temple's centre, but there was scarce room on its narrow summit to make the knobs for the two capstones which Saban feared would rest precariously.

He had the wrong fears. It was not the space that was inadequate, but the stone itself, for when the platform of timbers was built, and after the final capstone had been levered up layer by layer to its full height, and after it had been edged across until its tongue was above the slit in the neighbouring lintel, and when it was released to drop into place, the pillar cracked.

The capstones always fell into place with a jarring crash, and Saban always feared the moment, worrying that either the lintel itself or the pillars beneath would shatter under the impact. The hard stone contained faults that Saban had sometimes used to shape the boulders and he knew that some of those flaws must be hidden deep in the rock, though none had ever betrayed itself till now. The five lintels of the sun's house and twenty-nine capstones of the sky ring had all been safely raised, each had been levered across to its position so that the holes on its base lined up with the knobs on the pillars, and all had been released to fall with a crash, yet every stone had stayed whole until this final capstone was dropped. It did not fall with a crash, but with a flat cracking sound that echoed ominously from the circle's far side.

Saban went very still, waiting for disaster, but the silence stretched. The capstone was in its proper place and the pillar stood, but when he climbed down the stacked layers of timber he saw that the narrow pillar had a deep crack running diagonally across its face. The crack started at the stone's top and ran halfway down one flank. A slave jumped down beside Saban and put a finger into the crack. 'If that gives way . . .' he said, but did not finish the statement.

If it gave way, Saban knew, then the capstone would collapse. 'Don't even touch it,' he told the slave, and when Camaban came that evening Saban told him the grim news.

Camaban peered at the crack, then looked up at the lintel. 'The stone stands, doesn't it?' he declared.

'It stands, but for how long?' Saban asked. 'It should be replaced.'

'Replaced?' Camaban sounded astonished.

'We should bring another stone from Cathallo.'

'And how long will that take?' Camaban demanded.

'To move the stone? To shape it? To take this one away?' Saban thought for a few heartbeats. 'And we'll have to take both lintels off the narrow pillar,' he said, 'which is why I left the platform in place.' He shrugged. 'It might be done by next summer.'

'Next summer?' Camaban shouted. 'We are going to dedicate this temple in three days' time! Three days! It cannot wait! It is done, it is done, it is done! Of course it won't fall.' He beat the flat of his hand against the cracked pillar and Saban instinctively stepped back, but the stone did not shatter. Then Camaban tapped it with his small mace and afterwards, because he saw Saban was flinching, he picked up one of the heavy round stone mauls that had been used to shape the boulders and he beat it with all his strength against the cracked pillar. He smashed the stone again and again, grunting and sweating, filling the temple with the echoes of each hammering blow, and still the stone remained whole. 'You see?' Camaban asked, letting the maul fall, and then, his temper rising as it always did when his temple encountered an obstacle, he placed himself between the cracked stone and its neighbouring pillar and began to throw his full weight at the flawed stone, bouncing back and forth between the pillars. 'You see?' he screamed, and the slaves glanced nervously at Saban.

The pillar did not break. Camaban threw himself a last time at the stone, then tried to shake it with his hands. 'You see?' Camaban asked again, pulling his cloak straight. 'It is done. It is finished.' He backed away from the sky ring and stared up at its lintels. 'It is finished.' He cried those last words in triumph, then unexpectedly turned and embraced Saban. 'You have done well, Saban, you have done well. You have made the temple. It is finished! It is finished!' He screamed the last word and capered a few clumsy dance steps, then fell on his knees and prostrated himself on the ground.

And it really was finished. There was the just the last platform to dismantle and the debris of the long years to clear up. The stones of Sarmennyn were to be left in the low ground to the temple's east, while the timber of the sledges had already been piled into two great heaps that would be burned at the temple's dedication. That ceremony was three days away and Camaban, when he had finished his prayers, said that it was time the slave huts were pulled down and their timbers and straw added to the fire heaps. 'Huts burn well,' he said wolfishly.

'If I pull down the slaves' huts,' Saban asked, 'where will they sleep?'

'They can go free, of course,' Camaban said dismissively.

'Now?' Saban asked.

'Not yet,' Camaban said with a frown. 'I want to thank them. Should I give them a feast?'

'They deserve it,' Saban said.

'Then I shall arrange it,' Camaban said carelessly. 'They will have a feast on midwinter's eve. A great feast! And you can pull down the slave huts on the morning of the ceremony.' He walked away, though he continually turned to stare back at the stones.

Leir and Hanna both now lived in Saban's hut. The couple had come back from the island where Leir had left the lozenge, though there had been no reply from Derrewyn and Saban feared she was dead. Leir, far from being shocked at Hanna's parentage, seemed excited by it and demanded to hear the old stories of Cathallo and Ratharryn, of Lengar and Hengall, and of Derrewyn and Sannas.

'Derrewyn is not dead,' Kilda said stubbornly on the night of the temple's completion. The stones were deserted and Saban and Kilda walked hand in hand through the dark pillars that were touched with moonlight so that the tiny flecks embedded in the grey rock glinted like reflections of the uncountable stars. Somehow the stones seemed taller at night, taller and closer, so that when Saban and Kilda edged between two of the sun house's pillars it was as though they were enclosed by stone. Haragg's bones were shadowed, but the sour smell of blood lingered in the cold air.

'It seems smaller when you're inside,' Kilda said.

'Like a tomb,' Saban said.

'Maybe it's a temple of death?' Kilda suggested.

'Which is what Camaban wants,' a harsh voice said from the shadows that shrouded Haragg's stinking bones. 'He thinks it will give life, but it is a temple of death.'

Kilda had gasped when the voice interrupted them and Saban had put an arm around her shoulders as they turned to see a hooded figure stand up from beside the bones and walk towards them. For an instant Saban thought it was Haragg coming back to life, then Kilda suddenly released herself from his grip, ran to the dark figure and dropped at its feet. 'Derrewyn!' she cried. 'Derrewyn!'

The figure pushed back the hood and Saban saw it was indeed Derrewyn. An older Derrewyn, white haired and with a face so thin and skull-like that she resembled Sannas. 'You left the lozenge, Saban?' she asked.

'My son and your daughter left it,' Saban said.

Derrewyn smiled. Kilda was embracing her legs and Derrewyn gently disentangled herself and walked towards Saban. She still had a small limp, a legacy of the arrow that had pierced her thigh. 'Your son and my daughter,' she said, 'are they lovers now?'

'They are.'

'I hear your Leir is a good man,' Derrewyn said. 'So why

did you send for me? Is it because your brother will kill all the slaves? I knew that. I know everything, Saban. Not a whisper is uttered in Ratharryn or Cathallo that I do not hear.' She stared around her, gazing up at the tall stones. 'It already has the stench of blood, but he will give it more. He will feed it blood till his miracle happens.' She laughed scornfully. 'An end to winter? An end to sickness? An end, even, to death? But suppose the miracle doesn't happen, Saban, what will your brother do then? Make another temple? Or just feed this one with blood, blood and more blood till the very earth is red?'

Saban said nothing. Derrewyn stroked the flank of the mother stone, which reflected the moon more brightly than the stones from Cathallo. 'Or perhaps his miracle will work,' Derrewyn went on. 'Perhaps we shall see the dead walking here. All the dead, Saban, their bodies white and gaunt, walking from the stones with creaking joints.' She spat. 'You'll dig no more graves in Ratharryn, eh?' She crossed to the outer stones from where she stared at the glow of the fires from the slave huts in the small valley. 'In two days, Saban,' she said, 'your brother plans to kill all those slaves. He will pretend he is giving them a feast, but his warriors will surround the huts with spears and drive them to these stones to kill them. How do I know? I heard it, Saban, from the women at Cathallo where your brother goes to lie with your wife. They rut together, only of course they don't call it that. Rutting is what you and I did, what you and Kilda do, what your son is probably doing to my daughter even as you stand there with your jaw hanging. No, Camaban and Aurenna rehearse the wedding of Slaol and Lahanna. It is their sacred duty,' she sneered, 'but it's still rutting, however you decorate it with prayers, and when they have finished, they talk, and do you think the women of Cathallo do not pass on to me every word they overhear?'

'I sent the lozenge so you would help me,' Saban said. 'I want the slaves to live.'

'Even if that means Camaban's miracle does not work?'

Saban shrugged. 'I think Camaban is frightened that it will not work, which is why he is touched by madness,' he said quietly. 'And that madness will not end until he has dedicated his temple. And perhaps Slaol will come? I wish he would.'

'And if he doesn't?' Derrewyn asked.

'Then I have built a great temple,' Saban said firmly, 'and when the madness is over we shall come here and we shall dance and we shall pray and the gods will use the stones as they think best.'

'And that is all you've done?' Derrewyn asked sourly. 'Built a temple?'

Saban remembered what Galeth had said so shortly before his death. 'What did the folk of Cathallo believe they were doing when they dragged those great boulders from the hills?' he asked Derrewyn. 'What miracle were those stones going to work?'

Derrewyn stared at him for a heartbeat, but had no answer. She turned to Kilda. 'Tomorrow,' she said, 'you will tell the slaves that they are to be killed on midwinter's eve. Tell them that in my name. And tell them that tomorrow night there will be a path of light to take them to safety. And you, Saban' – she turned and pointed at him with a bony finger – 'tomorrow night you will sleep in Ratharryn and you will send Leir and my daughter back to the island. If Hanna stays in Ratharryn she will likely die, for she is still a slave of this temple even if she does rut with your son.'

Saban frowned. 'Will I see my son again?'

'We shall come back,' Derrewyn confirmed. 'We shall come back, and let me promise you something, and I promise it on my life. Your brother is right, Saban. On the day this temple is dedicated the dead will walk. You will see it. In three days' time, when night falls on Ratharryn, the dead will walk.'

She pulled the hood over her head and, without a backward glance, walked away.

Kilda would not go with Saban to the settlement. 'I am a slave,' she told him. 'If I stay in Ratharryn I shall be killed.'

'I wouldn't permit it,' Saban said.

'The temple has made your brother mad,' Kilda responded, 'and what you will not permit will give him delight. I shall stay here and walk Derrewyn's path of light.'

Saban accepted her choice, though without any pleasure. 'I am getting old,' he told her, 'and my bones ache. I could not bear to lose a third woman.'

'You will not lose me,' Kilda promised. 'When the madness is over we shall be together again.'

'When the madness is over,' Saban promised, 'I shall marry you.'

With that promise he walked to Ratharryn. He was in a nervous mood, but so, he discovered, was the settlement, which was filled with an uneasy anticipation. Everyone was waiting for the temple's dedication, though no one other than Camaban seemed certain what change would come in two days' time, and even Camaban was vague. 'Slaol will return to his proper place,' was all he would say, 'and our hardships will vanish with the winter.'

Saban ate that night in Mereth's hut where a dozen

other folk had gathered. They brought food, they sang and they told old tales. It was the kind of evening Saban had enjoyed throughout his youth, yet this night the singing was half-hearted for all in the hut were thinking of the temple. 'You can tell us what will happen,' a man demanded of Saban.

'I don't know.'

'At least your slaves will be happy,' another man said.

'Happy?' Saban asked.

'They are to have a feast.'

'A feast of liquor,' Mereth interjected. 'Every woman in Ratharryn has been told to brew three jars and tomorrow we are to carry it to the temple as a reward to your slaves. There's no honey left in Ratharryn!'

Saban wished he could believe that Camaban really intended to offer the temple's builders a feast, but he suspected the liquor was only intended to stupefy the slaves before the spearmen assaulted their encampment. He closed his eyes, thinking of Leir and Hanna who even now should be following the River Mai northwards. He had embraced them both, then watched them walk away with nothing except Leir's weapons. Saban had waited till they vanished in the winter trees and he had thought how simple life had been when his father had worshipped Mai, Arryn, Slaol and Lahanna, and when the gods had not made extravagant demands. Then the gold had come and with it Camaban's ambitions to change the world.

'Are you sick?' Mereth asked, worried because Saban looked so pale and drawn.

'I'm tired,' Saban said, 'just tired,' and he leaned back on the hut wall as the folk sang the song of Camaban's victory over Rallin. He listened to the singing, then smiled when Mereth's Outlander wife began a song from Sarmennyn. It was the tale of a fisherman who had caught a monster and fought it through the wind-stinging foam all the way to shore, and it reminded Saban of the years he had lived beside Sarmennyn's river. Mereth's wife sang in her own tongue and Ratharryn's folk listened from politeness rather than interest, but Saban was remembering the happy days in Sarmennyn when Aurenna had not aspired to be a goddess, but had taken such delight in the making of the boats and the moving of the stones. He was thinking of Leir learning to swim when there was a sudden shout from the darkness outside and Saban twisted to the hut entrance to see spearmen running south towards a glow on the horizon. He stared and for a mad instant he thought the vast glow of fire meant that the stones themselves were on fire, then he shouted to Mereth that something strange was happening at the temple and scrambled into the night.

Derrewyn, it could be no one else, had fired the great piles of kindling and sledge timbers that had been waiting for the dedication. She had done more, for when Saban reached the sacred avenue he saw that the slave huts were also burning, indeed his own hut was in flames and the crackling fires lit the stones, making them beautiful in the darkness.

Then a warrior shouted that the slaves were gone.

Or most were. A few, too scared to run away, or not believing the rumour that Kilda had assiduously spread all day, were huddled by the sun stone, but the rest had fled southwards along Derrewyn's path of light. Saban climbed the crest south of the temple to see the path, which had been made by ramming torches into the turf, then lighting them so that their flames marked a path to safety. The torches burned low now as they snaked across the hills to disappear among the trees beyond the Death Place. The path of light was empty, for the slaves had long gone. By now, Saban thought, they would be deep in the forest and, even as he watched, the guttering torches began to flicker out.

Camaban raged amidst the astonishment. He shouted for water to extinguish the fires, but the river was too far away and the fires were too fierce. 'Gundur!' he shouted, 'Gundur!' and when the warrior came to him Camaban ordered that every spearman and every hunting dog in Ratharryn be sent on the fugitives' trail. 'And in the meantime take them to the temple and kill them.' He pointed his sword towards the handful of surviving slaves.

'Kill them?' Gundur asked.

'Kill them!' Camaban screamed, and set an example by hacking down a man who was trying to explain what had happened in the night. The man, a slave who had stayed at the temple expecting gratitude, looked astonished for a moment, then fell to his knees as Camaban chopped blindly down with his sword. Camaban was splashed with the man's blood by the time he had finished, and then, his appetite unslaked, he looked around for another slave to kill and saw Saban instead. 'Where were you?' Camaban demanded.

'In the settlement,' Saban said, staring at his blazing hut. What few possessions he had were in that hut. His weapons, clothes and pots. 'There is no need to kill any slaves,' he protested.

'I decide the need!' Camaban screamed. He drew back the bloody sword. 'What happened here?' he demanded. 'What happened?'

Saban ignored the threatening sword. 'You tell me,' he said coldly.

'I tell you?' Camaban kept the sword raised. 'What would I know of this?'

'Nothing happens here, brother, unless you decide it. This is your temple, your dream, your doing.' Saban fought his rising anger. He looked at the flickering red flame-light where it touched the stones to fill the temple's interior with a quivering tangle of locking shadows. 'This is all your doing, brother,' he said bitterly, 'and I have done nothing here except what you have told me to do.'

Camaban stared at him and Saban thought the sword must swing forward for there was a terrible madness in his brother's fire-glossed eyes, but then, quite suddenly, Camaban began to cry. 'There has to be blood!' he sobbed. 'None of you understands! Even Haragg did not understand! There has to be blood.'

'The temple is soaked in blood,' Saban said. 'Why does it need more?'

'There must be blood. If there's no blood the god won't come. He won't come!' Camaban screamed this. Men watched him with appalled faces for he was now writhing as if his belly were gripped with pain. 'I don't want there to be death,' he cried, 'but the gods want it. We must give them blood or they will give us nothing! Nothing! And none of you understands it!'

Saban pushed the sword down, then gripped his brother's shoulders. 'When you first dreamed of the temple,' he said quietly, 'you did not see blood. There is no need for blood. The temple lives already.'

Camaban looked up at him, puzzlement on his striped face. 'It does?'

'I have felt it,' Saban said. 'It lives. And the gods will reward you if you let the slaves go.'

'They will?' Camaban asked in a frightened voice.

'They will,' Saban said, 'I promise it.'

Camaban leaned against Saban and wept on his shoulder like a child. Saban comforted him until at last Camaban straightened. 'All will be well?' he asked, cuffing at his tears.

'Everything will be well,' Saban said.

Camaban nodded, looked as if he would speak, but instead just walked away. Saban watched him go, let out a breath, then went to the temple and told Gundur the remaining slaves could live. 'But run away,' he told the slaves grimly, 'run now and run far!'

Gundur spat into the stones' shadows. 'He's mad,' he said.

'He's always been mad,' Saban said, 'from the day he was born crooked he has been mad. And we have followed his madness.'

'But what happens when the temple is dedicated?' Gundur asked. 'Where will his madness go then?'

'It is that thought which makes the madness worse,' Saban said. 'But we have followed him this far so we can give him the next two nights.'

'If the dead don't walk,' Gundur said grimly, 'then the other tribes will turn on us like wolves.'

'So keep your spears sharp,' Saban advised.

The wind changed in the night to blow the smoke northwards, and the wind brought a heavy rain that doused the fires and washed the last stone dust from the circle. When the skies cleared before dawn an owl was seen circling the temple and then flying towards the rising sun. There could be no better omen.

The temple was ready and the gods lingered close. The dream had become stone.

Aurenna came to Ratharryn in the morning, bringing Lallic and a dozen slaves with her. She went to Camaban's hut and stayed there. It was a strangely warm day so that men and women walked about without cloaks and marvelled at the new southern wind that had brought such weather. Slaol was already relenting of winter, they said, and the warmth reassured folk that the temple truly had power.

Many strangers were now at Ratharryn. None had been invited, but all came from curiosity. They had been arriving for days. Most were from neighbouring peoples, from Drewenna and the tribes along the southern coast, but some came from the distant north and others had braved a sea journey to see the miracle of the stones. Many of the visitors were from tribes that had suffered cruelly from Ratharryn's slave raids, but they all came in peace and brought their own food and so were allowed to build shelters among the berry-rich bushes of the nearby woods. On the day after the slaves fled Lewydd arrived with a dozen spearmen from Sarmennyn and Saban embraced his old friend and made room for him in Mereth's hut.

Lewydd was chief of Sarmennyn now and had a grey beard and two new scars on his grey-tattooed cheeks. 'When Kereval died,' he told Saban, 'our neighbours thought we would be easily conquered. So I have fought battles for years.'

'And won them?'

'Enough of them,' Lewydd said laconically. Then he asked about Aurenna and Haragg, and about Leir and Lallic, and he shook his head when he heard all Saban's news. 'You should have come back to Sarmennyn,' he said.

'I always wished to.'

'But you stayed and built the temple?'

'It was my duty,' Saban said. 'It is why the gods put me on the earth, and I am glad I did it. No one will remember Lengar's battles, they might even forget Cathallo's defeat, but they will always see my temple.'

Lewydd smiled. 'You built well. I have seen nothing like it in any land.' He held his hands towards Saban's fire. 'So what will happen tomorrow?'

'You must ask Camaban. If he'll talk to you.'

'He doesn't talk to you?' Lewydd asked.

Saban shrugged. 'He talks to no one except Aurenna.'

'Folk say that Erek will come to earth,' Lewydd suggested.

'Folk say many things,' Saban said. 'They say that we shall become gods, that the dead will walk and that the winter will vanish, but I do not know what will happen.'

'We shall discover soon enough,' Lewydd said comfortingly.

Women prepared food all that day. Camaban had revealed no plans for the temple's dedication, but midwinter had ever been a feast day and so the women cooked and beat and stirred so that the whole high embankment was filled with the smells of food. Camaban stayed in his hut and Saban was glad of that, for he feared his brother would miss Leir and demand to know where he had gone, but neither Camaban nor Aurenna questioned his absence.

Few slept well that night for there was too much anticipation. The woods were bright with the visitors' fires and a new moon hung in the west, though at dawn the moon faded behind a fog as the people of Ratharryn dressed themselves in their finest clothes. They combed their hair and hung themselves with necklaces of bone, jet, amber and sea-shells. The weather was still strangely warm. The fog cleared and a sudden rain shower made the people dash for their huts, but when the rain ended there was a magnificent rainbow hanging in the west. One end of the rainbow swooped down to the temple and folk climbed the embankment to marvel at the good omen.

The clouds slowly drifted northwards to leave a sky scraped bare and pale. By midday there were hundreds of folk from dozens of tribes up on the grassland about the temple and though there were scores of liquor pots no one became drunk. Some danced, some sang and the children played, though none ventured across the ditch and banks except for a dozen men who drove the cattle from among the stones then cleared the dung from inside the sacred circle. People stood beside the low outer bank and gazed at the stones, which looked splendid, clean, placid and filled with mystery. Folk complimented Saban, and he had to tell and retell the tales of the temple's making: how some pillars were too short; how he had raised the lintels; and how much sweat had gone into every single stone.

The wind dropped and the day became oddly still which only sharpened the air of expectancy. The sun was sinking in the southern sky and still no procession came from Ratharryn, though folk said there were dancers and musicians gathering about the temple of Mai and Arryn. Saban took Lewydd through the entrance of the sun and told him how the stones had been sunk in the ground and raised into the sky. He stroked the flank of the mother stone, the only stone of Sarmennyn remaining in the ring, and then he picked up some chips of rock that still lay on the grass about Haragg's bones. The rain had washed away the blood of the last sacrifice and the temple smelt sweet. Lewydd gazed up at the arches of the sun's house and seemed lost for words. 'It is . . .' he said, but could not finish.

'It is beautiful,' Saban said. He knew every stone. He knew which ones had been difficult to erect, and which had gone easily into their holes. He knew where a slave had fallen from a platform and broken a leg, and where another had been crushed by a stone being turned for shaping, and he dared to hope that all life's hardships would end this day as Slaol seared to his new home.

Then someone shouted that the priests were coming and Saban hurried Lewydd out of the temple, leaving it empty. They pushed through the crowd to see that the procession was at last coming from the settlement.

A dozen women dancers came first, sweeping leafless ash branches across the ground, and behind them came drummers and more dancers, and then came the priests who had their naked skins chalked and patterned and wore antlers or rams' horns on their heads. Last of all came a great band of warriors, all with foxes' brushes woven into their hair and hanging from their spears. Saban had never seen weapons carried to a temple's dedication, but he supposed that nothing about this evening would be the same for the crooked child was setting the world straight.

One of the approaching priests carried the tribe's skull pole and Saban saw the white bone start and stop as the priests placated the spirits. They prayed at the place where a man had fallen dead, wailed to the bear god where a child had been mauled to death, then stopped at the tombs to tell the ancestors what great thing was being done at Ratharryn this day. The sight of the skull reminded Saban of his false oath and he touched his groin and prayed to the gods to forgive him. Beyond the approaching priests the smoke from the settlement rose vertically into the sky, which was still clear of clouds, though the first faint shadow of night was dimming the north.

The procession came on again, dropping into the valley then climbing between the banks of the sacred path. The crowd had begun to dance to the approaching drum beats, shuffling left and right, advancing and retreating, beginning the steps that would not end until the drums ceased.

Camaban and Aurenna had not come with the priests who now spread themselves into a ring about the temple's ditch while the dancers swept their ash branches all about the chalk circle to drive away any malevolent spirits. The warriors, once the circle had been swept, made a protective ring about the chalk ditch.

The women of Ratharryn sang the wedding chant of Slaol. They danced to their own voices, stopping when the song stopped, then stepping on again when the beautiful lament resumed. The music was so plangent and lovely that Saban felt tears in his eyes and he began to dance himself, feeling the spirit inside him, and all about him the great crowd was swaying and moving as the voices swelled and stopped, swooped and sang. The sun was low now, but still bright, not yet touched with the blood-red of its winter dying.

A murmur sounded from the back of the crowd and Saban turned to see three figures had emerged from

Ratharryn. One was all in black, one all in white and one was dressed in a deerskin tunic. It was Lallic who wore the tunic, and she walked between Camaban and Aurenna who were arrayed in feathered cloaks. Camaban's cloak was thick with swan feathers while Aurenna, her hair as bright as the day Saban had first seen her, was swathed in ravens' feathers. White and black, Slaol and Lahanna, and Aurenna's face was transfigured by a look of ecstatic delight. She was unaware of the waiting crowd or of the silent priests or even of the towering stones because her spirit had already been carried to the new world that the temple would bring. The crowd fell silent.

Camaban had ordered two new piles of wood to be made on either side of the temple, but well away from the stones, and a hundred men had laboured all the previous day to rebuild what Derrewyn had burned. Now those new heaps of timber were set on fire. The flames climbed hungrily through the high stacks in which whole trees had been placed so that the fires would burn through the whole long midwinter night. The fires hissed and crackled, the loudest noise of the evening, for the drumming, singing and dancing had all stopped as the three figures came up the sacred path.

Camaban stopped by the sun stone, and Lallic, obedient to his muttered order, stood in front of the stone and stared towards the temple. 'Your daughter?' Lewydd asked in a murmur.

'My daughter,' Saban confirmed. 'She is to be a priestess here.' He wanted to walk closer to Lallic, but two spearmen immediately stepped into his path. 'You must be still,' one said and lowered his spear blade so that it pointed at Saban's chest. 'Camaban insisted we must all be still,' the

548

spearman explained. Aurenna was walking on into the long shadow of the stones and then she disappeared into the temple itself.

The crowd waited. The sun was low now, but the shadows of the temple did not yet stretch to the sun stone. There was a faint pinkness in the sky and the southernmost stones were touched with that colour while the inside of the temple was already dark. The pattern of shadows was becoming clear as the stones took on depth when, from the temple's darkened heart, Aurenna sang.

She sang for a long time and the crowd strained to listen for her voice was not powerful and it was muffled by the barriers of tall pillars, but those closest to the spearmen could hear her words and they whispered them on to the folk behind. Slaol made the world, Aurenna chanted, and made the gods to preserve the world, and he made the people to live in the world, and he made the plants and animals to shelter and feed the people, and in the beginning, when all that was made, there was nothing but life and love and laughter, for men and women were the companions of the gods. But some of the gods had been envious of Slaol for none was as bright and powerful as their creator, and Lahanna was the most jealous of all and she had tried to dim Slaol's brightness by sliding in front of his face, and when that failed she had persuaded mankind that she could take away death if they would just worship her instead of Slaol. It was then, Aurenna chanted, that man's misery began. Misery and sickness and toil and pain, and death was not vanquished for Lahanna had lied, and Slaol had moved away from the world to let winter ravage the land so that the people would know his power.

But now, Aurenna sang, the world would be turned

back to its beginnings. Lahanna would bow to Slaol and Slaol would return, and there would be an end to the misery. There would be no more winter and no more sadness, for Slaol would take his proper place and the dead would go to Slaol instead of to Lahanna and they would walk in his vast brightness. Aurenna's voice was thready and sibilant, seeming to come disembodied from the stones. We shall live in Slaol's glory, she sang, and share in his favour, and with those words the shadow of the topmost arch stretched to touch the sun stone and Slaol was poised, dazzling and terrible and vast, just above his temple. The evening was cooling and the first shiver of the night wind stirred the plumes of smoke from the fires.

Slaol is the giver of life, Aurenna sang, the only giver of life, and he will give us life if we give life to him. The shadow was creeping up the sun stone. All the ground between that stone and the temple was dark now, while the rest of the hillside was green with the year's last light. Tonight, Aurenna sang, we shall give Slaol a bride of the earth and he will give her back to us.

It took a few heartbeats for those words to register with Saban and then he understood Lallic's purpose, the same purpose that Aurenna had avoided at the Sea Temple in Sarmennyn, and he knew his oath was being returned to him in blood. 'No!' Saban shouted, shattering the crowd's solemn stillness, and one of the spearmen clubbed him on the side of the head with his spear staff. He struck Saban to the ground and the other man placed his blade on Saban's neck. Camaban did not turn round at the commotion, nor did Lallic move; Aurenna went on undisturbed.

We shall give a bride to the sun, Aurenna chanted, and we shall see the bride return to us alive and we will know the god has heard us and that he loves us and that all will be well. The dead will walk, Aurenna sang, the dead will dance, and when the bride comes back to life there will be no more weeping in the night and no more sobs of mourning, for mankind will live with the gods and be like them. Saban struggled to rise, but both spearmen were holding him down and he saw that the sun was now hidden behind the topmost arch and blazing its light all around the temple's outline.

Camaban turned to Lallic. He smiled at her. He raised his hands from under his white-feathered cloak and he gently untied the lace at the neck of her tunic. She trembled slightly and a whimper escaped her throat. 'You are going on a journey,' Camaban soothed her, 'but it will not be a long journey and you will greet Slaol face to face and bring his greeting back to us.'

She nodded, and Camaban pushed the deerskin tunic down over her shoulders and let it fall so that her white naked body shivered against the grey of the sun stone. 'He comes,' Camaban whispered, and from beneath his cloak he brought out a bronze knife with a wooden handle studded with a thousand small gold pins. 'He comes,' he said again and half turned towards the stones and at that instant the sun lanced through the topmost arch of the temple to send a spear of brilliant light towards the sun stone. That ray of light, narrow and stark and bright, slid over the capstone at the far side of the sky ring, through the tallest arch and under the nearest lintel to strike against Lallic who shuddered as the knife was raised. The bronze blade flashed in the sun.

'No!' Saban shouted again, and the spearmen pressed their bronze blades against his neck as the crowd held its breath.

But the knife did not move.

The crowd waited. The beam of light would not last long. It was already narrowing as the sun sank towards the horizon beyond the temple, but still the blade stayed aloft and Saban saw that it was shaking. Lallic was shivering in fear and someone hissed at Camaban to strike with the blade before the sun went, but just as Hirac had been paralysed by the gold on Camaban's tongue, so Camaban himself was now struck motionless.

For the dead walked.

Just as Derrewyn had promised, the dead walked.

There was a small group of people at the end of the sacred avenue. No one had remarked on their presence, assuming they were latecomers to the ceremony, but they had stayed in the lower ground as Aurenna sang the story of the world. Now a single figure came from the group and climbed the sacred path between the white chalk ditches. She walked slowly, haltingly, and it was the sight of her that had stilled Camaban's hand. And still he could not move, but only stare at the woman who advanced into the temple's long shadow. She was swathed in a cloak made from badger skins and had a woollen shawl hooding her long white hair, and the eyes that peered from the hood were malevolent, clever and terrifying. She came slowly for she was old, so old no one knew how old she was. She was Sannas and she had come to collect her soul

552

and Camaban suddenly screamed at her to go away. The knife trembled.

'Now!' Aurenna shouted from the temple. 'Now!'

But Camaban could not move. He stared at Sannas who came to the sun stone. There she smiled at him and there was only one tooth in her mouth. 'Do you have my soul safe?' she asked him in a voice that was as dry as bones that had been resting for generations in the dark hearts of their grave mounds. 'Is my soul safe, Camaban?' she asked.

'Don't k-k-kill me, p-p-p-please don't k-kill me,' Camaban begged. The old woman smiled at him, then put her arms about his neck and kissed him on the mouth. The crowd stared in amazement; many recognised the old woman and they touched their groins and shook with fear. It was then that Lewydd shouldered aside the terrified guards holding Saban to the ground and Saban climbed to his feet, seized one of the guards' spears and ran towards the sun stone where the ray of Slaol's dying light was shrinking. 'Now!' Aurenna shouted again, and the crowd was moaning and wailing in fear of the dead sorceress in her black and white cloak, and the spearmen did not dare interfere for they had seen Camaban's horror and it had infected them.

Sannas took her mouth from Camaban's lips. 'Lahanna!' she prayed in her grating voice, 'give me his last breath,' and she kissed him again and Saban thrust the spear with all his strength into his brother's back. He did not hesitate, for it was his own oath that had endangered his daughter's life and he alone could save her, and he struck high on Camaban's back so that the heavy blade smashed through the ribs and into his heart. Saban screamed as he struck and the force of his killing blow drove Camaban forward so that he fell, dying, but with the woman's mouth still on his.

Sannas clung to Camaban as they fell, then waited till she saw her enemy was truly dead before she pushed back her hood and Saban saw it was Derrewyn, as he had known it must be, and they stared at each other, blood on the grass between them and the light almost gone from the sun stone. 'I took his soul,' Derrewyn whispered to Saban. Her hair was whitened with ash and her gums were still bloody where she had pulled out her teeth. 'I took his soul,' she exulted. Just then Aurenna ran from the temple, screaming, and as she passed Saban she drew a copper dagger from beneath her raven-black cloak. There was still a patch of light on Lallic's face. The light shone on the sun bride and on the stone behind her, the stone which marked Slaol's midsummer rising and served as a reminder to the sun god of his strength. Slaol could see the stone, could know his power, and by seeing what gift was brought to the stone he would know what his loving people wanted. And surely he would give it to them? In that belief Aurenna drove the green blade through her daughter's throat so that the blood spurted out to spatter scarlet on Camaban's white-feathered robe.

'No!' Saban shouted, too late.

'Now!' Aurenna turned to the sun. 'Now!'

Saban stared in horror. He had thought Aurenna was running to rescue Lallic, not kill her, but the girl had collapsed at the stone's foot and her slim white body was webbed with blood. She choked for a heartbeat and her eyes stared at Saban, but then she was dead and Aurenna threw down the knife and shrieked once more at Slaol. 'Now! Now!'

Lallic did not move.

'Now!' Aurenna howled. There were tears in her eyes. 'You promised! You promised!' She staggered towards the temple, her hair wild, her eyes wide and her hands red with her daughter's blood. 'Erek!' she screeched, 'Erek! Now! Now!'

Saban turned to follow her, but Derrewyn put out a hand. 'Let her find the truth,' she said, still speaking in Sannas's voice.

'Now!' Aurenna wailed. 'You promised us! Please!' She was crying now, racked by great sobs. 'Please!' She was back among the stones and the ray of light had vanished so that the temple was all shadow, but rimmed with the sun's dying brightness, and Aurenna, weeping and moaning, turned to see that her daughter did not live and so she ran through the stones, twisting past the pillars to the entrance at the southern side of the sky ring where she fell to her knees in the wide gap next to the slender pillar, clasped her hands together and howled again at the sun, which now sat red and vast and uncaring on the horizon. 'You promised! You promised!'

Saban did not see it. He heard it. He heard the crack and the grating noise and the crash that made the earth shudder, and he knew that the last pillar of Lahanna's ring had broken and the capstone had fallen. And Aurenna's scream was cut off.

Slaol slipped beneath the earth.

There was silence.

Saban did not want to be chief of Ratharryn, yet the tribe chose him and would not let him refuse them. He pleaded that Leir was a younger man and that Gundur was an experienced warrior, but the men of Ratharryn were tired of being led by spearmen or by visionaries and they wanted Saban. They wanted him to be like his father, so Saban ruled as Hengall had ruled in Ratharryn. He dispensed justice, he hoarded grain and he let the priests tell him by what signs the gods were making their wishes known.

Derrewyn went to Cathallo and appointed a chief there, but Leir and Hanna stayed at Ratharryn where Kilda became Saban's wife. Slaol's temple, the one just outside the settlement's gate, was given to Lahanna.

The world was as it had been. The winter was as cold as ever. Snow fell. The old, the sick and the cursed died. Saban doled out grain, sent hunters to the woods and guarded the tribe's treasures. Some of the old folk said it was as though Hengall had never died, but had simply been reborn into Saban.

Yet on the hill there stood a broken circle of stone within a ring of chalk.

The bodies of Camaban, Aurenna and Lallic were laid in the Death House and there, in the shadow of the mother stone, the ravens fed on their flesh until, in the late spring, there were only white bones left on the grass. Haragg's bones had long been buried.

The temple was never deserted. Even in that first hard winter folk came to the stones. They brought their sick to be healed, their dreams to be fulfilled and gifts to keep Ratharryn wealthy. Saban was surprised, for he had thought that with Camaban's death and the capstone's fall the temple had failed. Slaol had not come to earth and winter still locked the river with ice, but the people who came to the temple believed the stones had worked a miracle. 'And so they did,' Derrewyn said to Saban in the first spring after Camaban's death.

'What miracle?' Saban asked.

Derrewyn grimaced. 'Your brother believed the stones would control the gods. He thought he was a god himself, and that Aurenna was a goddess, and what happened?'

'They died,' Saban said curtly.

'The stones killed them,' Derrewyn said. 'The gods did come to the temple that night and they killed the man who claimed he was a god and crushed the woman who thought she was a goddess.' She stared at the temple. 'It is a place of the gods, Saban. Truly.'

'They killed my daughter too,' Saban said bitterly.

'The gods demand sacrifice.' Derrewyn's voice was harsh. 'They always have. They always will.'

Aurenna and Lallic were laid in a shared grave and Saban raised a mound over them. He made another mound for Camaban, and it was that second grave that had brought Derrewyn to Ratharryn. She watched as Camaban's bones were laid in the mound's central pit. 'You won't take his jawbone?' she asked Saban.

'Let him talk to the gods as he always did.' Saban put the small mace beside his brother's body, then added the gold-hilted knife, the copper knife, the great buckle of gold and, last of all, a bronze axe. 'In the afterlife,' Saban explained, 'he can work. He always boasted he never held an axe, so let him hold one now. He can fell trees, as I did.'

'And he will go to Lahanna's care after all,' Derrewyn said with a toothless smile.

'It seems so,' Saban said.

'Then he can take her a gift from me.' Derrewyn climbed

557

down into the pit and placed the three lozenges on Camaban's breast. She placed the large one in the centre and the two smaller on either side. A robin perched on the edge of the pit and Saban took the bird's presence as a sign that the gods approved of the gift.

Saban helped Derrewyn climb from the grave. He stared a last time at his brother's bones, then turned away. 'Fill it,' he ordered the waiting men, and so they scraped the earth and chalk onto Camaban's body, finishing the mound that would stand with the other ancestors' graves on the grassy crest above the temple.

Saban walked home.

It was evening, and the shadow of the stones stretched long towards Ratharryn. They stood grey and gaunt, broken and awesome, like nothing else on all the earth, but Saban did not look back. He knew he had built a great thing and that folk would worship there until time itself was ended, but he did not look back. He took Derrewyn's arm and they walked away until they were free of the temple's shadow.

There were fish traps to mend and ground to break and grain to sow and disputes to settle.

Behind Saban and Derrewyn the dying sun flashed in the temple's topmost arch. It blazed there for a while, edging the stones with dazzling light, and then it sank and in the twilight the temple turned as black as night. Day folded into darkness and the stones were left to the spirits.

Which hold them still.

Historical Note

It is surely obvious that every character and deity in the novel is fictitious. The Stonehenge that we see is the ruin of a monument that was erected at the end of the third millennium BC, the beginning of Britain's Bronze Age, and we have no records of kings, chiefs, cooks or carpenters from that era. Nevertheless, some of the detail in the novel is drawn from the archaeological records. There was an archer, with a stone bracer to protect his wrist from the lash of his bow, buried beside Stonehenge's north-eastern entrance, and he had been killed, evidently at close quarters, by three arrows. The three gold lozenges, the belt buckle, the knives, axe and ceremonial mace were discovered in one of the burial mounds closest to the monument and are today on display in the Devizes Museum. Ratharryn is what we now call Durrington Walls and its vast embankment was one of the great feats of neolithic man, though today it is little more than a shadow on the ground. There were probably two temples within the embankment and a third, which is now called Woodhenge, just outside, and all of those shrines were close to Stonehenge which is here called the Old Temple or the Sky Temple. Cathallo is Avebury, the long barrow where

Camaban's warriors defiled the bones is at West Kennet, the small temple at the end of the sacred avenue is the Sanctuary and the Sacred Mound, of course, is Silbury Hill, and all those features can still be visited. Drewenna is Stanton Drew, Maden is Marden, Sarmennyn is southwest Wales. At Stonehenge itself the 'moonstones' are now called the Station Stones, while the 'sun stone' is the Heel Stone. The word 'henge' is deliberately not used in the novel, for it would have had no meaning. The Saxons originally applied the word only to Stonehenge, for only Stonehenge had 'hanging' (henge) stones (i.e. the lintels), but over the years we have broadened its meaning to include any and every circular monument that remains from the neolithic and early bronze ages.

What is Stonehenge? It is the question that occurs to most visitors and little at the site provides any answer other than the one propounded by R. J. C. Atkinson in his impressive book *Stonehenge*. 'There is one short, simple and perfectly correct answer: we do not know, and we shall probably never know.' Which is rather dispiriting, for without some idea of their use and purpose, the stones are diminished. We can appreciate the immense labour involved in the transport and erection of the monument, we can marvel that such a thing was built at all, but without a glimpse into the minds of the builders, it is somewhat meaningless.

It is, plainly, a place of worship, but worship of what? The usual answer is that the temple of Stonehenge is aligned on the rising of the midsummer sun, and that belief has led to much nonsensical misuse of the monument. The revived Order of Druids likes to worship there each midsummer, even though Stonehenge had nothing whatever to do with the Druids, who flourished long after the monument had decayed and who, in any case, probably preferred their rites to take place in dark, forested shrines. Undoubtedly there is an alignment on the midsummer sunrise, but it is not the only alignment at Stonehenge. John North, in his challenging book *Stonehenge, Neolithic Man and the Cosmos*, makes an overwhelming case for the alignment on the midwinter sunset, and it so happens that at Stonehenge the midsummer sun rises above the north-eastern horizon almost diametrically opposite the place on the south-western skyline where the midwinter sun sets (in 2000 BC the difference between the two alignments was less than half a degree), so any monument aligned on the one will, fortuitously, mark the other and, as both events are plainly important in the annual cycle of the seasons, we can suspect that both were marked by appropriate rites.

Professor North also suggests that celestial events were not observed from the inside of the monument looking out, but rather from the outside looking in. No doubt both means of viewing were possible; anyone wanting the best view of the midsummer sunrise would wish to be in the centre of the monument, but at midwinter sunset the observer would want to stand outside the shrine and look through its centre. That main axis, the line stretching from the avenue through the monument, seems to be the major astronomical feature which marks the summer rising and the winter setting of the sun. The four Station Stones, of which two remain, were aligned on major lunar events, but they form a rectangle and its two shorter sides are parallel with the monument's main solar axis.

Which raises the question of why such an elaborate

monument was necessary. After all, if marking the observed extremes of the sun and moon were all that was required, then it could have been done with just four or five stones. But the same is true of more recent religions. God, we are assured, can be worshipped as efficaciously about a kitchen table as in a church, but that is not a compelling argument for the demolition of Salisbury Cathedral. And cathedrals do have something to tell us about Stonehenge. If, four thousand years from now, archaeologists were to discover the remains of a cathedral they might deduce all kinds of things from the ruins of the building, but their first, and most obvious, conclusion would be that it faces the rising sun from which they would assume, reasonably enough, that Christianity worshipped a sun god. In truth the east–west alignment of most Christian churches has nothing to do with the sun. Nevertheless a theory would be propounded that Christianity was a solar religion (while the incidence of crucifixes would surely persuade our future archaeologists that Christians conducted horrific human sacrifices), and what might never be suspected are the vast range of other activities – weddings, coronations, funerals, masses, worship services, concerts – that went on within the building. So it is with Stonehenge. We can see the solar and lunar alignments clearly enough (and must hope that, unlike our notional future archaeologists, we are not entirely wrong about them), but we cannot see the other activities that happened at the stones.

Stonehenge, then, must have been a cultic centre used for a range of spiritual activities, but which was, nevertheless, aligned on significant solar events, which events must have been important to whatever religion was practised. But Stonehenge did not spring out of nowhere. The monument that we see is merely the last stage of a very long process that took hundreds of years, and remnants of that process are scattered throughout Britain. Most henges are circular enclosures formed by banks and ditches. That is a simple enough concept, suggesting the reservation of a sacred space, but it was complicated by the addition of wooden posts within the circles that were almost certainly used for the observation of celestial phenomena. Over time those circles of wooden posts became ever more common until, all across Britain, there were numerous timber henges: veritable forests of posts that were clustered in concentric rings within their earthen banks. There was one such timber temple at Stonehenge itself, another just to the north at what is now known as Woodhenge, at least two more at nearby Durrington Walls and a fourth, Coneybury Henge (the 'Death Place'), just a mile to the south-east of Stonehenge.

Later still some of the wooden posts were replaced by stones, and those stone circles are what we see today. They range from the north of Scotland to the west of Wales and to the south of England. Some are double circles, some have avenues approaching them, others have 'coves' like those at Avebury; no two are alike, yet two of them, separated by a mere twenty miles, though utterly dissimilar to each other, stand out for their complexity: Avebury and Stonehenge. It is no surprise, then, to learn that these monuments are the culmination of the tradition of temple building in southern Britain (in the north and west new temples were to be made for another thousand years), and that tradition is simple enough to understand. Neolithic man largely built his temples as circles, and used them to observe celestial events that were closely related to his religious beliefs. The difference between, say, the Rollright Stones in Oxfordshire and Stonehenge in Wiltshire is obvious, one is simple and the other is exquisitely engineered and awe-inspiring, yet at heart they are both the same thing.

Why were they built as circles? The easy answer is to say that they came at the end of a long tradition of circle building, though that begs the question. Sometimes neolithic man preferred to erect rows of stone, such as those at Carnac in France or the smaller rows on Dartmoor. He sometimes built mysterious earthworks that trailed for miles across the countryside (the Stonehenge Cursus, just to the north of the monument, is an example of this), yet overwhelmingly he decided on a circular shrine, and the commonest suggestion is that the circle reflected the heavens, the horizon or the nature of existence. Yet it seems unlikely that so powerful a tradition rests solely on metaphor; it is surely more probable that the metaphor reinforced a practicality, which could have been that the earliest worshippers of the 'henge' religions wanted to observe celestial phenomena that occurred all across the sky. John North suggests that they began with the long barrows, those strange mounded graves that can still be seen throughout Britain, and that the barrows' builders used the spine of the mound as an artificial horizon across which they sighted stars, planets, the sun and the moon. Timber poles fixed their sightings. But a barrow is really only useful for such observations from either side of its long axis, while a circular bank, a henge, can be conveniently used for every quadrant of the sky and the interior of the henge provides a useful place for positioning sighting poles, so the tradition of circular temples began.

When the builders erected Avebury and Stonehenge, then, they were working within a tradition, only they were taking that tradition to new heights of achievement. They undoubtedly wished to impress. God may be adequately worshipped from a kitchen table, but a person entering a cathedral is more likely to be filled with awe and wonder, for the builders did something marvellous that transcends the quotidian; just so with Stonehenge and Avebury. They are temples designed to echo the awesome mystery of the unknown. Neolithic man could effectively mark the position of the midwinter sunset with two short timber posts, but the posts would not have the same effect as approaching Stonehenge along its processional way and seeing the looming blackness of the lintelled boulders on the horizon. Then would come that heart-chilling moment when the land was smothered in the long shadow cast by the stones, and in the centre of that shadow was a last ray of the sun lancing down towards the Heel Stone. That shadow, and that livid shaft of light, was what the builders of Stonehenge achieved.

But just as a cathedral (the word comes from the Latin for a 'throne') is not made solely for the occasional enthronement of a bishop, nor was Stonehenge constructed just for the supreme moments of the solar year. It must have had many rites, many of them descended with the thousand-year tradition of henge building. We do not know what those rites were, but we can guess, for humankind's demands of the gods do not change much. There would be rituals for death (funerals), for sex (weddings), for giving thanks (harvest festivals), for petitioning (prayer meetings), for rites of passage (baptism, first communion or confirmation), for celebrating secular power (coronations or great state occasions), as well as the regular services which still punctuate the ritual year. Doubtless some of these activities were more prominent then than now, healing rituals, for instance, or those ceremonies related to the agricultural year. The best discussion I have found of what may have lain behind those rituals is in Aubrey Burl's book *Prehistoric Avebury*, for that monument was also built to encompass all the religious needs of a community. Stonehenge performed the same function, but, unlike Avebury, it also accentuates the midwinter sunset, and that suggests the temple was preoccupied with death: the death of the old year and the hopes of revival with the new year.

Death seems intimately bound with the henges. A child, its head split by an axe, was buried very near the centre of Woodhenge. There are burials at Avebury (including the dwarf crippled woman in the ditch), just as there are at Stonehenge. The existence of those graves, let alone the obvious celestial alignments, argue against the fashionable theory that the earth goddess was the primary deity and that she ruled over a peaceful, matriarchal society unsullied by violent male gods. There is far too much evidence of violence and death associated with the monuments for that happy theory to be true. The monuments are not cemeteries, though it does appear that for part of its history Stonehenge was used as a depository for cremated ashes, but the burials that occurred within the henges do seem to have been ritualistic: perhaps foundation sacrifices, or other deaths (like that of the archer at Stonehenge) which coincided with some crisis in the temple's history. There is a suggestion that the dead were laid out within the monuments, there to be flensed by natural processes, and that the bones were then taken and buried elsewhere. In mediaeval Europe it was believed that the closer you were buried to the saint's relics, which were usually kept on a church's altar, the quicker you would reach heaven on Judgement Day (the theory depended on being caught up in the ascending saint's slipstream); something similar may have applied to the great henges that, as at Stonehenge, stand amidst clusters of burial mounds. This congruence of temple and graves strengthens the idea that the circular henges were seen as a connection between this world and the other world where the dead went, a world that was almost certainly conceived as being in the sky for, long before there were any henges, graves were aligned on the sun, moon or prominent stars. The best example of this is the magnificent neolithic grave at Newgrange in Ireland where a passage was driven through the mound to carry the rays of the rising midwinter sun into the burial chamber. This stunning monument, which has been splendidly restored, was built at least two hundred years before the first simple bank and ditch were made at Stonehenge, suggesting that the relationship between the dead and the sky was well established in the fourth millennium BC.

Yet Stonehenge's history goes back to the eighth millennium BC. There was no circle then, and no stones, just a row of vast pinewood posts, perhaps like totem poles, erected in a forest clearing (positions of three of the four posts are today marked by white circles painted on the car-park, but in future, if we ever get round to presenting Stonehenge as it should be, they may be more appropriately commemorated). We know almost nothing about the posts, except that they seem too big to have been part of a building, and nothing whatever about the impulse that raised them, nor why that particular spot was chosen. Nor do we know how long they stood. Five thousand years later, in about 3000 BC, the henge that we know was begun. At first it was just a circular ditch with a high bank inside it and a lower bank outside, and just within the higher bank was a ring of holes named after their discoverer, the seventeenth-century antiquarian John Aubrey. The Aubrey Holes are another of Stonehenge's mysteries. There is controversy over whether the holes held any posts, but if they did all sign of them has long gone and, even more mysteriously, it appears that the fifty-six holes were filled in very soon after they were dug. Some of the holes contain the remains of cremation burials, but not all, and we really have very little idea of their purpose. We can blame those Aubrey Holes for the popular theory that Stonehenge was an 'eclipse predictor'; it is true that you can foretell the years of the eclipses by a complicated shuttling of markers about the fifty-six holes, but it seems an unlikely hypothesis. If it worked, why were the holes abandoned? And why was the system not copied at other henges?

Quite soon after the circle was made, the first timber posts appeared in its centre and at the north-eastern entrance which points towards the rising midsummer sun. This timber henge, similar to the ones at nearby Durrington Walls or the newly discovered timber shrine which stood at Stanton Drew, lasted for several hundred years, though some scholars believe that some time towards the middle or end of the third millennium BC the temple fell into disuse. Then, maybe two hundred years later, it was revived. The Station Stones, and a few other stones at the main entrance, were put up first. Almost certainly the Heel

Stone (the sun stone) was among those first boulders erected and it still stands, though leaning at an angle. It is not much remarked by visitors, yet it was probably the keystone to the whole temple. For a short time the temple was a simple arrangement of a few standing stones, no more remarkable than scores of other such shrines, and then something exceptional happened. Bluestones (so called because of their very faint blueish-green tint) were fetched from distant west Wales and erected in a double circle and it seems very probable that some of those stones carried lintels.

The bluestones are another mystery. There are no suitable boulders on Salisbury Plain, which is why all the stones of the monument had to be fetched across long distances, but why from the Preseli Mountains in Pembrokeshire? The hills near Avebury, twenty miles to the north, had an almost inexhaustible supply of boulders, yet Stonehenge's builders carried the bluestones 135 miles (actually much farther, for they were forced by topography to a circuitous route to their site). It was a stunning feat, though some theorists have attempted to dismiss it by claiming that the bluestones were deposited on Salisbury Plain by glacial action during an ice age. It is a convenient theory, but to be true it would surely demand that we should find other such bluestone 'erratics' elsewhere on the plain or in its vicinity, and we never have. The simpler explanation, however amazing, is that the builders wanted just those stones and so fetched them.

The journey would have been almost impossible to achieve on land, for the route from the Preseli Mountains to Salisbury Plain contains too many steep valleys which would need to be crossed, so there is general agreement among archaeologists that the stones were primarily transported by water. There is agreement, too, that the stones (weighing from two to seven tons) were carried on wooden dug-out canoes that would be joined together by a wooden platform on which the stone would be lashed. Two routes are suggested: either south about Lands End and then eastwards along the south coast to Christchurch Harbour from where the stones could be floated up the Hampshire Avon ('Mai's river') to a spot close to Stonehenge. The alternative, which I prefer, is a shorter sea voyage up the Bristol Channel, then up the Somerset Avon ('River Sul'), across a low watershed, then by river again. Anyone who has sailed the English Channel, and specifically the waters between Cornwall and Hampshire, will know of the many dangers that exist on that coast, especially in the form of massive 'tide-gates' where the fast tidal currents are compressed, often into venomous rips, by jutting headlands such as Start Point or Portland Bill. A voyage around the south-west of Britain would encounter those formidable obstacles, while a journey up the Bristol Channel would be assisted by a strong tide and prevailing winds. There is no evidence that neolithic Britons possessed sails, but we know the technology was in the Mediterranean around 4000 BC so it seems likely that the idea would spread as far as Britain in the next two millennia. A journey up the Bristol Channel, assisted by sails and taking advantage of the spring tides, could have been effected quite swiftly and without any of the massive dangers presented by the longer route south about the Cornish peninsula.

But however the stones were fetched, the extraordinary journey was made, and then something even more remarkable happened. The builders, having gone to immense trouble to move the stones from present day Pembrokeshire to Wiltshire, then decided that their new and still unfinished temple was unsatisfactory. They demolished it. The stones were taken away (except, probably, for the Altar Stone, which I have called the mother stone, and which also came from Pembrokeshire, from the bank of the River Clewydd near Milford Haven) to be replaced with the most prominent stones we see today: the sarsen stones. 'Sarsen' is not a technical name, but a local nickname, perhaps derived from 'Saracen', denoting the strangeness of these great grey sandstone slabs that once covered the downs close to Avebury. The stones that make Stonehenge came from the hills just to the east of Avebury and had to be dragged over twenty miles to their present position. It was not such a remarkable journey as the bluestones, but still an incredible feat, for the sarsens were much bigger and heavier (the heaviest weighed over forty tons). They are also among the hardest stones in nature, yet the builders shaped these vast boulders to make the five soaring trilithons and the sarsen circle with its wondrous ring of thirty lintels lifted to the sky. They also rearranged the stones in the main entrance, of which only one remains, the recumbent Slaughter Stone, which probably had nothing whatever to do with any slaughter. The name was given because of a reddish stain on the stone's surface which was assumed to be ancient blood, but is nothing more dramatic than oxidised metal dissolved by rainwater. It is at this point that the novel ends.

Could it all have been done within the compass of one man's lifetime? It is possible, and the radiocarbon dates (mostly derived from scraps of antler picks abandoned in the stone holes) are scarce and confusing enough to allow for the possibility, but most scholars would plausibly argue for a much longer period. I do not believe, however, that building Stonehenge was a leisurely pursuit. There is evidence that some of the stones were erected hurriedly (by being placed in holes too shallow to support them, whereas a painstaking process would have demanded that a longer stone be fetched and substituted), and unchanging human nature alone suggests that when a great work is undertaken there is an impatience to see it finished. I am convinced, also, that the design of the sarsen Stonehenge betrays an architect. The lintels and trilithons may have been copies of wooden originals, but the monument is nevertheless unique and daring, and suggests that someone designed it, and undoubtedly that designer would have been eager to see his idea finished. For all those reasons I suspect that the building took less time than is commonly assumed.

Yet Stonehenge itself was not finished when the great sarsens were installed. At some time, we cannot tell when, carvings of axes and daggers were hammered into some of the pillars. Then, just after 2000 BC, the discarded bluestones were brought back. Some were placed in a circle inside the sarsen ring while the rest were made into a horseshoe within the trilithons. That ended the building process and the ruins we see today are the remnants of that Stonehenge, though some two or three hundred years after the return of the bluestones more holes were dug for a completely new double ring of stones that would have encircled the lintelled sarsen ring, but those stones were never erected. It was about the same time that the sacred path, the approach avenue which has mostly been ploughed into oblivion, was extended in a great curve to the river bank. Then, around 1500 BC, the temple seems to have been finally abandoned, and it has weathered and decayed ever since.

I have mentioned my considerable debt to John North's book, *Stonehenge, Neolithic Man and the Cosmos* (Harper-Collins, 1997), and I borrowed the configuration of the abandoned bluestone henge from his suggestions. I found Aubrey Burl's books to be just as useful, specifically *The Stonehenge People* (J. M. Dent, London, 1987), and *Prehistoric Avebury* (Yale University Press, 1979). The best single introduction to the monument is David Souden's beautifully illustrated and comprehensive *Stonehenge, Mysteries of the Stones and Landscape* (English Heritage, 1997). I am also indebted to Rodney Castleden's *The Making of Stonehenge* (Routledge, London, 1993), and to the magnificent, cumbersome and awesomely expensive *Stonehenge in its Landscape, Twentieth-century Excavations*, edited by R. M. J. Cleal, K. E. Walker and R. Montague (English Heritage Archaeological Report 10, 1995). Lawrence Keeley's *War Before Civilization* (Oxford University Press, 1996) was most helpful. It is said that a picture is worth a thousand words, but Rex Nicholls's pictures, which illustrate the part-title pages of this book, are worth many times more. My thanks to him, and to Elizabeth Cartmale-Freedman who did much valuable research for me into late neolithic crops, living conditions and the findings from other archaeological sites. The errors, misjudgements and idiocies are all my own.

What makes Stonehenge so special? Some folk are disappointed by the ruins. Nathaniel Hawthorne, visiting the site from his native New England in the mid nineteenth century, wrote that Stonehenge was 'not very well worth seeing ... one of the poorest of spectacles; and when complete it must have been even less picturesque than now'. Perhaps, yet most visitors do find the stones awe-inspiring. For some people it is the association, over ten thousand years, of one spot of our planet with human-kind's spiritual longings. For others, it is the marvel of the lintels, unique for their time and still breathtaking in their architectural daring. That the monument survived at all is a miracle; over the years some stones were broken and taken away for building projects, while other stones, insuf-ficiently buried, toppled in gales. Yet the temple stands to this day, the names of its gods forgotten and the nature of its rituals a mystery, yet still a shrine for whatever aspir-ations we cannot answer by technology or human effort. Long may it remain.

Out in October 2005

The Pale Horseman

Bernard Cornwell

Uhtred, Northumbrian-born, raised a Viking and now married to a Saxon, is already a formidable figure and warrior. But at twenty he is still arrogant, pagan and head-strong, so not a comfortable ally for the thoughtful, pious Alfred. But these two, with Alfred's family and a few of Uhtred's companions, are apparently all that remains of the Wessex leadership after a disastrous truce.

It is the lowest time for the Saxons. Defeated comprehensively by the Vikings who now occupy most of England, Alfred and his surviving followers seek refuge in Athelney, a tidal swamp to which Alfred's kingdom has shrunk. There, using the marsh mists for cover, they travel in small boats from one island to another, hoping to regroup and find more strength and support.

Uhtred is still attracted to rejoining his Danish foster brother and the victorious Vikings. But he finds a growing respect for the stubborn leadership of Alfred, to whom Uhtred's support is essential if the Saxon strength is to be rebuilt and battle joined with the enemy.

The Pale Horseman is a splendid story of divided loyalties and desperate heroism. Uhtred and Alfred, Vikings and Saxons, are a winning combination for Bernard Cornwell.

ISBN 0 00 714992 1

The Last Kingdom
Bernard Cornwell

Uhtred is an English boy, born into the aristocracy of ninth-century Northumbria. Orphaned at ten, he is captured and adopted by a Dane and taught the Viking ways. Yet Uhtred's fate is indissolubly bound up with Alfred, King of Wessex, who rules over the only English kingdom to survive the Danish assault.

The struggle between the English and the Danes and the strife between Christianity and paganism is the background to Uhtred's growing up. Marriage ties him to the Saxon cause but when his wife and child vanish in the chaos of the Danish invasion, he is driven to face the greatest of the Viking chieftains in a battle beside the sea. There, he discovers his true allegiance.

'Bernard Cornwell is a literary miracle, producing the most entertaining and readable historical novels of his generation.'   *Daily Mail*

'Cornwell is a virtuoso of historical fiction.'
                                                                    Sunday Telegraph

ISBN 0 00 714991 3

Vagabond

The Grail Quest

Bernard Cornwell

Thomas of Hookton, having survived the battle of Crecy, is sent by the king on a mission to discover more about his father's strange inheritance. But caught up in a battle against an army invading the north of England, Thomas finds that he is not the only person pursuing the Grail, and that his rivals will stop at nothing to defeat him.

Returning to France, Thomas finds old comrades and rediscovers a lost love. Then, in terrible circumstances, he at last comes face to face with his enemy and cousin – the elusive Guy Vexille, Count of Astarac.

Vagabond is the second book in Thomas of Hookton's journey, which began in *Harlequin*.

'It is all spectacular, rattling good stuff: war and torture; love, lust and loss. The masterful writer who brought the world 18 Sharpe novels is meticulous in his research.'

The Times

Harlequin

The Grail Quest

Bernard Cornwell

It was the time when the English came across the Channel to take the battle to the French. The army was led by the King, the great lords and knights, but it is the archers, the common men, who are to be England's secret weapon.

Thomas of Hookton is one of those archers. But he is also on a personal mission – one he frequently forgets in the joy of fighting – to avenge his father's killing by a French raider and to retrieve his family's treasure. But the journey is far more complex and treacherous that he had expected, and the enemy who awaits him could harness the power of Christendom's greatest relic, the Grail itself.

The first book in the *Grail Quest* series ends in the great battle of Crecy, the beginning of what became known as the Hundred Years' War.

'A rich mix of bloody conflict amid political and religious turmoil – what a very fine writer Mr Cornwell has become.' *The Economist*

ISBN 0-00-651384-0

Heretic

Bernard Cornwell

When the English capture Calais, the war with France is suspended by a truce. But Thomas of Hookton still has to pursue the grail and confront his deadliest enemy: his cousin Guy Vexille.

Thomas and his men become raiders, but when he releases a girl condemned to burn as a heretic, his campaign is attacked by the church and Thomas himself becomes the hunted.

Thomas goes to the valley of Astarac, where he believes that the grail may still be concealed, but there are many others apart from Thomas who are searching for it. The prize will guarantee victory in battle and the games of hide and seek are deadly.

When Thomas finally succeeds in meeting his enemy, fate takes an unexpected hand. What had been a landscape of castles, monasteries, vineyards and villages, becomes death's kingdom and the need for the grail, as a sign of God's favour, is more urgent than ever.

'It is all spectacular, rattling good stuff: war and torture; love, lust and loss.'
The Times

ISBN: 0 00 714989 1